CALL YOU MINE

KENDRA MASE

CALL YOU

KENDRA MASE

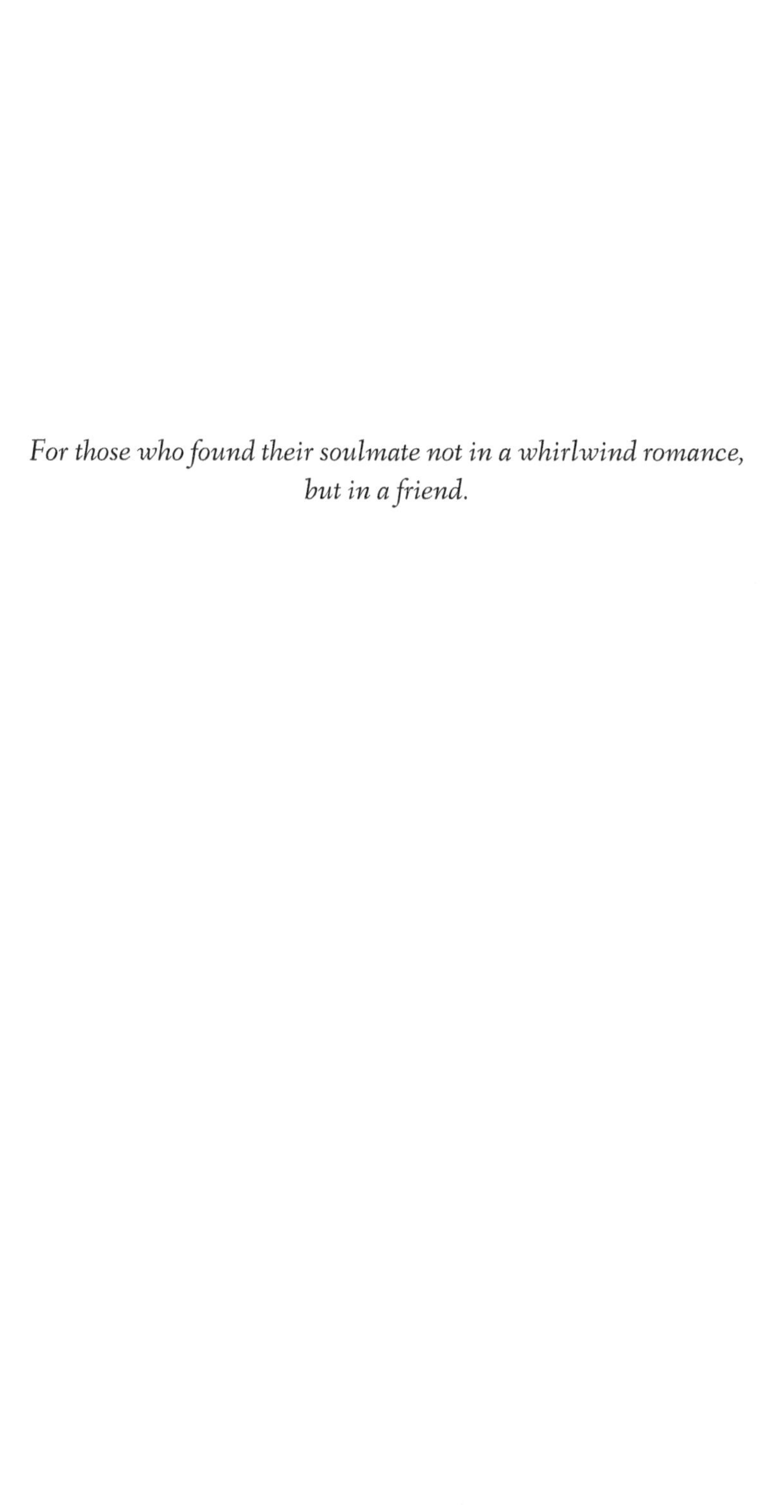

*For those who found their soulmate not in a whirlwind romance,
but in a friend.*

BEFORE

"YOUR CALL HAS BEEN FORWARDED *to an automated voice message system.*"

"Sylvia, it's Kieran. I know you don't want to talk to me. Honestly, I needed to call you. Could you just make this easy on me and pick up, so I don't have to talk to your voice mail? Pick up, pick up, pick up."

Beep.

"Come on, Sylv. Answer the phone. Or at least call me back. I need to talk to you."

Beep.

"Sylvia, you're going to regret not picking up this stupid phone. I know you, and you will. I'm basically going out of my way here to be the good person and call. Pick up the phone or at least call me back."

Beep.

"You're starting to piss me off, Sylvia. Look. You brought me to swearing. Dammit."

Beep.

"I can't believe you. What if this was an emergency? It *is* an emergency. Answer. Your. Phone."

Beep.

"I know you're there. Are you seriously just ignoring my calls and messages? It's my mom. I know things didn't go how either of us planned after Christmas, but it doesn't have to be this way. I still ... just call me back."

Beep.

"Sylvia. Please. Call me."

ONE

NOW

"SOME PEOPLE ARE JUST one-hit wonders, Leah." Miranda Yonders—*the* Miranda Yonders, one and only editor in chief of *Main Attraction* magazine—scrolled through what I assumed was her email. Her attention remained fixed on her computer.

The sleek silver was unmarred compared to mine. Over the years of writing, my laptop had become littered with stickers from the coffee shops I visited ever since I'd first arrived in the city. The stickers declared me to *espresso myself* and *die before decaf.* They might have looked childish, but in the beginning, they had also been a map of where I'd been. They were markers of where I hoped to go one day, where I'd have a fancy computer with a keyboard that didn't stick every time I typed a vowel.

That was years ago.

"It's Sylvia," I carefully corrected.

Miranda's sharply groomed eyebrows narrowed on me over the top of her eyeglasses. She took them off before taking her time, scanning me from the very top of my head, where I'd looped my hair into a tight bun, to the boring white blouse I wore. This way, I wouldn't "draw attention away from people during the meetings" when I came in to bring them their lunches. Because that was what I did every day.

I delivered sandwiches and coffee and sometimes fluffy pastries with powdered sugar if it was someone's birthday. Rarely were there any leftovers, and I couldn't bring myself to spend twenty dollars a day on a soggy croissant with a tomato and a slice of orange cheese.

It was a far cry from my original job title when Miranda had first taken me on. It was an even farther cry from the last time I could fulfill the job description I had been hired to do before being downgraded to sandwich girl. I was basically an intern.

Worse than an intern.

I took a deep breath, plastering a smile back on my face.

"Sylvia?" she repeated.

"Yes, my name is Sylvia."

Miranda blinked, shaking her head. "Right. Sorry. Like I said, it happens. Some people have one amazing pitch in them, and that's it. Your name will be up there with the magazine forever when people think of the great stories we've printed here, but otherwise?" She shrugged. "It happens. Not everyone can be consistent when it comes to creativity."

I didn't want to snap that I didn't think creativity came from ranking different hand creams every other week or body oils to use with your man, so I gritted my teeth as I responded, "I understand."

"I'm glad."

"But I do have some more ideas." I stopped her. "I have been coming up with a new angle to the self-love piece that we published last month. Remember, the one that got some commenter backlash? Since we are looking two months out, I thought it'd be perfect for Valentine's. We could reference brand partners, similar to our lotion piece? Or even the one on adult toys that Deena collated online, which got a lot of traction?"

Miranda grabbed a Post-it from the corner of her desk, jotting down what I'd said. I couldn't help the flinch the corner of my lips made. It almost felt like a smile.

Finally.

See? I wanted to ask her. *I can do this. I promise. I can still be a writer.*

"Yes, but we are going to have to let you go."

My heart stopped. "What?"

"We've been looking through our budget this past year. We've decided to make some cuts. So, we are going to have to let you go."

"When?"

"Effective immediately," said Miranda. "Due to the circumstances, you should still be able to claim unemployment if you want to go through that process. It will, however, probably take a bit for any unused benefits to kick in because of the holiday."

"I don't understand."

"Sylvia—"

"Is this because of when I sent my things down to lifestyle without asking you first? Or when I spoke up in the meeting the other day?" I asked, trying to pinpoint exactly when I apparently could no longer live up to expectation, even as a sandwich girl.

Miranda continued to shake her head. She almost looked sad.

No, that was pity.

She reached her hand out across the space between us, but not long enough for me to take. Her palm slapped down against her oversize desk calendar. "You just aren't living up to our hopes of when we hired you. You were a shining star. But, you aren't writing. Or you aren't writing anything good enough to be up to our standard. It's hard to stay on the top and all."

I didn't even realize that, at one point, I had been on the top. I hadn't even gotten to enjoy it.

"You understand where I'm coming from, right? Some people just aren't made to be in the magazine business. If you start writing some good pieces again, I'm sure you'll be able to freelance. Or perhaps, like I said, you just aren't cut out for this. It's not a bad thing. If anything, this is an opportunity. This is your time to find your place."

My place. My place that obviously wasn't here.

I tried to swallow but instead felt the spit clog in my throat. "I see."

"I'm glad you do. I don't expect you to finish out the day. Feel free to clean out anything you have lying around the office and you can head out immediately. I already informed human resources." Miranda tapped her pen before jotting something else down, or maybe she was checking off a list.

Firing me was part of her daily to-do list.

This couldn't be happening, and yet it was. Clearly, it was.

"You can go."

Slowly, I pushed myself out of the overly cushy leather chair and took a few steps toward Miranda's glass doors leading back out into the main office. I used to think the glass cubicles were cool and upscale. Now, I only had one thought about them.

I could not break down here.

"Oh, wait, Sylvia."

I twisted over my shoulder, my traitorous heart leaping. Could it be possible? After hearing my last idea, could she just give me one chance?

"Yes?"

"Please, try to be positive. Have a good holiday."

You too, I was supposed to say. Two words.

Instead, I yanked open the glass door into the rest of the bustling office, filled with tapping keyboards and the hum of the printer. I didn't have a space anymore to clean out. I grabbed my long blue peacoat off the hook and threw my crossbody purse over my shoulder. Then, I walked straight out of my dream job I had given everything to and everything up for, and onto the street.

———

After so many years, maneuvering one of the biggest cities in the world had become a habit. I walked until I could walk no more. By the time I thought about where I was going, I'd already swiped my subway card after being shoved left and right by other people, halfway to FiDi. The Financial District was a far cry from where I'd once lived with four roommates up in Morningside Heights.

I groaned as my phone continued to vibrate at my side. Yanking up my purse, I rifled through it until I pulled my phone free. My purse slapped back down against my hip.

"Hello?"

"Hi, hon. How's your day going?" my mother's bright tone asked on the other end.

Leave it to her to be in one of her rare good moods right when my entire life was going down the drain.

Well, I almost fell down the subway stairs, and now, I'm walking the rest of the way home, where I have to tell my boyfriend that I'm going to be mooching off of him for the rest of the year because I'm effectively unemployed.

"It's going," I settled with.

"That's nice. I'm sure everyone is slowing down as they get ready for the winter festivities. You're not coming home this holiday, correct?" my mother asked.

I sniffed, running my sleeve across my nose. I was not going to cry. Not yet. Maybe not ever. I refused on principle to let that snotty magazine have any of my tears, even metaphorically. If I convinced myself hard enough, I could tell myself that I'd suddenly developed winter allergies. Thick, awful, congested allergies.

"No, Mom. I told you before that I couldn't come home." I rubbed at my nose.

Of course, that had been before I was fired from my young self's dream job, which I had fought and given up years of my life for, but still.

"I can't make it. Sorry."

This year, for Christmas, I was going to be on the job hunt. If there was anyone who even hired during the holiday week. Half the city took off between Christmas and New Year's. The city emptied itself out like in August, when everyone fled to the Hamptons or Jersey to go to the beach to get wine drunk and dry out from the corporate shit show.

"Okay, that's perfectly all right. I just wanted to make sure. Your father and I are thinking about following through on some plans. I wanted to check in. Are you on your lunch break right now?"

"Kind of."

"Well, I'll leave you to relax. I know how I savored my downtime at work. Give me a call soon, all right? I hope you do something for yourself. I can't imagine it's nice to be alone on the holiday."

"I'm not alone, Mom. I have Ezra here," I corrected over the phone, reminding her that in one aspect of my personal life, I was exceeding expectations. That was, of course, if I hadn't lived in a small town all my life. There, at the age of twenty-eight, I should've been long married to a high school sweetheart and popping out a small trundle of children rather than reminding my mother that I did, in fact, have a boyfriend of two years she had once met over video call.

"Oh, well, that's good then. Have a good lunch. Keep me in the loop. Your father complains that you don't call enough."

The phone works two ways.

"I will."

"Good. Bye, Sylvia."

"Bye, Mom." I ended the call.

I forced myself to take a deep breath as I continued my steady pace down the block. Already, I was lying to my mother, but I wasn't ready to just blurt out that I had lost my job.

Even just thinking of it felt so permanent.

I'd lost my job.

God, right before the holiday.

I cringed as I stuffed my phone back into my coat pocket. I sounded like some sort of loser in one of those old Christmas movies I used to binge-watch.

My chest ached as I remembered exactly how I used to watch those kinds of movies every year. Two of us, curled up in a blanket and our feet kicked up on the coffee table. We wouldn't move for hours, alternating between gorging ourselves on popcorn or raspberry-filled shortbread cookies.

I couldn't remember the last time I'd had a good cookie, let alone my favorites. The reminder sat in my stomach like a rock.

I waved toward the afternoon doorman at my building—the place where I'd been living for the past eight months after moving in with Ezra. He insisted after looking at me like I was crazy when he saw I was living with so many other women. Any sane person would in Ezra's position. Unlike me, he had no problem paying off his student loans and had a more or less cushy financial planning position at a marketing firm, where he played with Excel sheets all day. Or at least, that was what I always imagined him doing—though he was rarely ever any help when it came to tax season.

My old post-war building had slowly been falling apart, as seen by the patched stairs on the fifth-floor walk-up. Ezra's high-rise apartment building, on the other hand, had a gym and a pool on the top floor. The living accommodations he had at his fingertips were the luxuries I never imagined I'd have in my entire life. Ever.

And moving in together was the next logical step in our relationship, wasn't it?

Luckily, there was no love lost from my past passive-aggressive roommates who had left more than just the occasional dirty dish lying around, though I was still trying to get through to Ezra how to clean the bathroom sink after he spit out his toothpaste.

That was the least of my worries now. I had approximately three to seven hours until Ezra got home. He'd walk in already slightly irritated after a long day, wearing his usual wrinkled suit. Dark hair would finally give into gravity and fall in loose clumps along his forehead. He'd ask if I thought about dinner even though he'd likely already have gone out with co-workers for drinks.

Then, I'd have to explain what had happened today.

Three hours. I had that much time to wallow, cry in the shower, and come up with a plan so that I could keep paying my part for rent—even though he never needed any help and often chuckled at my menial contribution.

Ezra, that hag at work fired me.

No, I should probably keep it mellow.

I lost my job.

It wasn't as if I could've done anything about it. It wasn't just me getting laid off. Miranda had said that it wasn't just me who was being cut out of the budget, hadn't she?

My heart thrummed in my chest as I stepped out of the elevator and fished for my key. I nearly put it into the lock and turned, but ...

The door wasn't locked.

My hand hovered over the knob.

Did someone break in?

Now, that would be the cherry on top of a sucky sundae of a day. I didn't even think that it was possible to be robbed in one of these buildings. I carefully pushed the door open, assessing for whatever it was I was going to find inside. My eyes landed on not one, but two people.

I slammed the door shut behind me.

"Are you kidding me?" I stared at the two of them on the couch. *My* couch.

The couch had been on the pricey side. But I couldn't help myself right after I moved in, and it was one design element Ezra agreed on me changing so I felt more included in his space. The couch was cozy enough that I could collapse into it at the end of a long workday.

It was a couch I had saved money to buy after moving in, even after Ezra teased me about it.

"Most girls dream of designer purses or the funny high heels with the red soles," he'd comment each time I found myself fascinated by housewares. "Is this the Podunk housewife coming out in you?"

When I had finally taken the plunge and purchased the plush piece of furniture, I had imagined the two of us curled up late at night, watching television, or sipping warm cups of tea in the morning with our toes perched on the coffee table, wearing only our socks. I thought of all the ways I wanted to be on that couch with him.

Now, it was certainly being used to sit more than one person. One of them was clearly not me.

Immediately, the two separated, quick to gasp at the sight of me. They flung clothing over themselves, tucking things back behind buttons.

I stared down at the caught zipper of Ezra's dress pants. He struggled with it, a look of both surprise and disgust written all over his face.

No wonder I hadn't seen such a view of him myself in such a long time.

He had been pushing me off. *Too needy. I didn't understand the pressure he was under at work all day long.*

"You're home early," he said, breathless.

I had met his coworker—his "work wife"—once at a company dinner. I'd insisted I go, only to stand in the corner, nursing a plastic cup of cheap white wine alone.

She remained half in his lap, trying to fix the front clasp on her cherry-red blouse. The shade was very cheery for the holidays. Her cheeks blossomed with a similar color. Somehow, she managed to be striking, the bright color luminous against perfect skin she probably got weekly facials for.

I couldn't remember the name of the stunning, well-educated coworker, or if I did, I didn't want to right now.

My head was already too full.

Her lips were flushed and swollen as she stuttered, "It's not what it looks like."

"Oh, well, that's good. It looked like you were about to go down on my boyfriend, but I guess if you are just staring at his penis for some sort of work reason, that's completely professional."

Neither of them said a word.

"A new marketing opportunity for impotence?" It was sad that my voice still teased at a laugh.

His coworker's mouth slammed shut.

"I think I'm going to go," Ezra's afternoon tryst said, slowly rising to stand.

"No, please. Don't." I put up a hand, eyes catching on my chipped nail polish. "Don't get up on my account. I'll leave."

The two of them murmured back and forth before the work wife at last headed out the door. The heavy metal shut with a slam, leaving me and Ezra standing across from each other in silence.

What were you supposed to say to someone you had just caught cheating on you?'

In soap operas, the woman scorned threw things. I could break things or scream—at the very least, surely. Yet I stood there. My stomach was hollow with embarrassment even though I had done nothing wrong.

My entire life was suddenly imploding. Everything I had thought meant something to me was scattered around me in bits and pieces that I couldn't even stand at this point to think about putting together.

I wasn't sure I wanted to.

I pressed the heels of my palms against my eyes. I made my way toward the bedroom, leaning around the mirrored closet doors for my suitcase, which still held most of my shoes, along with other pieces of my life that didn't quite match the decor. Ezra had barely pushed his things to the side when I moved in. He definitely hadn't thought that I needed floor space for my few sets of footwear.

That had been a sign, hadn't it?

So was the minimal indication of me anywhere in this apartment. There were signs all over, and I hadn't wanted to see them for so long.

But they all came around eventually, and today was that day.

I gritted my teeth as I shoved more of my clothes haphazardly inside my bag.

"What are you doing?" Ezra asked, his tone more annoyed than concerned.

"I'm leaving," I said.

He chuckled until he must've noticed I was still squishing things into my suitcase. "Oh. You're serious."

Tearing past him into the bathroom, I whipped my toothbrush from the holder, along with my travel bag of toiletries.

Another sign.

"It's not like I can follow you if that's what you want from me. It's not like you have friends I could track down," he said.

I flinched. *Way to go in for the low blow.*

"Come on, baby. Don't do this. We can fix this." He scoffed at my reaction. "Where else are you going to go?"

He was right. Yet, it didn't matter. For first time in years I wanted to be anywhere but here.

Absolutely anywhere.

"I'm going home."

"Home." Ezra repeated the word as if he'd never heard it in his entire life.

"Yes, home." Did he even know where my home was? Probably not. "First off, the fact that you think you can just gloss over what you just did is astounding."

"I'm not."

"You are. And that's fine. Because I'm done caring." I zipped my bag. Internal rage really made quick work of packing.

"Sylvia, stop."

"No, no, no. You stop. Because let me get this straight. You thought I wouldn't be home?"

"Right."

"So, you came back here to fuck your coworker on my

couch?" I raised my eyebrows. "Because, of course, I wouldn't be home."

At that, he seemed to be at a loss for words. His jaw was coated in a fine layer of stubble, dark and thick. It looked even more ridiculous with his mouth hanging open.

"You cheated on me," I said.

"I—"

"Are you seriously going to say that you didn't?" Laugh or cry—that was exactly the very fine line I had been walking on today, over and over again. "How long has this even been going on?"

"There are two sides of the story. It's not like I'm the only one who has cheated here." Ezra glared.

"Excuse me?"

"You." He ran his hand through his hair, ripping out more of the gel that I realized might not have been the reason his hair was always so perfectly tousled when he came home from work every day. "You have that little crush on that guy you've been hung up on for years."

"Oh, please."

"But do I comment on it or how you have a box of shit from him, which you hide, along with the rest of your stuff in my closet? No."

I rolled my eyes. That wasn't cheating.

All of that wasn't even Ezra's business. It wasn't a crush. I wasn't hung up on anyone. I had moved in with *him*. I'd told him that I loved him.

Somehow, I managed to think I had loved him last St. Patrick's Day after too many sour green cocktails.

At least a little. Enough.

"Look, Ezra. Are you listening closely? Because I don't want to have to go over this again. Currently, you disgust me. I don't want you to come after me. I don't want you to speak with me over the holiday. I'm going to take my things and get out of here because whatever was between us is over, and if I'm getting the picture, it has been for a long time. I need ... space."

Rolling his eyes, Ezra set his hands on his hips.

"So, I'm going to pack—oh, look, that's already done. Now, I'm going to leave." I hauled my bag up onto its side, and with one broken wheel skittering behind me, I walked past him. "Goodbye, Ezra. Happy holidays."

"Whatever."

Yeah. Whatever. I was going home.

Home.

If I could call anywhere that anymore, especially when it came to Marshall Falls.

TWO

BEFORE

"PLEASE, SYLVIA." My mom steered the two of us up to the white-columned porch of the historic colonial home.

The place looked like a mansion compared to the last apartment we had lived in. It still looked huge compared to the small house we moved into last week.

"This is my very good, very close friend. We actually met when we were about your age, so please, behave."

"I will."

"Her son will be here, and I have a feeling you two could be good friends."

I didn't say anything to that. I continued to walk—or rather, be dragged—up to the front door with a knocker in the shape of a lion before Mom stopped me with a solid hand on my shoulder. My feet almost fell out from under me, like we were on the playground. Kids would clothesline each other during a game of Red Rover—or they used to at my last school.

So far, the verdict was out about what kids liked to play in this town until I started school next week at Marshall Falls Elementary, where the walls were painted to look like a forest and the secretary had referred to me as a "little camper" when my mom signed me up.

"Sylvia? Are you listening to me?"

I blinked, not sure whether or not she had said anything. "Yes."

"Be kind and play nice," she pleaded.

I stared up into her dark-lined eyes. She had taken extra care to do her makeup this morning—every morning since we had moved here.

"He isn't as outgoing as you. He might need a friend."

A friend? The last time she had tried to set me up with a friend—well, we had moved now, so whatever sort of bad glaring her mother had toward mine no longer mattered. That had seemed to be the situation with a lot of things since we had moved.

"I'll behave," I bemoaned, slouching backward as she held on to my shoulders. I had nowhere else to look but at her and her frilly navy-blue sweater.

"Promise?" My mom held out a pinkie finger. She knew that it was nearly the only thing I held sacred at the age of seven.

I sighed, hooking my small finger with hers. "Promise."

"Good."

Mom knocked twice against the dark-green door, going for a third before it was whipped open.

"It's so good to see you!" A strange woman with wild, curly hair gripped my mother into a hard hug, not letting her go until she swayed this way and that, like a bear capturing her prey.

"It's good to see you too. You have no idea." My mom hugged the woman back for a minute before breaking away.

Her gaze turned to me. "And this must be Sylvia—or is it Sylvie?"

"Sylvia," I said, keeping my voice quiet as I stood still by the door.

I looked around the inside of the house. Like the outside, the inside was huge.

Unlike our new house, this one had two floors. Most of it was wooden planks, covered with a never-ending amount of fluffy, multicolored rugs. The walls had pictures of the family scattered everywhere with no real rhyme or reason. Two parents held a small boy, squinting with bright blue eyes at the camera, as if the flash had blinded him.

It felt like a hundred different people were there in the entry, staring at me. But everything was light in the house, even with it being so gray outside.

"It's good to finally meet you, Sylvia. My name is Lori," my mom's old friend said easily. "Your mom and I were really good friends, growing up."

I nodded.

"Speaking of ... Kieran!" Lori waved for the boy, who looked a little larger than the one in the pictures, to come off the stairs.

How long had he been sitting there?

The boy seemed about my age but moved slowly, as if he were an old man with posture issues. He gripped the railing the entire way down, his eyes never leaving me and my mom.

"Come here and meet my good friend," his mom insisted. "This is her daughter, Sylvia."

We gave each other awkward waves. To be honest, Kieran looked a lot less fun and more what I always imagined when someone said the phrase *teacher's pet*. He had fuzzy brown hair. Instead of squinting like the kid in the photographs on the wall, he also now had thick, dorky glasses that hung off the sides of his face.

"This is so nice. Getting the kids together. They're probably around the age we were when we became friends, right, Mer?" Lori gushed.

My mom smiled more down at me. I'd never heard my

mother called Mer before in her entire life. Even my dad called her by her full name, Meredith. Though that was usually only when he was grumpy.

He had been a little grumpy since we had moved here.

Lori still smiled. Her teeth shone, though they were a little crooked on the bottom as she turned her attention back to me. "You two should go outside."

The boy's shoulders slumped. "It's going to rain."

"Go for a little bit anyway. You need the sun to fill in those freckles. Go on," she encouraged. "Have fun."

My mom nudged me once more. "Behave."

I huffed, clenching my fists at my sides. "I said I would."

The moment we were out of the room, our mothers started to giggle.

Outside, the kid looked even scrawnier than he had when standing by the staircase, like a weird version of Harry Potter. The messy hair, the big glasses that didn't quite lay on his face right—all of it.

"I like your shirt," Kieran said in an attempt at conversation and pointed.

I glanced down at my sweatshirt.

"Why does it say *Estes Park?*" He sounded out the words.

I blinked at the print of mountains, faded from how many times it had gone through the wash. "Because that's in Colorado. We used to live there, and that's where Rocky Mountain National Park is. We went there one time because Mom said we needed to do something as a family."

"Have you lived there since you were born?"

I shook my head, narrowing my eyes. "No."

"Oh."

"Have you lived here since you were born?" I asked.

"Yeah." Kieran thought it over. "Kinda."

"Kinda?"

"Well, I spent nights over at my grandma's before."

"That doesn't really count," I said.

He shrugged.

"I lived in a lot of places. We were in Colorado and California, and we were in these little towns somewhere I can't remember since none of us liked it very long. My dad likes to move around a lot. My mom says that he can never sit still. I don't really get it though since I've seen him sit in the chair at home for long enough. We just moved here for now. My mom grew up here though. That's why she wanted to come back after what happened at my last school," I explained, wandering back and forth across the grass.

Kieran stood, watching. "Did you get in trouble or something?"

"No." Not exactly anyway. *Did his mom tell him something already?*

I wasn't a bad kid even if all the other moms had told my mom that I was, back in Colorado. I just made some bad decisions sometimes. At least, that was what Mom would say, usually with a huff of impatience or before sending me off to my room.

"Why?"

"I don't know. Your mom just sort of looked at you like ..." He looked away, back toward the house, as if he was preparing to run in the other direction.

Like I was always in trouble?

I clenched my fists again. "I'm not."

"Sorry."

"Why are you sorry?"

Kieran shrugged his shoulders again. His chin tilted downward until his glasses started to slip to the front of his nose. He pushed them back into place.

"Anyway, we're here because my mom wants to be here. She says that we are staying here for a while, no matter what."

"Where do you want to be?"

I hadn't really thought about it.

"Well, it's nice here. Most of the time anyway," he mumbled.

"Most of the time?" I asked.

"We get a lot of snow."

"And that's a good thing?"

"A lot of snow means no school for a lot of days."

Kieran had a point that I hadn't thought of before.

"Huh."

"You'll probably be in my class. Everyone's basically in one classroom since there aren't many of us," rambled Kieran as we walked through the grass.

We wandered around the back of the white house, and like everything I had seen in Marshall Falls, it felt like I was in one of those movies on TV. There was a fence all around the backyard. A garden was in the corner, which would've never fit on the balcony of where we had lived in Denver. There were even rose bushes with actual roses lining the side of the house. In the center of the yard, I was almost surprised when I looked up and didn't see a wooden house up in the big tree with low-hanging branches.

I smirked, walking toward the tree. There wasn't much in this town I understood, including the weird, quiet kid following me around every other step, but I knew where I would find fun when I saw it.

"What are you doing?"

"This is a perfect climbing tree," I announced, throwing myself at the thick bottom branch two more times before I was able to haul myself the rest of the way up. "Pull yourself up."

"I don't know if that's safe."

"It's perfectly safe! The branches are good and sturdy." I jumped on one for good measure. It barely wobbled. "This tree has probably been here for, like, a hundred years or something, right?"

"Probably."

I leaned against the thick center. "It won't let you fall as long as you're careful."

"I don't know."

I pulled myself up another branch and then another until I was high above Kieran and the rest of his yard. I could see the top of the garage, where there looked to be a whole other room. I could see the splashes of color on the rose bushes that looked more like dots than petals.

"The view is amazing up here. Come on up."

Kieran shuffled, still unmoving. "I've never climbed a tree before."

"Seriously?"

Kieran shifted nervously.

"No better day to change that!" I called. I climbed back down a branch. "Take my hand. I'll yank you the first way up."

"I don't know ..."

"Take a chance, Kieran. It's cool. See the view."

"Well, okay."

"Take my hand."

I waved it out at him again as he came closer to the tree. Reaching out, his hand slapped into mine. I pulled him up as he tried to lift himself into the first round of branches.

His feet scraped against the trunk as he tried to climb. He was right; he wasn't very good at this.

"Your hand is all sweaty."

He wiped both of them against his pants when he sat against one of the branches. He looked around where we were, a few feet off the ground. "Sorry. You're right; this is kind of nice up here."

"See? Now, we need to go higher."

"Higher?"

"Trust a little, Kieran."

He grinned when I used his name. It was the first time he had smiled along with me.

"Okay." He pulled himself up onto another branch.

"See? Still not so bad. It's like we are in a little tree house. Without the house."

He chuckled. "I see what you mean. It's kind of cozy."

"What's that place over there?"

"The garage?"

I shook my head. "The place above it."

"Oh, that's just an extra place. My mom used to bake stuff in there. She runs a bakery. It first started out of the house, but now, she has a shop and everything."

"That's neat."

"She makes really good jam cookies." He nodded thoughtfully. "She uses real raspberries and everything."

"Is that your favorite fruit?"

"Some of the time. I like apples too. They're probably my favorite. What's yours?"

"I don't know," I said. It was another thing I had never thought about. No one had ever really asked. "I do like raspberries."

Kieran's lips curled back up into a smile, looking around.

Rumbling sounded. The patter of rain slapped against the leaves of the tree. Our eyes met as we sat next to each other, and I looked into the striking blue of Kieran's eyes.

I'd never seen anyone who had such bright blue eyes. I could see every speck even through the sheen of his glasses.

Dots started to coat the lenses as Kieran looked up. "It's starting to rain."

Blinking, I reached my hand out. Before I felt anything on my hand, a fat blob of water spatted on my nose. I scrunched as I started to shift off the branch I was on. "Better get down."

"Right."

I was halfway down from the tree when I realized that Kieran wasn't following behind me. "Coming?"

"Uh-huh."

I narrowed my eyes at the strange nerd. "Need help?"

"Nope." Kieran's voice shook as he looked down. His eyes landed on me and then the ground. "I can do it."

"Okay."

Hanging from the final branch, I let go and landed hard on my feet. Dusting myself off, I cocked my head, looking back up into the tree. It'd felt like we were higher than we were, but Kieran still remained right where I had left him.

"Kieran?"

"I can't get down."

"Yes, you can. You're not that high up."

"I am. I am very high up, and I can't get down."

"Just move one branch at a time," I suggested.

"I can't do that either."

"Kieran!" My lips curled, and I looked back and forth toward the back sliding door of the house. No one was looking out at us. *Yet*, that was. "You need to get down here right now."

Because if he didn't get down, then I was going to have to go and tell his mom, and she would tell my mom. Then, my mom would know that I apparently hadn't behaved. It wasn't like I hadn't tried. I had.

It wasn't my fault he had never climbed a tree before. I hadn't really thought through the whole *getting down* thing.

I groaned up into the air, throwing my head back.

"I'm stuck. I can't move." A note of panic entered Kieran's voice as the rain started to turn from a pelt into a fine mist. His hands gripped the branch.

"Yes, you can."

"I can't."

"Kieran, you get your butt down here on the ground right now," I called, trying to sound intimidating.

With wide eyes, Kieran stared right back at me with as much conviction. He held on to the tree for dear life. "My butt is staying right here, stuck in this tree. I cannot get down. I'm stuck!"

We had to call the fire department to get Kieran out of the tree. He was like a cat. A very stuck cat that looked at me as if I were trying to make it lose one of its lives when I advised him to jump. When I mentioned the comparison to the firemen, composed of Marshall Falls top trade high schoolers, they laughed the entire time.

So did Kieran's mom, even as I meowed.

Kieran glared at me, even after his feet finally met the ground.

And just like that, I knew, even as he ran back in the house with frustrated tears rimming his blue eyes ...

He was mine.

THREE

NOW

"FELIZ NAVIDAD" played on a loop. At this rate, I was going to go insane before I reached my destination—if I wanted to reach my destination.

At the time when I had said I was going home, the idea had felt like the only one that made sense. Now, every minute the train got farther away from the city, the only thing thinking about going home to the small town of Marshall Falls did, where there were more trees than people who made sure to be constantly up in your business, was make me feel sick.

Where else could I have gone after basically kicking myself out of the one place I had to live?

I could've called up one of my old roommates maybe. We were still sort of friends—in the way that, occasionally, when we bumped into each other somewhere we'd smile and wave like estranged cousins. I could've even called up my old work friend from when we had both been in a string of unlucky and hardly paid internships, though I hadn't seen her in years. I wasn't even sure if she was in the city anymore.

It was odd that, in a city of millions, I could barely keep up with the very few friends I had made over the years in tiny spurts of outgoing necessity.

The trees turned thick, and the scenery quickly disintegrated from urban to rural outside the window. However, the trees were still bare, and the land surrounding me looked like a frozen tundra.

It was the perfect time to realize that, in my haste to get out of the apartment and away from Ezra in a sort of numb haze, I'd forgotten my coat.

I crossed my arms and sank lower into the crinkly gray leather seat.

I didn't know what I'd expected from Ezra. I'd known when we started dating after a run-in at a bar that he wasn't going to be the perfect one. No one would likely ever live up to the Mr. Right definition these days, but he was decent. No declaration of love would ever be uttered from his lips, certainly not while sober. But he was nice enough when he needed to be. He remembered my birthday and never made gross jokes to his friends when I was around. Ezra was ... steady.

Until today, that was.

Still, I had expected to feel *more*.

I'd expected to be so angry I couldn't stand it or so upset that I couldn't hold back the tears while begging him to love me even a little. Instead, I felt nothing.

I replayed my day over and over again. I watched myself, as if in a dream, from the moment I had been called into Miranda's office, already having a gut feeling about what was going to happen. And then the moment I had walked into the fancy apartment with the beautiful views, where Ezra had cheated on me before having the audacity to claim I did the same thing.

Oh my God. I covered my own face with my hands.

It was all so bad.

The thick lump in my chest made its way up my throat. The

pressure surged behind my eyes, yet still, I forced it down.

No, not yet.

I was going to get back to the city. I was going make this work somehow. It was going to be okay. I was not going to break down.

On reflex, I reached into my bag. Pushing aside shirts and shoes, I found the box Ezra thew in my face. He must've stumbled on it once or twice, but never said anything. You know, until today. It had been the perfect moment for him to decide to bring up touchy subjects after he got all touchy with his coworker.

Pausing, I slid my hand over the small shoebox. The contents calmed me down when I was on the precipice of a breakdown. I should've burned the entire thing before I moved in with Ezra and saved the possibility of him finding the strange coffin of my past, but I couldn't.

Every time I opened the lid, the stupid container of memories took my breath away. Inside, bent movie tickets stuck out from under a faded wine label and camp patch. Ripped pieces of paper were scattered around tiny trinkets. Old stories I'd written, torn out of school notebooks. The bracelet I used to never take off after it was given to me clanged around inside the box and weighed it down.

When I had first received the bracelet, there had been only one charm on it. Over the years, more and more charms were added. There was a cupcake, a cell phone, a little skyscraper smaller than my fingernail. The bracelet was the perfect gift because, for years, no one ever had to think about what I actually wanted. Charms were added until it became a full, gaudy accessory. I trailed my fingers across it, remembering each one.

I dropped the bracelet back inside the box. Everything looked so silly and ridiculous now. The worst part of the box— and perhaps the reason I didn't open it every day—were the photographs. My younger self, who wore more makeup than anyone should, smirked up at me. Arms were thrown around my shoulders in almost every snapshot. The person those arms belonged to grinned wide and proudly as he looked between me or the camera. The flash bounced off the shine of his glasses in some pictures.

Kieran.

It took me two tries to shut the box properly and shove it back into my overstuffed luggage.

I could still hear Ezra yelling at me as I had left the apartment about how I was clinging to my past—clinging to the little crush I'd been hung up on for years.

But that wasn't true. It wasn't.

I wasn't hung up on anything, let alone my best friend. There was no reason to be. We had grown up and grown apart. That was how childhood friendships worked, wasn't it?

That was that.

For an unknown reason, however, my heart continued to hammer in my chest. Every mile the train went on made me consider for a split second if I should throw myself out of the side of the passenger car and attempt a life of living as a recluse in the woods. Lots of famous writers did it, though I doubted I would get by without heat or indoor plumbing.

Hours later, I managed to settle by the time the conductor announced that we would be pulling into the nearest station to Marshall Falls.

The man leaned into my empty row, adjusting his boxy hat before swiping my ticket out from where it had been tucked above me with my luggage. "This'll be your stop."

I stood and grabbed my things that felt a lot bulkier now than they had when I got on. "Thanks."

"Happy holidays."

He waved as the side door of the train slid open, and I

hobbled onto the platform. I shivered in the air—at least twenty degrees colder than it was in the city.

"You too," I whispered, though the door of the train was already closing behind me. It kept going forward without me.

I watched the tin-can train leave before I forced myself to move. I yanked my suitcase behind me down the stairs one bump at a time. At the bottom, I reached into my pocket for my phone.

I probably should've called for someone to pick me up earlier. I pressed my phone against my ear, letting the dial tone ring and ring.

"*Your call has been forwarded to an automated voice message system.*"

I narrowed my eyes and tried my mom's number next.

"*Your call has been forwarded to an automated voice message system.*"

I huffed. "Par for the course today."

I tried one more time, though if anything, the service was worse.

"Hey, Dad. Mom told me that you wanted me to call, and, well ..." I drifted off as I left a message, looking at the thin layer of gritty snow covering the entire area.

They said everything was gray in the city from the buildings to the concrete, but Vermont took it one level further in the winter.

I tried to fake enthusiasm in my voice as I gripped the handle of my luggage and walked over to the nearest bench. "Surprise! I'm in town. It was sort of a last-minute decision, but I was hoping that someone could pick me up from the station. Call me back if you get this."

I slumped down into the seat.

What was the plan now? If my parents didn't call me back...

It couldn't be that hard to figure out, could it? I lived alone in one of the largest cities in the world for years. When I had first gotten to New York, I had been a fish out of water, and it was obvious that I had no idea what I was doing. But I made it work.

I had faked it until I made it.

Of course, in New York City, there were yellow cabs to get you wherever you needed to go. Now, I was just a washed-up fish, back in the tiny bowl of Marshall Falls.

The last time I had gotten off the train was nearly four years ago.

I had been so excited to come home back then. I was excited to see my parents and the rest of the town, all lit up for the holidays—the only real time I thought Marshall Falls looked at all like the pretty little town it tried to be.

Four years ago, I jumped off the train and onto the platform, racing down the steps with nothing but anxious giddiness pooling inside of me. I barely saw my driver back into town before I threw myself at him. He stood against the side of my dad's old cherry-red pickup truck, and I crashed into his arms with a string of laughter between the two of us.

"You miss me that much, Silly?" Kieran had chuckled, using my ridiculous nickname he had come up with.

I didn't miss how his arms wrapped around me tighter as he nearly lifted me off the ground until my face pressed into the space between his neck and shoulder. He carried the scent of vanilla from his mother's bakery and pine from whatever deodorant he'd worn since high school, and I sucked a deep breath in.

Now, I made it home, but suddenly, it felt a little more like I was waiting for the next shoe to drop. Not to mention, after another few minutes, it looked like I was walking.

FOUR

BEFORE

"IT WAS HIS FAULT," I argued with the principal. "He was the one who started it and was saying things."

"Things?"

I slumped back in the creaky chair that smelled like dust. I had done nothing wrong. Or maybe I had. I really had.

But it didn't mean I was the only one who had done things wrong. If someone had taught Dylan to keep his mouth shut when he had nothing nice to say, I wouldn't have to worry about punching him in the face when I had nothing nice to do in return.

The man in the light-brown suit, the principal of Marshall Falls Elementary, looked exhausted as he braced himself over his desk, filled with state college memorabilia. "It isn't about that, Sylvie—"

"Sylvia," I bit out.

What was it with Marshall Falls Schools and not calling someone by their actual name? It wasn't that hard.

Like it wasn't too hard for Dylan to learn how to be an okay person. I wasn't even asking for him to be nice. Just okay.

That way, I could be okay.

"We don't put hands on other students—*ever*. I'm sure that's no different from your last school, right?"

My eyes drifted toward the walls of positive quotes underneath predator animals as I held my pulsing red hand. It felt like it had its own heartbeat. "Yes."

"Is there a reason why your mother isn't answering the phone?" the principal asked with another long, heaving sigh.

My mom wasn't good about answering her phone on a normal day, but during the day, when I was at school, she was Secretary Meredith and no one else.

"Probably at work."

The principal opened his file cabinet. As the single new student at Marshall Falls, my folder was right near the front. He flipped it open before going back to the phone. Pressing it to his ear, he waited for another moment.

"Hello, this is Principal Rainer. Yes, everything is fine. I'm calling on behalf of Sylvia Calasis. She had a bit of a problem with another student today. I've been trying to get ahold of her mother. Right. Yes. That is what she said." He shut his eyes, continuing to inform whoever was on the other line of what had happened today.

Outside, the recess aide had to drag me away from the boy who now had a bloody nose in the nurse's office. They also pulled me away from Kieran. Kieran stared the whole time. His eyes were wide and rimmed with red. He followed me all the way to the office before being sent back to class, silent but watching.

"We will see you soon then," the principal continued in his strange, clipped tone over the phone to whoever he was talking to. "Of course. I will."

I stared at the principal as he set down the phone. He brought his fingers up to his forehead, massaging either side for a moment. Then, he picked up the phone again. It buzzed once.

"Hi there. Can you please send Kieran Rose down to the office with his and Sylvia Calasis's things? Yes, that's right. Thank you."

He hung up the phone. Finally, his gaze turned back up to me.

"Mrs. Rose will be here to pick you up soon."

Mrs. Rose? Kieran's mom?

I looked around as if she would suddenly appear with my own mom in tow, and the principal waved for me to stand up and took me back out into the main office area.

Over the past few months since we had first gotten to Marshall Falls, I'd seen Kieran's mom, Lori, a few times. I mostly saw her pick up Kieran at the end of the day, watching me walk a block before offering me a ride home. It was about the same amount of time Kieran and I spent together since the first time we had seen each other. We partnered during class when needed and sat together during lunch, where he had always packed something sweet to end on and often quietly left it for me to devour, mumbling about how he was full.

Other than that, however, we remained odd, friendless people who often found ourselves next to one another. I figured he probably still hadn't forgiven me about the whole tree thing.

Or at least, it seemed that way.

I could only imagine what his mom was going to think of me now. I was just another bad kid.

The one secretary did a slow look at me up and down before motioning for me to take a seat in one of the squishy, uncomfortable chairs by the door, near windows that showed everyone walking past who was sitting in the office in trouble. I sighed, slouching in on myself while I continued to hold one hand in the other in my lap.

Eventually, the steady squeak of white tennis shoes traveled up the hallway.

"What happened?" Kieran's mom gripped her purse to her side so it didn't whip away from her with the force she took the corner into the office with.

I stared at her. She wasn't mad? She didn't seem mad.

"I got in trouble."

Lori flashed a small smile. "Well, I can see that. What happened?"

I shrugged.

At that, her eyebrows lowered, as if she were unsure of how to react to my nonverbal answer. She dropped down into a squat in front of me. Even the secretary went back to whatever she had been working on, tip-tapping away on her computer.

"Did something happen to make you upset?" Her voice turned down, nearly whispering to me.

Yes. But no one cared about if something made me upset.

"You can tell me. I promise I won't get angry."

I took a deep breath, knowing that when an adult said something like that, they didn't mean it. Yet I took a chance. "They were making fun of his glasses."

"What?" Understanding dawned on Lori's face. "Kieran's glasses?"

"And other things. They were rude and stupid, and so then I was stupid."

"Hmm, that seems fair." Lori said, pressing her lips together in a hard line, though her eyes still gleamed like when she smiled.

I couldn't tell whether she was mad or trying to keep in a laugh. Though that didn't make any sense at all.

"Kieran is fine. He tried to get me to walk away, but ..." I glanced down at my hand.

Slowly, Lori looked down toward my angry hand. "I understand. You know that violence isn't what we do to make our voice heard, right?"

I knew this speech.

"Because you didn't want to hit him, did you?"

"Oh, no, I wanted to," I said.

I didn't think any of these people understood what exactly had happened. In my short amount of time here, it had already become clear to me that when it came to Dylan, there really was only one way that made him be quiet completely—and in record time.

I could tell that Kieran's mom must've had a good sense of humor because she was fighting another laugh, a peal of it snuck out before she got it under control. She glanced back toward the secretary, both of us seemed to expect her to be staring in disapproval.

"But you wanted to tell him that he was wrong too?"

In a way, I had done that. "He was wrong."

"And you know that. When you want to conquer a bully or tell the truth to them, even when they're screaming, you need to use your words. I have a feeling that you probably can think of some pretty good ones too. Right?"

"What if they don't listen?"

"Some people won't, but that's when we know we don't care about what they think if they don't care about what we do. Do you understand what I'm saying?"

"I think so."

"Good. Does your hand hurt?" Her fingers lifted my fingers up from my lap, prodding gently at the red spot.

"A little."

"We'll fix it up. Ready to go?" she asked.

"I have her stuff," a small voice answered for me.

Kieran was already in his coat and hat, standing in the middle of the office doorway. His book bag was on his back while the rest of my stuff dangled from his hand. The weight of everything nearly took him to the floor.

Lori patted my knee before standing back up, extending an arm around Kieran. "Wonderful. Come on, lovey. We're playing hooky for the rest of the day with Miss Sylvia."

Without a word, Kieran followed along, as if this sort of thing happened all the time. Lori corralled the two of us into her minivan even though I couldn't imagine she toted around anyone else but herself and Kieran—and maybe a dozen or two cupcakes for each bake sale.

She waited until we were buckled in before pulling out of the school parking lot and turning toward the main roads leading into the center of town. I figured that she was going to take Kieran home—or worse, drop me back off at my house to wait for the moment my mom or dad walked through the door and asked why I was home before the end of the school day.

I didn't think I could come up with a good enough lie.

Lori took another turn down the street before pulling up to the curb. She was nearly out of the car, along with Kieran, before I moved.

"Come on now. Just because you two are done working for the day doesn't mean that Mom is. Hop out." She waved her hand at me.

I followed Kieran from the backseat. We stood on the sidewalk in front of Rose Bakery, the sign drawn up with a buttercream flower above a mint-green porch.

Inside, the shop was just as light and bright.

Lori swooped around the back counter, leaning into the bearded man behind with an apron on. She gave him a quick peck of a kiss on the cheek. "Thanks for holding down the fort."

"Any issues?"

"None. I think Kieran and Sylvia could use a break for the rest of the afternoon."

It dawned on me that this was Kieran's dad. I blinked at the man, who raised his dark eyebrows at the two of us.

"Is that so?"

Kieran shrugged.

His dad laughed. "That hand doesn't look too good."

"I'm going to get her some ice," Lori agreed, heading toward the back room.

Kieran's dad bent down in front of me while Kieran moved along to the round booth in the corner underneath the biggest window. "I'm Dave. Can I see?"

I hesitated before I lifted my hand.

"Yeah, you see, when you need to use your hands, you have to use the flats of your knuckles more and make sure this thumb is right here." He fixed my hand into the right position. It hurt when he touched it, but I didn't stop him as I watched. "Like that. We don't want that and another call from the school though, understand? Those are emergency-only hands."

"Please don't encourage her." Lori shook her head as she came toward me with a striped towel wrapped around an ice pack.

"You're the one pulling them out of school in the middle of the day."

Lori cocked her head at Dave and gave him a look.

He put his hands up and walked away, giving me a wink as he did. "I'm headed back to work then, hon."

"Mmhmm." Lori instructed me how to hold the ice against the back of my hand. "Better?"

Honestly, it kind of stung. "Are you going to tell my mom?"

Lori hummed, thinking this through herself by the way her lips pursed. "Do you want me to tell your mom?"

"Not really."

"Then, we won't tell her. Not unless we have to."

The confusion must've shown on my face.

"But if it happens again at school, we will have to tell her," Lori amended. "Does that sound fair?"

"Okay."

"All right then," said Lori. "Since you two troublemakers aren't in school for the rest of the afternoon, I'm going to put you to work."

Kieran scooched back out from the booth and came back to stand in front of us. He motioned me to follow him and his mom back behind the counter. The shop was quiet, and yet it felt wrong to be going where I guessed all the stuff was made.

Even stranger? I was supposed to be in trouble. I was supposed to be told that I wasn't behaving again without being able to give my reasons why. I was supposed to be sent to my room without supper before my mom felt bad and ended up making me a peanut butter and jelly sandwich before bed.

Lori obviously didn't have that in mind.

"These are the ones I was talking about," murmured Kieran.

My eyebrows pressed together. "What?"

"The cookies I talked about before. When you were at my house that day," he said, shifting shyly.

The day with the tree, he meant.

I bit my lip so that I didn't smile at the memory of him up there, stuck in the leaves as the rain came down harder and harder. "Oh."

The two of us stood up on the small stools Kieran's mom pushed up to the edge of the wide metal counter in the center of the back room. The bakery looked small from the outside, but inside was wide and airy and full of color. The kitchen had shiny appliances lightly splattered with the remnants of what looked like lemon cake.

My stomach growled at the smell of whatever was already being baked in the oven.

Kieran chuckled as I clutched my stomach. Lori pull ingredients from the double-door fridge.

Mixing bowls, flour, sugar, butter, and raspberries were slid across the space in front of us. Kieran reached for the butter, pulling it out of its thin paper packaging and dropping it into one of the bowls, as if he had done this a million times before, not needing his mom to tell him what to do or even look at a recipe.

"You can eat one." Kieran nudged the punnet of bright red raspberries in front of me. "They're your favorites, right?"

I didn't know why it surprised me that he remembered. Then again, oddly, I remembered that his favorite fruit was a plain old apple.

The moment I placed the first berry on my tongue, I realized they were not just regular raspberries. My eyes widened as I chewed. They were somehow sweet and ripe and so fresh even though I hadn't seen any raspberries growing around here. I popped another raspberry in my mouth. The sweet tartness made my lips pucker before I reached for another.

"Don't eat all of them or else there isn't going to be enough jam for the next batch." Lori laughed.

She took two more raspberries out for each of us before turning around. On the stove, a flash of fire sputtered underneath a steel pot. She dumped the rest of the fruit inside, mashing the berries with a wooden spoon.

After rolling out the dough, Lori spread the trays between us, showing us how to roll the balls and set them on the trays.

"Then, you're just going to press your thumb right here in the middle," Kieran's mom advised.

I stared down at the shortbread cookies, wide-eyed. My mom rarely let me into the kitchen with her, let alone to bake by myself. The kitchen was her "me time," as she liked to call it. She preferred to make Hamburger Helper out of a box than have to explain and correct all the things I did wrong or complain about the mess I made while trying to help.

Kieran immediately went to work, just like he had done with the dough, carefully indenting each of the cookies with his small thumbprint.

"Aren't you going to do yours?" Kieran asked, looking at my half of the tray, which he was starting to get close to doing himself. His hands lifted up from the small globes of dough, and he narrowed his eyes. He used the back of his hand to press his glasses back up the bridge of his nose. "You can't eat them if you don't help."

"What if I do it wrong?" I asked.

"I don't think you can. Here."

Kieran grabbed my hand from where it had been stuck on the counter. One finger at a time, he pushed them down until it looked like I was giving him a thumbs-up.

He gave me one back.

I burst out laughing.

He brought my thumb to one of the cookies on the tray and helped press my finger down into the center. "See? Perfect. I'll finish the row next to it. You do the rest."

"How is it going?" His mom looked over the cookies.

For a moment, I thought she was going to fix the one or two that weren't perfectly centered.

She beamed. "They look great. If you want to help me scoop the jam in the center, you can clean up then and have a few as a snack when they come out of the oven, though they might be a little gooey."

"Yum." Immediately, Kieran reached for a spoon. Instead of putting the first dollop into the dip of the cookie, however, he put it directly into his mouth, taking the time to lick off the excess.

"Kieran, get a new spoon and save some for the cookies," his mother chastised, though she still looked as pleased as ever as she shook her head at her son. She passed a small teaspoon to me. "Now, if Sylvia wants a taste, she's welcome to it. I make it by hand from the raspberries in the yard at home, though I doubt you two got to explore them yet. It's why Kieran obviously can't control himself."

Kieran grinned wide at the two of us in proof, clearly unashamed. Raspberry seeds were stuck between his teeth.

***

Tucked into the small booth in the shop, Kieran didn't look at all concerned about the people coming in and out. Every time the door opened, a bell chimed with the new person arriving, and I looked up. I couldn't help myself.

I looked up toward the door, then back to Kieran. He had flour sticking to the underside of his chin and then back down to our little space we had set up in the corner since we had slid the trays of heart-shaped thumbprint cookies into the oven.

I recognized some of the people who came into the bakery. Others looked like I had never seen anyone like them before in my life—from the man with the bald spot and large messenger bag slung over his shoulder to the little old lady who had so much gold jewelry layered around her neck that I was surprised it didn't weigh her down. They came in for orders they had already placed, like a birthday cake. Or their eyes wandered over the case of cookies, cupcakes, and crescent-shaped buns.

All of them were from Marshall Falls. A few looked over at the two of us before moving toward the counter, mumbling something with a small giggle that caused Lori to lean over.

"Aren't they adorable?" Lori whispered, slightly too loud not to hear.

Then, they moved on to another boring subject, like the weather.

"Does your hand still hurt?" Kieran asked.

I took away the ice pack I had placed overtop. "Not really anymore." My fingers ached a little when I stretched it though.

It was still worth it.

"It was pretty awesome, what you did." Kieran peeked up at me through his too-long hair, which had flopped down over his eyebrows.

"You think?"

"Except for your hand looking like it's all red and splotchy, yeah. It was crazy," Kieran said. "But cool."

I chuckled. He had a point. "I didn't like the way Dylan or his friends talked to you or pushed you around."

He shrugged.

"Do they always do that?"

Another shrug. He reached for one of the cookies we had made. His mom had put them in front of us, fresh out of the oven. I reached for one too, watching as Kieran dunked it in his hot chocolate.

"Sometimes."

"Doesn't it bother you?"

His blue eyes met mine as he huffed and adjusted himself to sit better next to me. "Sometimes."

I reached over and took his mug of hot chocolate. I had said I didn't want anything, and Kieran's mom had listened, though she had given Kieran an extra-tall mug. I thought I understood why when I dunked my own raspberry-jam-filled cookie in for a second before popping it in my mouth. It was sweet and tart in all the most wonderful ways.

I groaned at the taste.

"Good, huh?"

I nodded.

He laughed before pulling out a few pieces of plain paper, doodling on them with the fat markers he always had in his backpack at school. There were only a few colors left from others taking them though.

"You're my friend, right?" I looked at him.

His eyes widened as he paused his chewing, looking up from where he had drawn what looked like some kind of combination between a dog and a dragon.

"I mean, you don't have to be, if you don't want to be."

Kieran hastily shook his head. "I kind of figured that we were already friends."

Oh. "We are."

"You sure?"

"You're *my* friend, Kieran," I said, this time certain, hoping he'd agree if I meant it.

Kieran was a pushover that way. He would be my friend whether he liked it or not now.

His lips pressed together before he peered down at his hot chocolate again. "I'm glad, Sylvie."

"It's Sylvia."

He passed me another cookie.

For once, I didn't feel like I was at some weird after-school program that preached Bible verses, listening to sing-a-long songs, or having another neighbor watch me until my parents came to pick me up. Warm and at ease, I took a deep breath.

Marshall Falls wasn't my home exactly, but I was home.

"Okay, Sylvia."

FIVE

NOW

WHEN I PUSHED through the front door of my childhood house, it was empty. The lights were off. No one was home.

"Hello?" I called out, slamming the door.

A slight shiver came over me. I might have dealt with cold city streets and snow, but Marshall Falls held air that felt like ice puncturing your lungs. Inside, the house felt no warmer.

"Anyone home?"

Nothing.

"Okay then."

I walked farther into the ranch-style house, and it was almost odd how quiet it was. My father had a habit of leaving on a light over the oven or even the television on if he knew he wasn't going to be long. Work should've been over for the day if he did a full shift, same for my mother.

Maybe they went to the diner for dinner?

I narrowed my eyes through the kitchen and down the hall toward my old bedroom. I flicked on the light switch. Though the room was cleaner and sans the posters I used to have on the plain beige walls growing up, it was nearly exactly how I left it.

My phone buzzed against the side of my purse. My mother's name flashed across the screen.

"Hello?" I tucked my phone between my ear and shoulder.

I unzipped my suitcase and duffel bag before pausing. I had no idea what I planned on doing here. I was sure most of the dresser drawers still had all my old stuff inside that I never took with me, and I wasn't going to be here that long. Or I didn't think I was. It was probably better if I lived out of my suitcase until I decided what to do.

Dropping my hands down, I held my phone up to the side of my head as I looked around the space again. It was smaller than I remembered.

"Sylvia," my mother sighed as if she was frustrated.

"Hi, Mom."

"Did you make it home? You know you could've called anyone in town to come and pick you up. The neighbors next door were going to pick up their daughter from college anyway, I believe, today. Or maybe that was tomorrow ..."

I ignored the fact that my mother probably thought it was okay for me to sit overnight at the train station while risking hypothermia. "Yes, I made it home. Where are you guys?"

"Oh good," was all she said.

"So, are you guys in town somewhere or ..." I let the question drift off.

"Well, that's the thing, honey."

I paused. "Is something wrong? Are you okay?"

"Yes! Of course! I didn't mean to scare you. That was the thing I was trying to tell you earlier when I called. I wanted to make sure that you weren't coming home. You haven't in a few years, so your father and I figured that it was time to mix it up a bit." She hesitated.

"Mix it up?"

"We're on a cruise! For two weeks!"

"A cruise?" I blinked, making sure I had heard her correctly.

My mother and father, who hadn't taken a vacation in twenty years, were now on a two-week voyage somewhere in the middle of the ocean?

"Cruises are cheaper this time of year, and the weather is milder, even in the Caribbean. We really didn't think that you were going to be home, sweetheart. I double-checked, didn't I? I called you nearly every day last week."

I sat down on the edge of my bed. The duvet crinkled beneath me. "You could've just told me what you were planning. You didn't say you were going on a cruise."

"We figured on Christmas we'd video you a sort of holiday well wishes. We wanted to try and be spontaneous. You haven't been home for the past few years so ..." She paused again. "I can't tell if you're upset."

"I'm not," I responded quickly. "I'm surprised. Not upset."

"Your father is already trying to get me to cancel and somehow get off the boat before we have to do the safety drills."

"No. Don't do that."

"Thank you. It can still be a good holiday."

"Mmhmm," I agreed, looking around my old room again. There was a cobweb in the corner.

"You'll see all your old friends," my mother went on. "I think Jenna has been doing lots of stuff with her new baby—or I guess not so much a baby anymore. She's about two now, I think. Amy Walmer still works over at the elementary school. They'll be going on holiday vacation by the end of the week. I'm sure she'll be looking for someone to go spend time with. You two used to be friends a bit, weren't you?"

There was no one else in the world I wanted to spend less time with than Amy. Or at least in the small world that was Marshall Falls.

"Kieran—"

"Kieran's still in town?"

Of course he was still in town. I didn't know why I had asked that.

My mother laughed as if the idea was ridiculous to her too. "I'm sure he'll be at the lighting ceremony later. That's also happening this evening at the gazebo in town. It's such a shame that the two of you haven't been able to see each other in so long. You were so good together."

"We weren't together, Mom."

"Good friends," she corrected herself with a huff.

I took a deep breath, hanging my head between my shoulders.

"If you really want us to come home and stay with you, we can. We'd probably lose out on the trip money since we wouldn't be able to reschedule—"

"It's fine." I stopped her. "Really."

"You're sure?"

I nodded to only myself. "Positive."

"Okay." I could hear my mother's grin. "I'll take tons of photos to come back and show you by New Year's. You'll still be here by then, right? You'll need to stop by the store and get some things as well since I planned on leaving and I don't think I have anything stocked. You know what I mean."

"That's ... great."

"Perfect." My mother's plan was all coming together. Everyone was happy as far as she could tell. "Oh, I wish I were home with you. It has been so long since your father and I have gotten to see you. Anyway, you really should go to the town gazebo lighting tonight. It's little late this year since some of the lights needed to be replaced," she explained.

After using the same decorations from the '50s, I wasn't surprised.

"You should absolutely go and catch up around town. I'm sure people will be thrilled to see you. Wear something warm."

I nearly cut her off. I knew how to dress myself.

"I know. I just wanted to remind you."

"Okay. Have a good vacation."

"We will, and I'll check in. Relax and enjoy your time at home, Sylvia," she said, a demand lining her voice.

"Have fun," I said, trying to sound a little more chipper. "Talk soon."

"Talk soon. Bye."

I hit the button to end the call and dropped my phone back down beside me. The house was still quiet and empty.

I'd lost my job. Found my somewhat-steady boyfriend of two years cheating on me. Nearly cried on public transportation but hadn't. Now, I was alone at Christmas.

I almost wanted to jinx myself and ask what else could possibly go wrong, but even I wasn't going to risk that sort of vengeance.

Taking a deep breath, I wandered the room and rummaged through drawers. I stared down at the old band tees from concerts I never went to. I dug through the crazy patterned socks covered in seasonal patterns, gifted to me. Most of them had been given to me by Kieran.

He would laugh every time I opened a new pair, noting the amused and overly excited look on my face at a pair of socks. He'd clap his hands together the moment I yanked apart the packaging and slipped on the new pair. Full of ruffles or snowflakes over my toes.

The reminder of them as I looked over the Valentine's Day pair covered in little cupids complete with bow and heart-shaped arrows made my chest ache.

Socks were intimate.

Socks were something that someone wore nearly every day.

Every time I looked down, they were a little reminder. For the past few years, I couldn't remember the last time I had worn any socks that weren't a dull, simple gray, bought in a pack of six or ten, hidden beneath boring brown loafers or slipped inside my favorite pair of ankle boots that zipped up the side.

I never thought to buy anything fun for myself. Neither had Ezra nor anyone else. Never anyone but Kieran.

Kieran, Kieran, *Kieran*.

Already, since I had stepped back into Marshall Falls, it was like he was a ghost, haunting me.

Grabbing a pair of the socks, I shut the rest of my drawers and swung the lid of my suitcase open where I had slid it onto the floor, out of the way. In comparison to the rest of my room, the clothes inside of it were oddly subdued. Grays and blacks and the occasional muted pastel sweater were unceremoniously stuffed inside from my speedy escape. Leaving on the loose cream sweater, I slipped on a pair of dark jeans. I shimmied them over my hips, sucking my stomach in to slip the button through.

The jeans were much different than my work slacks, which fit more like yoga pants. The jeans, however, did make my butt look nice. I turned back and forth in front of my hazy closet door mirrors.

The last time I had been home, I had stood in front of the mirrors just like this. I wore a tight sweater dress and patterned lace tights. I wanted to look nice when I headed over to Kieran's house for his mom's annual holiday party. I curled my hair even though it would turn into a mess the moment I got there. Kieran had sprinkled tinsel over me like fairy dust that sparkled in the red and green Christmas tree lights.

Blinking out of the memory, I checked my phone. No messages were waiting.

I had told Ezra I didn't want him to follow me, but I figured I'd at least get a text.

Since I had moved in with Ezra, I had started to believe he'd been, at minimum, emotionally cheating on me with his—quote—"work wife." I brought it up. I let him know how it made me uncomfortable when I didn't see him as much as I used to.

He brushed me off. He told me I was jealous and just like all the other catty girls he'd dated in a string before me.

And nothing shut me up faster than not wanting to be just like everyone else.

I could barely even remember the last time we'd had sex.

Too needy. Too clingy.

And after a while, I stopped caring. That way, I didn't have to hear him defend himself by tearing me down slowly, as if my job at the magazine I had worked so hard to get three years ago wasn't already doing that enough throughout the work hours.

Too efficient. Too personal. Too off-brand.

And on and on it had gone until I snapped and let it all fall apart around me today.

I looked at myself in the mirror one last time. I was a strong, independent woman who had taken on the city.

Wasn't I?

"I failed," I whispered. I stared at myself, expecting another wave of tears to come over me, but nothing happened. Looked like I still wasn't ready to let them loose.

"I failed," I said a little louder and then again until I was screaming and out of breath. "I failed."

I was right back where I'd started.

SIX

BEFORE

"THE MUD IS PERMANENTLY CRUSTED to my knees. Seriously, I don't think my feet are ever going to recover from being so waterlogged. When I went to bed last night, my feet were so wrinkly that I could feel them against the sheets," I complained, stretching my feet out in front of me.

My toes squelched in my previously white sneakers.

Now, they looked like they'd gone to war and lost.

"Here I thought, you would be more upset about how you haven't eaten anything but peanut butter and jelly sandwiches for the past three days," said Kieran, grimacing as he looked down at my shoes.

He didn't look much better. In fact, if possible, he looked worse. Kieran's skin looked grimy with a layer of dirt. His glasses had turned a little crooked on one side after a particularly intensive team building activity that also left me with a red mark that was starting to bruise after that snake, Amy Walmer, elbowed me in the jaw.

I still thought she had done it on purpose. Everything she did to ruin my life seemed to be on purpose.

At the beginning of sixth grade, I went to the bathroom once and ran into Amy and Jenna. They were cool and talked to nearly everyone, including the boys. They also always seemed to coordinate when they peed. This time, as they chatted in front of the mirror, admiring Amy's perfect strawberry-blonde curls, I joined them. My mom had insisted I at least try to find more girlfriends, though I didn't see the point. I had Kieran.

I offered my watermelon-flavored lip balm. Jenna accepted gladly, smoothing the scented gloss over her mouth before complimenting my fresh bob haircut. I still thought the hairdresser lady had cut it too short.

I laughed at a joke they told and included myself in maybe joining them in hanging out in the coming weekend if they didn't mind, as if we'd never met before. Though my words turned stilted, awkward, the more they stared at me, carefully nodding.

Right before they left, Amy's expression turned sad.

"You have to understand," Amy pleaded. *"You seem real sweet and all, but some people just don't fit in."*

Then, she shrugged. There had been no malice in her words, and it made the comment sting all the more.

Two years later, I still couldn't help but think she was right.

Another reason I hated Amy Walmer.

"The food here is gross," I agreed with Kieran.

"At least the rain stopped." Kieran leaned out from underneath the covered porch of the girls' cabin. His hair was still stuck to his head from running across the fifteen feet between the two cabins. He leaned back on the bench, letting his feet swing.

I whipped my yellow raincoat's hood up over my head. I cinched the strings closed until only my face was still sticking out.

Whoever had thought it was a good idea to send dozens of thirteen-year-olds into the woods for a week for the sake of environmental education while living in one of the greatest hiking spots in the country obviously wasn't thinking clearly. Especially when that week included never-ending water-soaked clothing from the cold, pelting downpour, a dead snake in the cabin closet, and not being able to do any of the activities, like climb the mountain trail—which was said to be the best thing about this whole painfully educational trip—all because of said rain.

Kieran raised his eyebrow, trying not to laugh.

"It's not funny."

"You're right." He nodded slowly. "This is one torture after another."

Finally, he was seeing things my way.

A group of boys came out of cabin B. They grabbed on to each other as they headed toward the middle of the camp, where everyone else was slowly trickling in for the next activity they had for us. By the sounds of it and the fact that everyone was being given red and green bandanas, it involved square dancing.

This is camping hell.

Whistles shot up on us toward the porch as the boys jostled one another into a tree. They snorted in between sardonic laughter.

"Aw! Look at the lovebirds!"

"Shut up, Dylan!" I snapped at him, lifting myself off the bench.

They continued laughing as they walked away down the path, jumping in every ankle-deep puddle along the way.

"I don't know why you let them get you angry," said Kieran.

"They're just stupid."

"Well, yeah. But we know that. You think we should go to lunch?"

"If we go to lunch, then we have to go on the rainy afternoon bird-watching expedition," I said, pouting. "And there will be no birds because of the rain. And that means more time for Dylan to come up with stupid bird jokes."

Kieran paused before nodding.

"And if we go to lunch and the disappointing bird-watch, then we will have to go to dinner to eat another peanut butter and jelly sandwich," I said.

"I thought you said you didn't mind them."

That was beside the point.

"At this point, there's only grape jelly."

"The horror."

"And if we do that, we'll eventually have to ..." I shook my head.

"Square dance?" Kieran asked.

"Square dance," I confirmed.

"We could hide in the bathroom."

We could, but the bathroom smelled like a combination of farts and baby wipes. We were finally away from school. I'd honestly been sort of excited about this whole experience for ages. Now that we were here, well, I hated it. This entire adventure education week of outdoor fun sucked big time. Everyone raved about it in older grades. It was becoming clear that either they had no brain cells and no concept of having a fun time or we were severely missing something.

"I really wanted to climb the rock pile to the top of the trail," I muttered.

Kieran pulled his knees up until he turned into a small ball next to me.

The final few girls left inside of my cabin. The screen door slam shut behind them as they laughed and made their way past us.

How in the world are there people who enjoy this?

"I thought it would be cool too," said Kieran. "It didn't even rain that badly yesterday. But the counselors did say it was slippery."

According to who? No one, apparently, was willing to take the risk to go up and see.

No one but me.

Eyes widening, I turned to face Kieran.

He didn't notice I was staring at him until he did a double take. "What? Why are you looking at me like that?"

"Do you trust me?"

"I feel like that's a loaded question."

I smiled. "Do you want to go on an adventure?"

He looked at me again, this time assessing. "I have a feeling I'm going to be going on one either way."

I tipped my chin down slowly, not blinking as I stared at him, leaning forward until he had to lean back out of my personal space. "I think you're right. Let's do it."

"Do what?"

"Let's climb to the top of Marshall Falls Peak."

Air caught between his teeth. "I don't know, Sylv."

"I do. Let's do it. It's not that hard. Everything is marked, and it's not a complicated trail. We could be up there and back before anyone even noticed."

"Not to be rude here, but we aren't the most athletic people," said Kieran. "In fact, I'm pretty sure we're the opposite."

"Come on." I nudged him. "You know you want to."

"Yes, and no."

"You do."

"I'm getting less sure by the second," said Kieran.

"If you go with me, I'll ..."

He waited.

"I'll write you another story."

"The last time you wrote me a story, I couldn't sleep for days," he deadpanned.

"I'll ease up the horror. I'm out of my dark suspense period."

"I can only hope. I've never been much of a horror person."

"You read Stephen King," I argued, much like after he called me at one in the morning to complain about how my ghostly slasher story I had written had ruined his dreams.

"I skim the gory parts," said Kieran. "It's not the story I like. I'm there for the whole craft of it. I mean, what other person can hold a reader's attention for over a thousand pages?"

"Nerd."

He didn't argue.

"Fine. I'll write you a love story."

"A love story?"

"Perfect for your sweet, romantic disposition."

He considered it. "With a happily ever after?"

"Is there any other kind of love story?"

Kieran stared at me, his expression shifting and his cheeks turning pink before settling back to their normal color.

"Let's get out of here," I repeat, looking Kieran right in the eye.

It was now or never, and even if he didn't have faith in himself, I did.

He nodded. "Deal."

"This had better be one good love story." Kieran huffed and puffed as we walked up the hill, and then before us was the rock pile.

Though the rain had lessened to a mist before stopping altogether, maybe the counselors had a point—the rocks did look a bit slick. Nonetheless, I climbed up the first boulder with a grunt.

I peered over my shoulder at Kieran, who assessed the sharp rocks before going toward the one beside me. He pulled himself up with just as much grace—meaning very little.

"Perfect for your mushy heart." I guaranteed it.

This hill was a lot steeper than I'd thought. Or at least my body thought so.

My lungs ached. My mouth felt like it was bleeding. A metallic taste lingered under my molars. When we had first began our trek up the trail, everything started well enough. Kieran had pointed out different types of leaves and plants that were edible if we became desperate, and I had jumped in puddles until my new pair of pants were soaked through.

Then, we made it to the dreaded rock pile. I remembered them saying how half of every class ended up turning around at this point, either from fear of falling off the side of the mountain or from pure exhaustion.

But I was determined. Kieran and I were not going to be one of that half.

"Holy crap, this is a big hill."

Sweat beaded above my eyebrow. "Talk to me about something."

"I'm climbing a mountain with you," he said.

"I already know that."

"This might be the craziest thing I've ever done, Sylvia. I'm not sure I have anything else to talk about right now other than how disgusting the guys are back in my cabin. I doubt you want to hear about that."

Probably not.

Reaching for the next foothold, I lifted myself up onto the next ledge and waited for Kieran to make his way next to me. We caught our breath, and we began again.

"I wanted to do this," said Kieran.

"Yeah?"

"I'm just reminding myself of that fact right now. I really thought I was in better shape."

I huffed a laugh. "So did I."

"I mean, they talked about this trip and this hike like it was the biggest thing that was ever going to happen to us while at school here," Kieran mused as we struggled, one step at a time. "It's becoming even crazier to me that so many people apparently made it to the top of this mountain to talk about it nearly every year during their graduation speeches."

"They must be some in-shape valedictorians."

"Exactly."

Unlike Kieran, however, I noticed what he didn't. That most of those speech givers at graduation, who came back now as camp counselors or graduated at the top of their class at Marshall Falls High School, never ended up leaving. They thrived. They made it to the very top of the mountain and saw the glorious view people oohed and aahed about. Then, they stayed right here in Marshall.

I told Kieran so.

"What do you want to do after graduation? I thought you wanted to become a writer, you said." Kieran gulped down air after each word.

"I do. Maybe." More than that I wanted one thing. "I want to live an exciting life."

"Well, I think we are doing that," said Kieran.

"No. I mean, like, run away."

"From camp?"

"From Marshall."

A quiet moment settled between us, save for the ragged sounds of our breaths.

"I thought you liked it here."

"I do," I said. "Sort of."

I grunted as I yanked myself up onto another rock. I reached back for Kieran's hand, and he immediately slapped his palm into mine, letting me hoist him up.

"Thanks."

"It's fine. I just mean that I want to see more of the world. I want to travel and live in the city and go to parties. I want to meet fabulous, interesting people." I could already see it in my head. The fancy parties with tall glasses that clinked together and secret societies that people actually wanted me to be a part of.

"I thought you hated people."

"When did I say that?" I asked.

Kieran shrugged. "I don't know. I just sort of assumed."

I smacked his arm with my hand. He teetered off the ledge before grabbing the rocks.

"Hey! Are you trying to kill me?"

"That was rude."

"I figured it was honest, but okay."

I rolled my eyes.

"So then"—Kieran regrouped—"where would you go first?"

"First?"

"I assume you won't end with New York, if that's where you're talking about."

"I was."

"Then, where?" he asked again.

"Europe," I said.

Kieran nodded, as if this had been expected.

"Paris first," I elaborated. "Then London. Venice."

"Venice?"

"The place with the river rides."

"The gondolas?" Kieran chuckled at my crude description

of the little boats people lounged in under the sun while they were pushed along.

"Those." I pointed back at him.

"Okay. We can do that."

"We?"

"I'm obviously going to be coming with you," said Kieran. "But I'll want to stop in Rome if we are going to Italy."

I stared at him. I never saw Kieran outside of Marshall, but it wasn't hard to imagine. Though, over the years, he had lost the freckles he'd had when I first met him, he still always got sunburned when he stayed in the sun too long, right along his cheeks. He'd be the definition of bronze dusted.

He'd look like a budding Greek god.

"Fair."

"I figure we'll have to try all the flavors of gelato too," he insisted.

"I like the way you're thinking now, Kieran."

He grinned. "Better than peanut butter and jelly sandwiches."

"If I have to eat one more PB with grape J, I might scream," I said. "Italy also has pizza."

"And noodles. So many different types of noodles."

I moaned, taking a pause on the rock. We should've brought water. All in all, I hadn't exactly thought this expedition through. "With all the cheese. Just imagine the cheese, Kieran."

"Oh, I am. And pastry, though I would have to tell my mom hers was still the best."

I barked a laugh. As of now, Lori's pastries were the best.

"Maybe we should get to the top and run away from home," said Kieran.

"Maybe we should just leave and run away forever."

"Into the sunset?" Kieran teased.

"Of course into the sunset," I concurred. "That's exactly

what we'll do. We'll run off into the sunset together and never return to Marshall Falls ever again. The world is our oyster!"

Kieran laughed between his gasping breaths from exertion. Even his glasses looked sweaty.

"If we survive this little adventure of yours today, okay," said Kieran. "At this rate, we are never going to make it back down before dinner, let alone before the sun goes down."

When I looked up at the sky, a light breeze traveled across my face. I hummed as Kieran groaned with the simple, cool pleasure.

We could do this. I was sure of it.

"We're already this far. You just wait." I smirked, helping him up the next round of rocks until we were back on a steep path toward the top, covered with thick pine trees and sky. "You're going to thank me for this one day."

Kieran shook his head, but at least he was smiling again as we hauled ourselves up onto another ledge. Both of us looked up, so close yet so far away from the top.

"Probably anyway," I added.

"Probably."

One step after another, we encouraged each other to make it up the hill, not yet worrying how we were going to get back down. Or at least, neither of us vocalized those concerns. By the time we made it to the next marked section of trees, the sun was already setting, taking on a dull hue as the afternoon ended and evening teased the top of the trees with the golden hour.

We glanced back and forth. With relief unfortunately came the understanding that we were definitely not going to make it back down in the amount of time we had thought.

"I think this might be one of the last turns." Kieran took a few steps ahead of me, jogging with a sort of second wind to look around the bend.

"It'd better be. My legs hurt more than my wrinkly old-lady feet."

"Good thing your life goals don't include being a dancer," he teased as he fell back beside me.

How dare he bring up how, last year, all I had wanted was to fulfill my childhood dreams of being a ballerina! It wasn't exactly my fault that it had turned out that I royally sucked at being anything close to graceful, according to the musical director. Seriously, I had heard her say it during auditions. I had gotten a spot in the chorus for *Singin' in the Rain* and promptly quit.

I'd rather spend time with Kieran after school at the bakery anyway.

"You laugh now, but you're going to have to carry me back down—"

My ankle scraped over the edge of a small rock, taking the rest of me with it. I flew to the ground. My hands took the brunt of the fall. Smears of mud and dirt slid up toward my elbow, along with tiny rocks. The sharp edges embedded themselves into my skin.

Kieran reached back, but didn't quite catch me before it was too late. "Are you okay?"

"Ow, ow, ow."

"I tried to catch you." Kieran's eyes went wide as he looked down at me, frozen with his hands extended.

"I know." I winced.

"What is it?"

"My ankle."

Finally, he reached the rest of the way down for me, trying to pull me back up to stand. I flinched as I put weight on my foot.

"What happened to your ankle?"

"I don't know. I'm not an ankle doctor! I twisted it or something. All I know is that it hurts, okay?"

"How bad does it hurt?"

I shook my head, testing myself to stand on it again. It still stung, but a little less so. What burned the most was the heavy feeling climbing up my throat and behind my eyes.

I sniffed. "This was stupid. We are so stupid."

"What are you talking about?"

"We should've never come up here. We are not going to make it back down before it's dark out, and we are going to get in trouble, and you're going to hate me."

"I'm not going to hate you."

"You are."

"No offense, Sylvia. But if I was going to hate you, it would've happened by now." Kieran's mouth quirked up at the side.

"I was still stupid to think this was a good idea."

What if it was him who had fallen? There was no way in the world I could carry him back down. We might be the same size—something that haunted me most days when I compared myself to other girls who were slowly developing things I wasn't, like boobs and hips that could hold a denim skirt up—but there was no one way I would be strong enough to carry him down.

It was like we were seven years old all over again and I was watching him get stuck in a tree. It had been funny at the time. We were alone. We only had each other.

Yet now, he was the one shaking his head at me, a calm determination on his face.

"No, we aren't. This was a good idea. *Carpe diem.*"

"Carpe what?"

"Seize the day," Kieran explained. "It doesn't look too bad. It's not swelling or anything yet. Maybe you just need to stretch it out. You shocked yourself or something."

Maybe. I tried to roll it in a circle, flinching at the mild pain. But maybe he was right. It wasn't that bad.

"Come on," said Kieran. "We're making it to the top."

"What?" I asked. "You complained the whole time that I was crazy."

"Well, you're always a little crazy. That's why I like you, Sylv. Are you fishing for compliments again?" Before I could answer, he swung my arm around him. "Just hold on to me and start to stretch it out. You might've pulled it or something."

"You're going to carry me?"

"You're going to have to try and walk."

Though Kieran was somewhat larger in size, he was still one of the smaller boys in our class. We were both the same height.

"We're almost there."

"Ow."

"Now, you're just complaining to complain," mumbled Kieran.

A little. To be honest, the sharp pain subsided, leaving behind a much more bearable ache. Still, I didn't let go of Kieran. We were going to make it to the top. Together.

"I got you. Hold on."

"Here I thought I was going to be the one hauling you the rest of the way up," I murmured into him.

"At this point, we're making it, no matter what, Sylvia. Just hold on and don't fall off the edge."

"So encouraging."

He squeezed me tighter as he laughed, taking the final steps out of the trees and onto the precipice of the renowned rock pile and higher. He was right. We were going to make it. It was just a few more steps, and we would've gotten here without a single problem, all by ourselves. It was just me and Kieran.

We stared out into the open expanse before us.

"Wow."

"Whoa."

Taking a step out closer to the edge, I hobbled enough that Kieran stepped to quickly catch up with me. Waving him off, I extended my arms out on either side. This must be how a bird felt, ready to take off in flight into the world.

"That's definitely a view."

"Uh-huh."

Turning back to look at Kieran, I dropped my arms. I expected to find him looking out at the view in front of us as the sky went from pink to orange to even the lightest of purples. Instead, he was looking straight ahead. He was looking at me.

My eyebrows turned down as I studied him. He was somehow at peace after the day we had, eyes hazy and soft as he took a deep breath. His shoulders slumped as he took a step up toward me, leading me down to the dirt ground to sit.

Heavy aches already started to make themselves known in my legs from the hike.

Kieran curled his body around me, warm and cozy, like it always was. I tilted my chin up toward his face, and I stared at Kieran from his too-short hair that the barber had sheared off to the spattering of freckles, mixed in with the beginnings of pimples, up the side of his face.

His glasses were slipping, and I reached up and pushed them back up his nose.

"Thanks."

I looked back out at the view again as it began to get darker. "Thank you, Kieran."

"For what?"

"Trusting me."

"Eh"—he shrugged—"we still have to get down, don't we?"

I couldn't help myself. After the entire trudge up here, I looked at him and laughed. We were the two people in this year's class that could say they saw this view and sat right here.

"I'm sure we'll figure it out."

"We're going to be in so much trouble."

"I'll take care of it." It was another way of saying, *I'll take the blame.*

"Are you sure about that?"

"For you?" I took a deep breath and shook my head once as I leaned against him for just another second. "Always, Kieran."

"It *was* worth it."

"Told you so."

"You still owe me my story though."

I smiled down at my chest before looking up at him. "Figured."

Kieran nudged me with his shoulder. I knocked him right back.

We sat there for a while, watching colors I'd ever seen in photos and paintings. When it was just dark enough that we knew it wouldn't be long until we had to pull the flashlights out of our backpacks—one of the only things we had thought to remember from our camp checklist—we made our way back down the path one step at a time.

Going down the hill was a lot faster than trying to get up, especially when we were met with a half-dozen angry teachers and high school counselors who had noticed that we were gone when they took attendance at the pre-dinner sing-along.

At the bottom, I looked back up to the top. Kieran caught me and grinned before we turned the corner into camp. My arm was held by one older girl with a scowl on her face, as if I was about to make a run for it now.

I let myself be tugged along and grinned right back at him. I was going to have to write him his love story, but right now, this moment felt like a pretty good story all by itself.

SEVEN

NOW

"THREE! TWO! ONE!"

The tree curved against the white-painted gazebo in the center of town. Strings of lights flickered before finally bursting to life. The fat tree limbs looked like they were about to drop off from the center under the weight of Christmas cheer.

It was the first time I had seen the event from this angle.

My arms crossed over one another as I looked directly upward at the tree. Usually, at this time of year, years ago when I had come to the gazebo lighting ceremony, I would be running around somewhere with everyone else.

Or rather just one someone else.

We'd sneak in and out of people's trucks for the warm air. We'd also sneak sips of drinks people had in the cabs that would make us feel warm all over with or without mittens.

I always seemed to forget gloves every year—a fact very much felt when the countdown started. Everyone came out of their hiding places. They stood in a horde out in the dark and cold. Every year, my best friend in the whole world would only roll his eyes and smirk. He'd grab my hands and rub them between his before tucking them into his own thickly lined coat pockets.

Blinking, I didn't see anyone who stood out in the town center.

A smattering of applause went up through the tiny crowd, as if they hadn't seen the same display year after year. The slight alterations to the tree were the handmade ornaments adorning the branches. Every year, the high school woodshop students made them. They were the same students who would take turns swiping each of the ornaments by the new year until the tree was completely bare. The senior with the most by the end of the holiday season won, though no one ever really asked what.

Or maybe I just hadn't been as preoccupied with the thrill of it as others were.

I had been preoccupied with a lot of other things, yet somehow, I had ended up right back here.

Though I hadn't planned on coming to the tree lighting, I couldn't stand to be in my house, and my mother's well-meaning, albeit irritating, nudge to go into town and not be a hermit had finally been enough.

Each movement felt heavy, especially under the glow of Christmas lights. It was probably the sleep deprivation. Pulling late nights at the office and taking over work shifts during my lunch hour were to make a good impression and move up the invisible success ladder.

And for what?

I shuffled my feet. People started to move around, the lead-up to the main event over and done with. I pressed my lips together. I knew that if I kept biting them, they'd get chapped, yet I couldn't stop. Each time a pair of eyes glanced at me, they quickly glanced away again, as if they realized that they had caught sight of something they didn't see often. An outsider.

I shouldn't be here.

My eyes caught on a group on the other side of the gazebo. My heart stopped. I hadn't seen them in four years since I was last in town, and yet there they were. All of them were right in front of me. Jenna and Gabe stood with their kids, bundled up in an obscene number of layers. Next to them, Dylan and Landon laughed loudly, pulling more than just my attention. Amy rolled her eyes and shoved her leather-gloved hands back into her white puffer jacket.

And where they were …

I quickly turned on my heel. None of them had noticed me. Good. I made a beeline in the other direction. My feet carried me as I ducked my head into the edge of my too-thin jacket I'd packed.

Everyone was having a great time. I shouldn't have been surprised, and I wasn't. If anything, I was worried what that meant and what I could've seen if I hadn't run away like a coward. I wasn't supposed to be here to see or be a part of it.

Then again, I should've been doing a lot of things that just weren't happening.

For example, I should've been working on some last-minute projects for my job. Or even better, my plan should've worked out when I left Marshall Falls. I should've been writing, like the dream always was from the moment I first noticed bylines and realized all the articles were written by amazing people.

I wanted to be one of those amazing people. I should've been one of those amazing people ever since I had the chance to work at one of the best lifestyle magazines in the country, *Main Attraction,* four years ago.

By now, hell, I should've even been promoted to an editor of a whole section. At home for the holidays and curled up with my keyboard and a blanket in my lap, watching the first snowfall outside the window in my chic, ridiculously expensive New York apartment. I should've been listening for my loving and non-cheating boyfriend to come home so we could decide on what we should eat for dinner since I hadn't figured it out yet, too entranced by what I was working on because I loved the city and loved my job and loved the creatively brilliant life I'd always imagined for myself.

Should've ... should've ...

The internal pity party all came back around to one thing.

I shouldn't be here.

I inhaled, and my breath caught in my chest. Pressure built in the back of my throat and to my eyes again. This was it. I was going to break down in the middle of the sidewalk in Marshall Falls. With my luck, everyone was going to know about it by their morning coffee.

My nose ran down into my jacket collar, which was wet and freezing against the underside of my chin. My skin rubbed against it as I caught exactly what I was standing next to.

I nearly growled at yet another stupid reminder I hadn't needed about exactly what a big mistake it had been to come back here.

"Great, just great! Of course I'm standing here!" I yelled.

No one, other than the dark and empty shop with a turquoise-blue door, was there to hear me.

Rose Bakery didn't respond, obviously. But why not add Marshall Falls lunatic to the roster of what everyone could gossip about tomorrow?

Rose might not be like any pastry shop in Paris, but it was the perfect, cozy shop to forget your woes in a chocolate crois-sant. I'd spent enough time inside—dipping peppermint delights in thick, hot chocolate, made with a real brick of dark chocolate instead of the powder—to know that she had managed to instill even the tiniest bit of magic in this often-cold and unchangeable town.

I could hardly remember the last time I'd had hot chocolate

at all in favor of bitter drip coffee. Probably not since I'd last been inside the shop.

I hardly remembered a lot of myself, it seemed.

"Just fantastic," I muttered softly.

"Sylvia?"

Swallowing, I froze, lips parted.

I turned toward the voice I would recognize out of an entire crowd. But now, on the street in front of his mother's bakery, there was only him.

"Hi, Kieran."

EIGHT

BEFORE

"I JUST DON'T UNDERSTAND why everyone is making such a big deal about us deciding what we want to do with our lives, let alone what schools we are applying to."

I wasn't even going to comment that the schools they seemed to be pushing for everyone to apply to were within a three-hour radius. They were much more concerned about my extracurriculars, or lack thereof.

It wasn't my fault that I didn't participate. I had Kieran, and though he seemed more apt to volunteer and be a part of tutoring programs, I just never really thought about it. I was too busy. I was also still shocked that my parents hadn't upped and moved us again over the years.

Why bother joining a team or a club if I wasn't going to be there long enough to be in the group photo they put in the yearbook? Why bother even joining the yearbook with all the other girls who wanted to make sure they got the best not-candid candid shot of themselves on their class page?

I huffed and leaned back against the bookshelf behind me, holding the rows of old forgotten Shakespeare reference textbooks, and kicked my feet up. My boots, the heels rubbed off since it had started snowing, balanced on the edge of the *theater theory* shelf.

Since we had decided the lunchroom wasn't for us last year, Kieran and I had turned the narrow reference aisle in the back of the library into our own dusty oasis during the lunch block.

We'd chat until the librarian gently told us our laughter was too loud to be getting any actual work done, like we were supposed to be doing. Sometimes, there were random snacks we brought from home since the times we didn't bring anything at all meant that Kieran would have to stifle his laughter during History after lunch, where my stomach would start to growl— something he found oddly amusing.

Today, we had almond butter and jam sandwiches, cut into four small, bite-size squares, courtesy of Lori.

Kieran scrunched his nose at my feet so close to his face, swatting them another inch to the right. They were more to his shoulder now. At some point within the past few months since we had transitioned from lowly freshmen to lowly sophomores, Kieran had turned into a giant. A tall, gangly giant, but a giant nonetheless, compared to me, who was suddenly beginning to find myself turning round in all the places I'd rather not.

I barely noticed the change in Kieran until he stood next to his father, helping with a new delivery shipment at Rose Bakery. They were nearly the same height, if not nearly the same size as one another, though Kieran didn't have to ever worry about taking on Dave's mountain-man burliness.

"I don't know." Kieran lifted a shoulder. "It's nice to have an idea of what you plan to do after school."

"And what do you plan on doing after school, Kieran?" I asked him, raising my eyebrows.

He opened his mouth and then closed it again. "Well, I don't know exactly."

My point.

No matter how many quizzes they gave us during study hall to determine which job fit us, none of them felt right. Or at least not to me. Certainly not to Kieran, who spent hours staring over his results that he should be a pilot even though he had terrible eyesight or a teacher even though he was objectively awkward around kids.

My quiz had told me that I should be a secretary. A secretary!

I would not believe those results were at all conclusive.

"Just because you're not active with clubs at school—" He caught my glower and rolled his eyes at me hard enough that his glasses nearly went with them. "What? You're not. You could still do something or put in the essays you need to write with your applications."

Now, I had to write another essay for college? What was the point? What would I even write?

Please let me into your school that I will be paying an obscene amount of money for. I hopefully won't do anything stupid. Please and thank you.

God, maybe that stupid, judgy counselor, who had gone to the school where she was sitting in now, might've had a point. I was doomed.

I hung my head. "Like what?"

"You like writing when you want to."

"Please don't suggest the newspaper."

The school counselor already had. The weekly updates they handed out before announcements was consistently dry, to say the least, and I could imagine the kind of trivial assignments they would give the newcomer. Especially me after the student editor once overheard me say I'd rather die than write for Marshall Falls High.

"I wasn't going to," Kieran assured. "I was going to suggest that you start a blog."

"A blog?" I cringed.

"People blog all the time." I didn't answer, and he backtracked. "They totally still do, don't they?"

"They do. Sort of. Interesting people blog. People who live in cities and do cool things," I tried to explain even though it sounded more like I was arguing.

Kieran glanced around us at the library, as if that could be taken as a point in his favor. "We do cool things."

"Do we?"

"Just wait a second," said Kieran. "I might have found the answer to your problems."

"All of them?"

"Well ..." Kieran reached into his backpack.

He slapped down what was clearly not a copy of a new book, which I could borrow to fill the void of my impending future, from Pauper's Used Books in town.

In his composition notebook, one page was nearly filled with bullet points.

Kieran adjusted his glasses on the bridge of his nose, trying not to touch his face near the slowly fading acne that cascaded down his jawline. He waited for my reaction.

I slid the notebook toward myself. "What's this?"

"This is the stuff you could write about. You could write about us."

I glanced down at the page. "Kieran and Silly's Adventure List?"

"Ignore the title."

"I don't think I can." I was already grinning.

I set the book I was no longer reading to the side. Maybe a secret plan of his was already working. I might not have wanted to suddenly blog, but I was feeling a little better than I had been when I first sat down across from him.

For the past three years or more, ever since camp, we'd been talking about going on a real adventure. I didn't think that adventure would take place here in Marshall Falls, but right now, beggars couldn't be choosers.

And if the school counselor was correct, if I didn't get my act together, I was going to make a career out of begging on the streets.

But this ...

Kieran had put a lot of effort into this.

There was the gazebo lighting, baking our favorite short-breads with the raspberry jam from scratch, watching all the famous films, water balloons ...

I looked up at him, pointing my purple fingernail down at that activity. "In winter?"

"You'll see."

I was sure that I would see how one could get hypothermia if we managed to cross that one out. I focused back on the paper. "Karaoke?"

"It's another senior-year tradition. We'll work up to it."

So would our confidence considering neither one of us could sing, apparently. This was a tradition I had never heard of unless we went to two very different schools.

Kieran's light-brown eyebrows pushed together. "Terrible challenge?"

I leaned back so he couldn't take his handwritten to-do list away from me. There were also doodles in the margins, like the ones he jotted down on his notes during class. Little three-dimensional Christmas presents and snowflakes lined the edge.

"I didn't say that."

"You didn't need to."

"It's a great list. Fantastic actually." I watched as his ego boosted a whole half of a point in real time, which was a vast improvement for Kieran. "There's only one problem with it."

"What?"

"This might take us years." I put a hand to my head. My charm bracelet my mother had given me last year for Christmas banged against my forehead, the three charms clinking together like a chime.

"I don't know." Kieran looked sheepish. "I figure we can manage it by graduation."

"So, two years?"

"About that. More like two and a half," he corrected quietly. "Have faith in me, Sylv. I did promise you an adventure even if you never paid up with my story since we talked about it. There it is."

And if there was one thing that Kieran did, he kept his promises.

I glanced through the list one more time. Here it was. Our Marshall Falls adventure. I had faith we'd make it through all of them and have a good time. It wasn't the sort of outlandish adventures my mind could come up with, but they were also a thousand times more doable than convincing a millionaire to jet us off to Amsterdam for the week.

I really needed to write him the story I had been starting and stopping—at least two dozen times by now—which he hadn't forgotten about either.

"I figure that some of them might even give you good writing material for the blog. A recipe. A story at the very least, if things go horribly."

"You think?" I raised my eyebrows. "With us, they're bound to."

I could try to fill a small website with engaging articles and pieces. I wasn't exactly stylish or even as bookish as Kieran. I was just Sylvia. Only Kieran ever seemed to think that was enough.

I twisted the page around, narrowing my eyes at the one

open checkbox between us again. "Isn't the gazebo lighting tonight?"

"And the tree. See? We can already make progress."

"Because the whole town getting together to watch some electricity flicker on every year isn't cheesy," I teased. It sounded like one of the holiday movies we would also eventually have to watch.

Kieran didn't try to convince me otherwise. He nodded, mighty proud of himself. "Yep."

"Spontaneous for us."

"I try," he agreed, reaching back for his water bottle and one of his tiny sandwich bites we'd laid out. I grabbed one too. My mouth was full when he added, "Everyone will be there. Practically."

"Everyone?" I swallowed down the dry combination of almond butter and white bread.

"The town. The student body, along with everyone who had woodshop this semester, to add their ornaments. Amy and Jenna and the rest of their friends will be there too."

"Amy?" I cringe.

He snorted. "She's not that bad."

Sure she wasn't. Kieran, after all, wasn't the one who had to deal with Amy's chronic case of the stink-eye whenever she looked at him. It was much more of a stink-eye for one disease, clearly directed at me whenever I walked in a room that Amy Walmer was also gracing with her presence.

"All of them are bad."

"You just have to make more of an effort to talk with them. In fact, they're trying not to be complete assholes anymore."

I paused at Kieran's phrasing. He never usually swore, not unless it was serious, so he was trying to get through to me.

"I think it occurred to all of us that our class size isn't that big."

Tiny. Kieran could say it was tiny. Our graduating class was going to be lucky to reach three dozen people, if that.

"We're going to be stuck here with each other until at least graduation."

But after that, we were going to be out of here. So, what was the point of playing nice with the people who, for years, had made fun of us until the upperclassmen made fun of them, too, when we made it up to the high school? It might have evened the social playing field, but I still didn't have to like them.

"Amy's mom practically runs the events in town after she took over for the mayor's wife. We are the ones who rarely go to any of them," he insisted, still trying to sway me.

"Fine. If you want to hang out with them, you can. I'll go with you and spend time with Satan's spawn of Marshall Falls."

He chuckled, thinking I was joking.

I was, but only a little.

"Thank you."

"I said I'll go. It's on Kieran and Silly's Adventure List after all. What time?"

There were no details on his list from what I could notice unless there was a separate binder for such things. I pressed my lips together so as not to ask and possibly ruin the surprise.

"Seven o'clock. For you though, six thirty."

"Ha-ha." I twisted the list back around to him for safekeeping. "I'll be on time."

"No amendments to the list?" Kieran clarified, taking the notebook and shutting the cover. He carefully slipped it back into his book bag.

"Did you think there would be?" I leaned across the space between us, over the final pieces of sandwich, and gripped his wrist. He zipped the book bag back up. "I'll think of a few extra ones."

"Good."

"Just please tell me you don't plan on laminating it."

"Pshaw."

"You totally plan on laminating it."

"Well, if it's going to travel with us on these adventures ..." He attempted to justify having our trusty librarians laminate the single piece of slightly crumpled, lined notebook paper. And they would do anything for their sweet library patron. They basically fawned over him.

I smirked, shaking my head back and forth.

"You love it, and you know it."

"I certainly feel something toward all of this," I confirmed.

We parted ways and went back to class. Kieran tottered off toward the honors hallway while I remained forever more in the perfectly acceptable college prep math. I half-listened to the fresh-out-of-college teacher. The other half of me wrote down some ideas that might be good for a blog.

Maybe Kieran was right. I needed to somehow gather some inspiration. Or maybe it was stupid to think I had anything anyone wanted to read about, let alone for me to write so I could become big and famous with magazine editors sending me emails, begging me to write for them, or publishers trying to sign me on for a four-book deal even though I never considered myself much of a fiction fanatic.

Because *that* sounded exactly like what I dreamed of for myself after I left little Marshall Falls even if my career personality test had said otherwise.

I stuffed my stack of multicolored pens back into their pouch and zipped everything up and away.

Kieran waited for me outside the building, falling into step beside me as everyone flooded out the doors for the day. As if noticing the way my face pinched and how I clenched the straps of my bag, Kieran gave me a wide breadth space until we came to the fork in the road between Peach and Caracas.

I pushed away from him as I turned to go up one more street home while he hopped out of my way, heading in the other direction.

"I'll see you at six thirty!" he called.

Looking over my shoulder, I gave him a thumbs-up. "I'll see you at seven!"

He rolled his eyes and turned his head up toward the gray sky.

I scrolled down and checked my blog. I had managed to set it up the moment I got home and took the family laptop into my room, claiming it was for a school project before my mom could object.

A thrill built in my chest. This could be a good idea. A great idea. This blog could get me a step ahead of anyone else.

How many people could say they had hundreds of possible readers by the time they got to college?

I could shove that in all those college recruiters' faces.

My website wasn't the prettiest, but it would do with how easy it had turned out to be to claim a little space on the internet as mine. I'd even written a welcome post already, sitting right at the top.

Not that anyone would read it or even know my tiny website of nothing even existed.

Yet.

Shaking my head, I clicked out of the internet browser, glancing at my latest look for tonight in the mirror. I hoped I appeared chic and less like I had pulled an oversize sweater out of my mother's closet. I was pretty sure it was from the '80s, sans shoulder pads—I thanked the world for small mercies. The color was the prettiest blue.

I heard my parents as I pulled my second layer over my head, tucking my tank top into my waistband. Grabbing my bag, I slung it over my shoulder, taking a deep breath.

Sneaking farther down the hallway, I was careful. I didn't want my footsteps to creak. Gently making my way toward the living room, I carried my boots in my hands. The closer I got, the more I could hear the sharp pitch of my parents' voices.

Their previous whispers became piercing bursts of resentment.

"The job would include a pay raise," my father argued, hushed.

"Along with the increase in the cost of living up that way. Have you thought of that?"

"Sylvia could be there to get in-state tuition and be close by still. She could go to Harvard—"

"Sylvie is not getting into Harvard," my mother snapped.

I stayed mostly hidden, trying not to feel the jolt of irritation that came with the fact that my mother thought I could never manage to get into an Ivy League. I never thought that I could, but hearing her say it brewed something sharp and bitter in my chest.

"Tufts then. Or some other school. I'm sure there are plenty."

Still, my mother scoffed, crossing her arms over each other as she shook her head.

"This could be good for us."

"That's what you said about this move and all the others before that. You promised that this would be the last one. That even you wanted to settle down and make a home—not just get a nice house." My mother bit out each statement. "We've made friends here, Richard. We have neighbors and a life. Your daughter has even made friends here. She has another two years of school before she graduates."

"She'll make friends anywhere."

"That's not the point. This was not part of the deal, Rich," my mother insisted, using his full name. "You know it. Just because you're bored—"

"Bored?!"

"Yes, bored. You get a little bit bored and decide to upend our entire lives just because you've entered a slow patch in the middle of winter. It's no wonder where Sylvia gets it. The constant wanderlust! You want to do something different and see the world. Put down the computer. Let's go on a trip. Let's book a vacation somewhere. We keep saying that we are saving for one every year. Go to Europe or Maine or anywhere for a week."

"So, you admit that Sylvia will be on board." My father raised his voice in a sort of triumph.

Silence swept over the house as my mother scoffed at the few words he had managed to latch on to.

She shook her head and kept shaking it. "We are not doing this again."

"Just consider it."

"I'm done considering it!"

Carefully, I snuck out the front door, careful not to let it slam behind me. I jogged the rest of the way up the block and toward the center of town.

NINE

NOW

"KIERAN."

When romantic comedies went on and on about when the main character found "the one" and they used the phrase "heart stopped," I always rolled my eyes. I turned the page.

But when I saw Kieran Rose, my heart stopped.

When I looked at Kieran, I saw him. All of him.

I saw Kieran from his goofy, always slightly unsure smile to his tortoise-framed glasses, which he had only ever changed once at his mother's insistence during sophomore year. He had promptly returned to them the next day. I saw his mousy-brown hair, which he never let get over his ears but was always floppy up top. I saw him at the age of five even though I only ever saw pictures of the toothy, stuttering child his parents were so proud of. I saw him standing before me at sixteen with his dad's car keys, begging me to drive slowly so I wouldn't go over a curb—which I had. I saw him at eighteen, bright and shiny at graduation, playing with the tassel on my hat.

I saw Kieran, shivering in the cold in front of me the last time we had stood just like this. We had been outside, mouths parted, waiting for the other to speak and hopefully have the right words. The snow had been high and heavy, and neither of us had had anything good to say, let alone the right things.

And now, maybe that last part was still true. Neither of us said a word. We were like ghosts coming back to haunt the other.

I swallowed, and the action triggered something in my brain. "I ..."

"Still not dressing for the weather, I see," Kieran commented, cutting me off. His eyes lingered as he gazed at my apparel, or lack of it.

I felt every pinpoint where he looked at me. I could feel the way he stared at my shoes, which didn't do well in snow, all the way up to where my jacket wasn't properly covering my neck.

I cupped my bare hands, trying to fit them back up my sleeves.

"I didn't pack well," I said, though that was a lie. I had packed everything.

Kieran's chest rose with a deep breath. He likely considered his next words. Kieran didn't usually speak without playing the conversation out in his head first. It was the biggest reason I always thought he'd be a better writer than I was.

Imagine the dialogue of someone who worked through a thousand different ways a conversation could go without even opening their mouth.

"I didn't know that you were coming home," he said.

"I didn't either." I tried to add a humorous droll. It came out flat. I waved a hand back toward the center of town that would be crowded with families for the next hour at least. "I got a grand *welcome back to Marshall Falls for the holidays*."

Kieran parted his lips, chapped and pink from the cold, but said nothing before sucking them back into his mouth, biting them between his teeth.

"It was kind of unplanned, coming back here. I didn't think—"

"You said you'd never come back," said Kieran, his voice deep and steady. He clearly remembered the last time we had spoken as well as I did.

"I did say something like that."

"You said exactly that," Kieran insisted.

"Okay. I wasn't expecting to see you when I decided to come back home or tonight. I mean, I thought I saw you before at the lighting ceremony, but then I wasn't sure. But here you are." I tried to hide the shake of my voice.

"You still call this place home?" he asked.

I guessed I did.

Kieran took my lack of an answer as one. "I was hoping that I wouldn't ever see you again."

I blinked, feeling the punch to my stomach. "Ouch."

"Not really, Sylvia. Not ouch. You left."

"You know why I left."

He had let me leave.

"And?"

"I was hoping that if I did see you ..."

"What?" Kieran snapped, his forehead creasing in thick, concentrated lines. "Did you think when you saw me that we could pretend that everything was okay?"

"Well, no."

"What option did you want? Did you want us to smile and wave at each other like you hadn't done what you had? Did you think everything could go back to normal?"

"Of course not."

"Then, you just wanted to stand there in front of me and give me some fake small talk, like it hadn't been four years?" Kieran asked. "Like you hadn't ignored me even after I tried to reach out and talk to you? After you missed—"

"Kieran ..." I didn't know what to say, but I didn't want any of that. I didn't know what I thought or wanted or what I needed to do right now when, lately, everything I decided and did was wrong.

Before I could figure out the right thing to explain it all, on the verge of letting him know just how much the past four years had hurt me, likely just as much as him, Kieran's voice broke.

"I needed you."

My nose scrunched. The burn of tears rushed back up behind my eyes.

Shadows stretched between us, and neither of us could bridge the gap.

"I, um ... I—"

"No." Kieran shook his head. "I think it's my turn to talk."

"Okay—"

"I needed you. After what happened between us, I needed you so much more than you ever knew, no matter what happened that Christmas and the holidays, and where were you?"

I wasn't here.

"You weren't there. You didn't even pick up the damn phone. You were selfish. You weren't the person I had grown up with every single day. You weren't my best friend. You weren't anything you had said you were to me—wanted to be."

I shook my head. "I know."

"No, you don't. Because after everything, all that felt like a lie too." Kieran spat each word before he could hold it back for being too forward or too harsh. His lips quivered with emotion.

It would've been better if he had walked over and hit me or shoved me into the snow. But he was right. That wouldn't even begin to make us even for what I had done.

"So, go on." He gestured.

"What?" I breathed, surprised it had even come out in a cloud of hot air.

"Go on and tell me whatever it is that you want to tell me now," said Kieran. "Explain."

Explain.

"You really have nothing to say?"

I had so much to say. I had everything to say to him, and yet for some reason, I couldn't piece the words together. I stood there, gaping at him.

"Four years can do a lot to a person, huh?" he murmured, just loud enough that I could hear. "I just thought—"

He just thought what?

I watched pain and fury cross Kieran's face. He could never have one without the other. Four years could do a lot to a person, yet I still recognized the one in front of me, mostly anyway. It was still Kieran. Kieran at twenty-eight and twenty and sixteen and thirteen—when I had first started to see just how stupidly pretty he was, even after the braces and terrible fights we had when we disagreed.

He must've seen all of that looking at me too, only he didn't like it.

I swallowed and hoped I'd choke on my own saliva. Put myself out of my misery.

"You want to pretend that everything is okay here and now. That's on you. But I told you before and I'll tell you again ..."

I shook my head as he fought with himself to say it. But I'd never seen Kieran this way before. I'd never seen him so angry.

"I would've been happy if you'd never come back. I would've been so fucking happy if I'd never met you that day you came knocking on our door with your mom."

There they were.

Those were the words I always thought I would hear in terrible nightmares, but now, it was here, right in front of me.

When I didn't say anything back, Kieran nodded once more. He turned and headed inside the dark and empty bakery.

I crossed my arms over one another. I twisted around and took the long way back up toward home, feeling the heavy weight of tears cresting in my throat and pounding behind my eyes as I tried to breathe evenly.

I couldn't imagine how many times he had thought those words to himself. I had known he'd be upset.

Yet it hurt anyway.

It hurt more than losing my job this morning. It hurt so much worse than seeing Ezra getting a blow job on my stupidly expensive couch I had saved up months for. It unnerved me more than the silence hanging around my head, no words, no sounds, no nothing to fill the void.

I slid inside the house as quietly as I could out of habit so as not to wake my parents after a late night out, but no one was home.

It was just me.

I made sure to turn the lock behind me. I slumped down the hallway back to my room, shedding my clothes on the floor as I made my way to bed. I'd taken most of my favorite stuff with me when I finally left home, including the nice sheets that used to be warm and thick on my bed.

So, now, I yanked on the clearance department store sheets my mother got in case she ever decided to turn my childhood space into a guest room even though we never had any guests. The sheets were thin and cold, but I didn't really deserve much else.

I clutched the puffy duvet tightly around my shoulders. I squeezed my eyes shut and let out a heaving sob. I cried in my nest of blankets until my ribs hurt. I let myself cry, whether it be from pity or because my body felt like it was going to shatter completely after today.

It was over.

I had thought everything was over from the moment I stepped off the train into Marshall Falls, but I was wrong.

It was over from the moment Kieran had looked at me like I'd never left, but with all the pain, as if he had hoped he'd never have to see me again, and he had told me so.

Because that was the point after staying away all these years, wasn't it?

TEN

BEFORE

"HEY!" Kieran caught my attention.

He waved over to me as he stepped away from the horde of town people. The rest of the school was already here, along with families. That included the group of kids from school, like Dylan, Jenna, Landon, and Amy, who were casting us looks. Or maybe it was just me they were staring at, like they weren't sure who I was.

"I was just going to come and get you. You made it just in time."

I pressed my lips together, crossing my arms for some type of warmth. Should've grabbed my heavier jacket. Though that would've meant that I would have to cross the kitchen to get to the closet, and that was one more thing I hadn't wanted to do today.

Kieran dipped his head to get a better look at me, seeing the way, I was sure, my mascara was smeared with how cold it was. My eyes were still red.

"What's wrong?"

I shook my head. "It's nothing."

He stared at me.

"It's really nothing," I repeated. "It's just my parents. What else is new?"

"Fighting?"

It wasn't the first time. Not recently. I had tried to ignore it for the last month, trying to believe that it wasn't happening. Not the fighting exactly. What the fighting was about.

After so long, I shouldn't have been surprised that my dad was trying to get us to pack up our things in boxes in an effort to widen our lively horizons, or whatever he wanted to call it, so that leaving a world that we had built for the past almost decade, longer than anywhere before, felt thrilling and romantic.

We never stayed in one place for long, even after my parents promised that we'd stay here for a good long while so I could call a town home. And oddly enough, that was what happened. Marshall Falls, at some point, had become home. Here with the middle of town and Rose Bakery and Kieran.

"My dad is getting restless here, apparently." *Again.* I sniffed, trying to pretend it was the cold getting to me.

"Wasn't he saying something like that last spring?"

"He did." I dipped my chin. "But now, he's looked into other job openings, including one that comes with a promotion, near Boston."

"Boston," Kieran repeated, as if trying to calculate the miles. "Would've thought you'd be more excited to get close to a big city like that."

"Or maybe he'd try to go to Boston, and we'd all end up in Indiana for some completely ridiculous, unknown reason."

It didn't matter. Nothing was set, and yet it felt like someone had taken a sledgehammer to my midsection.

Kieran was right after all. All I ever wanted was to get away. All I ever wanted was to get to a city with bright lights all day and night. I'd drink coffee at fancy coffee shops and meet interesting people. Now, I might have my chance if my dad ended up convincing us once and for all to get out of Marshall Falls, and yet...

I looked at Kieran. He stared down at me, and a similar expression as mine passed over his face. Or at least, he showed what he was feeling. I locked the fear and sadness down tight, unable to witness my own disappointment, which shouldn't have been disappointment.

"So, that's it? You're moving?" Kieran asked.

My voice softened into almost silence. "I don't know. Maybe. I wouldn't be surprised."

Without a word, Kieran wrapped his arm around my shoulders. He would always be there if I needed to cry, but I so far in our relationship, I hadn't.

"Are you okay, being here?"

I nodded. "Yeah."

"You still don't mind if we hang out with everyone? We can leave if you want," said Kieran. "We have two more holidays to get this knocked off the list."

"No, it's good. I just needed a second. Let's go," I said.

I burrowed further into Kieran's side.

His dark eyes scanned carefully over the entire town square. "Kieran—"

"Oh, I'm so glad you're staying!" A blur rushed into us—or rather into Kieran. His arm slid away from me with an oomph.

"Hey, Amy."

"Good to see you," Amy squealed. She pulled back away from hugging him. She looked so tiny next to him. She smoothed her golden strands of hair sticking out from beneath her earmuffs back down toward her fake fur lined shoulders. "For a second there, I thought you were going to be pulled away. I wasn't even sure if you'd come to begin with, but I'm glad that you took me up on my invite."

I glanced back up at Kieran as he lifted a hand to the back of his neck, face flushed from the sudden contact.

Invite?

I had wondered why the gazebo lighting was oddly near the bottom of our adventure list when the rest felt more intentionally chronological. It was starting to make sense.

Kieran shrugged good-naturedly as he looked from Amy around to the rest of the many decorations the town had seemed to put up overnight. "It's been a while since I last saw the lights. My parents used to bring me every year when I was little."

"I think it's the best way to start the holiday season." She fluttered her eyelashes.

I forced myself not to barf, which Kieran noticed a lot more than Amy's blatant desire to make herself as close to him as possible. I looked between the two of them, trying to decipher if it had always been this way.

If he wanted her, he would do something about it. Right? So, for now, she was just pitiful.

At least in my silent opinion.

Amy turned in my direction. Her eyes widened, as if I hadn't been standing there right next to her the entire time as she threw herself at nearly every guy in a ten-foot radius. "Hi, Sylvie."

I waved an unenthusiastic hand. "It's Sylvia."

"Isn't that what I just said?" She giggled.

I looked up at Kieran. I could see his careful request for me to be nice staring back at me, just like everyone had done as I grew up.

But I was nice, and I did behave, whether or not anyone cared with the final product of me doing so. It sure didn't feel that way when I had my mother constantly on me, the school counselor, and now, even my father, who I could only assume would be right by the door, trying to sway me to convince my mother into this new move we could take.

His type of adventure.

And then what was I to do? What did being nice and good ever end up getting me in the end? All it seemed to do was continue the torture of standing awkwardly next to Kieran and realizing that I was a seventh wheel.

"A group of us are gathered right over there if you want to join. Dylan and Rebecca both have their ornaments in the running this year." Amy smiled brightly, reaching out for his hand.

Kieran let her take it, much to her obvious delight. I slowly trailed after them. Crossing my arms over one another again, I tried to trap the heat that I had lost the moment Kieran's body heat left.

Amy led him farther into the crowd, circling around the gazebo and tree, both still unlit. Many held to-go cups of hot chocolate, bundled in all their hats and scarves. That included the small junior class, who stopped talking as Amy burst through the middle of them.

"I found Kieran. He was hiding on the edge of the crowd."

A few of the guys smiled.

"Hey, man."

Kieran lifted a slightly shy hand in greeting, as if he'd done this before.

"Now, the entire gang is together," said Amy, clapping her mittened hands together. "I can't believe this is one of our last years of doing this before we all go off into the real world."

Because this one was so fake? I wanted to tease, but held my taunting words back.

A few of the guys cheered at her words as they talked, checking the time they still had left to wait as more people joined in the center of town.

Amy kept herself tightly situated beside Kieran. Holding on to his arm, she grinned up at him. He smiled back as he answered some sort of question.

A new, uncomfortable feeling churned in my stomach. I glanced to my other side. Jenna leaned up against her boyfriend.

She looked me over, holding a small smile, unsure. "I like your sweater."

I glanced down at it, part of it peeking up through my jacket. "Thanks."

"Did you thrift it or something?"

"Or something. I found it in the back of my mom's closet."

"That's cool. I could never wear my mom's clothes. She has far too many cat sweaters. Which are just ..." Jenna shivered in horror.

A small laugh escaped me.

"I can't believe we haven't seen you out more. It's nice, everyone all together. It's not like the junior class is that big and—"

She didn't get to finish her thought before Amy stepped up next to her. "Hey, I have something I want to show you really quick, all right?"

Jenna glanced between me and Amy. "All right. Nice to see you, Sylvia."

With a dip of my head, I tried not to watch as Amy took Jenna the two steps away to situate her best friend closer to mine. Kieran was slowly coming out of his shell, but this might have been the first time I'd ever seen him with everyone else, smiling and laughing and having a great time.

Maybe we should've started our list together earlier. For so many reasons.

Jenna's boyfriend leaned back and forth on his feet as he gave me a smile.

"I've seen you around, right?" Gabe asked, pointing at me.

For a moment, I was unsure if he was kidding. "We have Chemistry together. Every day."

"Ah, right." He snapped his fingers, as if I were the one who had now made a joke.

Carefully, I extracted myself from between them all, mumbling a half excuse of needing air. I heard Kieran's hesitant yet oddly powerful laugh ring behind me as I took a few more steps. I wanted to somehow go up and insert myself with the rest of them. I wanted to tear Amy's claws off Kieran and position myself right where I should've been standing—beside him.

Jealousy and nerves swirled in my gut again. Not that I was jealous.

I was jealous of Kieran's time and attention maybe. Who could blame me after having no one else who seemed to care if I was even there or if I left for Boston or Indianapolis or wherever my father wanted to take us tomorrow?

Not when they could have fun and bubbly Amy at their side instead.

I shut my eyes as I made it to the other side of the sidewalk in the center square. Small kids ran around, brushing the fine layer of snow flurries off the bench slats before climbing on top for a better view. They laughed and giggled in their puffy jackets, which made them appear more like fat marshmallows than anything else.

"Hey, I wasn't sure where you went." Kieran trailed up next to me, cocking his head to the side.

"Sorry. You can go back and hang out with them. I just felt sort of on the outside, I guess. I'm fine with it," I quickly assured.

Kieran sighed. "I know Amy is kind of ..."

A bitch?

"Not really welcoming for some reason."

That was one way of putting the undeniable fact that they were rude and trying to make their own little exclusive club where only one person couldn't seem to join. At least it wasn't just me who had seen it.

"Unless they're you."

"What do you mean?"

I raised my eyebrows. Mostly because I had caught him looking at Amy and her backside more than a few times before at the football games, whenever her cheer uniform flung up in the back with every toe touch.

I didn't elaborate.

"Are you okay?"

"Of course. I'm great. I'm perfect. Just peachy." The words came out of my mouth a little too fast.

He noticed all too easily. "Why does that not sound convincing?"

"Because." Because it wasn't. My shoulders slumped. "I'm just being selfish."

"We can all be a little selfish sometimes. Tell me what's going on in there." He tapped my head. "Is it still about your parents?"

"I'm just ..." I shook my head, inhaling a breath that didn't quite make it back out from where it had ballooned in my chest. "When it comes down to it, being here and being around all them, I want to be. But I can't because then I realize that I'm no one. I know that sounds dramatic, but I'm starting to piece together that, really, it's just honest. I have nothing to say and nowhere I'm meant to be, like everyone else seems to fit in. I'm completely invisible."

"You're not invisible. Not to me."

"For now," I said. "You'll be fine if I leave. Sure, maybe you were this odd, little literary genius of a dweeb before I came along ..."

"Really hitting me with the compliments here."

"Stop it. I'm serious." I didn't need him to make me laugh

right now. "Look at you. You've blossomed into Kieran. I'm always just Sylvia. You have these friends and this town, and maybe it wouldn't be such a bad thing if it turned out my dad did convince us to leave Marshall. I was only meant to be here for a little for some cosmic reason or whatever."

Maybe that was it. Instead of getting my own stories, I was just assisting in everyone else's.

"Sylvia, take a breath."

"You know I hate being told that." It made me want to start hyperventilating until I was curled up in a tiny ball on the ground.

"Do it anyway," Kieran ordered.

I did.

"No one will ever take your place in my life. It doesn't matter who they are. You are Sylvia. You're my ... you're my best friend."

"Even if I'm not here?"

"Always, Sylv. And that's not going to happen. My mom will practically hide you in a closet if she even hears about you moving away too. You're like the daughter she never had."

Neither of us knew that, but I didn't fight the spare positivity Kieran had to share.

"Take another deep breath."

I took a shallow one, but he didn't correct me. He rubbed my hands between his bright red mittens before he easily slipped my two hands into his lined coat pockets. Warmth was his hands holding mine there, not letting me run away.

He turned his attention back ahead. "Now, just you wait."

For once, I did as I had been told. Kieran stayed next to me as the mayor counted down.

The switch was turned. The lights flickered before they blared. One line of our checklist was already complete. And the town of Marshall Falls came alive.

ELEVEN

NOW

I LAID in bed for as long as I could, unable to move due to the overwhelming sorrow thing I had going on and was clearly excelling at. Eventually, the need to use the bathroom and eat something won out. Bodily needs really messed up the entire *spinster bound to bed* persona.

I moved from the bed to the couch, though that didn't mean I had left any of the blankets behind. Quilts trailed me from one room to the other. Old reruns ran on the television as I bundled myself up.

It was freezing in this house.

I drifted in and out of sleep and ate half the frozen meals in the freezer, which looked nothing like the way they were pictured on the box. The only thing that disturbed me from my depression was the light chime of my phone somewhere on day two of my holiday spiral.

I reached for the jeans I had left on the floor after I tried to get dressed once this morning to then realize what really was the point of pants? I pulled my phone out of the back pocket. The screen exploded with light, bright enough for me to squint.

My heart stung as I saw the single message at the bottom. It was from Ezra.

I hesitated before I opened it.

Don't be stupid, he had typed.

Don't be stupid. I stared at the words, rereading it two more times.

Don't be stupid?

Rage bubbled in my chest. Anger and hurt were so potent that I wanted to hurl my phone across the room.

I didn't respond.

I swiped into my email. All that was there was a written copy from human resources about being fired from *Main Attraction*. Oh, and an ad from somewhere I no longer shopped, offering twenty percent off. I narrowed my eyes at the final unopened email below it. I must've missed it a while ago.

My domain for my old blog was being auto-renewed.

I hadn't even known I'd been renewing it.

Looking at the button to check the link, I clicked. The website buffered for so long, I almost turned back before the once-obsessed-over blog loaded one section at a time to life. The template design was awkward. The top title was all out of whack on my phone screen.

I scrolled down anyway.

One of the first things on the site, front and center, was the article that had changed everything. Or nearly had.

The simple post had spread like wildfire around the internet with over two hundred comments before a somewhat-decent magazine saw it. At the time, I thought that was viral. *Groundbreaking.*

That was what the website that offered me my first internship said. Though their start-up went right into the ground not long after. A few fancy parties and headlines on New York's infamous *Page Six* had sent the place downhill, no matter how many times my manager had assured it was all good publicity if people were reading.

I skimmed my retired blog from page one to page two and three. Photos were the first things, along with my many book recommendations and lists, that assaulted me. One by one, pictures of a younger me and a smiling Kieran with a terrible shaggy haircut and smudged glasses couldn't help but be there.

Our ill-fated hikes were all documented. So was our junior year at the falls and the time Kieran came to visit me in the city. We somehow ended up all over the place that day. I didn't understand how we had managed it. In the end, all of it had become the perfect writing portfolio. From Kieran's big, floppy hat at the beach so he wouldn't get burned, which he always did anyway, to his horrified face as I took a picture of him in a sterile black chair during one of our last spontaneous decisions. The caption read, *He told me not to post this.*

It was all there.

Ezra had thought I kept a time capsule of Kieran and my childhood together in a shoebox in the back of my closet, but no. If there was ever a sort of memorial to a life I thought about every single day, it had been put on the internet for the entire world to see.

I looked ... happy.

Hot tears slid down my cheeks. Not moving, I stared until my phone drifted to sleep. I dropped it back on the floor and shut my eyes, trying to stop the never-ending flow of emotion that had overtaken me during the past forty-eight hours.

I had to be running low on tears by now. I had thought I was done, yet it didn't seem to be the case. My shoulders silently shook. I curled further under the mountain of blankets, feeling even more like a child than I ever had before while at home.

However, I knew one thing. It was still the holiday, which

meant that my mother had more than just a few bottles of wine to add to the cheer.

Pushing away the heavy quilts tucked around me, I strutted toward the kitchen in nothing but my old bathrobe. For once, I was grateful for my mother's preparedness, occasionally stashing liquor and bottles of red wine under the counter in case someone came over to the house, though they never did. Her wine taste was terrible, but it would do.

I yanked off the spiral of red ribbon around the neck while searching for the opener. Popping out the cork, I grabbed a glass —I wasn't a complete heathen after all—and proceeded to pour the wine as close to the very tippy top of the glass that I could. Leaning in, I sipped the first layer with a loud slurp.

I'd had better wine in my life, but right now, this was heaven. This was needed.

Halfway down the glass, I refilled, glancing back once more to my phone. I nodded in silent confirmation to myself as I looked around the silent space. The television was my companion, still rumbling with a laugh track in the background, as if it, too, thought my life was hysterical.

Okay, it was time to get down to business.

I let myself sulk. That was reasonable. Now what? I needed to know what exactly the plan was.

Just because Ezra didn't want me in the city with him didn't mean that I couldn't live on my own. I was independent and confident enough to do so. As I opened the first page of recent apartment listings on my phone, I nearly choked.

In the past year, prices even for the tiniest of studios had skyrocketed. Plus, I was going to need a job to get approved to live in a legal apartment.

I needed a job first. That was clear.

I needed to somehow start a job search over the winter holiday, like HR was checking their emails and job opening responses at all on a normal week, let alone one of the most distracting times of year. And who knew what would happen when they decided to ask for a reference? I had put years into *Main Attraction*, and I had been no more than a glorified coffee slave who didn't even make a good drip.

I had caught more than one of my coworkers grimacing in the morning when I was the first one to make a pot.

An hour later, I paced the house and looked in the mirror in my room, continuing to scroll through options that didn't completely make me want to gouge my own eyes out. My robe hung off one shoulder. My slippers looked even sadder in the daylight. The dark brown color that I had dyed my hair with was taking on a dull sheen on the bottom while the top looked like it hadn't been washed in days—which, in all fairness, it hadn't.

I was the epitome of sad, old cat lady. Without the cats.

I chuckled to myself and took another sip of wine and went back to scrolling. I sorted through all my old contacts, trying to remember where anyone I used to work with now worked. Maybe they could put a good word in! That was it.

I could call ...

I could call Kieran.

Wait. No. What?

I looked down at my almost-empty glass of wine again, as if it had been the one to come up with that ridiculous idea.

I couldn't call Kieran. Mainly because he hated me and never wanted to speak to me again.

He had said so.

Wandering back toward the kitchen, I reached for the bottle of wine and poured the last few drops into my glass.

That had really gone way too quickly.

Taking a sip nonetheless, I set my phone aside and stared at it.

I wanted to call Kieran. He always knew what to do. He was the planner and the list maker. He could figure out this entire mess for me with a snap of his fingers—if he was still here, watching me implode. He would probably even laugh at everything that had happened to me in the past week if he cared enough to try and lighten the mood.

At this rate, I doubted Kieran would even be surprised.

I was, after all, one big screwup.

I pressed my lips together. I was going to figure this all out. I had to keep telling myself that. I was good on my own, and I could do this.

But then there was still that furious, pained expression on Kieran's face.

Maybe it was the wine talking again, but before I left, I needed to do something. I needed to make sure that he knew that I was sorry and that I did have something to say.

Swinging around, I yanked out drawers in the kitchen until I found a pen and a pad of paper. It wasn't ideal with snowmen trailing up the borders, but it would do.

I had so much to say even if, for the first time in my entire life, I wasn't able to completely get it out.

Even if I couldn't figure out my life and make it better right now, I was going to do this. Then, everything would be better.

Or at least, it would be a start.

Not having time to pull out the hot tools from the bottom of my suitcase, I wrestled my hair back into a claw clip. At least the tangles would be out of my face even if it was unable to help the slight greasy quality.

I tugged on a thin jacket, along with a crossbody purse I must've left here years ago.

All that mattered right now though was that I was buzzed on crappy, dry wine that had been hidden away in my mother's kitchen for who knew how long, and it had taken me at least seven times, but I thought I'd finally gotten this note right. Or not-note.

I was always better at revisions anyway.

When I had first started writing it, I had tried to write Kieran a letter. I explained what had happened and how I wanted to call but couldn't and how much I loved him. I had poured everything into it before shoving it out of the way.

Kieran liked to read, but I knew that there was one thing he loved even more. There was one thing that Kieran couldn't pass up, and if that was what it was going to take for him to even slightly forgive me enough that he didn't wish me dead whenever he saw me, I was going to do it.

I was going to make the ultimate Win Back Kieran Rose's Love and Affection List there ever was. Though I didn't title it that.

Duh. I was tipsy, not stupid.

Now, there was one thing left to do. Make sure that Kieran got this note. To-do list. *Whatever.*

At seven thirty at night, Marshall Falls was nearly silent. I filled the void with my heavy breathing as I made my way to Kieran's house. The windows were dark against the white siding, and no one seemed to be home. Luckily, I knew where next to check this time of year. I turned back toward town center and then one street farther until I saw familiar lights and a door being pushed open, guarded by someone's grandpa taking a smoke.

It was easy to forget that Marshall Falls only had one bar. In New York, there were hundreds of places to blow off steam. There were the classic dive bars as well as the up-and-coming spaces with cocktails that had the names of famous movie actresses and that looked more like works of art than overpriced alcohol. In Marshall, there was a single place for everyone in town to meet up for a holiday drink after work.

It was also the one place I knew for a fact Kieran would be after seeing the rest of the crew back in town all together. Or at least I could hope.

I noted the few direct stares I got for letting in any of the cold before I made sure it shut behind me. It didn't take long for me to find what I was looking for—or at least, what I thought I was looking for.

Bingo.

I picked out his quiet, off-kilter laughter before I noticed anything else. In the corner booth, a group of my former classmates shoved themselves together into almost a pile so that they'd all fit.

They all had one thing in common.

They all somehow looked ... happy.

That included Kieran, who was at one end. He pulled away and headed back toward the restrooms. He didn't even look in my direction.

I clutched the silly pieces of paper I had stuck in my pocket before I left the house.

What was I thinking?

I was clearly still far too sober.

I pushed off the rubber heel of my boot and quickly maneuvered toward an open space at the bar.

TWELVE

BEFORE

I CLICKED my pen a few more times, forgetting why I had picked it up at all until Kieran looked at me.

"I will take that pen and break it if you don't stop," he threatened.

I stared down at the pen, clicking it one more time to close the point. "You wouldn't do that to my poor pen."

Kieran looked between me and the pen seriously. His head gave a little dip as he came to his conclusion. "I would."

"Violent this evening." I set the pen aside on the bed next to our stacked textbooks. "What's gotten into you? Did your date with Amy not go well?"

"It wasn't a date."

I raised my eyebrows. "It was a date."

Kieran sighed.

"You took her out. It was just you two, right?"

He nodded.

"You ate food somewhere other than at your mom's bakery. You dressed in something other than your normal half-buttoned shirts."

"I like my shirts."

It was why he had one in nearly every single color known to man. Even I had one or two that he had outgrown through the years in case I got something on my clothes while cooking with Lori and him. My talent in that aspect never grew, but Lori never seemed to mind the mess I always ended up making.

"It was a date."

"Fine. It was a date," Kieran finally admitted.

"Did you kiss her?"

Kieran lifted his eyes up from his homework and stared at me.

"What? It's a normal question."

Sighing, he lifted his glasses up and rubbed his eyes. "You're making this weird."

"I'm not. You're the one who won't admit that you had an actual date with Amy Walmer."

He rolled his eyes. "Yes, I kissed her."

I blinked. I had known that he did. If Kieran had any balls at all, of course he'd kiss her. Still, I hadn't expected to pause as long as I did. Something pulled in my chest.

"What?"

"Nothing," I said. "Sorry. How was it?"

"I don't think I want to talk about it."

"Why not? Was it bad? Was she bad at it?"

"No, Sylvia, she was not bad at it," moaned Kieran.

"Were *you* bad at it?"

His cheeks flared pink. "No. I don't think so."

I narrowed my eyes. "Have you kissed someone else before?"

"It was a fine kiss, Sylvia. It was a good kiss, okay?" he exclaimed, exasperated.

Both of us sat for a moment.

I pressed my lips together, not sure whether it was to stop

myself from saying something I'd regret or laugh. "Okay. Sorry. I just thought ..."

"What? That you'd give me some pointers?"

I inhaled, feeling the tease as more of a hit to the chest. I looked back down toward the family laptop I'd inherited as of last month when my mom got a new one from work. I focused on the faded letters of the keyboard.

"Low blow, Kier."

It wasn't my fault that even while trying to hang out with Kieran and the rest of his friends, it was abundantly clear no one cared if I was there, let alone the fact that out of the smallest school in the world, it felt like no one was interested in me. Unlike Kieran. Over the past year, Kieran had somehow started to fit in.

Not even Dylan was attracted to me, and he was interested in just about everyone.

"That was." Kieran shook his head. The space between his brows creased. He took off his glasses and rubbed the lenses with the edge of his shirt. "You're right. I'm sorry."

"It's fine. Sorry I pushed."

"It's fine. It's me. I just don't get it."

Now, it was my turn to be confused. "Get what?"

"Amy, I guess," said Kieran. "I don't get why she likes me really."

"Do you like her?"

He shrugged. "I guess so."

I cocked my head to the side, studying my friend. I tried to notice if there was anything different about him. For example, this strange shyness that came over him in my presence. I thought we had gotten over it years ago.

"This isn't exactly a guessing situation."

"Why not? I'll get to know her more and then see if we are compatible together."

"Compatible?"

"It's nice and all. She's nice. Yeah, I know, most of the time," he corrected when he noticed my expression.

"You're treating love like it's an equation in math," I scoffed.

"Who says I'm in love?"

He had a point. Hearing him say it somehow made the weight in my stomach ease, too, even though that was completely crazy, right? I was worried that, soon enough, Kieran would pull away from me altogether. Even if it hadn't happened yet, it didn't mean that, eventually, he wouldn't finally see how good he was, like everyone else was starting to.

After a little while, finishing another paragraph of the post I was working on for the end of the week, I looked back up at him.

Kieran did a double take when he noticed I was staring. "What? Do I have something on my face?"

"You'd marry me if I was sad and depressed and alone at thirty, right?" I asked, meekly.

Kieran blinked. The corner of his mouth curved up in that endearing sort of way that made me know he was either going to say something nice or stupid. "I'd marry you right now."

Rolling my eyes, I threw my bookmark at him.

He whacked it away.

"Stop looking at me like that," I chastised.

"Like what?"

"Smiling."

"Why shouldn't I be smiling?" Kieran asked. "I'm planning our future wedding. I'm thinking ... backyard. My mom would be thrilled, don't you think?"

"Stop."

"We could have a white cake with the raspberry filling you like. She'd probably insist on making it."

"Shut your mouth right now and stop making fun of me."

I lunged across the bed to land on him, as if I could stop his mouth from moving.

"Little blue flowers. You'd be in a lace gown, all white and virginal."

"KIERAN."

Kieran gasped with laughter as we fought against each other's hands. I stared down at him as we laughed and his hands dug into my stomach, tickling me until I choked on the air between us, unable to pull any into my lungs as I broke with unwanted giggles.

"Stop, stop, stop it! I can't breathe," I cried.

Kieran laughed more, hands smoothing down over my shirt. I twisted my legs around him to sit up. Finally, we stopped.

My hands lay on his chest as I looked down at him from above, my hair falling into my face from where it had previously been twisted into a loose bun. I made no move for a moment as our chests rose and fell rapidly. I froze as I leaned over him. His eyes drew a line back and forth from my eyes and then down lower.

Carefully, we pulled away from each other, maneuvering our bodies until we were back to sitting up, side by side. I shifted the top of my shirt back over my chest, where it had been yanked down.

Kieran cleared his throat as he reached back for his book, marking the page before setting it aside again. "You know, we could go somewhere to eat food after school other than the bakery. If you want. I just thought we were comfortable there."

"We are," I agreed, looking back down at my laptop as I pulled it back into my crossed legs.

Both of us sat there, looking around the room before peeking at the other.

Quickly, I gestured back toward my laptop to change the subject. "Anyway, you still haven't helped me with this mess."

"What mess? You've been working for the past hour and a half nonstop."

"I meant the other thing," I said. I still couldn't quite look at him, knowing I would see flushed cheeks mirroring my own. "I still need to decide whether or not I should apply to the writing workshop this summer."

"The one in the city? Your mom said you could, didn't she?"

"She only said that because she thinks I won't get in."

"I think you'll get in," said Kieran. "If there's anything you are made to do, it's write."

Honesty had rung in his tone and in his expression as he looked at me. "You should just hit the Submit button. I know you already filled everything out."

I had.

"You're overthinking it."

"I am not." I completely was, but that hadn't been the sort of response I had hoped for. I wasn't sure what I had hoped for exactly, but not Kieran's specific brand of frankness.

"Okay then, you're not. I still think it would be cool. You'd be good at it. Imagine yourself when applying to school or even after. You can always say you got your start in a fancy writing workshop for college students when you were a student at Marshall Falls High."

"I'm not sure that will mean that much, and seriously, I doubt they'll even look at my application."

"Why would you say that?"

"For one thing, I'm not that interesting," I said.

Setting aside my laptop with the tab for the application I had indeed already filled out still open, I bit the skin around my nails.

Kieran paid my anxiety no attention as he continued to clean up his side of the bed before moving onto the rest of the room, like he needed something to do with his hands. He shoved his small pile of discarded clothing that had been sitting on the chair in the corner into the hamper. "I wouldn't write that on your résumé."

"Ha-ha."

He pursed his lips in a smirk. "You always have plenty to say. Your post the other week was pretty good."

So far, I had created a few book reviews—some including comments from Kieran in a book club fashion—as well as a few random pieces on the time Kieran's uncle and cousin had taken us hiking up toward the renowned falls and even more well-known hiking trails that tourists flooded in the spring.

People really enjoyed those photos and the unfortunate story of how a shared hammock did nothing to protect us from the torrential downpour that happened that night. We had both looked like drowned rats, though Kieran's uncle and cousin had thought it was hilarious. So had my mother, who wondered what in the world had prompted me to go camping to begin with.

The experience as well as the page views had come to be my answer.

Thank goodness that sort of spontaneous adventure wasn't repeated on the list.

"It's stupid to even apply."

Kieran raised his eyebrows. "No, it's not."

"It is. I know my writing isn't good. No matter how good I want it to be, someone always reads it and says, 'It's really pretty but confusing.'"

It was the best and worst kind of insult, all rolled into one. I might not have the talent like the girl who won the writing competitions in school, but I had to believe that my determination to write every day meant something.

"You can do it," he encouraged. "You're the most interesting person I know, Sylvia, and anyone would be stupid to toss you aside."

But in Marshall, I still couldn't help but figure that didn't say much.

Reaching slowly across the space between us, Kieran tapped the top of my computer screen. "Do I need to shut it, or are you in full trance?"

Slowly, I lifted a hand as if I was going to swat him. Instead, I placed my palm right on top of his hand. "Aw. Look at us."

His eyes softened as he raised his eyebrows in amusement. "Adorable."

The cuteness lasted for a second before Kieran turned serious again.

"Hit the Submit button," Kieran insisted.

"I can't."

"Hit it."

"No."

Kieran reached across and hit the Enter key. "There."

My eyes widened in both horror and sudden relief. "Kieran."

His eyes were just as round. "I really didn't think that would work when I hit the key. They should have more of a secure submission platform."

"Well"—I gestured to the screen thanking me for my application—"it did."

"You mad?"

I shook my head, still a little dumbfounded at how easy that had been. Or at least easy for Kieran.

I was glad. I had just applied to one of the coolest programs for young writers in the country. They were going to look at my work, and I was going to be able to go to the city. I'd meet interesting people, and I'd have things to write about.

Looking up at Kieran, I smiled.

He sighed with relief, as if he'd been holding his breath. "Good. Now, let's go."

"What are you talking about?" I looked down at myself. "I thought we were just going to spend the weekend here and wait for your mom to get home to make us one of those amazing grilled cheese sandwiches."

I had been really looking forward to that sandwich ever since she had made one for me the first time. She added basil and crisped the outside with butter. Who knew that bread and cheese could produce such happiness?

He laughed, shutting my laptop once and for all. "Later."

"Promise?"

"Promise."

Good. I sat up, twisting myself around so that my maroon-striped socks were tucked under me.

"Now, we have our next adventure to complete," Kieran said.

"What is this adventure that does not involve grilled cheese right now? I assume it's also not another movie marathon?"

"Something to write about later."

"It's the list, isn't it?" I raised my eyebrows.

He shook his head like I was kidding. He reached into one of his drawers, tossing me one of the thick sweaters his grand-mother gave him every year, and he waited for me to put it on. This one looked like it must've been from his middle-school years, threaded in a deep blue color.

"It's always about the list, Sylv."

A FEW EYES at the bar turned, questioning who the hell I must've been to have walked in so confidently. To most of them, just like at the lighting ceremony in the center of town, I was an outsider.

I adjusted myself on the barstool, slipping my purse over the low back. I kept my jacket on, hand in my pocket, holding on to the note.

This was so stupid. What in the world had I been thinking, coming here? If I had any sense at all, I would turn myself right back around and head out the door and go home to sleep off whatever insanity the bottle of wine I had chugged was laced with.

"What can I get ya?"

I blinked, clearing my throat. I hadn't spoken to anyone but myself all day. The young bartender with a swoop of dirty-blond hair over the crown of his head assessed me, up and down.

"Anything?" he asked, rephrasing.

"Dirty martini," I requested, unthinking about my average order I'd been giving for the past three years, ever since Ezra had judged me for my boring vodka tonic. Up until then, it was my safe bet nearly anywhere I went, not to mention half the price.

The young bartender rushed to pour another pint for someone else before turning back to me with nervous eyes. "Right. Is that the one with the olives?"

I was about to say it was. I thought better.

We were back in Marshall. Even if he did manage to make me a decent martini in this crowd, I'd then have to question just how long those olives must've been sitting in the back of the fridge and what was just green and what was mold.

I waved off the question. "I'll just have something else instead."

Behind me, I heard another low guffaw of laughter.

"Make up your mind?" The bartender raised an eyebrow.

I sighed, forcing myself not to turn around. I looked up at the pendant lighting instead. "Whatever you have that's strong."

"Coming right up." A short glass clattered in front of me. Dark liquor was poured in. "You want ice?"

"Uh, no. That's good."

Whiskey might not have been my favorite, and it might not have been the classiest of options, but I wasn't going to wave it away. I carefully lifted the tumbler up to sniff before tipping it back. The harsh burn of alcohol singed from the tip of my tongue to down my throat.

I cringed until I felt the small amount slip down into my chest, creating a warming sensation. It felt like someone was giving me a hug from behind.

I could use that right now.

"Let me know if I can get you anything else."

Swallowing, I gave the kid a thumbs-up. It earned an amused laugh, all for me. At least I didn't appear completely miserable. Maybe one or two more of these, and I could see myself as being even pleasant tonight. Maybe I could even manage to walk myself up to the corner of the bar and confront my entire graduating class. I'd slap the stupid list, which was now burning a hole in my pocket, in front of exactly who it was meant for.

Bam. Just like that.

Though that list sounded completely stupid now, didn't it?

I needed to get out of here.

"Are you trying to hide? Because if you are, you're doing an awful job at it," a voice spoke up beside me.

I stopped breathing.

My heart steadied the moment I saw Jenna with her short brown bob, smiling back at me before engulfing me in a hug.

"Oh, wow." I held her for a moment before she pulled back.

"I heard you were back in town!" she screeched happily. She kept a hand on my arm, not letting go. "Why didn't you come over to our table? You had to have seen us. Or heard us."

I shook my head. "I couldn't."

She tugged at my hand. "Why not? Come on. It's so good to see you."

I let myself be pulled along, making sure to grab my glass along the way. I took a deep breath by the time Jenna presented me. I felt like I was back in high school all over again, only worse.

Conversation trickled down to nothing.

Yeah, it was definitely worse.

"Look who I found!" Jenna sang.

For the first time in years, I got to look at everyone.

Some of the people I knew from high school looked better, some worse than when I had last seen them. A few of them looked exactly the same since we had graduated. Others slouched with wide stomachs and tired eyes, which I was sure matched my own in some respects.

Dylan's eyes widened at the sight of me. "Sylvia Calasis, no fucking way."

I lifted my hand in an awkward wave, letting go of the piece of paper in my pocket. My good intentions to fling the completely logical and not-at-all-crazy list at Kieran so that he would maybe not hate me for the rest of my life and walk out so that he didn't need to say anything else was going up in flames.

"Sit!" Jenna insisted.

All of them scooched to one side, opening a space on the edge of the bench, including Amy, who stared at me without a word near the center of the booth.

"Whiskey?"

I shrugged, lying, "It was what the bartender recommended."

Jenna's husband, Gabe, snorted. He reached for my tumbler across the table and switched it with a beer.

After a sip, I paused. "It tastes like fruit cereal."

"I know, right? It's awful," said Gabe, beaming, as if he had tried to pull the biggest prank on me.

I thought it was pretty good actually. I took a bigger gulp. In fact, it was much better than this entire night had turned out.

Dylan watched me next to him, scrunching his nose, as if his face wasn't quite sure what sort of shape it wanted to take. "I swore that was you over by the door when you first came in. I was just about to tell everyone that the one and only Sylvia Calasis just walked in here like she'd never left."

"The one and only," I repeated, the words bitter on my tongue.

Trying to wash the taste away, I took another slug of my drink. It was almost gone.

"That's right." Dylan smirked. "You're all famous now, huh?"

"If that's what you want to call it." I was in no position to argue with Dylan. "How are you doing?"

"Me?" he asked, as if I'd asked him the most complex question of the day. "Good, good. You know how it is."

"That's, uh, good."

"Most of the time, yeah." He chuckled, waving to the bartender to get him a check. "Sorry I have to say hi and leave, but I promised my mom I wouldn't wake up my dad again after last week, when we were all out. I'll see you soon anyway. You'll be around for the holidays, right?"

"Looks like it."

"Awesome. It's good to see you."

"Thanks, Dylan."

He leaned back. "Course. See you, everyone."

Everyone waved toward him, including Amy, who once again took the moment to look me over. Her eyes flickered behind me. Before I could see what she was looking at, I heard.

"Sylvia."

I took what was surely a second too long before I turned to face Kieran. Looking straight ahead, I got an eyeful of his navy-blue sweater before I leaned back to meet his eyes. "Kieran."

His lips parted before he found the words to ask, "What are you doing here?"

"Nice to see you too."

"What are you doing here?" Kieran repeated, as if I hadn't heard him the first time.

I glanced toward everyone else, who didn't seem to pay any attention to our awkward interaction. "Oh, ya know, living life in the grand falls of Marshall."

"A little drunk?"

I let my head shake to either side, as if testing his theory. "Not yet. I just got here."

"Right." His voice turned tight, put off from my correction. "Your cheeks are red."

He knew me too well.

"It's the holidays. The goal is tipsy, isn't it?"

"Cheers to that," Gabe said, pushing to stand out of the booth. "Do you want your seat back, man?"

Kieran shook his head.

Everyone got another round of drinks. Jenna filled me in on the kids, and Gabe told a story about something that had happened this past summer at the lake house they all went to.

I listened, though carefully didn't interject.

The entire time, Kieran talked occasionally, but stopped himself. His attention always ended up coming right back to me, as if I was about to say something awful.

You know what? Kieran could see me however he wanted to see me right now. I was trying to make things right. I was trying. But you also know what? I was tired. So very tired. And now, soon, I'd be tired and drunk since this evening was obviously not working out how I had expected it to.

"Hey." Jenna waved a hand at me. "You okay there?"

I blinked. "Yeah, thanks. Just zoning out."

"We're finishing up for the night. I'll see you before New Year's? If you're around, you should absolutely come over to our house for dinner on the twenty-third. We know it's Kieran's mom's famous get-together night, but we figured it would be fun for all of us to have something of our own. You'll come if you're around?" Jenna reached out to squeeze my arm again.

"That sounds great," I said unthinkingly.

It did sound nice after all, and I realized I had downed another beer in the past hour. I barely registered that there was a new glass in front of me.

Jenna looked back at Amy, who was staring at the interaction. "You're coming with us, right? I know you have to get up early."

"You're right," said Amy, moving slowly as she focused on Kieran. "I do."

"You're leaving?" Kieran's brow wrinkled.

Amy glanced between Kieran and me. For some reason, since I had come back home, I hadn't even thought about Amy other than when my mother mentioned her, let alone thought about Kieran and Amy.

He gave her a hug goodbye, looping his arms around her.

Were they back together?

It made sense. Of course it made sense.

"Yeah, I'm headed home. My extended family just got in, and my mother already warned me what would happen if I ignored them any longer."

"*'Tis the season* also means *'tis the time for familial torture*," joked Gabe, though he seemed perfectly serious. "We have to relieve the babysitter too. Do you need a ride, Sylvia?"

"No," I said immediately. "I still have a drink to finish. I'm good."

Everyone made their way toward the door. I watched one man, however, clamber back into the booth. He waved at the young bartender, who looked just as confused as me.

"One more, please," Kieran requested.

"Coming right up," the bartender said as he turned toward the drafts.

He was staying.

My brain tried to comprehend it, but couldn't, slowly malfunctioning.

"Wow, I really know how to end a party." I reached for my pint glass. "I thought you'd leave with everyone."

"Doesn't look that way."

Now would be the perfect time for me to whip the note out

of my pocket and put it on the sticky table between us. Then, everything would be done. He would take it, or … he wouldn't.

But then, I could say that I tried to at least end on okay terms.

Yet, even as I reached into my pocket, I squished the piece of paper further. I couldn't do it.

"So"—Kieran stared at me—"why were you looking for me?"

Lifting my hand from my jacket pocket, I rested it against my fresh glass. "Who said I was looking for you?"

Kieran waited, taking a sip of his drink.

"What are you drinking?" I asked, studying his cup.

"Ginger ale."

"Ginger ale?"

He pushed it toward me, and hesitantly, I took a sip. Flat ginger ale.

I cringed. "Oh."

"Oh," he agreed, looking down into his cup. "You still didn't answer my question."

"I think I did."

"Didn't," he countered. "I know you hate being around all of them."

"I do not."

He raised his eyebrows, yet still, I didn't back down. It wasn't that I hated being around them. It was just that I didn't fit in. I never quite fit in.

I sniffed, still evading.

"Do you remember that one time when we were in here for senior night?" I asked.

He was the one who didn't answer now.

Stubborn mule.

"It was awful. Everything about it. The people, the shitty food, the even shittier sodas, mixed with maraschino cherries, which they called mocktails. Disgusting." I slapped my hand against the tabletop, right on a sticky spot. *Gross.* "It was a good thing that we pregamed beforehand."

"Because you were a terrible influence."

"No, I was a great one. How else would you have lived?" I said. "And you know it was mainly Dylan's idea."

Kieran took another sip of his soda.

"The only thing that wasn't terrible about it was marking off that one line on our stupid list we had back then. You almost weren't going to do it," I reminded.

"No one should ever be forced into karaoke."

"You made the list," I argued.

"I never thought you'd hang around with me long enough to actually complete it," he said simply.

"You don't mean that," I said, giving a pained chuckle.

Kieran didn't reply.

"We sucked at singing, both of us, but I think we were still the best act. At least we knew the words to our song."

"Only you would think that."

"What do you mean?"

"We weren't the best. That wasn't how the night went."

"Yes, it was. We knocked *sing karaoke like complete idiots before graduation* off the list," I told him.

"Do you seriously not remember what happened after that?"

My eyebrows tilted down above my nose. I did remember that night. Maybe not perfectly. It was nearly a decade ago. I remembered the senior tradition and how I'd had to drag Kieran out of the corner even though it had been all his idea to begin with.

But, yes, I specifically remembered everything after, though I didn't think that was what he was talking about. Not exactly.

I gulped down my fruity beer, hitting the bottom long

before either of us attempted to speak again. He was still here though, sitting with me. That had to mean something.

Kieran's eyes widened at my talent. He slowly shook his head when he saw the thought cross my face. "You need to go home."

"No, I don't. Not yet anyway."

He shook his head again—or maybe he never stopped. "One more, and then home before the alcohol that you obviously had before you got here hits you, along with all this, and you're too drunk to walk."

"What? Not going to fight with me?"

"I'm done fighting with you, Sylvia." His voice was steady and somber.

I didn't know why that statement made me sad. But it did. The simplicity of the statement, short and sweet, hit right in the center of my chest, like a softball, heavy and not meant to collide with bones at all, let alone fragile ones, protecting important, life-altering internal organs that kept my heart beating.

It meant something that Kieran was sitting across from me, but I raised my hand for the bartender. I couldn't help but easily see that it might never be for the reason I hoped ever again.

Swallowing the thick emotion, I dipped my head toward my hands. "Well, okay then. Message received."

FOURTEEN

BEFORE

"WOW, ALL THESE PLACES LOOK AMAZING." I opened the next brochure as we sat in the hallway outside of the library during lunch.

One of the desktop computers in the library, or maybe it was the printer, had gone up in smoke yesterday afternoon, causing a whole *fire drill gone wrong* fiasco. The people in the office had decided it was best to force everyone elsewhere while the windows were open to let the frigid winter air in.

A big piece of paper, drawn on with a permanent marker, demanded that everyone who walked by **STAY OUT**.

I leaned against my book bag, using it as a backrest, as Kieran and I looked through his latest college haul.

He and Lori had gone east last weekend to tour three more schools and visit his aunt. It was a boring weekend. While Kieran was gone, I mainly remained plastered on the couch or my bed, trying to get ahead of my blog posting schedule and creating a new frequently asked questions page even if no one was really asking me any questions frequently yet.

The latest trifold paper Kieran handed me featured an old building with a clock tower. One of the numbers was missing.

College students were pictured laughing as they lay on the grass strewn with textbooks on advanced chemistry.

The caption beneath read, *Start your premed journey with confidence.*

Was Kieran going to go into premed? I hadn't asked. Or if I had, it was a while ago.

"If I get in," mumbled Kieran. He pointed to the next page with a picture of dorms with tiny windows.

"You're going to get in. Any school would be stupid if they didn't let you in." I rolled my eyes.

Premed or anything else, Kieran could have his pick. It was probably why Lori and Dave wanted to give him so many options. Their miracle baby could play the field.

"We'll see."

"Which one are you thinking of?"

His answer changed every other week, the more he researched. Kieran was always researching where the best colleges were, though they often never extended past the tristate area. The farthest one away from Marshall Falls he had looked at was a state over.

"This college looks cool. Is this the one you went to last weekend?"

Kieran leaned over my shoulder. "Yeah, that's the one I wanted to tell you about. I tried to take more pictures, but they came out blurry. It was so cool there. Everyone looked like, well, they looked like they were living. It's far enough away from here."

"Important," I agreed.

"They have a great English program."

"You are deciding to major in English now?"

"Not sure yet. But I meant for you."

"Me?" I asked.

"Yeah." Kieran grinned. "I think there's even a concentration for writing."

"Really?"

"They told me on the tour that their acceptance rate was about sixty percent or so. That's not awful. Maybe if we try a little harder this semester, it will come together."

"What do you mean?" I peered down at the other booklet. "I'm doing all right."

His gaze caught on something behind me as everyone made their way through the halls to their next classes. I peeked back with him until I caught exactly what he was seeing.

Landon and Amy stood, coming out from the music hallway.

Kieran focused once more on me as he started to pack up, shoving papers into his bag. "I said, we, as in both of us. It's not like you're battling me over valedictorian though."

I handed the brochure back to him. He set it with the others, careful not to crease them.

"Wow, I never knew you were so judgmental when it came to grades."

"I'm not. I just care about you. I thought that maybe after you saw all this, you'd get as excited and motivated about moving on as I am," Kieran said as he took a step toward Landon and Amy, who were waving him toward the English hallway. "You're the one who made me excited about college to begin with."

"I am excited." *Sorry that I don't have the kind of parents who take off work to shuttle me around to colleges every weekend.*

I held back my comment. I knew it was bitter jealousy that bit into me like a thousand needles, poking and prodding until I wanted to scream. Or more likely, run away. It had been getting harder to ignore lately.

Kieran, my friend and only my friend, had somehow turned popular along the way. If not popular, he was still much more well liked than me.

It was a struggle not to remember him with thick glasses and a quiet disposition when I had met him in elementary school. I didn't understand it. I always kind of thought that if there was anyone who would make friends, it would be me, and I'd bring him along to get out there, living life. The tables had turned.

"I'll see you at the end of the day?" I asked, looking up at him.

Kieran held his smile, hiking his backpack on his shoulders. "See you then."

"I don't know, Sylvia." The guidance counselor, Ms. Hart, looked over my papers.

I waited for her to ask me something. Instead, her gaze remained locked on my past report cards, as if they held the answers to the universe. She swept a blonde curl, which looked as dry as the Sahara, over her ear as she squinted at my transcript.

"I won't discourage you from applying to a reach school, but you should be sure you have more attainable options as well."

"*Reach* school." I repeated the words.

"I always encourage students in your position to apply to schools that they might not be a shoo-in for academically. There are absolutely other things that can push you over the top. There are personal statements, extracurricular activities ... I know we've talked about those previously. There are even in-person interviews if you can get to the school for a tour and sit with your department."

I blinked at her, thinking of Kieran and all the schools he

had already visited. Had he sat down for interviews with the head of whatever department he wanted to get into? He hadn't said that he did.

Then again, who wouldn't like Kieran once he got out of his turtle shell and started talking?

"I have a blog."

Lifting her gaze back up, Ms. Hart raised her eyebrows in surprise. "That's actually very good. You can make sure that you mention that in your personal statement. You say you want to become a writer. Like a journalist for the news?"

I shrank further into the blue woven chair. "Sort of."

"That's the kind of initiative and determination that college officials will look for when it comes to acceptances. It's good, but I still want you to keep your expectations reasonable."

"Are they unreasonable?"

"Not exactly." Ms. Hart tapped the papers together and set them aside. "Sylvia, I feel like I can be honest with you. Can I?"

"I guess so."

"Marshall Falls is a small school. We both know that. There are other schools in the country, the state even, that are more prestigious. They have students working at a much higher level than you are currently. Those students are enrolled in all advanced placement classes. They have high SAT scores. They have been trained to get into a few of the schools you've written on your list. They are prepared for academically challenging colleges that you and most of the students here in Marshall Falls simply are not."

"So, you set us up for failure?" I asked.

"I didn't say that. We let our students dictate their own future. We have offerings available, but we don't push. Most adults grow up in this area and stay here. There's not an issue with that. We have a strong community, but, Sylvia, the kind of life you are trying to pull off in your final hour?" Ms. Hart sighed. "You can try. I will be here to help you, but I just don't see it happening unless you are ready to show something that isn't on these papers that they're going to be looking at, just like I am."

I chewed on the inside of my cheek as I looked for the right words that wouldn't have me yelling in Ms. Hart's face. How dare she say that! I tried hard. I did enough. There were people who did less than I did.

"Okay."

"I don't mean to discourage you," she restated.

"You haven't." I pushed myself to the edge of the seat, reaching for my backpack. I swung it over my shoulder.

"Sylvia—"

"Thanks," I cut her off before she could continue. "I should probably go before I'm late for Geometry."

"Please, come back and see me if you need anything. No matter what you decide, I'm here to help you."

The day went on slowly. I wrote new article ideas in the margins of my math notebook. The teacher didn't even shake his head as he passed my desk and continued lecturing about the thrilling topic of isosceles triangles. He was all too familiar with my personal learning process by this point in the year.

I still got okay grades when the tests came around, so he never said anything, not even when I once asked him if he had an extra pen after I ran out of ink. I had been drafting a post on my and Kieran's latest baking adventure. The amount of chocolate chips we had put in the brownie batter after I decided the recommended one and a half cups wasn't enough eluded me.

People loved that post and the photos we had taken, covered in flour behind Lori's wide kitchen island at the house. She had nearly beamed when she came home from work and looked at the two of us—the perfect messy chefs in frilly aprons and construction paper hats.

Love the direction this blog is going! So fun and real. Can't wait to try the recipe with the heart sprinkles this Valentine's! one commenter had written.

My blog, *The List*, was getting recurring commenters.

How could anyone at any college think that this wasn't worthwhile? These were all words, too, just as important as those on the flimsy printouts Ms. Hart had, describing my time in Marshall Falls.

Dozens of people had told me that the things I had written were good and getting better every day.

The look Ms. Hart had given me, however, when she saw I was planning on applying to NYU made me want to hide. She obviously thought I was halfway to stupid and would never stand a chance at getting in.

Just wait until I become a world-renowned writer. Marshall Falls High would probably even invite me back as a speaker for graduation, like senators and actors were, to inspire the next generation.

I still felt unsteady and unsure through study hall until the bell rang. Grabbing my things, downstairs, Kieran was talking with Amy. I made my way to the doors, him falling into step beside me.

"How did your meeting go with the counselor?"

I shrugged. "Fine."

"Just fine?"

I sighed. I could never withhold the truth from Kieran. If anything, he was the only one who could possibly patch the uncertain hole that had opened somewhere between my heart and stomach.

"She doesn't even want me to apply to half the places I want to go. You just wait though. I'll show her. I'm going to apply wherever I want, and then I'll wave the stupid acceptance letters in her face."

Kieran didn't say anything.

"What?" I narrowed my eyes, pausing on the sidewalk so I could face him. "You don't agree with me?"

"I agree with you," he said with little emotion.

"Then, why aren't you saying anything?"

"I don't know. I just think maybe you should listen more to the counselor," Kieran advised. "You were the one who set up the appointment."

"It was your advice I go and see what else I needed to do to apply since my mom has no idea, unlike yours."

My mother had suggested I go to cosmetology school or business school to become a secretary, like her. She had practically preened over the result of that career personality test after snooping through my book bag. I should've just gone to Lori to begin with if I hadn't been so impatient. She would've helped me, no matter what I wanted to do.

Kieran hesitated. "Do you want me to be honest?"

"I'm really starting to hate people asking me that," I muttered.

"You're angry now because you haven't been putting in the work this past year and now it's coming back to haunt you."

"What?"

"You don't care enough to study to get the grades or do your homework half the time. I'm not going to let you look at work again either. I'm clearly the one enabling you no matter how much I want you to do well and get into schools with me."

"What are you talking about?" I leaned back as if I hadn't heard him correctly. I couldn't have.

"Amy saw us sharing the homework answers the other day before class, and she didn't think it was a great idea either."

"Oh, so this is about Amy and your new besties."

"They could be your friends too."

"I try to be friends with them. Turns out, they obviously don't think much of me," I snapped. "Neither do you, it seems. I care. I care a lot."

"Really?"

"Of course I do. I've told you that I do. Sure, I don't get things done on time most days, but that's because I'm focused on my blog. That's what is important. I'm getting new readers every day."

"You read under your desk."

"So?" So did he. Or he used to. "That doesn't mean I don't care. It means that I'm willing to do anything in the world to escape this one for the few hours I'm stuck in that building like a prisoner."

"I get that, but ..."

"But what?"

He shrugged.

"I didn't know you thought I was such a slacker who couldn't get in anywhere," I said softly.

Would I be able to get into school? I always thought that I would, and now ... well, I was a lot less sure than I had been before. What if I didn't get into the schools that Kieran wanted to go to? What if I didn't get in anywhere?

What would I do then?

Would I just be another Marshall Falls graduate, living in town and working at the diner or bagging condoms at the pharmacy for the rest of my life?

"I just thought we were going to do this together," Kieran said.

"And you're saying now that you don't want to? Or you think I'm some failure that isn't going to get into any school with you? A few hours ago you were showing me brochures."

Kieran stared at me, mouth parted and his hands on either side of his frame in exasperation. "I really don't know what you want me to say right now."

Maybe I wanted him to say that he cared about me. I wanted him to mention that maybe he was worried about me and was willing to help. I just wanted someone in this stupid world to see that I was floundering and had no idea in hell what I was doing while everyone else seemed to.

The pressure of tears built in the corners of my eyes. "I don't know what I want you to say either."

Just something. *Anything.*

"Are you on your period or something?"

My eyes turned up toward him, and I was certain he saw the watery fury in them. "Are you kidding me?"

He shut his eyes.

Who the hell was this person in front of me? Where was the Kieran I knew and loved and who stood by my side? Had he been transformed over the weekend by snooty academics showing him around? Was it Amy?

Or was he right?

I cared. I did my best, and yet, according to everyone in Marshall Falls, my *best* wasn't enough.

I couldn't even get accepted to a little writing workshop that I had applied to with his encouragement last year or the year prior when I had done it in secret so there'd be no one to disappoint other than myself.

"I'm sorry you can't see that I'm trying my best. It might not be as good as you are, but I'm still the person who wants to leave this town and do something great while you want to stay here now that you have people who fawn all over you."

"That's not fair."

"No, it's the truth. It's always been the truth. I want to leave and see the world and do great things, no matter what my grades say. You already can do whatever you want and go wherever you want. Sorry if I asked you for help here and there so that I could maybe reach your level of opportunity when you're wasting it."

Kieran shook his head, looking down at his feet. "I need to go home."

"Fine." I might've swallowed my tears as they found a new home in the center of my chest, heavy and tight. "Go."

"I will."

"I just said to."

Kieran huffed. He turned away, stomping through the snow down the street. He left me standing next to the building I wanted to run from most hours of the day. Now, I wasn't sure where I wanted to go. Where should I?

Usually, I'd walk back with Kieran. I'd be fed snacks at the bakery or work through homework with him in his kitchen, depending on how much we had to do.

I had nowhere to go without Kieran.

I had nowhere to go.

FIFTEEN

NOW

ONE MORE DRINK turned into three, which turned into Kieran hauling me most of the way up the street before I yanked away from him. I promptly upchucked the little contents of my empty stomach onto gravel and slush.

"Brings back old times, doesn't it?" I attempted to joke.

Kieran pulled me back against him and continued our trek back down the street.

"At least your hair is pulled back," he commented.

Tears slipped down my cheeks. At first, I thought they were just from the awful taste in my mouth, but then they ran faster than I could push them away.

I sniffled. I was screwing this entire thing up. I couldn't believe that I thought making a silly little new list for us could fix what had happened between us. Kieran was right. I was just ruining everything more.

I was pretty sure drinking myself sick and almost throwing up on his shoes constituted ruining it.

"Come on, Sylv. We are almost there."

Sylv. I was back to Sylv again? Well, that was something. Probably anyway.

I hiccuped, trying to regain control over myself before I fell further into thinking I was somewhere familiar and safe enough to have a complete breakdown.

"Let's just get you home and into bed," said Kieran.

"I'm sorry, you know."

He groaned. "Sylvia."

Now, we were back to Sylvia. Who knew that my own name could turn so sour?

"I'm so, so sorry. I'm sorry, and I didn't mean what happened. You know what I mean? You do, don't you? I know I'm sorry, and I'm fucking this all up. I was supposed to have a plan. I had a plan—"

"Stop talking."

I pressed my lips together. I only made it a few steps. But who was surprised, really?

"I'm sorry," I murmured again into his coat sleeve.

"You need to stop talking."

"Forever?"

"Yes," he said.

A long moment passed while I stared at him. Kieran snorted, though he didn't sound very amused. Not-fun-loving Kieran was back in the house. Or rather, outside the house. Beside me—

I waved it all off.

"But we both know that you couldn't manage that."

I sniffed again, not sure what to say to that. There was still no humor in his tone.

There was a plea, aching. "Just let me get you home."

"It's all falling apart."

"What are you talking about?"

"Everything," I insisted.

"I'm sure that's not true."

"It is," I whined. "Why else would I be here?"

The next few steps were nothing but snow crunching and the sound of his breath escaping into the air in white clouds. "I can't imagine it's actually for the holidays."

"You knew I was lying about that?"

"Yes." He nearly laughed again. It sounded painful, but it was also a nice sound. "Why would you come back here? Your parents aren't even in town."

"I had nowhere else to go."

Kieran snorted. "That I don't believe."

"You should."

"What about your fancy, fabulous life in the city?"

"Why do people keep thinking that it's all that fancy? It's gray and gross most of the time unless the sun is out." My hand gripped his coat sleeve. "And I don't think I'll ever have that life, no matter how hard I try."

"Don't cry."

"I'm not."

"You are."

I reached up and touched my face. A new wave of tears was there. "You would too."

"Because your life is so hard?"

Again, I said nothing. I wasn't supposed to tell him, but I guessed, well, I had to tell someone. And it was always Kieran even if my brain couldn't comprehend that it shouldn't be anymore.

I took a deep breath, preparing to tell him everything.

I wanted to tell him everything that had ever happened to me—from the moment I had left him four years ago before the train ride back to the city to the terrible roommates who had brought bugs home as pets. I wanted to tell him about Ezra and how when I had seen him getting a blow job by someone other than me, I had felt nothing other than disgust that he was getting his gross-ass germs all over my couch.

God, I was never going to get that couch back.

A whimper escaped.

"Sylv."

"Don't say my name like that," I said.

"What are you talking about?" Kieran asked, looking down at me.

"Don't pretend you care. Okay? I know I'm a big loser with no friends, and I'm an awful person and an awful friend, and I know that I'm invading your life like a disease again, and I'm sorry. I'm really sorry."

"Now, you're just being dramatic."

I swayed, leaning more of my weight on Kieran. I tried to keep my feet underneath me as he started to climb the front steps to my childhood house with its little brass lamps on either side of the door. They looked like they needed to be cleaned, giving off a yellow glow.

I looked up at him, biting my lip. "Did you forget about me?"

"Where are your keys?"

I kicked at the doormat.

I ignored his grumbled complaints about how unsafe such a hiding place was before we made it inside. The light in the kitchen was left on, illuminating the empty space.

"Oh."

Kieran took even more of my weight as I slumped. "What's wrong? Are you going to be sick again? I didn't think you'd had that much to drink."

I looked around. Same flattened-out rug. Same couch I had spent most of the day yesterday on. I expected there to be a new permanent indent.

I shrugged. "I almost forgot it wasn't Christmas here. In the house, I mean."

"Yeah, your parents didn't really get into the spirit before they left, did they?" Kieran assessed.

He surely didn't see one decoration. Not even the Santa cookie jar my mother used to put out religiously on the counter the day after Thanksgiving was there.

"Not even the fake tree," I muttered.

"Your folks always did use one of those plastic ones, right?"

I nodded. "It wouldn't be so hard to just stick it together. Yet nope."

"Why don't you put it up?" asked Kieran.

"Then, I'd have to brave the basement." And that was one thing that never got any less scary as I got older.

"I could get it for you if you really wanted, Sylvia. I doubt this was how you wanted to spend your holiday."

He had that right. Sort of.

I wasn't sure how I had planned to spend my holiday here or in the city. Though in the city, back at my apartment, I would probably be working and trying not to make a big deal when Ezra casually didn't invite me to go along with him to his work holiday functions.

I snorted, as if that was the biggest issue we'd had.

"No." I turned down the offer as we walked down the hall. "The whole fake-tree thing never went over well with me anyway. The only time I ever had fun decorating the tree was when I did it at your house with your mom and your dad, drinking eggnog in the recliner until it was time to put the angel on top. It always smelled like oranges and dust from the old plastic tubs full of decorations in the attic."

Kieran didn't say anything as he opened the door to my room. He paused when he turned on the light. "Why is it so cold in here?"

If we didn't look at each other, it could almost be as if we were still kids again, our surroundings unchanged.

Then, he took a deep breath and took another step with me inside. "Sylvia, look at me."

I looked up at him. The illusion shattered.

"Is something wrong with the heat in your house?" he asked.

"Heat?"

"Yes, the thing that keeps you warm inside during the winter. Is it on?"

I hadn't really checked. I was always wrapped in a blanket or layered up in enough sweatshirts or booze that I hadn't noticed. Though, now that he mentioned it ...

I burrowed deeper into Kieran for body heat. "Did you get one this year?"

"Get what?" he asked, distracted.

"A tree," I clarified. "I mean, I'm sure you did everything, like always. It was part of my list to get you to like me again, but—"

"You made a list?"

I shrugged. "Yeah, it was stupid though. It still is stupid."

Kieran didn't say anything until he cleared his throat. "I didn't actually."

"Huh?"

"I didn't get a tree this year."

"But your parents always get a tree."

"They did," Kieran agreed.

Where had Kieran, the guy who was always full of Christmas cheer, gone? He had always been the one to push me into caroling and tree trimming and even making a huge mess while icing sugar cookies at Rose Bakery.

Kieran yanked back the puffy duvet on my bed with one hand, setting me down on the mattress with the other. With little movement, I toed off my shoes and looked down at my fun socks. As I wiggled my toes a bit, my feet flexed the winter-themed design of snowmen with oversize orange noses before I curled in on myself, lying down. The world felt like it was swaying a bit, as if somehow, I'd gotten on that cruise ship with my parents. I floated back and forth.

I forced myself to keep watch as Kieran continued to fuss with my sheets, pushing them under my body so I'd stay on my side.

"I'll be right back," he said. "You stay here."

"I have nowhere else to go."

"I'm going to check on the heat."

I watched him as he went. Kieran, always so responsible.

In the past few years, he'd aged. I could see it. If not completely physically, I could see it in his shoulders. They were stiff and steady, like he always was, but Kieran was no longer a boy trying to hold it together.

He was a man. A full-grown man. He had dark stubble and everything that probably needed to be shaved every day.

People didn't age after all in the city, not really. They just grew, and they kept moving, never noticing.

I must've drifted off for a second because I was blinking my eyes open when Kieran jostled my shoulder.

"Come on."

"What?"

"Back up you go. Shoes." He shoved my boots back on my feet, though I was pretty sure they were on the wrong ones.

"Where are we going? You're right; I'm tired."

"You can't stay here. Your heat is shot. I'll have Landon come out and look at it in the morning, but you'll freeze if you stay here tonight. I can't believe that you have been living in this."

"Only for a few days."

Kieran harrumphed. He pulled me back up to standing, layering a coat and blanket over my shoulders as I was guided back out into the cold. I let myself be led by Kieran this time, leaning my weight against him all the way toward Peach Street.

By the time he pulled me up a flight of outdoor stairs, I finally opened my eyes back up.

"Are you still with me?" he questioned.

"Where are we?"

"My place."

"You have a place?" I looked around in the dark. "You don't live at home?"

"Sort of. It's warm. You should be thankful."

I was.

"Just get inside." Kieran pushed open the door and led me in, shutting it quickly behind us, as if he was afraid the heat would get out.

I immediately understood where I was. I had been in the apartment space above the Roses' garage once before, when we were kids, more out of curiosity than anything else. Now, it was completely renovated and cast in an amber glow from the lamps Kieran had turned on.

I looked around from his queen-size bed, pressed against the panel wall, to the small living space he had somehow managed to make look homey with only a couch, coffee table, and television, which I also recognized as coming from the Roses' main house. His parents must've upgraded.

I dropped down onto the couch. It was still as comfortable as I remembered. Kieran set a glass of water down on the table and knelt in front of me.

"What are you …"

He yanked off my shoes and put them next to the wood coffee table. Reaching up, he unzipped my jacket, rolling his eyes at how thin it was as I shrugged it off.

"Your eyes are the prettiest, you know? I always thought that, but I was worried that you would get offended since the boys in school used to tease you about looking like a girl. That changed though. I mean, *fuck*. Look at you. Now, you're the prettiest, handsomest man, I think, ever."

Kieran didn't say anything. Continuing to shake his head, he reached for the throw blanket behind me. He wrapped it around my shoulders, suspiciously constrictive.

"Seriously," I insisted. If I couldn't do anything else, at least I could boost his ego a few notches.

"I'm sure that's just the extraordinary amount of beer you drank talking. Or maybe it's whatever liquor you drank before you showed up at the bar. Lie down on your side and go to sleep," Kieran murmured.

"It wasn't liquor."

"That so?"

"Wine," I clarified for him. "At first anyway."

Kieran's shook his head. "For you, that's worse."

He had a point. Wine drunk for me was a different kind of drunk. This kind though was a terrible, sloshy mixture now.

Ugh. It even sounded disgusting.

I leaned down, covering my face with my hands. "None of tonight went to plan."

"Yeah, well, I didn't plan on spending tonight dragging your ass all over Marshall, but here we are." Kieran ran a hand through his brown clump of hair.

"You didn't answer me," I said after another few seconds, noticing he hadn't moved. "Before."

"I answered your tree question back at your place."

"Not that one."

Kieran sighed. "What was the question?"

I breathed in, taking my time. Maybe if I held him at least with my words forever, he wouldn't leave. Not again.

Not like I had.

"Did you manage to do it?" I whispered.

"Do what?"

"Did you forget about me?" I asked.

"What are you talking about?" Kieran asked, though his eyes averted, going anywhere but meeting mine.

It didn't stop me. Obviously, I was far past care for that. "When I left, were you really able to forget me?"

I could still hear his voice. It had echoed off the ice that coated the road that night four years ago.

"If it's the last thing I do, I'm going to forget you ever happened to me, Sylvia. It'll be like you were always nothing to me."

Even remembering his words made me flinch. I always thought about them when I felt like this. Drunk and regretful.

It wasn't so different from how we had been that night when everything changed.

Kieran remained still. He sighed.

I blinked slowly at my old friend, unwilling to fall asleep. Not until he answered, no matter how heavy my eyelids were.

Kieran's voice was as quiet as it had been all night. "No, Sylv. I didn't forget about you. Not for a second. I didn't even try."

SIXTEEN

BEFORE

I HIT publish on the article I had drafted during Geometry. Afterward, I followed my usual routine and looked through my latest updates.

It was odd how, one week, I'd had nothing, and as of the last month, people were finding my little blog. Not only were they finding it, but they were also enjoying what I did, no matter if it came at the expense of other things going on at school or in class.

When it came to my blog, I was magnificent. I was a classy, put-together person, living in a small town and on a never-ending adventure, brought on by a list with my best friend—*see post number two for more information.*

Yet in Marshall Falls, no one noticed. I was no one.

I scrolled down my latest comments.

The List *has become one of my favorite things to read each day when I need a pick-me-up! Have you ever thought about creating a book club? You always have such great picks,* a commenter had written.

A small smile curled the corner of my lips, but I couldn't

bring myself to reply. Kieran was usually the one who gave me his latest favorite books to read. Right now, I was lucky if either of us would manage to talk about something as easy and wonderful as books after what happened today.

By the sounds of it, he hadn't even been reading anymore. He didn't have the time with all his new friends who thought I was stupid and ridiculous and would likely never get into college, like them with all their AP classes they bragged about.

I got that I wasn't the best student always, but I never thought Kieran openly thought that kind of stuff about me. Sure, I had thought that, sometimes, he was goofy and had little social cues, growing up, but he was always mine. Kieran was my best friend, my person, my everything and anything.

Unconditionally.

The thought that maybe Kieran's affection wasn't so unconditional after all hurt more than what Ms. Hart had said during my counseling appointment. I was about to become just like most of the student body and stay right here in Marshall Falls. Maybe I'd even stay in this house until I withered away and died. I'd be as special as the dust accumulating on the baseboards.

Slapping my laptop closed, my charm bracelet jingled around my wrist. The snowflake charm jostled against my initial. I carefully set the computer on the floor next to my bed, where my backpack was open. Papers were sprawled out onto the floor in a mess. Yanking on my purple floral comforter, I pulled it over my head until I encased myself in my own little cave. In here, everything was warm and safe, and there was only me.

I wanted to be a writer. To be a writer, I needed to do one thing. I needed to live.

I didn't need school or friends here at Marshall. I didn't

need anything at all but myself and a pen and paper if things got desperate. I needed to go on adventures, like the ones on my and Kieran's list. If that would even happen now.

But the world sucked, didn't it? I was just trying desperately to make the most while living in it. I hadn't realized that was such a heavy task until now and that maybe Kieran didn't want to be in it, like I'd always counted on.

I shut my eyes and let everything go into darkness.

My bed dipped on one side.

I knew exactly who it was before he said anything. His awkward movements felt around the mass of pillows and throw blankets until he found an opening.

Kieran crawled into bed with me, like I usually did in his. I flinched when his sock-covered feet brushed my shins.

He felt like he'd been pacing barefoot through the snow.

"What are you doing?" I peeked out from under my comforter. The clock on my nightstand blared with three red numbers. "It's one in the morning."

"I couldn't sleep."

I lifted my blankets, and Kieran crawled into my makeshift cave.

We were silent for a long time. We both knew if my father found him in here, there were two ways this situation could go, and with my dad, it was hard to guess even though he knew I snuck out to Kieran's late at night on more than a few occasions. Lori gave us each a *look* when she caught us there.

But right now, I didn't care. "I'm sorry."

"You don't need to be."

"But I am anyway."

"Me too," whispered Kieran. "I'm sorry I said what I did. I

didn't mean it like that. Like, what I was trying to say was just that I was going on these college trips without you, and I kept hearing all these statistics of how many people got in and from where while we were walking around campus, and all I could think about was if I could see the two of us there. It's hard to see anywhere without you."

"Wow," I said.

Kieran breathed a short laugh at my response to his carefully laid out apology. "I just want to make sure you know how hard I'm rooting for you—for both of us—not to completely flop once we leave this place, like I know you will. So, I'm sorry."

"So am I. I just don't like when you compare me."

"There's no comparing you, Sylv. You are—well, I can't gesture under all these blankets; seriously, I'm starting to sweat —but you are on an entirely other level no one else could ever attain."

"What a liar."

"Nah, but I am sort of an ass."

I chuckled. I never thought I would ever think those things about Kieran until today, though I knew it was partially my fault too. "Happens to all of us."

"It's sad that we can't even go all of five hours without each other."

"Codependency is chic these days I hear."

He quietly laughed. "You should write about that on your blog. Open a dating section each week."

Definitely not. "Nothing to write."

"For now."

Probably forever, but I wasn't going to start a whole new argument.

"I'm going to do better too," I hushed after another moment. Both of us slipped into a languid sleep, eyes closed but still talking. "You were right."

"I was?"

"I haven't really given them a chance, Dylan and Jenna and everyone."

"And Amy?" Kellen asked.

Opening my eyes, I rolled them even though he couldn't see. Ever since things had burned and fizzled between Kieran and Amy in the past year, I knew they were just friends, but I still didn't like her.

"And Amy. I'll try anyway."

That was all he could ask of me.

"I'm sorry," I repeated.

"Should I write that one down in the history books?"

I try to whack him with my hand but hit a pillow instead.

Kieran's laughter was a rumble. "It's nice to feel like you are part of a group. A family. You'll see."

"I have my family," I whispered, hoping he understood. I let my head fall onto him, somewhere between his chest and shoulder.

He smelled like the bakery. Warm cinnamon and sweet buttercream icing seeped from his pores where most guys smelled like corn chips and sweat.

You, I wanted to say. *You're my family.*

"You're going to get into a great college and do all the things you want to do after school, no matter what—you know that?"

I shrugged.

"You are," Kieran said firmly. "You even said it. You'll still apply to everywhere you want to go, both with and without me, and we'll see what happens."

"I can't believe it's going to be our last year."

"I know."

"We still have our list to complete."

"I know."

"We still have all the time to figure it all out. Don't we?"

"We do," agreed Kieran, slipping further away from me as sleep took hold. "It's going to be all right, Sylv. You are going to have everything you could ever want in life. You're a force. I just know it. Now, be quiet. You stressed me out, and I'm tired."

"I believe you," I whispered.

SEVENTEEN

NOW

MY LIMBS WERE MADE of lead. I pushed off the mountain of blankets someone had laid on top of me, creating a heavy, warm cocoon in my bed. Or not my bed.

I sat up. Immediately, I regretted it. I put a hand to my head and groaned.

Where in the hell am I? I put the pieces together in my hungover brain.

Kieran had brought me here. This was Kieran's apartment. Small and filled with books he'd collected over the years, the space still managed to be undeniably clean and put together in a way no one in my entire life other than Kieran had ever been. There was no denying that was exactly where I was.

When we had been growing up, Kieran's parents contemplated renting the space above the garage out, talking about how it was wasteful not to make use of the apartment space.

Now, it looked like they had decided to rent it out.

To Kieran.

As if on cue, the door leading outside opened, and the man of the hour stepped through. Without a word, he shut the door and made his way inside, moving toward the kitchen.

He flicked on the light, and I couldn't help my cringe, though Kieran wasn't paying attention to me anymore as he opened the fridge and poured a glass of water. He walked over, replacing the old, untouched glass from last night with a fresh one, alongside two small pills.

Without pausing, I reached for them, hoping for some sort of relief.

"I called Landon this morning, and we were already over at your place," said Kieran without inflection. "Your heat isn't working. There was also something about your water heater being out. Honestly, I have no idea what he said other than you've been living in a freezer."

"Oh."

"Which, honestly," Kieran went on, "does concern me even more, considering it means I have no idea when you last showered."

"I showered," I grunted. Though, of course, I couldn't remember when that had been. I resisted the urge to raise my arm and sniff.

"You will need to find someplace to stay until your parents get back and fix everything. Landon couldn't get ahold of them."

I blinked. Right. That made sense, though I was still pretty sure I could manage living at my house with a few extra layers. It would be better than going through town and having to ask for a room at the inn that usually catered to the hikers during the summer season. Because then, I would also need to figure out the money to pay for it.

"I'm sure my mom will let you stay in the main house." Kieran problem-solved, as if he could sense my inner turmoil.

"No," I said quickly before I could stop the terror that rang through the word. I couldn't do that—even if I had no idea what else I was going to do so that I didn't freeze indoors. Death by frostbite would be a completely new sort of low when it came to braving the winter weather.

Kieran narrowed his eyes.

I rephrased, "I'll figure something out."

As if thinking about fighting me, Kieran shook his head. He walked away from where I hadn't moved on the couch. "Whatever."

Yeah, whatever. I took a deep breath, feeling my forehead crease. Now, I had another thing to add to my mess of a life right now. I needed to reorganize my internal list since it was clear now that I was becoming a list maker.

Number one, find some place to live for the next week so I didn't freeze to death in my sleep.

Two, figure out why exactly Kieran was looking at me now like I had not only ruined his life, but was making him constipated.

And three—

My eyes widened as Kieran brushed up against my jacket and a small piece of paper fell onto the floor. Kieran bent down and swooped the note up between his fingers.

"Stop!"

"What is this?"

I made grabby hands toward him, though they weren't very helpful. He wasn't looking at me, even as I jumped up from the couch. I felt like I was going to die.

"Do not read that! Give me that."

Before I could make it over to him in my still slightly drunk state, he was halfway down the list. "Is this the list you were talking about last night?"

"It doesn't matter."

I reached for it once more. Unfortunately, I forgot just how tall Kieran was. He lifted the piece of paper above his head and continued to read with a tilt of his chin.

"It's just a list."

"A list for what?"

"A list …" I drifted off. "I'm trying to get back into the holiday spirit."

"These are all things that I like to do," Kieran murmured. Suspicion laced his tone.

"So?" I countered. "Are you the only one who can enjoy the holidays?"

"You hate the holidays."

"No, I don't."

He raised his brows.

"I'm trying to turn over a new leaf. I might be home alone in my childhood town, but that doesn't mean that I can't make it worthwhile," I said.

"Right." He clearly didn't believe me as he looked back down to the list. "You want to get a tree? After you asked me if I had gotten one yet."

"It's traditional."

"And string it with white lights, specifically, not the rainbow ones? And it does say *specifically* in bold."

Had I written that?

"Of course."

"This is a stupid list."

"You're right. We should throw it away. Right now." I glanced back down at my jacket, looking toward the other pocket, where I saw another piece of paper sticking out.

What the hell is that?

Kieran was just about to turn his head before I refocused on him. I pushed him lightly, and my touch reinvigorated his confusion.

"And you want to watch the old movies that you once claimed were completely boring and snooze-worthy?"

"For someone who doesn't like to see me, you sure do take a

lot of stock in my short reviews from years ago. Maybe my film tastes have changed."

"Uh-huh ..." He extended the note back to me.

I stared at it for a second before taking it from him. Glancing down at it, I carefully folded it into fourths.

I didn't know what I'd expected. The list admittedly was a very stupid, tipsy idea, but I hadn't thought it would cause Kieran to look at me with even more distrust.

"Look ..."

"What?"

"I made the list for a reason."

"And that was?"

To make you possibly care about me again after I ruined everything.

"The house is—*was*—too quiet and weird. I needed something to be right. So, I made this." I wasn't lying. I needed something to be right even if it wasn't Christmas. "It's none of your business."

"So you said before, and I agreed."

I didn't stop talking. "It's mine so that I don't get day drunk every day and cry and sing Christmas carols to my mother's kitten knickknacks, which are oddly more disconcerting than I ever remember them being. Okay?"

Kieran blinked. "Okay then."

"Okay." I took a deep breath.

"You should probably go and take a shower now," said Kieran as he turned back into his kitchen. "Towels are in the closet, and I brought some of your clothes back from the house when I was there with Landon this morning. Seriously, you threw up at least two times on the way home last night, and you stink."

I watched him reach into the fridge for something. With his

back turned, I finally tucked my head into my own shoulder and sniffed.

EIGHTEEN

OUR SMALL YET ROWDY group of Marshall Falls High seniors rounded at the edge of the trail. Most cried with laughter, all the while shuffling from the cold in thick winter boots. Excitement filled the air. Applications to college had been turned in. The holidays were closer than ever since the freak snowstorm had come early and shut down the schools. There was less than a full semester left until all of us left the oddly tight-knit group we had become in the past few months.

Kieran was right about not actively excluding myself from his friend group. Even if none of them openly liked me like they liked him, it was nice.

Most of the time anyway.

My boots came untied three times before Kieran knelt in front of me.

"You look like a child who has never been out in the snow before," he teased with a dip in his voice so only I could hear his gibe.

"That's because I haven't been out in the snow since we were children."

And even then, the two of us had never gone out in the

snow when school was closed unless ultimately forced by one of our parents. We had been bundled up and thrown into the snow piles, encouraged to make snowmen or find the friends we didn't have at the time to sled down the hill behind the grocery store. The dumpster would stop us on our way down.

Kieran chuckled as he triple-knotted my laces. He patted them down, tucking them into where my socks overlapped at the top. "There. Now, that should do it."

"Why, thank you."

"It's my honor," he joked. His cheeks flushed from the cold.

Today was the day we were about to cross off what was perhaps our most looked forward to list item.

Two guys held the large plastic container, full of sloshing water balloons. They grunted as they made sure the lid was in place before lifting the heavy basin between the two of them.

"Is everyone here? Are we ready?" Gabe, as our ringleader, called out to what had to be at least half the senior class. He cupped his hands around his mouth, and his words echoed between the trees. At the outcry of agreement, he tugged his striped knit hat his mother had knitted over his ears.

All the guys laughed and kept pace as they mounted the hill from the parking lot right on the outskirts of town. We followed the marked and somewhat-shoveled trail. Kieran stayed at my side for most of the way before smiling at me.

"I'll be right back," he said, running ahead.

Kieran nudged Gabe, who smiled at him, and they talked about something or another. I was too busy trying to keep up as I huffed and puffed. Next to Kieran, Amy laughed at something someone had said before leaning into him.

In her bright white puffer, she looked like a snowball in its natural habitat.

I giggled to myself.

"Hey. How are you doing?" Jenna asked.

I nearly did a double take. At some point, she had appeared next to me. She was huffing and puffing—worse than I was, if possible—as she tucked her dark hair back under her hat, which looked similar to Gabe's.

"I'm all right."

"Good. Gabe's been looking forward to this for the past three months." Jenna swung her arms at her sides. "I don't remember it being so steep."

"I'm just out of shape," I admitted.

Though my blog was slowly but surely coming along, it didn't require a lot of exertion.

"I thought you, as the track star, would have some more endurance."

Jenna laughed before she paused, as if deep in thought. "Yeah, you have a point."

I laughed. When she didn't chuckle along with me, however, I narrowed my eyes at her hesitation. "You all right?"

"Yeah, it's probably nothing. I can't believe that we only have this semester left before graduation."

"Neither can I."

"Have you heard back from any colleges yet?" Jenna asked.

I shook my head, stepping over a slippery, snow-covered rock. Jenna took notice to move around it as well. "Have you?"

"I got an early decision from Marshall Falls Community last month. I'm still waiting to hear back from other schools."

"What other schools?"

"A bit of everywhere, honestly," she said. "I couldn't make up my mind, so I applied to all the average universities Ms. Hart had recommended. I also added a few she hadn't. I'm just nosy to see if I could get into somewhere big."

"Like where?"

"Harvard, UMass, Bennington, UVM. I got very bored

while Gabe was at baseball practice last spring and went a little crazy."

"Fancy."

"Expensive," Jenna added.

"That too," I sympathized. "You aren't going to commit to Marshall Falls Community yet though?"

"Not yet. I have time," said Jenna. "I know that's probably where Gabe is going even though he's waiting to hear back from his other top school. They might offer him a small sports scholarship, which would be nice—not that the two are that far away from each other."

"You are planning to go to the same place though?"

I thought about my and Kieran's plans. At first, it had seemed obvious that we were going to go to the same college, but now, as the letters started to come in and everyone was getting accepted to different places ... I was beginning to become less and less sure of the possibility.

His and Ms. Hart's words last year hadn't stopped ringing through my mind. I wasn't a great student. I would be lucky to get in anywhere that Kieran was basically guaranteed.

"Not sure. Probably? To be honest, I didn't think I would ever consider it this much. I thought by now, I would be ready to run out of here with Gabriel, no questions about when or where." Jenna drifted off, looking around at everyone and everything—from the overcast gray sky to the way snow hung on thin branches of the canopy above us. "I'm going to miss this."

I stared at Jenna for a moment longer, hearing the laughter that echoed through the trees with all of us together.

The class of Marshall Falls was small, and though it took some time, somehow, we had all managed to blend, much like the community activities where all the parents seemed to know each other as more than just acquaintances.

They were just like us.

They had grown up here.

Only they never left.

It looked like we would be the ones to break that cycle.

For a long time, I'd thought it was only me making plans, but everyone had some sort of idea what they wanted, and Marshall Falls itself didn't seem to be a complete decision maker in the end. We were all trying to do what was best for ourselves. Gabe and Jenna, who I couldn't imagine spending a minute apart, let alone a school year. Landon, who took the bus every day to the technical college. Even Amy seemed to be under high stress over her applications that she had sent in, including the ones far away from Marshall Falls.

Smiling, I nodded. "I think I will miss it too."

"It's nice to have all the memories stored though."

"What do you mean?"

"Your blog," said Jenna, as if it was obvious.

I blinked with surprise. "I didn't realize ..."

"I found it with some of the other girls last year. It was nice to reread some of our adventures and the little things around Marshall. You're a good writer," she complimented.

"Thanks," I said, though it came out soft like a whisper.

"Seriously, you really captured this place without coming outright and saying it. I didn't always think you understood it since you moved here with your family without being a part of growing up here completely, but you do, huh? Marshall, whether we want it to be, is special. It's ours."

Just like Jenna, I looked forward at everyone else. My eyes caught on Kieran, smiling his crooked grin and fixing his glasses as he sniffed from the frosty chill in the air. The one side of my mouth curled up.

Jenna watched me with unwavering eyes.

"What?"

"Nothing." She pressed her lips together in a not-so-hidden smile. "Nothing at all."

We made our way around the swerving path until the trees started to get farther apart, and in front of us was one of the major tourist attractions of Marshall Falls, which brought the most money in to make the area livable at all.

In the summer, families took their kids to hike and play in the basin of water at the bottom of the small waterfalls. In the winter, the water was encased in a thick wall of ice. Slippery tendrils spread out from where the water fell, frozen in time and season.

The ice sparkled in the stripes of sunlight that peeked through the clouds.

Jenna sighed with relief when we finally stopped before taking a light jog to meet up at the front of the group. Like a true leader, Gabe didn't help, but motioned for where the other two guys next to him should put the bucket of filled balloons. He clapped his hands before rubbing them together with anticipation.

"Looks like we're ready!" Gabe called out.

Landon dropped the one side of the plastic container and popped the lid.

"Are we sure it isn't going to break the ice and make it all come down on us?" Jenna asked her boyfriend, looking up at the frozen falls.

"Please, Marshall Falls hasn't seen a winter like this in years. It's thick. It won't break," Gabe assured her. "Plus, they do this every year. If it didn't break then, it won't now."

Jenna flashed the small gap between her teeth. "Let's do this then."

Gabe handed her a purple water balloon.

"Start us off then. One, two"—he stepped back—"three!

Jenna threw the first balloon.

The moment it met the sharp edges of the ice, the plastic popped. Water splattered. Against the ice, deep purple food coloring turned into lavender. Jenna gasped before turning back to Gabe, who picked up another to hand to her before grabbing one of his own.

Immediately, everyone joined in.

The ice turned pink. Then a crisp, sharp blue. More and more of the balloons were thrown against the ice, which tore through the thin plastic, as if it were nothing, coating itself in color.

I was tossed a balloon. I almost didn't catch it before it was in my hand. Not a minute passed before I threw it up into the air with the rest. My shoulder strained in my puffy coat. I nearly slipped forward with the movement before an arm caught right under my elbow.

"Woo!" Kieran clapped his hands, and I nearly jumped away. At some point, he had come to stand right back next to me.

I grinned up at him.

"Get it now?" he asked, referring to when I had first looked at it on the list and not understood how water balloons in winter could ever make sense.

Voices rang out with each new color splattered on the ice.

Handing me one of the balloons, he looked at me. "Ready to knock off another adventure from our list together?"

We stepped forward, sturdy on the ground as we planted our feet.

"Ready, set ..."

"Go!"

We both threw our balloons at the same time, watching as they encountered ice and rock. As we threw, we screamed every time, just like everyone else.

When I had first seen the amount of water balloons, I had

thought the guys had overestimated. If anything, they had underestimated. Balloons were gone. Color stained the ice in front of us in an abstract rainbow. Everything was right as we stood around and breathed with heavy gasps for air, as if we all had just run the three miles from the parking lot.

The frozen falls, in a way, were even more beautiful than they were at peak season, spattering and raging.

And we just kept on adding color.

Kieran snapped a few pictures on his phone. "For your blog."

Amy looked over at us, smiling with Jenna and her other friends, reaching for each other's gloved and mittened hands. She watched as I swung myself into Kieran's arms. Screw everyone who wanted to stop me.

Kieran grunted but took my weight on without question as I hugged him.

The past few weeks and months had been stressful, no matter how many of these sorts of things we tried to do to make it otherwise. The end was coming in a sense, just like Jenna had said, and for the first time since I'd been in Marshall, I wanted to hold on.

"God, I love you, you weirdo."

He squashed me into his side. "Love you too, Sylv."

<h1 style="text-align:center">NINETEEN</h1>

NOW

FOR THE GARAGE apartment once being a makeshift at-home bakery for his mom, Kieran's water pressure in the shower was glorious. It also made me realize just how cold I was. Letting the droplets scald me, I scrubbed at my skin with Kieran's bar soap that smelled like fresh linen.

Getting out of the shower, I swiped my hand across the condensation on the mirror. My hair was a mess as I attempted to calm the wet knots and waves. After wrapping the towel around my center and swiping a blob of toothpaste over my teeth with my finger, I made my way back out into the apartment.

I cleared my throat. "Kieran?"

No one answered, though I didn't need help with anything. By *some clothes* that Kieran had brought back from my parents' house for me, he had really meant my entire suitcase, which I hadn't unpacked, along with the handful of other clothes I had left strewn around my room.

I dug through the half-folded clothing pit and pulled on my pair of jeans and a tank top. Remembering about the magic of layers, I added a thick maroon sweatshirt overtop. For once, I felt sort of cozy.

It had only taken me twenty-eight years.

I was really representing Marshall Falls now, specifically the community college. Kieran had gotten me this sweatshirt as a part of a Christmas gift during our first year at university, both of us creating the other a care package.

He had insisted I try to keep warm for once, fashion or no.

Looked like it was finally coming in handy. I had worn it that day and never again. I never noticed how soft the lining was on the inside.

Now, I really looked like I never left this place.

Every day, when I looked in the mirror, more of the Sylvia I had thought I knew well over the past few years seemed to be disappearing. As if, if I imagined hard enough, I could almost picture what I could've been like if I had decided at the age of eighteen never to leave Marshall Falls. I could've gone to the community college a town over, and this crewneck could've been my uniform throughout the cold months. I could've stayed in town instead of taking the internship hundreds of girls wanted.

I could've stayed.

Right here.

I could've never known better.

With a deep breath, I shoved down my emotions, leaning into the nerves more than anything else, especially when I lifted my gaze out the window and saw Kieran down below outside. He headed around the front to where his car was.

I grabbed the nearest coat and scampered down the wood steps. I passed the tree that Kieran had once gotten stuck in and where we had often studied beneath the first week of school every year. I kept going until the side garage door opened and nearly ran into someone.

I rocked back on my heels. My heart caught somewhere high between my throat and lips.

A wide and slightly scruffy man stood in the doorway. He raised his eyebrows in gentle surprise until they were nearly tucked beneath his old forest-green ball cap. "Is that Sylvia Calasis I see in front of me?"

I pushed a small smile at the man's sense of humor. I gasped a short laugh. It was hard to believe my own eyes, considering I never thought I would see Kieran's father again for the longest time. "It's me."

"How are you? It's so good to see you, sweetheart."

"It's good to see you too. I'm ... I'm okay."

"Are you sure?"

When I had been young, I couldn't see any of Dave in Kieran. Now, I saw it in the older man's smile and the little mannerisms Kieran made. It was undeniable.

I waved my arm somewhere behind me. "I was just ..."

"Are you looking for Kieran?"

"Sort of."

"I figured you'd be around when I heard you were back in town." Dave nodded knowingly.

I wanted to cringe. What exactly did he know?

He dipped his chin. "He always works on Thursdays."

It rang a distant bell in the back of my still-throbbing head.

"His car is still out front if ya want to catch him. I'm sure he wouldn't mind a visitor if you don't mind helping him today. Especially not you."

I definitely wasn't as confident in that as Dave was.

Kieran's dad waved me around toward the front of the house as easily as if I were a kid again and he was shooing me to his son's room, where he'd be holed up for hours, studying for final exams. "Go. Catch him before he leaves."

I pointed in the direction he was talking about. "Okay."

"Tell him that his mom needs his help tomorrow to get supplies for the party. You are welcome to come by as well. Anytime," his dad called. "I'm sure she'd love to see you."

A hole in the middle of my stomach opened into a pit at the mention of Lori. Yet I took a step back off in the right direction. "Will do."

———

I was going after him after all. That was clear even if I now had little to no plan about how this was all going to work out as I approached Kieran's car. For one thing, I didn't think I was going to be this forward about it.

But if there was one thing I knew about Kieran, it was that he wasn't very good when I wasn't forward with him.

I climbed into the passenger seat.

"Sylvia." My name was a startled sound as it came out of Kieran's mouth. "You're wearing my coat?"

"Hi." I slammed the door shut and reached for the seat belt. I didn't bother to answer his question. It was clear I was.

"What are you doing?"

"Your dad said you were going to work at the bakery. I'm coming with you."

Kieran scoffed. "No, you're not."

"I am."

"No."

"Yes," I argued, watching a mixture of emotions cross his face. "It's part of my list."

"That stupid list?"

"Yes," I said, realizing exactly how I was going to make this work. "I'm sorry, but you're involved now. Number six."

"Number six?" Kieran looked around as if someone were

filming this joke of a life ours had become in the past twenty-four hours.

"Raspberry shortbreads."

He rolled his eyes. "Go inside. My mom already has a dozen in there. I doubt she'd be surprised if I told her you ate them all."

"I have to make them," I insisted.

"You *have* to?"

"Yes. Put the key in drive, and let's go. I'm not getting out unless you want to test out those buff-ish muscles of yours and throw me out. Or, ya know, yell at me. Are you going to yell at me?" I stared him down for a solid minute to make sure.

There was nothing worse than a Kieran scorned.

"Please?"

Finally, he huffed.

The key turned in the ignition. He didn't say another word until we both arrived at the bakery. I stopped before the stairs. Just in this spot, Kieran had yelled at me the other day, but that wasn't the reason I paused.

"What?" asked Kieran. "Are you coming in or not?"

After a moment, looking at the lights already on inside, I made my way through the front door. A young girl who looked about high school age and had a face covered in big splotches of freckles stood behind the counter. She wore a sweatshirt with *Rose Bakery* embroidered on the front.

I followed Kieran to the kitchen. When he pushed through the door, it was like walking through time. I took in the silver countertops, the fridge, and double ovens. A few dozen orders in baby-pink boxes greeted us.

An apron slapped into my chest.

"If you are going to make cookies, you're going to make some for the shop too," informed Kieran.

"All right." After a second longer than it should've taken me, I found the loop of the apron to go over my head.

"First, you need to start the dough since we don't have enough in the fridge left over for a whole batch." Kieran rattled off instructions, tying his own apron through muscle memory. "Get the silver mixing bowls over there and add two cups per batch—"

"I remember," I said softly. It cut him off all the same.

Frozen in his tracks, Kieran nodded before he went to the other side of the kitchen. "I'll let you get to it then."

For the next few hours, I worked off my hangover that still made my head feel like it was full of bricks. Carefully, I walked myself back through the recipe I hadn't made in years and never truly thought I'd make again.

Growing up, Kieran and I'd make these cookies every year. Often, they weren't reserved for the holidays. I liked them too much for that. It almost became a gambling currency to us at one point. I would write Kieran stories in nearly every genre, and he'd promise to make me cookies even if it often meant that we were the two making them while his mother complained that she was going to have to start planting more raspberry bushes.

I only had to look at the recipe Kieran had printed out and set in front of me a few times. These cookies were practically ingrained in me, which meant that, technically, I could've been making these shortbreads all the time. It just didn't feel right. Not until now.

I pressed the cookies into their forms and simmered the jam for the center over the stove. I was slow compared to how Kieran worked, but for once in the past few days, few weeks or even years, my mind was quiet.

I wondered if any of my blog readers from years ago would believe that I was back in Marshall Falls. I wondered if any of them had even cared when the blog posts became further and further apart before stopping altogether after I got to the city—a place where I thought the inspiration to write would come in boatloads instead of drying up altogether.

That was what had happened.

And yet, as I set the timer and let the shortbreads bake, I thought about writing about making the cookies, just like Kieran and I had done in high school, where I had pictures of us covered in flour by the end.

I was slightly less messy this time around.

After I waited the perfect amount of time, courtesy of Lori's recipe, I pulled out the cookies and scooped them off the tray and onto the cooling rack. I started a new batch in the oven, then another.

When they were all done, half drizzled with white cream, I reached for one. I looked over the edges, and they weren't perfect, but I still felt as if I were in a dazed dream. Biting into a cookie, I couldn't stop the obscene sound that escaped.

Damp pressure pulsed behind my eyes.

It's been too long.

Coming up alongside me, Kieran didn't ask. He grabbed a cookie right next to the one I'd chosen and popped the entire thing into his mouth. Chewing slowly, he took a deep breath, looking like a chipmunk.

He didn't say anything before swallowing. "Do you want to check it off the list now, or should I?"

They're that good? I wanted to preen as I reached for a second cookie, just to make sure.

"I left the list back at home—your place," I said.

"Guess that part will wait then," said Kieran. "I'll, uh, help you box these up."

He wrote my name on one stuffed box in bold black letters as we cleaned up.

"Thank you."

He wiped down the final mixer.

"I mean it. Today was probably one of the best days I've had back at Marshall Falls since..." I left the words hanging before rephrasing. "Since I've gotten back."

Kieran pulled off his apron in a way that shoved his hair up toward his forehead. He knocked his glasses down his nose.

I chuckled, unable to help myself as I reached for the back ties of my own apron. I couldn't have looked much better with my tight bun on the top of my head and in my Marshall Falls Community College sweatshirt.

Kieran took a moment to look me up and down. Did I have something on my face?

I snuck a third cookie when he wasn't looking.

"Grab your box and then the one next to you," he directed.

"Closing time already?" I asked, glancing up at the clock. It was two in the afternoon.

"I have one more thing I need to get done," said Kieran. "I already promised I'd do it, and since you're here, I figure you don't want to walk back home."

He'd be right.

"You really trust me enough to come along? Just like that?" he asked, as if amused.

"I do." I wasn't sure I understood. I always trusted Kieran. That, if nothing else, hadn't changed. His little smirk, however, made me second-guess myself. "Do you want me to come with you?"

Kieran flicked a wrist to the counter. "Grab another box if you can so we don't have to take as many trips to the car."

"Okay. Where are we heading? On a delivery?"

"We need to head over to the school actually."

"The school?" I felt like I sounded like a parrot, asking so many questions.

Kieran had never made me feel like this before. Nervous.

"Yeah." He offered up no more information as he smirked. "I figure maybe it will help if you come along anyway."

"Really?"

"The ultimate goal of your list is to get you in the holiday spirit, isn't it?"

"Right." I dragged out the word.

He handed me my coat, and I quickly slipped my arms into it as the air from him opening the door swept over me in one freezing rush.

"What are we doing again, going to the school?" I asked.

"I thought you said you were going to trust me."

TWENTY

BEFORE

COMPLETING our list was a slow but steady process. As of the past few weeks since the ice balloons though, nothing new had been checked off. At this rate, I wasn't sure we were going to complete it by our self-imposed deadline of graduation. I didn't bring up the likelihood, however, to Kieran, and he didn't bring it up to me.

We sat in front of each other on the edge of his bed, two plain envelopes sitting between us. One was addressed in block printed letters to Sylvia Calasis. One was labeled for Kieran Rose. Each of them had a return address to Marshall Falls Community College.

We both swallowed as we nodded to each other. Kieran's fingers shook as he picked up his letter.

"One, two, three!" I ripped into my envelope. "You get in?"

Kieran grinned up at me. His eyes were still scanning his thick piece of paper. I already knew what it said. "Yesss."

Dropping my own envelope and note, I pulled him into my arms. "Congrats, Kieran."

"What about you?"

His clear acceptance fluttered to the side, along with my

rejection. "It's community college."

Everyone got into community college. Over ninety-one percent, whether or not they had a larger than average incoming class this year, according to their stupid rejection note. Especially then.

I wasn't a horrible student. Sure, Marshall Falls Community was tiny, almost as tiny as Marshall Falls High. I didn't understand.

I tried to smile. I took a deep breath. It didn't bother me at all. At least, I had to make Kieran believe that.

He blinked a few times. "It's not a big deal."

"It's a big deal for you though," I insisted. "You should celebrate all of the places you're going to get into. It's amazing."

"I guess." He watched me closely.

"Plus, we're both still waiting on other schools to come in. It's still early. This is only the second one."

The second one I had gotten rejected from and he had gotten into.

Still staring at me like I had just received word of my own demise, Kieran nodded.

"What?"

"Nothing," he whispered.

I narrowed my eyes before I let them soften. "I think I want you to say it."

"Sure?"

It was probably a lot better than all the things I was thinking in my head. I figured my heart would race when I got in somewhere. Excitement would flood my brain that I was going to do something exciting with my life. I was going to meet new and remarkable people and maybe leave this small town for good. I would do the great things I always imagined even if it felt like more of a task than it ever had before now that it was here.

But that didn't happen. I never got those letters. I never got anything.

Yet, instead of disappointment, my heart stopped. My body didn't seem to know what the correct reaction was.

Because now, with every rejection, I felt almost ... relief.

I was a coward. Worse than that probably since I also had a great feeling for Kieran. I was happy for him.

I am.

"You can be upset," he told me.

"I know."

He set the letters aside and reached out for me. I almost flinched before Kieran pulled me into a hug.

"I'm fine," I mumbled into his shirt.

"I know you are."

"You'd better." I snuggled into his chest, and he held me that way for a while. It was just the two of us again in those seconds. It was just me, and it was just him, who smelled like vanilla and coffee today.

"A year can change everything, Sylvia."

I inhaled and shook my head at him as I pulled out of his arms. "Maybe. But it isn't going to change us. I mean it."

"I know you do."

"You're my person, Kieran."

Before he could stop himself, he wrapped an arm around me and pulled me in tight. Maybe he was the one who needed the hug.

I wrapped my arms around his middle and squeezed.

"You don't even know. You could get your acceptance any day now," Kieran said optimistically.

"And I have my blog."

He smirked into my hair. "You're right."

"It's taking off ... slowly, I guess." I pressed my lips together so I didn't smile at my own downplay.

"More than slowly. Didn't you just say that other people are mentioning you on their own blogs now as their inspiration for starting theirs? That's amazing, Sylv. I've always believed in you and your writing."

We carefully untangled from each other. I didn't want to get sappy and tell him that he was the person I had to credit for my inspiration to start the blog that was picking up traction to begin with. Recently, even some brands had wanted to send me books now for if I ever did start that book club I had mentioned and kept talking about every other week, and cheers of encouragement came from my readers. I'd been so distracted with everything going on in our senior year that I hadn't been able to move forward with it all yet.

"Plus, we have the list," I said.

Kieran pulled me into an odd side hug. It was as if he couldn't stop touching me, making sure I was here in front of him right now. As if he was really thinking that he was going to have to leave me behind.

Maybe he was right.

"We always have the list."

The bed dipped underneath us. The house was quiet with both Kieran's parents still at work. Kieran's house always felt like home more than mine ever did, and now, I soaked it all up, feeling like I could stay here, just like this, forever.

"Speaking of the list, are we still going to go out tonight?" Kieran asked, his voice low.

"To karaoke? We have to."

"I'm really regretting that number on the list."

So was I, but now, I also really wanted to see Kieran try to sing after the spectacularly awful rendition of "Memory" from *Cats* that he had sung in the elementary school choir. His voice might've gotten lower, but I doubted he could manage to hold a tune.

Then again, I was pretty sure that made two of us by the

way Kieran cringed every time we drove around town in his dad's truck with the music turned up. It still wasn't loud enough to cover my belting out the lyrics of whatever was on the radio.

I lifted my head. "Dylan did seem very excited about the after-party."

"Like his parents don't already know what he has been planning for the last month. He's been blabbing about it ever since they told him they were going out of town."

Kieran snorted as both of us remembered the time in the school parking lot. Dylan hadn't exactly been discreet. His mom and dad both worked at the school. Both had been walking out the doors at the same time Dylan revealed his plans to everyone, leaning on the back of Amy's used Nissan.

"You should get changed."

"What's wrong with what I have on?" Kieran asked, standing up and doing a small turn around to show off his Barnett University sweatshirt. Another one of his spoils from the many college tours to places he was going to receive acceptance letters from any day now.

I gave him a look.

He huffed. "Fine, I'll change. But if we're walking, I'm wearing the hat Gabe gave me."

I watched him yank on the speckled blue knit. It covered half of his face before he rolled it up along his fuzzy, flat bangs that were captured against his eyebrows.

I bit my lip. "Wouldn't dream of you not."

It took a few minutes for him to switch around his shirt, trying on a few options before I gave him the final nod on yet another henley, but this one without the stripes.

He was fixing the hem as we headed down the stairs. Lori dropped her keys on the kitchen counter, getting off the phone with likely one of her sisters. She was nearly always on the phone with how many aunts Kieran had.

"You two look nice."

I gave a small twirl, which delighted both Kieran and Lori, It didn't matter that I didn't look any different from any other day. I wore my tight jeans with a single hole in the one pocket that was meant to be there and a loose sweater with a tank top underneath so that Kieran wouldn't get on my case about layers. I didn't want to have to worry about carrying around a coat all night.

"Are you two going out tonight?" Lori asked. "Another list item?"

"Maybe if we get bored," Kieran said.

I elbowed him in the side. "We're knocking karaoke off the list once and for all."

"That's right. I remember when the school rented out the pub down the street."

"It's a bar, Mom."

"Same thing." Lori smiled, as if her amusement wasn't already palpable. Her eyes flickered behind me as Kieran came up at my back. "Be careful. Keep an eye on each other. Call if you need anything."

"We always do."

"Good. Makes a mother feel better. Though I'm not going to ask any more questions!"

"Probably for the best."

Her eyes flared with amusement. "Take care of him."

"I think that's the guy's job, Lori."

She rolled her eyes and waved us out. "Be careful. Make good choices!"

I chuckled at Kieran's snort as we made our way out the door. Kieran zipped up his coat along the way.

He looked at me. "Where is your jacket?"

I shrugged. "It's not that far of a walk. I'll be fine."

"You're going to freeze."

"Yes, *Mom.*"

He nudged me with his shoulder before reaching for my hands. He grasped them tightly between his soft gloved palms, rubbing feeling into them. "Better?"

I wouldn't admit that it felt like heaven. "I was fine."

"Sure you were." Kieran held my hands, not letting me move more than a step ahead of him to race from the cold until we made it to the bar down the street, already surrounded by other high school students and unfortunately a few teachers who looked around at the dozens of tiny plastic cups around the bar.

Each cup was filled with different kinds of soda—from the strangely bubbleless Diet Coke to orange fizz.

"Not much of a setup, is it?"

"It's not so bad. It's one of those high school traditions I thought," I said.

"Oh, it is," Dylan said with a glint in his eyes.

"Am I missing something?"

"It doesn't mean that they completely outsmarted us from a good time," said Landon. He nudged Dylan.

Jenna rolled her eyes at their antics. "What are you talking about?"

Dylan flashed what was inside of his oversize coat alongside Landon, who did the same.

Gabe burst out in laughter as he held on to Jenna tight. Her own eyes looked tired but lit up at the sight of what I could only describe as travel-sized bottles of liquor, laughing along with the rest of us.

"Now, it's really karaoke night. Come one, come all as we pregame my very own house party later."

"You realize that it's just going to be us there, right?" Jenna spoke up.

Dylan was unconcerned. "All we need."

I stuck out my cup to him before taking Kieran's. His eyes widened in warning as Dylan filled it with a little more than a shot.

"Liquid confidence. How else are you going to get up there with me?"

"Kieran's singing tonight?" Dylan barked a laugh. "Oh shit, this is going to be good."

Kieran took his cup back and slugged back a sip. It didn't taste any different to me, but he winced. "Thanks for that."

"I expect my thanks in a serenade."

He took another sip of his cup until it was half gone. I laughed.

We found our seats, along with everyone else milling around the bar. Eventually, when our names were called—I had made sure the two of us were on the list as of a week ago—I tugged Kieran onto the stage. His head fell back as if trying to pull me back down into the booth, but his legs followed along with me until we were set up between two microphones.

I held on to him as we sang the words, off-key and out of tune, but no one seemed to care. Kieran held me tighter as we swayed this way and that until the song was finally over.

I motioned with my hand toward him, down and up again. He repeated the same gesture.

Check.

After a few more sodas, laced with something more than sugar, we all snuck out the doors with those who didn't plan on staying at the school event all night. All of us, along with a few others who'd overheard Dylan's parents were out of town, ran down the street toward Dylan's house.

A few of us gathered in the kitchen, where the guys

attempted to set up a poor excuse for beer pong. Gabe looked like he was either going to be sick or turn into a ghost before the night was over. His face turned paler and paler with every hour that passed until, finally, Jenna nudged him off and went somewhere else in the house without him.

It took everything I had not to offer him a trash can. The rest of the guys surrounded him, including Kieran. I watched as his eyes widened and settled in a small nod.

Did they get some bad news with acceptance letters today too? It wouldn't surprise me. Every other day at school, someone was either cheering or near tears about schools they had or hadn't gotten into. Or worse, had gotten into, but knew they couldn't go. There was a strange combination of excitement and terror in the hallways.

I was beginning to know it well.

"What's going on with him?" I asked. "Did something happen?"

"I'm not sure I'm supposed to say."

I nudged Dylan, leaning in closer to him. "Is something wrong?"

"No, it's not that."

I waited. I knew better than to walk away now, especially with how red Dylan's cheeks were from all the alcohol he consumed. He was about to crack.

"He didn't say I couldn't tell anyone. Everyone's going to know soon anyway, I guess."

"What is it?"

Dylan's voice was low so only I could hear. "Jenna's pregnant."

My eyes widened. "What?"

He took another sip of his drink, long and slow. "They just started to tell people, but apparently, she's already a few months along. The two of them have been trying to keep it under wraps until the acceptance letters started to be sent. So far, she got into almost all her schools that she had applied to, but she doesn't know what she's going to do now."

"Oh, wow." *Oh my God.*

I looked across the room to where the guys surrounded Gabe, Jenna nowhere in sight.

Kieran's voice could be heard above everyone else. "Absolutely. You're going to do amazing, Gabe. Don't worry."

"That's easy for you to say, man."

"It's all going to work out, no matter what."

Gabe tucked his mouth down to the edge of his beer bottle, trying to take a deep breath under Kieran's hand, resting on his shoulder.

"Imagine you as a dad," Kieran said.

"I always wanted to be a dad."

"And it's going to happen, maybe a little sooner than you thought ..."

Gabe snorted. "A lot sooner."

"Yeah, but if there's anyone who will be great at it, it's you," insisted Kieran. "And you got all of us here. We're a family. We all are going to be right here for you too."

For now.

Dylan had just said it. Jenna had been getting dozens of acceptance letters, and she wasn't the only one. They were marked with terrifying postage from all over the state, the country in some cases. We weren't all going to be here for very long, and that included Kieran.

Because Kieran was going to get into every school he had applied to, and then there would be no holding back as he took on the world with his amazing attitude and kind words and perfect ... everything.

Kieran nearly always had the right thing to say. He could pull a person off the side of the cliff or pull me back from a panic attack just about to set in. He was perfect as his hair swept over his forehead, right above his glasses as he continued to talk to Gabe. His friend wrapped him in a hug, knowing that Kieran would never push him away.

What would happen if I didn't get into any schools by the time we graduated and everyone moved on without me? I'd make him, because the last thing I would ever do would be to hold him back here when he had so much to offer the world and not just Marshall Falls.

Probably more than I did, and that wasn't just the universities talking.

He was right; a lot could change in a year. For the first time, I wasn't so sure I liked it. Change.

For so long, I had thought I was my father's daughter. Now, I felt stuck right here, staring at Kieran as if I had never seen him before and also as if I had never known anyone better in my entire life, even myself.

I didn't want to lose him. I didn't want to let him go even if I had to.

He's mine.

The thoughts sincerely settled in my chest. Jenna came back inside from the patio. Amy and Dylan and Landon and everyone else tagged along.

All these years, no matter how hard I tried to make it otherwise, I never wanted to be a part of any of them. I didn't want to be any of their people they called their friends.

Not when I could be next to Kieran.

Kieran might like facts, but there was one I could never admit aloud.

I stared at him across the room, and he met my eyes, soft and easy.

I loved my best friend, Kieran Rose.

TWENTY-ONE

NOW

I SHOULDN'T HAVE TRUSTED Kieran.

I didn't remember Marshall Falls Elementary to be so small. The hallways were narrow, and the intermixed blue tiles were faded from polish and years. I had spent two years in this school, right next to Kieran, growing up, yet the moment I walked through the front doors, it felt as if I had wandered into an alternate reality.

The secretary, I was nearly positive, was the same one who had often looked at me disapprovingly as a child. She handed me a visitor badge.

Kieran clipped his badge to the edge of his coat.

Unsure where to put mine, I held it awkwardly between my fingers, careful not to drop the pink bakery boxes stacked in my arms. One step at a time, we made our way down the first-floor hallway. Kids yelled alongside bangs of things falling—or more likely being thrown to the floor.

"Sounds like someone's having fun," murmured Kieran.

"And not like a prison for tiny tots at all," I murmured in agreement.

Kieran chuckled as we paused at one of the doors. He

knocked twice with the edge of his foot. Inside, the teacher with short waves in her hair and a wide polka-dot skirt turned around.

"Oh, thank God. You made it. For a second, I thought I was going to have to break into the emergency snack stash. Then, I'd have to restock all the cheese crackers again," Amy rambled before she seemed to realize who was standing in front of her. Shock was cleverly hidden on her face. Her eyes raked between the two of us. "Kieran … and Sylvia."

"Cookie delivery," replied Kieran.

I lifted my own boxes up, as if in offering. "The long-lost manual labor is also here," I attempted to joke.

Obviously, my self-deprecation was lost on this crowd.

Amy dipped her head in a small nod. She turned her attention back on Kieran. "I was unsure if I was going to see you."

Kieran shook his head, as if that was ridiculous. "I promised."

Slowly, Amy smiled. "You did. The kids have been looking forward to their little holiday party. You are welcome to stay if you want. They should be back from music any minute now."

"Cool. Do you want me to set up the stuff—"

"On the table near the back. My class mom should be coming in any minute to help wrangle everyone too," said Amy.

I set down the boxes. Kieran tipped his head in thanks as he opened the boxes into little platters for the kids. This way, they could choose between the raspberry thumbprints, gingerbread, and sugar cookies to eat off snowman-themed plates. After hovering for a moment, I wandered across the classroom to where Amy was.

Rushing to the other side of the blackboard, I reached up to lift the other side of the streamers Amy was hanging, spanning one edge of the board to the other.

She glanced down from where she stood, tacking each side down. "Thanks."

"No problem."

"I didn't expect to see you here," Amy said after she got back down from the chair, brushing off her hands as she looked me up and down.

"I didn't expect to see you wearing pink polka dots."

Amy raised her eyebrows, as if surprised I had bitten back. "They used to be red."

"Festive."

"So, you and Kieran have been together for the day?" she asked almost casually.

But I knew Amy. I also knew that in most of my time with her, except for a few small occasions, she rarely spoke to me unless she needed something or had no other choice.

"He's helping me get into the holiday spirit," I explained. "I also needed help getting home last night after everything."

"That's nice," said Amy.

I watched as Kieran continued to organize the snack table before smiling back at the two of us. His eyes still tensed when they landed on me.

"Don't do it."

I turned, unsure I had heard her correctly. "Don't what?"

"Don't get his hopes up. Don't do whatever it is that made him like he was a few years ago again."

"Oh, I—"

"I really don't want to hear it," sighed Amy. She walked away.

What I had done?

I knew exactly what Amy had been talking about, and yet ... I hadn't realized that anyone had noticed what must've happened other than the two of us. I figured they had just assumed we grew apart, and when we were together, we were just Sylvia and Kieran.

We were always *just* Sylvia and Kieran.

Kieran's eyebrows furrowed into one scruffy brown caterpillar as he looked away from Amy and toward me.

He mouthed a question with concern, *Are you okay?*

I quickly nodded, giving him a thumbs-up.

Once the kids returned to the classroom, the entire idea of a winter holiday cookie party turned into chaos.

It was odd, looking at all the seven-year-olds running around the room. They were the same age that Kieran and I had been when we met.

The average rambunctiousness was increased by sugar and the *make your own sugar cookie* station for those who wanted buttercream on top, also provided by Kieran, much to most of the kids' delight. They had all obviously met him before, Amy close at his side to watch for anyone making too much of a mess, chatting continuously about something I couldn't hear over the high-pitched voices and laughter.

I still couldn't help myself. I watched as they talked, trying not to be obvious. Amy touched his arm. Puzzlement crossed her face at what she saw before she lightly smiled down at another student.

The one room mom clapped her hands, and all the students fell silent for a single moment. She motioned for anyone to come over to the newly setup craft station. Everyone could make their own unique snowflake out of coffee filters.

A group of second graders not licking icing off their hands rushed toward the table.

Reaching down to my own new best friend's plate, I ate

another one of the raspberry shortbreads that seemed to be the least favorite of the kids anyway.

The little girl in pigtails looked up at me as she munched away at icing. "Mmm."

"Mmm." I chewed in agreement.

"Are any of them yours?" The class mom snuck up next to me.

"Oh." I startled, standing as I brushed off the wayward cookie crumbs. "No. I'm just a last-minute helper."

"You look familiar."

"Rich and Meredith are my parents," I offered, knowing that she'd connect the dots eventually.

Small-town perks.

"Of course!" She smiled. "Sylvie Calasis, right? I think I remember you from school years ago. You were a few years behind me. I'm Mina. Mina Stanton, formerly Kisner."

"It's Sylvia actually."

"Sylvia, sorry. Anyway, you look good with the kids. You're just home for the holidays then?" Mina asked. "It must be nice to catch up with old friends, like Kieran and Amy."

"It is," I agreed.

"I can only imagine. I'm not sure how I would handle being away from here for so long. At first, that's all I wanted to do, but it's comfortable here."

How long had I told myself that just being comfortable wasn't enough?

I took the chance to look back at Kieran and Amy again, putting out a game for the kids.

Mina's eyes followed mine. "I don't know how the two of them haven't gotten together yet."

Slowly, I dipped my head. "They used to be together in high school."

"Really?"

"On and off."

"Huh, I guess who knows then how long it will take for them to realize they should get together? The baker and the teacher. It sounds kind of cute, don't you think? A little small-town romance novel in the making." Mina giggled at the thought, automatically reaching toward the table in front of us to clean up the crumbs one of the kids had left behind.

"Yeah. Cute."

"Sorry, we've recently been on a romance novel kick with the book club in town," Mina said. "If you stick around after the holidays, I'm sure we'd love to have you. You read, right?"

Any other time, I would wonder what she meant and if she knew that people had jobs to get back to after the holiday, only now, I didn't. "Yeah. Maybe. I think I might be looking for a change of pace after being in the city for so long."

"Track me down or let Amy know. She'll pass along the details." Mina grinned. "It's been a little chaotic since our last book club leader left, but it's still a good time once we all agree on the book of the month."

"Sounds like it."

"It definitely is. There's one person in the club who brings the wine, and Jenna makes these amazing lemon bars. You went to school with Jenna too, didn't you?"

"I did."

"See, it would be perfect." Mina sighed with glee, as if the little life she was making for herself and now me was all coming together. "I'd better get back to the kids over there before we get carried away with the markers. I'll be back if I can."

"Have fun," I said softly, feeling eyes on my back. Twisting, I expected the heavy gaze to be Amy watching me.

It wasn't.

Kieran stared at me with his lips pressed into a tight line.

I wrapped my arms around myself on the ride home, waiting for Kieran's car to heat up. Cold air flowed through the vents, slowly warming until that was all I could hear, aside from Kieran's blinker as he took the turn back toward the center of town. He was always a good driver. He was a much better driver than me anyway. Both of our fathers had taken turns, trying to teach us, and ... well, Kieran never ran over a curb or hit a fire hydrant so ...

I curled my legs up toward the center of my body, careful not to put too much of my shoes on the seat.

"Did you mean what you said back there?" asked Kieran.

I peeked up over my shoulder. He pushed his glasses further up his nose as he glanced at me. Then, just as simply, he turned back to the road and came to a stop.

Narrowing my eyes, I tried to remember if we had talked at all back at the school. It had been oddly silent since Amy had greeted us. Kieran had turned on his outgoing personality for all the kids. Now, I figured he was recharging in the silence. I knew to leave him to it. It was clear that his brain was still churning on something as he bit the side of his tongue and waited for my response.

"What do you mean?" I asked.

"At the school," Kieran clarified, "when you were talking to Amy's class mom."

"Mina," I filled in.

"Right. Mina. You said that you were looking for a change of pace. You said you might be moving out of the city."

I blinked. "I did say that."

"Did you mean it?"

I hadn't thought he'd been able to hear my conversation with Mina at all.

The sun was going down in the distance over the mountains. Oranges turned to nearly red before dying out.

After another moment, the darkness settling, I nodded slowly. "It's been on my mind. Kind of anyway."

Kieran turned, watching me closely. We sat at a Stop sign for longer than anyone probably should. Then again, this was Marshall Falls. No one was behind us and would honk their horns good-naturedly if they were.

"What?" Under his gaze that normally relaxed me, I wanted to slip farther down the passenger seat until my knees were also in my jacket.

Kieran looked like he was about to say something else, but shook his head.

"Did you still want to go get a tree?"

TWENTY-TWO

BEFORE

I WAS in love with my best friend.

The unsaid words burned in my throat. I couldn't help myself after they were there. I thought about them over and over and over. I burned and burned and burned.

I was in love with Kieran Rose.

There was only one thing to do, and considering I was at Dylan's house party. I needed to get hammered.

After a half-dozen cheap, bubbly beers and sugary, raspberry-colored wine coolers, my stomach grumbled unhappily. I bent over from where I sat on the edge of the kitchen counter, leaning in Dylan's arms. He picked me up, settling me on the floor. I bet his parents had left the house a lot cleaner than they were going to find it when they came home unless Dylan did some serious cleanup. The kitchen tiles took on a hazy, sticky quality.

I squealed as we swayed.

His lips pressed in close to my ear. "Look at us. I always thought you were kinda cute, you know."

I didn't, but I didn't answer. I let my hips bend back into

him as we leaned this way and that to the sound of music playing from the living room.

"You want to maybe see my room upstairs?" Dylan asked, voice rumbling in my ear.

I bit my lip as my head lifted to look at him. His eyes were brown pinpoints staring back at me.

"We should get going," Kieran interrupted, stepping up next to Dylan and me.

"You want to go?" I watched him take another glance around the space, not uncomfortable, but clearly not as comfortable as he had been the last time I noticed him with Gabe and the rest of his friends.

He was right; it was getting late. Though Lori didn't mind that he was out, he never liked to push her too far if she attempted to stay up for him on the couch.

Dylan looped his arms around my waist. "You don't have to go yet, do you?"

"Kieran—" I lifted a hand toward my friend. I had to keep reminding myself of the word. *Friend.*

"You can stay with me." Dylan grinned. "Kieran doesn't need to take the party with him. Right, man?"

Slowly, I started to nod, waiting for Kieran to agree too.

Dylan pulled me further into him.

"Sylv?" Kieran remained where he was.

"Kieran?"

"Do you want to go?" he asked again.

I bit my lip. My hand settled on Dylan's shoulder. I glanced at him and back at Kieran. Any other time, I'd agree right away. We'd leave together, just like I wanted to right now. I always wanted to be with Kieran. Then, we'd probably spend some time at his house while I sobered up before heading home for real—if I went home.

I was in love with Kieran. I was in love with my best friend.

Dylan wasn't my friend. He was, well, *Dylan.* Sure, I'd never been extremely attracted to him. It was hard to be attracted to anyone after seeing them snort orange juice in the school cafeteria before panicking when they got a nosebleed. But Dylan was nice enough.

Pleasant.

And he wasn't Kieran.

I nodded firmly this time. "You can go. I'm going to stay a little longer."

Dylan's smile widened at my choice.

Kieran looked between the two of us, though his expression gave nothing away. "You sure?"

I took a deep, long breath. "Yeah. I'll call you later. Okay?"

"Sounds good." Kieran's words were short and clipped before he pressed his lips together. He loitered, unsure as he rocked back a single step. "Call me if you need anything."

Dylan's eyes trailed from my head to somewhere around my boobs. "We'll be all right. See you, Kieran."

Was I really doing this? Was I going to let this go? I should. That would be the normal thing to do. I expected the feeling in my chest to loosen, but instead, emotion squeezed tighter.

Then again, when I glanced over Dylan's shoulder, Kieran was already gone.

I blinked at the empty space.

"Do you want to go up and see my room now?"

I licked my lips as I focused back on Dylan. "Sure."

A hand slid down past my elbow and into my hand. He led us back toward the front staircase. Landon and someone I didn't know were curled up, chatting on the couch. Another group of girls remained on the shag living room carpet. One tipped back with laughter at something someone had said.

Amy.

Her gaze landed on Dylan and me as we made our way up the first few steps.

Three doors down, Dylan's room looked as I'd imagined. His desk was cluttered, and his dresser was lined with a row of small baseball trophies. The walls were blue—likely the same color blue his mother had picked out when she was pregnant. His bed creaked as he pulled me to sit on the edge.

"This is it," he announced, extending his arm around the place.

Slowly, I took it all in. "It's nice."

"Thanks."

Dylan's hand slid from where he held my hand, warm and a little slick, down to cup my knee. Leaning closer, I inhaled.

I wasn't stupid. I knew exactly what was going to happen. I read about it enough. Only now, it felt as if my years of reading romance novels was going out the window as Dylan's mouth started a slow descent over mine.

Tilting my head, I met his mouth. His lips settled over mine and slipped against me with a thick layer of saliva. He moaned heavily. My eyebrows pinched together. I needed to not be awkward as he pulled me closer, trying to settle me on his lap, but I felt stiff, like a wooden board.

The thick comforter bunched around our legs. He sucked my lips into his mouth until I pulled away with a resounding pop.

Dylan's scratchy palms roamed over my stomach, slipping up under my sweater as his hands became a little more adventurous. His mouth also took their lead, pressing wet kisses over my neck and shoulder. His hulk of a frame hovered over me until I was forced to lean back, hips crushing onto my thighs.

I took another breath as I stared up toward his empty ceiling, swallowing. "Um ..."

"You okay?"

"Yeah, I mean ..." I met his eyes as they pulled back up from where he was about to burrow between my boobs. "I don't want to have sex."

"Oh." Dylan pulled back. "That's fine."

He went back to kiss me again. I let him. He cut off my airway, and I counted those seconds.

One ... two ...

"Actually"—I broke away—"I'm sorry. I think I should go."

"Did I do something?"

"No. You were great," I assured him. "Thanks. I just didn't realize how late it had gotten. I'm sort of dizzy."

He nodded, as if understanding rather than annoyed, although that emotion flickered over his expression. "Gotcha. Too much to drink?"

That might've been a quarter of the problem.

"I forgot you don't hang out with us a lot. You're cool, Sylvia. How come I never saw that before?" Dylan asked.

He might've been the first one to ever say that to me. Besides Kieran, he was probably the only one who ever talked to me like I was a normal human being who had grown up beside them all since I had moved here. It made me almost want to stay there, next to him, for one more minute.

"Well"—I waved a hand, tucked close to my jeans—"thanks."

"Maybe we can still go out sometime? Next week?" he offered.

"Okay. Maybe. Yeah."

"Awesome," he sighed. "Do you, uh, need me to help you home or something?"

"No." I stood. "I'm good. I'll see you."

"Bye."

I put my hands to my face and let my fingers run down my cheeks. How stupid was I? I just kissed Dylan, who had kissed half the school. Even though, I really didn't know how he managed it.

I'd always expected kissing to be … I didn't know … better.

It had felt nice for a second there—to be wanted.

Then it just felt like chapped, crusty lips were trying to eat my face.

I barely made it back down the hallway to the stairs before I heard sniffles. Pausing, I leaned through the doorway of another bedroom. Inside, Jenna sat on the edge of the made bed, taking deep breaths as she stared at the wall.

"Hey."

Jenna nearly leaped out of her skin at the sound of my voice. She quickly swiped a hand under her nose. "Oh, sorry. Hey."

"Are you okay?" I took a step inside, cupping my hands in front of me.

She huffed a short laugh. "I assume you know?"

Debating on the appropriate answer, I sighed. "Not going to lie. I think everyone knows."

Jenna waved off the information. "There's no point in trying to cover it up anymore. Soon, I'm going to get massive anyway, and the cat will really be out of the bag."

"Do your parents know yet?"

She shook her head. "We're going to tell them tomorrow. Neither of them will be surprised. They always joke about there being soulmates in every Marshall Falls graduating class, so I don't think they'll be too mad. They always joke, too, about wanting grandbabies."

"That's good at least. You don't have to worry about it," I said. If I went home and told my mother I was pregnant, I wasn't sure what she'd do. Likely, she'd flip.

"Yeah, I don't know why I decided to wait so long to tell

them. I know it's been weighing on Gabriel," she said. "I kept saying it was because I wanted to enjoy senior year. I wanted to do all the traditions and get my letters from colleges."

"And did you get in?"

She nodded, shutting her eyes. Carefully in the silence, I sat down next to her on the bed.

"It just wasn't meant to be," whispered Jenna, looking down at her hands in her lap. "I did say that I was going to miss this place, and honestly, I can't picture a better place to raise this little boy or girl. I always sort of imagined it. I imagined me and Gabe getting married with a little wedding at the church in town with all our family. I imagined us getting a house and sending our kids off to school at Marshall Falls and taking them on hikes on the weekends."

She picked at the skin around her nails.

"It's everything I wanted." Her shoulders shook at the tears that began to trail down her cheeks.

It might've been everything she'd ever wanted, but maybe just not right now.

"Like I said, there's always been talk about how there's a couple who are soulmates in every class in Marshall Falls," said Jenna, keeping her eyes locked on me. "It sounds like superstition, but I've always liked that story."

"It would be nice."

"I'm just not so sure it's us."

I paused. "What are you talking about?"

"Me and Gabe. I don't know if we're the soulmates." Her eyes turned pointedly at me. "Especially not when there are two other people who act like they were made for each other and can barely spend a moment apart."

I blinked, slowly understanding what she was talking about. "Me and Kieran? It's not like that."

"I might be a teen mom who apparently makes bad decisions, Sylvia, but I'm not blind."

I shook my head.

"Don't waste it," said Jenna. "Someone deserves their complete happy ending."

"Who says that can't be yours?" I asked.

"I'm going to make mine. You just need to go and take it. Consider it a baby gift to me so I don't have to watch this strange soap opera going on between the two of you any longer."

"There isn't a strange soap opera."

"Fine then," Jenna sighed. "I assume it didn't work out with Dylan?"

"You're making me like you less."

She laughed. "I heard that he kisses like a washing machine."

I laughed with her. That was an accurate description.

"You sure you'll be okay up here?" I asked.

"Gabe will come and find me soon. He's more worried about his parents tomorrow, but I don't think it'll be that bad. Really."

"Okay. See you on Monday?"

"See you then, Sylvia."

TWENTY-THREE

NOW

"I LIKE that you actually decided on a coat today."

I glanced down at the coat, which was slightly larger than my average one. "We already went over that it's your coat."

Kieran found a spot along the sidewalk to park a block away. In the distance, in front of the grocery store, was the only Christmas tree stand in Marshall Falls. That was, unless you wanted to drive out and chop a tree down yourself. I could see the soft glow of lights hanging from the store sign.

A woman taking out her small wiener dog looked at us oddly as we were nearly at a jog, walking toward the sparse trees. Even the dog paused, jumping in and out of the snowbank to stare.

Kieran nodded to the woman, whose attention then landed on me, but I couldn't place her if I tried.

"Still, very impressive."

I nearly tripped over my own feet. "I thought I'd try this new thing today called not freezing."

"Seems like a valid option most would choose," he confirmed.

I stuffed my hands further down into the coat's deep, plush

pockets. "I figured there are a few things I'm still not too old to try."

"What is up with you and your age? You're twenty-eight."

"Twenty-nine soon enough," I corrected.

Kieran still stared at me with a *so what* expression.

I shrugged. "I don't know. I guess I've always looked at everyone else doing what I love around me."

"And?"

"And ... so I look at how they're doing."

"And how are they doing?" Kieran asked as if he really had no clue what I was talking about.

I scoffed. "They're usually doing fun, great things. Everyone is succeeding. They're landing pitches and writing the kinds of articles I always imagined writing—or better yet, being in them. They're something and someone. They are also, most of the time, twenty-three and, for some reason, embracing life. When I notice that, it becomes clear that I ... haven't."

I peeked up at Kieran. He slowed his steps so that we were at a leisurely pace instead of sprinting. I could've cried with relief, but held it in.

"Not that I didn't try," I added.

"Obviously."

I couldn't tell if it was a jab or not, but I ignored it. He deserved a jab or two. I wasn't dense enough that I thought all the things he had said the other night were suddenly gone. But he was out and standing next to me right now. Not only that, but he was talking to me!

If I had to take a few punches to the gut, I would. "It's not that I think my life is over or that I can't still do things, but I feel a little late."

"Since when have you cared about showing up anywhere late?" asked Kieran.

I let out a short burst of air through my nose. He had a point.

"You should still get yourself a real coat though."

"I have a real coat," I muttered, seeing he was teasing.

"Oh, yeah? Where is this mysterious article of clothing?"

"I left it in the city, I think." I wasn't sure in what closet I would've left it in though. Either way, it was gone now. "I was in a rush."

"Why were you rushing?"

I realized what I had hinted at. "No reason. Just excited to get home."

He huffed a breath, as if that was the last thing he'd believe.

"How have they been? Your parents?" I asked finally, taking a deep breath. "I saw Dave."

"You did?"

"Yeah, this morning, I nearly ran into him. He seemed surprised to see me," I said.

"He's not the only one," Kieran muttered. "I'm sure you'll get a few more of those looks until you head back out of this place."

"What do you mean?"

"I mean, that none of us expected you to be back," he said. "You gave the town something new to gossip about by coming back."

"At least I'm popular for once in my life."

"If that's what you want to call it. Dad's fine. Mom has been getting ready for her party."

My eyes widened at the mention of the famous Rose holiday get-together. The entire house turned into a winter wonderland of green garland and sugary sweets that made my stomach ache for days afterward.

"She still hosts it? Your dad did say that. He said that she needed help picking up some stuff though."

"I'll ask her what. It's fine. She never stopped hosting though," Kieran informed me, sounding as if the very thought of his mother taking a year or two off from her annual holiday party was ridiculous. "Even after her cancer diagnosis, she never let it put a damper on her favorite time of year. We all pushed through for at least one night every year for her until she eventually was in remission. Now, she's back to putting everything together and bossing us around."

I chuckled. "I didn't know."

"Maybe if you had picked up the phone."

I took the next hit.

"What, not going to say anything?" he asked, almost taken aback by my silence now.

I shook my head. "You're right."

Kieran didn't reply.

"Is that what you want me to say? You're right, and I'm wrong. What else is new?"

"That's not how it ever was between us."

"I didn't think so either," I whispered, taking a deep breath. "But then again, you don't seem yourself. Not completely anyway."

"Maybe you just don't know me anymore," said Kieran.

That nearly felt like a punch to the gut as well. "Maybe."

He watched my face.

I forced myself to look forward.

"I haven't been exactly in the holiday mood myself. Okay? Sorry if that, combined with *everything else,* makes me not so cheery for you."

I had a feeling I was the *everything else* in this scenario. "Why?"

"There's been a lot going on," Kieran admitted, but nothing more. "Just because you left doesn't mean that life ever stopped in the past few years."

"I know that. I didn't mean it like that."

Kieran swallowed. "I know you didn't. Sorry."

"What, can't help yourself?"

He didn't say anything.

"It's fine. I'm sorry." My words sputtered at the silence he left between us. It was okay when I was taking the blows and letting him berate me or do anything so long as he was talking to me. "I apologize if I ... let's just ..."

"We really need to stop saying sorry," said Kieran.

I pressed my lips together. "Sorry."

He shook his head. Was that a teeny-tiny smile I saw?

"Because ..." I said, unsure of exactly what I was about to come up with before the words flowed out. "I have nowhere to go. I need to do something. Anything to make at least the next week feel like I'm not completely messing things up or doing something wrong. I need to somehow find happiness. I need a change."

"*Here* isn't known for evolving too much."

"At least this place has never let me down," I whispered. *At least not any more than I ever planned.*

Kieran studied me for another minute before nudging me forward with his arm. "Let's go get a tree. Then, you can show me the rest of this holiday list of yours again."

"To make fun of again, you mean?"

"I never make fun of a list. Yours, on the other hand ..."

I rolled my eyes and made sure to hide my smile. It felt too real, too familiar, and I knew better. If there was one thing I ever knew in my life, I knew not to get my hopes up.

***

The tree lot looked like it had been ransacked by overenthusiastic Christmas fiends. I touched the short branch of one of the thinner trees. The very top came to my shoulders. Needles scattered to the ground until the branch was nearly bare. I quickly walked away from it.

"This is just plain sad," I murmured.

"Eh, it's not that bad," Kieran said. How he managed to stay at least somewhat optimistic in the face of defeat was always astonishing.

He rounded the last average-sized tree left on the lot. Or at least the one tree that still had most of its original intended needles still clinging to life. Most.

"The boy's right. It ain't so bad," an elderly gentleman intoned. He came up alongside us in a plaid scarf and army-green knit cap.

Mr. Benson had become a holiday staple in Marshall Falls and had run the small tree lot for as long as I could remember. He wore the same brown plaid coat every year. The shape hung loose over his shoulders.

"You can fill in the empty spaces with some popcorn strings or cranberries, if you got 'em. Tinsel would do the trick."

"Tinsel?"

We'd need a few pounds of the stuff to cover the gaping divot in the side.

"Tinsel and a few ornaments fix just about anything, I figure."

Kieran tipped his chin in swift agreement. "Very good point, Mr. Benson. Guess this is the one."

"Good choice. I always liked to pick out a tree last minute. Some people get everything ready and end up just staring at it all for weeks. I like to keep the fun going. Once, I didn't even put the star on until Christmas Eve. A final celebratory moment, though my kids didn't see it as fun as I did. Best time of the year," Mr. Benson mused. "Best time of the year."

"That it is," Kieran said.

Both of us turned and gave each other a look, as if we were on the same page about how we currently felt about the time of year. I almost smiled at the new inside joke we had.

"Here's some extra of the sparkly stuff on the house too." Mr. Benson eyed me. "Tinsel can fix damn near anything, I tell ya."

I squinted down at myself, as if I had a sign saying that I was basically the prodigal best friend coming back home to cause issues. I wasn't sure if tinsel could fix all of what was between me and Kieran.

I took the bag anyway.

STRAIGHTENING MY CLOTHES, I hastily made my way back down the steps of Dylan's house. Framed photographs of him and his parents at various sporting events were hanging up on the wall.

Everyone remained where they had been before Dylan and I went upstairs, in a variety of disarray. Feet were flung over the arms of the couch. Others half sat, half laid on the floor.

Amy glanced at me from where she was on the floor, her tight sweater riding up over her belly button. She eyed my frame before she burst out into bubbling laughter.

A few others glanced in my direction, along with her, as I stepped off the final stair.

"Did Dylan not last long?" she called out.

Her comment set off a round of girlish giggles.

Maybe that was the real reason they never invited me along to hear such gossip. There were only so many people in Marshall Falls they had to gossip about after all unless they wanted to do it to their faces.

I wondered if they even noticed that Jenna was missing tonight as they gorged themselves on wine coolers, not that I was doing much better. In fact, now that I was back downstairs with everyone, my face felt hot and red—and not from embarrassment.

Though that was probably part of it.

I opened the front door and shut it behind me. I just stood there for a moment.

I should probably go home. It was late, and the streets were slowly being coated in another layer of ice and snow as flurries fluttered from the sky. Yet I stepped off the front porch and down toward the street.

The cool air slid around me with its flecked caress and squall. It swooped around my feet as I ventured out onto the silent, snow-covered street, knowing exactly where I planned to end up.

Home.

The thick patches of snow crunched under my shoes with each step. Fishing through my pockets as I made it to the end of the next block, I lifted my phone and pressed it to my ear. A stagnant buzzing filled my ear.

"Pick up, pick up, pick up," I muttered to myself. My breath came out in bursts of white, like ghosts surrounding me.

The sharp ring rang three times before the call was finally picked up.

"Sylvia?" Kieran answered, voice groggy and tired. "Are you okay?"

"I think you were right," I said. I bet he liked it when I said that. Then again, I thought I said it pretty often.

"What?"

"I think I'm a little drunk." I kept walking, swiping the hair away from my face as the wind blew. "Just a little though. I guess that just means tipsy, right?"

He snorted, his voice relaxing back into a gruff, sleepy tone. "I figured."

I hummed. Finally, I came to a stop. I swayed on my feet in the cold, back and forth in the middle of the street, trying to send some heat down to my toes.

Over the phone, Kieran started to rustle out from what I imagined was his bed. "Sylvia?"

"Yeah?"

"Where are you?"

I looked down the familiar street. "You were also right earlier about how I should've worn a coat. It really is cold out here."

"You're outside? Seriously, Sylv? It's the middle of winter. Are you walking home?" He shot question after question.

"I didn't want to go home," I admitted. "Not yet."

"Where are you?" he asked once more, a little agitated.

"You're right, concerned Nancy. I should just go home," I sighed. Though I really didn't want to do that. In my heart of hearts, after all, I technically was home. Or as close to the feeling of home as I might ever get.

Kieran grunted. "Stay where you are and don't move."

I smiled. So worried and irritated—when he was like this, Kieran's voice turned low and forceful. "Why?"

"Why? Because, Sylv, I'll be there in a second. I don't want you to turn into a Popsicle. That's all we need—for you to freeze to death. The police will see your last phone call was to me."

"That's a tad self-serving."

"It's *you need to get your ass out of a blizzard* serving. Plus, you know I'm too pretty for prison."

I had told him that before.

"How long do you think it takes for someone to fully freeze

into the previously mentioned Popsicle form if they lie down?" I ask, pressing my lips together so that I didn't laugh.

"Don't you dare lie down!"

Still standing, I looked up. "The sky has big, dark, puffy clouds."

"Do. Not. Move," Kieran commanded. "Are you at least still wearing something warm?"

"This is me we're talking about. Of course not."

Another grumble.

"But what are *you* wearing, Kieran Rose?" I couldn't help myself this time. I chuckled.

"Stop. I'm putting on my shoes now."

"I always wondered if you were a boxers or briefs guy."

My friend made an exasperated sound. *Friend.*

My chest rattled as I took another deep breath.

"Just hold on," said Kieran.

"Knowing would make getting your Christmas gift a whole lot easier," I said simply.

The front door of the house I stood in front of whipped open. Kieran took a step outside before he saw me. His shoulders slumped in between relief and irritation.

I stared at him and smirked. He looked adorable in his plaid pajamas and unlaced snow boots. He hit the End Call button on his phone, pulling it out from where it had been tucked between his cheek and shoulder.

"What are you doing?" He stomped toward me.

I slipped my phone back into my pocket. "I told you, I didn't want to just go home."

"Did your night with Dylan not go to plan?"

I shrugged. "I also wanted to see you."

Shaking his head at the whole scenario, Kieran looped an arm around my shoulders before twisting us back toward the front door he had come from. "Come on. You're freezing."

"But not in Popsicle form."

"Not yet. We couldn't have that." His boots squished in turned-over slush, leaving heavy footprints. "You cause me stress, you know that?"

"Sorry."

"No, you're not."

I didn't correct him. He was right. Mostly right.

Wrapping my arms around my best friend, I held on tight so I wouldn't fall up the slick steps of the Rose house. It looked even more classically beautiful in the light of yellow streetlamps.

Perfect home. Perfect life. Perfect Kieran.

"I'm not perfect," he muttered.

Did I say that aloud? Maybe I was a little tipsier than previously thought. But it felt nice now that I was with him. I felt light. Floaty.

Kieran hefted me closer as if he was trying to pick up all my body weight. We passed the kitchen and went upstairs to his room. The moment I stepped through the doorway, the scent of clean sheets and Kieran settled over me.

"You should know that by now," Kieran said.

Walking over to his bed, I jumped in, curling up with his blankets and pillow. I breathed in the sweetly distinct comfort.

Kieran stared at me for a long moment before he climbed in next to me. He pulled up the big comforter until we were in our own cozy nest. "You're so odd."

"You should know that by now too."

"Trust me, I do," he said quietly. "You didn't answer. How was the rest of the party and your ... *time* with Dylan?"

I didn't really want to talk about that. However, then again, I didn't know what I wanted to talk about. I had gotten here, and Kieran was back in front of me, and I was warm with him. That was all that mattered.

"How long do you think until Gabe officially proposes to Jenna now?" I asked.

Kieran raised his eyebrows, knowing I was changing the conversation. "He was already planning to propose to her at graduation."

"Do you think he'll still hold out until then?"

Kieran shook his head. He nestled farther down into his pillows until we faced each other. Our noses nearly touched. "Absolutely not."

"That was really nice, what you said to Gabe before, about being there for him and everything about him becoming a dad," I whispered.

Kieran pondered, in deep thought. "Would that be so bad? Being in Gabe's position?"

"Pregnant your senior year?" I didn't need to think hard. "Kind of."

"No, I mean, having your life right in front of you, ready to go. You have purpose and love and a family already. That's kind of great, I think." Kieran's voice drifted off.

"It could be," I said, though I wasn't sure I agreed. It sounded terrifying.

His eyes flickered back and forth between my eyes and lower, as if trying to figure out what I was going to say next, focused on my lips.

"You didn't answer me before," said Kieran.

"What was the question?" I asked, knowing what he was talking about already.

"Dylan." He repeated his question, voice sharp, "How was it?"

I focused on him. "Wasn't the same without you there."

"You were getting on just fine."

I narrowed my eyes. "Are you jealous?"

"No."

My heart picked up a beat as I settled my voice between teasing and honesty. It was a very fine line between us. "A little?" I held up my fingers in demonstration.

He shut his eyes, shaking his head. Neither thing helped cover the tiny smirk on his lips as he turned to lie on his side.

"Thanks for coming to find me before I turned into a Popsicle."

"Always, Sylv." He nodded. "When I tell you to call me, I mean it."

"Kieran."

"Hmm?"

"Nothing happened, you know, between me and Dylan," I said.

"It's fine if it did," he replied quickly. "I would be a hypocrite to get all bent out of shape about it when you know about Amy and me, which is ... what it is."

"We didn't do anything," I repeated. "I mean it."

"I believe you."

"You do?" I asked. *Good.* "At first, I thought I wanted to."

"Why?" he asked.

"Because we were at karaoke, and then we were back there at the party, and everyone was having a good time."

"Were you having a good time?"

"For a while, I thought I was." I licked my lips, leaning into the part of my brain that I could still call inebriated. "But I couldn't stop thinking about you and looking at you, and I knew that I should. Stop, that is."

Kieran's eyes widened. Without his glasses on, I could see his reactions plain as day. His lips parted. In terror? In understanding? I wasn't sure which one I preferred. All I knew was, I didn't like the way my heart raced.

"Sylvia ..."

"I think we should have sex."

His eyes popped open wide. "What?"

My heart started to calm down. This was reasonable, rational even. "I think we should do it together."

"Now?"

"No time like the present."

"Sylvia."

"Come on," I whispered. My fingers traced over his cheek. *God.* Even his freckles were oddly adorable.

"You. Me. It wouldn't be weird. It'd probably be better this way for the two of us together. We could get it over with. Like you said."

"Like I said?"

"A year could change everything." I repeated his words when we had opened our acceptance letters. Or lack of acceptance. "What if I don't see you again? What if something happens?"

It couldn't change us. *It couldn't.* But if it did...

I huffed a laugh into his neck, feeling the way his body responded with a row of goose bumps.

"Sylvia."

"We should do it."

"Nothing is going to happen."

I expected him to pull away. Instead, Kieran reached out and pulled me into his arms. He wrapped me up in him until my face was pressed into the crook of his neck. Sweet cinnamon and whatever deodorant he was wearing mixed together.

I breathed it in. "But what if it does and you leave me behind and—"

"You're drunk."

"I'm not that drunk."

"The fact that you have to say that makes me think otherwise. You won't even remember this. Sleep, okay? We'll talk about it in the morning."

I moaned pitifully into his ear. I burrowed into his sweet warmth, making my way down toward his chest, where I could hear his heart beating a steady tune.

Would we talk about it, really? Us? I wasn't so sure.

Nonetheless, unable to argue, I curled up until I felt like I was making a special hole just for myself in the center of his chest.

The next morning, when we got up, his mother was unamused that we had found ourselves in the same bed yet again. Her look said more than her stern lecture did as we sat down at the table.

Neither of us brought up what we had talked about last night. Kieran probably thought it was just as he'd said as we ate Cheerios out of the box. I had been drunk. I had no recollection of any of the crazy words that had come out of my mouth after midnight.

But, oh, I remembered it all.

TWENTY-FIVE

NOW

MR. BENSON WRAPPED up the tree in record time. Once we drove home, we untangled the tree from the roof. Lights were on in the main house, his mom likely popping in and out from the shop during the day. A cat lounged in the one side window, catching the hint of sun peeking through the heavy gray clouds.

"You guys got a cat?"

"What? Oh, yeah. We got the cat for my mom a few years ago when she was in treatment. She said she always wanted one."

"That's kind of nice." I cocked my head at the way Kieran's shoulders had slumped when I brought it up.

Maybe it made him think back to when his mom had been in treatment or when she had been sick and no one knew what was going to happen so getting a cat wasn't a bad idea. Maybe it made him think about how I hadn't been here during it all. Because I hadn't been.

He probably was starting to remember just how terrible of a human being I was, let alone a friend.

"It hates me."

"What?" I snapped out of my thoughts, immediately seeing Kieran's drawn expression.

"The cat. The thing hates me," said Kieran.

"You're kidding." Slowly, I couldn't help it. I started to smile.

"I'm not."

"And here I thought you two would be BFFs."

Kieran always struck me as a cat person. The one at the used bookstore in town sure seemed to like him enough.

"Clean, subtle in terms of affection, indoor people ..."

He rolled his eyes as we passed the tree in the backyard. "It encouraged me to move out."

"Aw, poor Kieran," I teased. "No longer the favorite."

He snorted. We paused before the stairs leading up to the second floor of the garage. "Ready to lift?"

As ready as I was going to be.

"Ready, set, lift."

Both of us dragged the tree up the stairs. By the time we reached the top, I felt as if I had run a mile. My breath turned labored. With a push, Kieran put the tree upright against the one wall and twisted the frame into place. A hundred needles fell, scattering to the floor.

Both of us looked at what we had brought into the house with renewed appreciation and confusion.

"There, see?" Kieran took a step back to look at our new addition to the holiday. "Not so bad."

"It's really the ugliest tree I think I've ever seen."

Kieran barked a laugh. "Yeah, probably."

On the floor of the garage apartment, it once again felt like I had entered the coziest cave I could've ever imagined. The lights were dim, and the Christmas tree had the white—not multicol-ored—lights twisted around its branches, giving off an efferves-cent glow.

We decorated the tree to the light sound of Christmas music Kieran had put on the radio. Old handmade ornaments and decorations I remembered from growing up were slowly added to the branches.

Kieran bent down as he looked inside the final box, peeking inside to the ornaments. "Okay, maybe you're right. This is a lot of crap, isn't it?"

He pulled out the second strand of lights, though with how small the tree was, I doubted that we'd need it. I reached for them anyway and picked apart the knots.

"I really didn't realize you'd moved out of your house."

"To my parents' garage." Kieran rolled his eyes, embar-rassed. "It's not like I moved across the country or anything."

"Big step up in the world," I said anyway. "Or a step to becoming a serial killer. Either or."

"Definitely not my job of choice."

"I was always the spider killer out of the two of us."

"You were," he agreed. "Still watching too many true crime docs?"

I shook my head, focused down on my task. It was easier to talk this way, with somewhere else for my eyes to focus when not drawn up to his face. "Not really anymore."

"No?" He raised his eyebrows, a flicker of surprise taking over his face. It might have been the first real reaction he'd had to me all day.

"After a while, Ezra got sick of me waking him up because I was too freaked out to go to bed."

Back when I had first started watching the documentaries that were on late at night after sitcoms, I couldn't help but keep watching. The background noise had turned into a sort of deranged obsession. Afterward, I'd lie in bed, convinced that every creak in the floorboard was someone coming to rape and murder me, and for some reason, I doubted they would leave a very good ransom note. I'd end up calling Kieran, who would laugh sleepily at me but nonetheless stay on the phone until I fell asleep.

My mother hadn't been very happy about the phone bills I racked up back then.

"Ezra." Kieran repeated the name. "Your boyfriend."

Definitely not. Yet I paused. Kieran already looked at me like I was a wreck. I was. It didn't mean I was ready to admit it proudly out loud.

"You're pretty serious now, huh?"

I took a deep breath. "I wouldn't say that."

"It's been a few years, hasn't it?" he asked. "That's, what, close to marriage material?"

"It's been about two years," I corrected, though in Marshall Falls time, we were already married.

We were the opposite of serious now though.

The easy conversation slowed back into a lull.

Finishing up my strand of lights, I laid them out straight so they wouldn't tangle again. I smoothed them down over the carpet before looking up to Kieran. He was doing the same, and then he found the plug on the one end and set it around the side of the tree so that we would know where to start.

"It's really weird, seeing you here instead of at the house," I said.

"It's weird, seeing you too."

We stared at each other. Finally, I looked away and grabbed the bag of tinsel off the coffee table. Neither of us had ventured to touch it yet.

"Well, I guess it's about time to add some of our lovely gift from Mr. Benson."

"Sylvia, don't—"

I yanked on the packaging. Instead of peeling open, the entire thing exploded.

Tinsel went everywhere. Tiny, iridescent strips of plastic coated my legs and stuck to Kieran's face.

His eyes were closed, and then he blinked one eye open and then the other. At least it wasn't glitter.

I pressed my lips together so I wouldn't laugh. "Well, don't you look like you're getting into the spirit."

"Look at what you've done."

"Tinsel can fix everything," I mocked, my voice deeper than before.

Both of us burst into a round of laughter. It felt good, laughing as the shiny pieces of tinsel stuck to us and the carpet, where it had exploded.

Kieran could only shake his head, but said nothing about the mess. "You stay here and keep decorating. I'll check on the food."

I'd almost forgotten about the boiling pot he had started on the stove a while ago. For some reason, I couldn't wrap my head around the fact that he was cooking dinner or anything for me right now.

A flash of light crossed over my face, and I looked up toward the window as it continued past the detached garage.

"Probably just Mom getting home from the shop," said Kieran, noting my interest.

With a brush of his hands against his jeans to disperse some of the tinsel, he headed toward the small kitchen. Opening the drawers, he dropped utensils on the counter before continuing to rifle through the cabinets for a colander. The pot behind him bubbled.

I couldn't pull my eyes away from the main house. Kieran's mom was inside, right now. Lori was there.

His mom, who he had begged me to pick up the phone for. Four years ago, he had just wanted me to pick up the phone so that he could tell me what happened and let himself cry.

But I didn't. I hadn't answered the stupid phone, and I had tried to tell myself that it was the right thing to do.

But I still couldn't come up with any good reason.

I hadn't answered the phone.

My jaw clenched.

Kieran wrung his hands once before letting them fall to his sides, emotionless, as if he knew exactly what I was thinking about.

"Kieran."

"Huh?" He braced himself on the countertop as he watched me pick at another ornament clip, making sure that it was tight enough on the bulb.

"I just ... I missed you, is all," I said quietly. "Sorry, I shouldn't have said that."

He tipped his head in a single nod. "I, uh, missed you too," he said, though his words were short.

Gently, I lifted the final ornament and clipped it to the branch, careful that the needles didn't crumble under the weight. Backing up, I collided with the small couch in the center of the room. I sat down as I looked at the tree.

Kieran clicked off the stove and dumped the water out of the pot.

I just kept looking at the tree. It was an ugly tree. Even the tinsel hadn't fixed it, but it helped. Every little piece helped.

"Here." Kieran held two bowls, handing me one.

I reveled in how warm the ceramic felt in my hands.

"You're right. It's not a terrible tree," I said. "Just an awful one."

"Eh." Kieran stabbed a few noodles and shoved them into his cheek as he talked. "I think we could've done worse."

There was no doubt in that.

"Thank you."

"For what?"

"For getting a tree with me. I seriously didn't plan on even attempting it."

"You know I can't resist a good list."

That I did. Even slightly wine-tipsy me had known it.

The carbs sitting in my bowl stared back at me with garlic, butter-filled glory.

"Is there a reason you are looking down at your pasta like it just delivered bad news?" Kieran asked, sitting down next to me.

I shook my head.

"I've gotten better at cooking over the past few years, so I hope that's not it."

"No," I said. "You're a better cook than me. I just have a lot on my mind. I should probably figure out where I plan on living now, huh?"

Kieran nodded, as if he understood and was debating something.

"I also haven't had pasta in a while," I admitted.

"Why not? Hasn't that always been, like, your main food group?" he asked around a bite.

"My ... Ezra was very worried about my carb intake."

"What?"

I shrugged.

"You sure know how to pick 'em," Kieran mumbled.

I remembered the first time he had said something similar to me. He was right then too.

"That's the stupidest thing I've ever heard."

It sounded pretty stupid to me now too.

"I can't believe you haven't eaten pasta for, what, a year?"

Maybe longer.

I mixed all the seasonings together on top with my fork.

"Well, we'll fix that, won't we?"

At least that was one thing.

"Christmas pasta?" I lifted a forkful to him in a sort of cheer.

He lifted his back, clinking overstuffed forks. "Christmas pasta."

Along with the bakery, Kieran had also seemed to inherit his mother's amazing talent and taste with all types of food. I stared at him as he smiled down at his bowl at the tiny happy sounds I made with each bite.

"Thank you again."

"It's just a bowl of noodles," he said.

I took another bite. I meant to thank him for everything today. I still couldn't comprehend it all—that I had woken up this morning, still a little drunk, and now, I was sitting here in front of a tree with Kieran. It made no sense.

I needed to stop worrying about it. All I needed to think about was this pasta right here. Another pleasureful noise escaped me. I barely had to chew as the noodle melted on my tongue. So much better than those stupid strings of zucchini Ezra always said tasted basically the same. They hadn't, just like his morning juices he'd tried to get me on didn't taste like fruit. It'd tasted like licking the underside of a lawnmower.

Unable to stop himself this time as I chowed down, Kieran chuckled. He peeked up from twirling his fork. "Now, I know what I'm making you for every meal for the rest of time."

"And I'll never complain."

After we finished eating—I had eaten seconds and nearly thirds—Kieran cleaned up and settled back on the couch. He didn't ask what I planned to do next or what was next on my made-up list but shifted over on the couch.

I sat next to him. He reached for the blanket behind us and draped it over our laps once a movie started playing on the television next to the Christmas tree.

What a picture-perfect little home he had made for himself. All by himself, unless Amy ...

I shook my head, letting myself bask in the silence for a little while. I didn't want to think, and this might be the closest I would get to it.

My eyes fluttered shut, then opened again. I must've fallen onto Kieran's shoulder at some point. If possible, the place seemed even darker than before, and I must've missed a crucial plot point in the movie because the two main characters were currently yelling at one another.

"You okay there?" Kieran curved his head to look at me.

"Tired."

I didn't move. I didn't want to lose his touch yet, so I kept my eyes closed.

Opening them was a risk I didn't want to take. Plus, then I'd be alone again.

And when I was next to Kieran, it became so clear to me that I might not have been meant to be alone.

"You seem ..." Kieran watched me as he carefully shifted, stretching his one arm out. I must've been crushing him for some time, but he hadn't jostled me once.

"What?"

"I noticed when I took you home last night."

I narrowed my eyes. "What, Kieran?"

"I thought that you said you were just home for the holidays."

"I am."

"You brought home all your stuff though," he said.

I had nothing to say because he was mostly right. I had shoved all I could into those suitcases, only to then realize that it wasn't much.

"And you brought it all here. I wasn't snooping. I just

noticed," said Kieran. When I still didn't respond, he went on. "I can tell that something more is up. You don't seem happy."

I shrugged, trying to play it off. "What is happy, really?"

"For a minute there, earlier when we got the tree and then again, oddly, when we saw Amy at the school, I thought maybe you were, but ..." He shook his head, looking me up and down now. "Can you just tell me?"

"Tell you what?"

"What's going on, Sylvia?" he asked, his voice soft, careful.

He didn't seem accusing when my eyes were still clenched tightly shut.

"It's nothing. I'm just home. Like you said, I'm home for the holidays, and I'm supposed to go back to the city and then ..." I drifted off, not sure where I was going with all this anymore.

Hiding everything after today felt sort of pointless. But also, it was my last shred of dignity, wasn't it?

I shook my head. All we did was talk about me.

I wanted Kieran to know that I was here. I was here for him, even when I wasn't when it mattered, and maybe that was all that mattered, and nothing would be the same, but I didn't want to be that person. I had to prove to someone I wasn't that person.

"What about you? What else is new? I'm sure you have more to tell me if you are willing."

"I work, and I come home." He shrugged. "My life is an endless loop. Tell me what's going on with you."

I hesitated. If he wanted to know, I guessed there really wasn't a point to holding it all back anymore. "At least you still have a job."

His eyes widened and voice rose as he shifted, forcing me to open my eyes again. "You lost your job? Sylvia, is that what's going on?"

I looked away, huffing.

"What are you talking about?" asked Kieran. "Please, just tell me."

"I can't."

"Why?"

Because it was clear that he cared and was upset. I didn't need to make him more upset with me. "Then, it was all for nothing. All of this was all for nothing, and you'll throw it back in my face."

"When have I ever thrown anything in your face?" Kieran looked more disgusted than upset now. I wasn't sure if that was better.

"I lied," I finally whispered. The weight on my chest didn't dissipate. If anything, it grew. "Or I kept things from you now today. I've wanted to tell you."

"You did?"

I nodded. "Because I really can't do it anymore. My body hurts, and I'm tired. I absolutely hate it all. Everything. This stupid life."

"I get that."

He probably did.

"But at least you didn't have to walk in on your boyfriend cheating on you."

"What?"

Another casual attempt at exposing my truth might as well have hit him like a freight train.

"Or your girlfriend. Whatever." I closed my eyes and opened them, trying not to blink. I saw it all over again.

Kieran latched on to one thing. "You and Ezra aren't together anymore?"

"He broke up with me. Or I broke up with him." The details really weren't all that clear. I wasn't even important enough to have him respond to what was so clearly the truth for longer than I had wanted to admit when he wasn't even hiding it. "He was seeing someone else. He'd been seeing her for a while, I think."

"That asshole."

I shrugged.

"No, he is. Only an idiot would cheat on you."

"He was an idiot," I agreed.

"Clearly." Kieran shook his head, as if none of it made sense. "Like, really? He didn't realize what he had right in front of him. You're smart—"

"Please, I'm not that smart."

"And creative."

"I haven't written in over a year."

"What?" Kieran's forehead creased.

"I tried, but I'm dried up."

"Are you saying you're old again?" He narrowed his eyes.

"No," I groaned. "There just aren't any more words."

"I really doubt that's true."

"It is. Even at my job, before they kicked me to the curb, they knew it. No matter how many ideas I came up with that could've made it into that stupid magazine ... nothing. I was basically doing the job of an intern."

"And what was that? Didn't you proofread when you were an intern for that other site?" Kieran asked.

I had, which made this even worse. I was surprised he even remembered what I had done—all my extra side gigs and internships—before I thought I had my big editorial break.

I peeked up at him. "I was a sandwich girl."

"A what?" Before Kieran could help himself, a laugh burst forth.

"Don't laugh at me."

"I'm not. I promise I'm not." He was still laughing. "But you need to tell me what a sandwich girl is before I picture you standing on the street corner, wearing one of those ridiculous hoagie costumes."

"I ..." I took a deep breath. "I picked up disgusting, bland sandwiches for everyone in the office who wanted them nearly every day."

Kieran laughed again. "With your fear of touching deli meat?"

"I know. It was like a horror story."

Serving out sandwich after sandwich and knowing everyone's nauseating lunchtime orders was a nightmare that I had lived daily for the past two years at least.

Why didn't I leave?

I even started to chuckle, holding it in until my chest was shaking from the effort. "I handed out sandwiches and occasionally made copies. I wasn't even writing. I sucked at the one thing they had hired me for."

The laughter started to slow.

"So, yeah, that's where my life is at. It's one big shit show, covered with mayo, basically." I put a hand to my forehead, leaning down on it so my hair could hide my shame. "Since the moment I went to New York, I was obviously destined to be a failure."

"That's not true."

It was kind of true. "It didn't take much to see it."

"You were really good at covering it up," said Kieran.

I had tried. I tried really hard to make it seem like everything was good and fine—*great*. Even when it wasn't any of those things. I would say otherwise on phone calls. I would tell people the good stories. Sometimes, I'd even tell stories that weren't mine, that I had heard from other coworkers, which would be sure to cause a chuckle out of my mother. But half the time, they were dreams.

They had just been stories.

"I really didn't know, Sylv. At least not completely. I thought after your first year, things got better."

"How could you have known?" I picked at my nails until all the nail polish was nearly completely scraped away. "It's not something I prefer to broadcast."

"To be honest, I always wondered why you stopped your blog after you got your big break and everything. I kind of worried about it for a little while. You stopped posting on social media and online. I stopped hearing from you."

For so many reasons.

"I worried that you lost yourself somewhere along the way."

Both of us were more casual and relaxed than we had been all day.

"Life hasn't been all roses around here either." Kieran smirked at his own pun after a moment of silence. "Like I said, I go to work at the bakery or do odd jobs around town with my dad. I come home. I cook and bake and watch terrible television."

Sounded like my life the past few days.

Kieran shrugged. "I might be happy enough, but it's still not everything we, as kids, planned for our lives, is it?"

No, it isn't.

"Then again, at least I didn't turn into a sandwich girl."

I wanted to do something, to laugh or to cry. Maybe I'd even scream. I had plenty to scream over.

Instead, I shoved Kieran back into the pillows. I shook my head at him.

There was failure and hope and loneliness and the fear that I had messed up not only the past few years, but also most of my life with decisions I thought would lead me toward something extraordinary.

Only they hadn't.

I took another deep breath, swallowing down the overwhelming coating of upset stuck in the back of my throat. "I never understood it, so I never asked."

"Asked what?"

"Why didn't you go to the big school?"

"Oh." Kieran seemed shocked by the question. He took a deep breath as he considered his answer.

I curled my legs up and inward toward my chest until I hugged them. "You applied to so many places. Even that one private university that you loved after your tour—that was your number one choice, and you got in. You got in everywhere. I didn't. So, why didn't you go? Why didn't you leave here? It wasn't like we were holding out for each other. We still didn't go to the same place."

"No, we didn't." Kieran focused on me. "I think that's just what you never got, Sylvia."

"What?"

"That in the end, then and still, I liked it here," said Kieran. "All my life, even when we were making plans to run away and see the world, I always figured I would come back. It was comfortable, and I know that's kind of stupid. I see that now. But I liked Marshall Falls the entire time, growing up, even if you didn't. So, after weighing my options and seeing my mom sad about me leaving, I stayed. I never regretted it. Not for a long while anyway."

"But you did regret it."

"I still do. Sometimes. I've never really been the hero in my own story, have I? That was you. I never even gave myself the chance."

TWENTY-SIX

BEFORE

I SHUT the mailbox and stared down at the piece of paper in my hands.

I blinked, not quite comprehending. The envelope was full. The paper was thick. I barely paused before I tore the seal where I stood right on the edge of the driveway. All that mattered was the crisp tearing sound as the slightly damp envelope ripped open.

Inside, I still expected to see a short, formal letter. It was going to read just like all the others had that I received.

Dear Ms. Sylvia Calasis,

After careful consideration, we regret to inform you ...

I didn't call Kieran or save it in case he had some more acceptances coming in from schools so that we could open the envelopes together, much to our bittersweet sadness when we realized again that Kieran was the smart one, the funny one, the one everyone wanted at their school and I wasn't.

No. This time, after seeing the three bold purple letters branding the outside left corner of the piece of mail, I couldn't wait.

I could still hear my mother's voice ringing through my head from two years ago while my parents had bickered back and forth. *"There's no way Sylvia is ever going to get into someplace like Harvard."*

I would've been lucky to get into the nearest community college.

But I wasn't going to the nearest community college. I wasn't going to go anywhere near here, like I had given myself over to the idea of, with or without Kieran, who didn't seem to care much either after the third or fourth rejection letter I had received.

Unlike then, however, this wasn't a rejection.

Dear Ms. Sylvia Calasis,

After careful consideration, we are pleased to inform you ...

I was going to NYU.

I BLINKED MY EYES OPEN. The furnace still flickered with warmth. The lights on the tree were still on. I was curled up on my side. A thick blanket was tucked around me, and Kieran lay next to me. We were tightly packed together on the couch whether or not we had intended to be.

After we had started talking again, more had come up. Stories, honesties ...

We put another movie on, but at some point, the two of us must've fallen asleep that way. It was just like we used to do when we were kids and I didn't want to go home. Because deep down, back then, I had known I was already there.

I stared at him in the dark. My heart ached.

Carefully, I adjusted myself until I was out of his arms. Both wrapped around my shoulders, bear-hugging me to his chest. Kieran's nose twitched, as if he was upset about something in his sleep. He sighed and stretched without waking.

Reaching for my phone on the coffee table, I settled back into my spot. Opening my internet browser, I paused, looking back at the website, which was still an open tab.

The List.

It needed more than a little work to update it from where it was, and it would be easier done on my computer, but I started to move some things around and rework the graphics. I chose new colors and updated my profile page. Surprisingly enough, a few things did change. I had a few more bylines, however piti- ful, to add since I had been twenty and last cared to update it.

More than a few, it had turned out, though they stopped around four years ago.

Slowly but surely, *The List* I had made in high school and updated daily was almost looking as if it was taking on a new life as a full website rather than a single-paged blog. By the time I looked up at the clock again, over an hour had passed.

Working on it was almost ... fun.

When I turned my head toward the window, the tree outside shook from the wind. A light was on in the main house kitchen. Or had it always been on? I didn't think it had been.

Before I realized what I was doing, I carefully set my phone back down on the table and stood. I reached for the coat next to the door. Not mine, but Kieran's still, I realized after it was already over my shoulders. It was wide and smelled like butter- cream frosting since I had taken it off in the bakery earlier.

I glanced back toward Kieran, unmoving as he slept and looking oddly comfortable. I didn't want to just leave him there. What if he woke up? What if he thought I had snuck out in the middle of the night and left him there without warning after everything today?

A form moved past the kitchen window of the main house.

Holding myself tight, I moved down the steps and toward the back door.

Taking a deep breath, I paused outside in the cold.

Come on, Sylvia. Put on your big-girl panties and become a goddamn badass woman already, like you planned to.

When I knocked on the glass slider, the woman inside

jumped. Her eyes caught me outside. Her shoulders visibly relaxed as she opened the door and waved me in.

"Get in here before you freeze to death," she scolded.

I stepped through, looking around the house. The space smelled the same, though the kitchen looked like it had new countertops. Or maybe I'd just never noticed them before until now.

"I thought I saw you up there with Kieran," Lori whispered. She waved a hand for me not just to stand in front of the door, though kept her voice quiet. Kieran's dad was probably asleep. "Do you want some tea? I was just making some."

"I'm okay."

"Are you sure?" Lori raised her thin eyebrows.

I hesitated. "All right."

"Good." Taking the bubbling kettle off the stove, she poured the hot water into two mugs. "I've been having trouble sleeping through the night. I've made it a bit of a habit. Tea and a book. Of course, my taste isn't the best."

I glanced over at the breakfast nook, where a pink bodice-ripper sat with a creased spine. On the cover, the heroine swooned into the hero's arms.

"I love those."

"Then, maybe I have better taste in reading material than I thought."

She passed me a mug of tea. I carefully took it, following her toward where she must've been sitting. "Sit. Make yourself comfortable."

I sat down.

"I always wondered where Kieran got his love of reading from," I said after another minute.

"My mother and I dropped him off at the library probably a few too many times during their summer reading activities. Instead of coming back to find him doing arts and crafts, he'd always be holed up somewhere, at least three picture books deep."

Both of us chuckled at the image. Kieran had probably held up the colorful pages close to his long eyelashes to make out each word. Another reason it had taken everyone so long to notice their charming, gifted boy had been seeing the world in a blur until the second grade.

Lori studied me as I looked toward the floor and took another deep breath, but I didn't blow it out to cool down the tea. I set the mug down on the edge of the table.

Lori took the chance to reach out, her hand setting itself on top of mine. "It's good to see you. You look gorgeous, as always."

"Thanks."

"Of course," she said. Her blue eyes, the same dark and stormy shade as Kieran's, peered at me with nothing but kindness. I couldn't understand it. "I'm also very glad that you came to see Kieran. I think he missed you."

"I highly doubt that," I whispered.

"I don't."

I was going to argue with her until I thought better, pausing. "Honestly, I feel a little bad about it."

"What? Coming to see him?" Her eyebrows pinched together.

"And you. I'm sure that he would've been happy if he never saw me again after ..."

He had even said he never wanted to see me, and I thought I was starting to understand why. Until today anyway, when everything started to feel, well, nice again. It would've been a lot less painful, maybe for both of us, if I hadn't come back or spoke to him or made this silly list to weasel my way back into his days. It was a recipe for heartbreak, wasn't it?

All over again.

Lori shook her head. "I very much do not believe that for a

second. I hope you don't. He loves you, no matter what happens. I will admit that I never got the full story, but I've started to piece it together."

Even more of a reason I didn't understand why Lori didn't completely hate me right now.

"I've always believed some people come into our lives for a reason," she said. "And I believe that you came into my son's life for a reason. You showed up here at the age of seven like a hurricane and drove yourself into his life when he needed someone more than maybe either of us will ever know. And you're back here. I don't mean to say that you are soulmates or anything like that, Sylvia, but I've never seen anything as close to soulmates as you two."

From where she spouted her truth into her cool tea, his mom lifted her gaze back up toward mine. At some point, my eyes turned cloudy and filled with tears.

"Oh, honey."

I put up a hand and shook my head. "I'm so sorry."

"You don't have to be sorry." She pulled me in closer to her.

"I am though. I'm so sorry. Kieran called me all those times after he found out you were sick, and I couldn't bring myself to answer the phone. I couldn't bring myself to call him back. But even after everything, he called me."

He still trusted me.

"I was such a coward for him and for you. To think if I wasn't here and something happened..." I could barely forgive myself now, let alone if the worst had happened. Everything rushed to the surface, and I couldn't help myself as I hiccuped. I leaned my forehead down into the palm of my head. "I'm just— everything isn't how it should be, and I know it's all my fault."

"Everything?"

"Basically."

"Now, that's impressive."

"What?"

She shook her head. "Everything is your fault? It's your fault that you came here to Marshall Falls and met my son? Is it your fault that you two became such wonderful friends? Is it your fault that my cancer came back? Is it your fault that it looks like you are falling apart and my Kieran has looked about the same since you were last here years ago? All that and everything else in the world is your fault too? My goodness, Sylvia, I didn't know you were so powerful."

I rolled my eyes. "You don't get what I mean."

"I do."

"You don't even know everything," I argued, sniffing.

Lori took a deep breath. "Tell me then."

I stared at her. Then, I told her everything. I was unable to hole it up inside of myself any longer. I told her everything I had told Kieran, and more. I told her every little piece of myself, as if I had come to a midnight confessional.

I told her that when I had met Kieran, I had known that he was going to be my best friend.

I told her that when we had gone to camp for the first time, I had looked at him next to the sunset, like in one of those unironic romance films, and knew I wanted to kiss him.

I told her that when Kieran had started dating Amy and other girls, I had known that it wasn't just a silly crush I had on him.

I told her that I had been devastated when I left for school, and finally, it set in that Kieran wasn't going with me. I told her it was then that I had really realized that I was in love with him and how many times I had tried to let him go. That I'd been with so many guys who I thought could truly, always tell that there was someone else my heart was set on, and that was why they often treated me so badly—to punish me. Or maybe, like Kieran had insisted, I knew how to pick 'em just right.

Because he had hurt me too.

I told her about what had happened four years ago, and by the end of everything, I felt like I was out of breath and rubbed raw from every moment of every day I had spent with Kieran all my life and every second I had spent without him.

"You need to tell him."

"He has a life, Lori."

He had friends and worked at the bakery, and if he just gave it another chance, I was sure he could be happy with someone else, someone better, like Amy, who Mina had said looked picture-perfect next to him.

I swallowed. "I can't."

"All I'm going to say, Sylvia, is, if there is anything I've learned as an aging woman who has seen her life and everyone she loves flash before her eyes, there's nothing I wouldn't give to keep them and hold on. But it's up to you. Because you're right. My son has grown in the past few years, more than I think anyone has, I've noticed. That's partially because of me and my illness, but you played a big part as well. I'd hate for you to have to witness someone else reap the benefits."

TWENTY-EIGHT

BEFORE

"THE GIRL in the room next door to me has now officially committed hall-cest with the majority of the guys," I said through the phone. I pressed it closer to my ear. That way, I could almost feel like I could hear Kieran shaking his head at my change of conversation. "I think there's only one guy left for her to completely conquer the entire hallway, and he's gay."

"Hall-cest?" Kieran asked.

"It's like incest, but with the people on your floor. Ultimately still awkward and a little disgusting," I explained.

"It sounds like it."

"I wish I had that confidence because, seriously, she doesn't even flinch when she walks down the hallway in her towel, knowing that nearly everyone now has seen her naked at this point."

Kieran chuckled. "You do have that weird mole on your butt."

"I do not." I gasped in outrage.

"Sure you don't."

"What else is new?" Kieran asked. He might've already asked, but we still had at least a few more minutes before we had to hang up.

"Besides the fact that you sound like you've become a part of the living dead?" I questioned.

"Besides that," he groaned. "I need a coffee."

"Since when do you drink coffee?" I asked.

"Since last week. It has been an enlightening new hobby of mine."

"Drinking coffee is a hobby now?"

"If it isn't, it should be. There's one good place to get it on campus, and I have to basically hike there before the afternoon work study students take over. Then, the coffee sucks."

I barked a laugh. A few people in the hallway glanced at me where I sat on the bench near my last lecture of the day. I had one more class today in an hour, but I didn't want to leave the building and have to come right back. Even though I was kind of hungry.

I tucked the phone between my shoulder and ear as I turned my book bag over and rummaged through my bag. I swore I had left a protein bar in there somewhere.

I covered my mouth and tried to keep my voice low. "You're ridiculous."

"And sleep-deprived. What's new?" he repeated as he walked wherever he was going on campus.

A few voices drifted in the background. I listened to his very unathletic-sounding huffs and puffs.

"I think I completely flunked a test today."

"Great. Then, we both are right on schedule," sighed Kieran.

"You?" I asked, astounded.

"Yeah, I don't know, but it definitely didn't feel good when I walked it up to her desk and walked out. Barely anyone else was finished."

"Maybe you just knew the material."

"Maybe I just thought I knew the material and thought I would be able to breeze by in English."

"I doubt that."

If there was anyone who could succeed at a college-level English course without trying, let alone any of the other classes, it was Kieran.

"We'll see," he sighed.

"Your call has been forwarded to an automated voice message system."

"Do you regret being at home yet?"

"Nah, I end up on campus most days anyway. They have a special lounge for commuters, and the couch is surprisingly comfortable," said Kieran.

"I'm sure other people thought that, too, and have done things other than sleep on it."

He groaned. "I've been trying not to think about that. I also stay in my friends' rooms when they're around."

"You made friends?" I asked.

"Yeah, don't sound so surprised."

"Who are they?" I asked, latching on to this new information as tightly as I clutched the phone to the side of my head. It didn't pass my knowledge that the background of wherever he was sounded a lot livelier than the silence of my dorm room. "Where are you?"

"Out."

"Like, out at a party?" I asked. "You shock me, Kieran Rose. Your friends, are they nice?"

"They are. They took me to a different party the other week. It was at a fraternity and everything."

"Look at you, living the college experience."

"It's weird. I'm not sure I like it."

"You're not supposed to like college parties," I said. Or so I'd heard. "If you do, then you're the weird one."

"I don't think so."

I adjusted the phone again.

"Gabe was there. He seemed surprised to see me, but nice. He introduced me to some of his friends too."

"He always makes friends."

"Yeah, though he didn't stay long. He wanted to get back to Jenna. There was a Ben and a Shelby and a Lana."

"Cute?"

"Eh, Ben was trying to grow a beard—unsuccessfully—so I wouldn't say that."

I rolled my eyes. "Ha-ha."

"Miss you," said Kieran.

"Miss you too. I'll call you again this week if you're free."

"For you?" Kieran laughed. "Always, Sylv. You sound tired. Get some sleep before you keel over and I don't get to hear your pretty voice again."

"You are absolutely drunk."

"Nah. Only a little," he admitted, stepping back into where the noise was even louder through the phone. "I'm surprised you aren't."

As I hung up and fell back against my pillow, instead of him being out, I imagined Kieran doing the same exact thing.

"Your call has been forwarded to an automated voice message system."

"Your call has been forwarded to an automated voice message system."

"Sylvia."

"Kieran."

"So, my mom bought me a ticket for my birthday."

"A ticket?"

"Yeah, a train ticket. As you know, it isn't too bad of a trip from Marshall Falls to New York City. My mom apparently doesn't think so either," said Kieran.

"You're coming to the city?" *He's coming to see me?*

A barking giggle I had never heard before came out of my mouth.

I grinned into the phone, holding it tight in both hands as I rocketed up to stand. I might have even done a little jump in place.

Kieran laughed, loud and clear through the receiver. "I'm coming to the city."

THE NEXT MORNING, I woke up back on the couch. It was softer and warmer than I remembered, partially because Kieran had given me the entire blanket at some point when he moved back to his own bed.

Pushing myself up, I looked toward a creaking sound. Kieran stood with his back to me in the closet doorway.

"Good morning."

Kieran jumped, startled.

"Sorry."

He shook his head. "Morning."

There was another moment of silence.

"Thanks," I said. "You know, for letting me stay here last night again and everything."

He shrugged.

"The tree looks worse in the light of day, doesn't it?"

Kieran finally let loose a small snort of a laugh. He rubbed his hand down the back of his neck as he took a step toward me and the tree. Now that it was light out, we could see the bare spots straight through to the thin trunk, just barely holding everything up.

"Yeah, it kind of does."

I let my lips purse to one side. "I talked to your mom last night."

Kieran's eyes turned back to look at me through the corner of his glasses. "You did?"

"She said that I could stay inside the house if I needed somewhere to go," I told him.

We had talked about a lot of things last night, before and after we talked about him. Though I wasn't going to tell Kieran that. I still wasn't sure what exactly I wanted to tell him after last night. Everything, however nice right now, still felt wrong between us, and I didn't know if time would fix it.

Kieran's lips parted before he found his next words. "That's good. I figured it'd be fine."

"I don't know though."

"What are you talking about? You need a place to stay," Kieran argued, though it came out as more of a whine about even having this conversation.

"Yeah, well ..." I came right out with it, remembering his mom's words from last night. I didn't want to miss out on Kieran either, even if I wasn't sure he felt the same way anymore. "I told her that I was going to stay here."

"I didn't agree to that."

"I mean, I have to see my tree." I waved toward the final decorated tree next to the old television. The lights were still on from last night, and Kieran immediately went to unplug it. "How else will I stay in the holiday spirit? And my cookies are still in your kitchen now for me to eat over the next few days."

"There are thirty cookies left in that box. You are not going to eat them that fast."

Did he really want to throw down that kind of challenge?

"Please?" I asked quietly. "Can I stay here?"

"Sylvia ..."

"For old times' sake?" I asked before I could stop myself. The old times probably wasn't the best thing to bring up in the way of convincing Kieran to do something.

Kieran paused nonetheless, considering it. "Fine."

"You'll let me stay?"

"You're sure as hell not going to stay in that junkie motel near the edge of town."

I nodded viciously, as if he was saving me from a grave mistake. I would much rather live on the side of the road or in my freezing house than stay there.

"Just so you don't become a Sylvia Popsicle, sleeping outside to prove a point." Kieran went on, trailing right where my mind had gone.

"It would be a Marshall Falls tragedy," I agreed, turning to my makeshift bed and the rest of my things that were already slowly being left around Kieran's space. "No one would ever look at you again after having that on your conscience."

"Sylvia?"

I turned back. A hesitant look clashed on Kieran's face. Skin creased, and there was a frown deeply set into the mouth that usually remained neutral.

"This doesn't mean anything, you know. This is just you, staying here because you need somewhere to stay."

Shaking my head, I looked down toward my lap. "I understand."

"No." Kieran pulled my attention back to him. "I need to say it, okay? Things can't go back to how they were years ago. No matter how hard we try, we can't just go back to being just friends or whatever sort of image you have in your head when we think of each other. Things between us will never be how they were."

"Okay, Kieran."

"You get it?"

"I get it."

Kieran was never going to be just my friend who I loved ever again.

We could never be *just* anything to each other. And friends? Kieran and I had always been so much more than that.

"You're sleeping on the couch."

"Sounds perfect."

"Okay," he said softly as he turned back toward the bathroom. "Let's leave it at that."

Soon enough, the shower started.

Let's start a new adventure, Kieran, I wanted to whisper.

Even if it would probably be our last.

If I thought my body hurt after yesterday, running around town from the bakery to school and getting the tree up in what had felt like record time, I was sorely mistaken. By which, I mean, after a few days of constantly moving, my body felt like it was so sore that I could collapse into a puddle of goo.

"You really thought you were going to stay with me at my place for free?" Kieran asked around lunch.

My arms were about to give out from carrying boxes out from the bakery to the van.

It had turned out that Rose Bakery was a lot more popular than I previously remembered. Even Kieran's dad got involved with all the orders they had to deliver.

Rose Bakery was a hot commodity in a small town where having a proper pastry was practically a godsend.

Every twinge of a muscle felt like Kieran was trying to punish me rather than make any kind of amends. I couldn't blame him. Making me do manual labor was high up there on what my sort of hell would look like. Yet it sure made Kieran smile, so I wasn't so sure.

I switched off baked goods to the front desk after Lori sent home their non-family employees. A group of teenage girls worked the front counter. When they hung up their aprons, they laughed about how they were getting together with their group of friends for a party now that they were on school break.

I wondered how many ornaments would be left on the tree in the town center by morning.

Not long after the last customer left, who had been working at one of the small bistro tables by the window, Lori said that she needed to finish decorating a cake for a wedding two towns over and would close when she was done.

"Don't worry about staying with me." She waved me out the door. "I want to take my time. Usually, I have Kieran bothering me to take it easy by this time when he's not out on deliveries. It's not often I have an empty kitchen to work in anymore."

I headed out, leaving her to her artistry, switching the front sign to Closed. Turning that sign when Kieran and I had been little was one of my favorite things. We used to argue about who got to do it after school when we spent time here until Kieran realized he had a lot more opportunities to do so than I ever did.

Eventually, when I got back to Kieran's apartment, I took a deep breath and got to work, reorganizing my things in my suitcase. That way, it didn't look like it had exploded. I washed my hair and tucked it into a loose bun before changing into my pajamas.

Kieran walked in once I was firmly tucked in on the couch with the lamps and tree light illuminating the studio. My laptop screen loaded and lit up my face in the dark. For once, I wasn't afraid to click on one of my latest emails.

When I opened it up, I saw my mother and father grinning on some beach, basking in the sun. Her cheeks were burned, and my dad looked like he was enjoying himself even if he didn't want to.

I chuckled.

"What are you laughing at?" asked Kieran. He shook off his coat and hung it up next to mine—or rather his, the same one I'd been wearing, though I should probably get my own soon.

I turned the computer around to him while I reached for another blanket.

Looking at the few photos they had sent, Kieran smiled. "They look like they're having a good time."

"Definitely looks that way. Who would've thought my father would end up on island time?"

Kieran's freckles bounced when he snorted.

He moved away toward the closet, yanking off his sweatshirt as he went. I stared at him until he turned back. He raised an eyebrow.

Clearing my throat, I took a deep breath, as if I were thinking about something important. I surely hadn't been looking at the way his arms filled out his Rose Bakery T-shirt under his sweatshirt. No way.

"So, now what?" I asked.

He blinked. "What do you mean?"

"What are we doing now?"

"Do I look like an entertainment coordinator?"

"I don't know, but you'd probably make a good one." I peeked over the edge of my laptop. I made no move to do anything else. "Just wanted to make sure my daily penance to sleep here had been paid."

Kieran rolled his eyes and went back to changing.

"Where are you going?"

"I need to head back out and help Gabe assemble something so that it's ready for Christmas morning. I'm just happy he isn't waiting until the night before, like last year."

"They really are like a little family now, aren't they?"

"More than a little one. Who knows with them? They say that they are done, but with Gabe, they could pop out another kid by summer."

"I don't think it works like that," I informed him.

"What are you doing now that you are caught up on Meredith and Richard's adventures through the Caribbean?"

I glanced down at my laptop again and my many unopened emails. "I'm not completely sure. I was going to check my email, but then I thought better."

"Why?"

"Well, whatever is in half these emails is going to be depressing, considering I'm unemployed and I'm sure HR is going to come at me with a few more emails to remind me that I have no lasting benefits. So, I could open those right now or, you know ... better to not."

"I think you're making the right move then. What are you doing for the rest of the night? There's food in the kitchen if you want to make something."

"I ..."

"Still not sure?" Kieran chuckled before he stopped himself. "I'll leave you to it then."

"I could come along and help," I said. "If you and Gabe would like."

"You could be good with a power drill?"

"If I believed."

Kieran shook his head. "Nah, you look cozy."

Then, you should join me, I almost said, but kept it locked behind my lips.

"Stay here and do whatever it is you're doing. It's better if you don't get into any more trouble while you're in town."

"I was helpful today."

Kieran didn't comment on that as he changed his shirt to a

long-sleeved one before heading back toward the door, swinging on his coat once more.

"I'll be back later." He paused, looking at me. "We can, uh, watch a movie if you're still up when I get back."

"A movie?"

"We can knock another task off your list. Famous holiday movies and whatnot. You can choose. They're all in that drawer there under the TV. If you want to." Kieran went on.

Slowly, I dipped my head once. "Okay. That sounds good."

He grabbed a scarf last minute to wrap around his neck. The door shut gently as he headed back out into the darkness now that the sun was nearly down every day at four in the afternoon.

"Just me and you again," I muttered, eyes glancing back at the last tab I had opened last night. Pausing, just like last time, I clicked the link and opened my old blog's home page.

Damn, I was good. *The List* had taken on a whole new style after I played around with the fonts and a new, more cohesive color palette. Yet I narrowed my eyes at the little bell at the top of the page.

I had a new comment.

Wait. I had a new comment?

That made no sense. I hadn't posted anything. No one would likely ever be able to find this blog now that it was in the deep, dark, oversaturated pits of the internet, let alone dead hobby blogs.

Does anyone see this? I check out The List *occasionally, but just noticed it looks entirely new! Does this mean what I think it does?* the commenter had asked.

I wasn't sure. What did she think it meant?

Did she think that the blog was up and running? Because it wasn't.

The last post was from a little over four years ago. Though

the devoted readers had been steady for a while after that, it wasn't as if they would still be there if I started blogging again. Would they?

Blogging was a slowly dying craft, especially since social media had taken lifestyle blogs to an entire new height within the past decade. Most of the good writers had turned into lifestyle celebrities and influencers that constantly danced across my phone when I ended up in an endless scrolling cycle just for something to do.

Still, I couldn't help myself. I fixed up more pages and updated links. There wasn't much more to do. My old blog looked a lot better. Everything was organized correctly compared to when I last used the site.

Blogging used to be my favorite thing to do in the world. Every minute was spent coming up with new fun series or posts. I hadn't written anything new or even just for me in a long time.

A very long time.

My phone buzzed.

It was probably Kieran telling me he needed help after all. I let out a disgusted sound after I lifted my phone up to see. I should've left it stuffed between the couch cushions.

Ezra's message, per usual, was short, though not, in any world, sweet.

For God's sake, RESPOND. Do you want me to think you're dead or something?

My blood boiled as I stared at it directly underneath the last message he had sent, basically asking me to get over myself and "not be stupid."

I lifted the phone to my ear to listen to the voice mail also left.

"Call me back. This is a misunderstanding. Right? Look, my parents are still expecting me to show up to dinner with you at Christmas, and you need to get back here so that I don't look like a complete jackass in front of them and their business partners coming. Don't ruin Christmas over this." He huffed, as if he was really put out. "Call me back, Sylvie."

I didn't answer his text messages so far. He had threatened that he wouldn't come after me when I left.

And I didn't want him to.

I replied, typing out a short message. *I'm at home with my family for the holidays. Please do not reach out again.*

Before I could set my phone down, it rang.

Ezra was never one for boundaries, was he?

I answered. "Hello?"

"What the hell do you think you're doing, just freezing me out?" Ezra snapped across the line. "Here I thought you weren't like one of *those* girls, Sylvie."

"It's Sylvia," I immediately corrected him before I could stop myself. I didn't want to stop myself. "And what kind of girls are *those girls*, Ez? The kind whose boyfriends take a hint? I told you that we're done. I'm at home. I'm sorry if you made plans for this holiday, but I'm not going to be a part of them."

"You said you'd go to the holiday thing with me and meet my parents."

"You said that you weren't cheating on me," I shot back before I fought to calm my voice.

"I wasn't cheating on you."

My silence said enough.

He scoffed. "Well, it's now or never. If you don't come with me, I'm going to have to take Tabitha home."

Tabitha? For some reason, that name didn't ring a bell. I could only hope she had been the woman on my couch.

I was never going to get over that couch.

"Then, I guess it's never," I snapped.

Silence hung between us. I curled my legs up and set my

laptop to the side as I listened to Ezra's breathing before he sighed in a great, big huff.

"Can I guess what's really going on here?" he asked.

"If you want to."

He went on as if I had never said anything. "You're back in your little hometown, sleeping with that guy you said was nothing."

"No."

"I don't believe that."

"You don't have to."

"Fine then. You want to, right? Depressingly pining. You went home, and now, you're hoping something great is going to happen and that everything is going to work out," Ezra surmised. "Waiting and waiting until you're going to realize that it's not going to happen. Then, what, Sylvie? You threw away everything with me and in the city, and for what?"

"You don't know what you're talking about."

"I'm sure you think you do. But do you really think that whatever kind of story you are trying to have play out right now is going to work? You think that he's going to magically still be available or even still want you after all these years, after whatever the hell happened?" asked Ezra. "You're willing to bet it all on that guy?"

My heart stopped in my chest. Was that what I was doing? I mean, I wanted Kieran back. I wanted my best friend.

I loved my best friend.

The idea still took the breath out of my lungs. But it was true.

I had, and I *do*.

Why else was I sitting here in his apartment?

I glanced around the empty space of Kieran's studio. It felt big in the silence.

I looked from the warm heater to the stack of blankets next

to me. I looked at the book Kieran had marked diligently with a paper bookmark. I glanced down at my old blog next to me and then finally found myself staring at the list, sitting still on his tiny coffee table. A pen had sat next to it ever since Kieran had checked off the tree and cookie making.

It was still there for the rest of the lines, filled with his favorite holiday things, to be marked off, as if I was hoping he'd eventually realize that all his favorite things throughout the years always had me next to him.

"Maybe I am," I whispered.

"You know, I was going to introduce you to someone who might've even cared about what you wanted to write. We had our bumps in the road or whatever, but we could've made something. I guess I just hope you're happy with your choice," he said, though he sounded anything but.

"I hope you are too. Goodbye, Ezra." I hit the button to end the call and sat in the quiet apartment for another moment, waiting to see if he'd call back to continue his next rant.

That was one thing I had first found charming about Ezra. He was passionate. He always worked through something in his head and could go on about it for hours.

Now, I was tired of listening.

Deleting the voice mail messages he had left, I silenced my phone before I focused back on my laptop. Clicking the corner, I opened a new document.

I stared at a familiar empty screen, patiently waiting for me to make a decision. A choice.

I used to think stories were for new beginnings. But the good stories never started right at the beginning. They started where they needed to be told.

I set my hands on the black keys, covered with flecks of powdered sugar. I watched the cursor blink, blink, blink.

I hit one key and then another one. After the third, I

thought maybe Kieran had had more of a point than I realized the other night. I had lost a lot of myself over the years to who I wished I was. But when I was writing and posting and sharing life with him and with others, I never felt more like I was already exactly who I was meant to be.

New beginnings are all about choices ... and sometimes, you have to go back to start again.

THIRTY

BEFORE

"YOU'RE HERE!" I screeched, slamming into him.

My entire body weight fell into Kieran's arms as I squeezed. He squeezed me right back, picking me up a few inches so that the only parts of me touching the ground were my toes.

A few people moved out of our way, throwing some nasty looks at the two of us as they did so.

Well, screw them.

If I hadn't thought that before, I thought it the moment Kieran pulled back to look at me with happiness coating his every feature.

Kieran grinned wide, laughing from the moment he had tried to catch me and keep hold of his slouchy duffel bag, all at the same time. "I'm here."

"It doesn't even look right." I went on, flopping back down to my own feet as we stood in the center of the train station. Immediately, I tugged him to start walking. His other hand looped his bag around his shoulder. "You. You're here. You're here in New York."

"How many times are you going to need to say that before it sets in?"

"At least nine," I said. "You're here!"

He chuckled, his eyes widening the moment we stepped out of the station and onto the gray sidewalk. Sirens filled the air, and people pushed past from all directions.

"Wow. There's so much going on."

I glanced down at our clasped hands as he squeezed close to my side. His thumb subconsciously swiped back and forth over the metal charms on my bracelet.

"Just stick with me," I said.

Kieran stayed close all the way back to campus. I led him through Washington Square Park. He watched in awe at the amount of people constantly everywhere—kids skateboarding around the fountain and performers strumming guitars or selling paper cranes. Groups of students from NYU and around the city lay out on blankets on the lawn with their sunglasses on, reading or taking a nap, using their backpacks as pillows.

"It's wild that you live here."

He hadn't even seen the half of it yet. Then again, neither had I really. Today was going to change that.

I led him inside the residence hall, and we trailed up the stairs, but that was as far as we were going by the time I made it to room 512.

Popping the door open, I reached for his bag. Kieran handed it over and watched as I threw it in, landing somewhere next to my desk and closet.

"All right then, let's go." I closed and locked the door before he could look inside.

"You're not going to let me see your room?"

"Later. There's plenty of time for that. Right now, we have a day to seize, Kieran Rose. I just can't believe that you're here."

He shook his head. "That's number five."

"Four more exclamations to go of how happy I am to see you," I said without an ounce of humor.

I might've underestimated exactly how many times I needed to say that I just couldn't believe this. It was something that we had talked about all the time, but in the back of my mind, I hadn't known if it would ever happen.

Ever since I had left Marshall, I couldn't help it. I felt like I had stepped out of one universe and into another, and occasionally, aside from our phone calls, everything felt far away. I wasn't sure if it was a good or bad feeling either.

Except for, sometimes, when I called Kieran late at night and he didn't pick up. Then, even in the loudest city in the world, everything felt too quiet.

Back down the five flights of stairs, we pushed the doors open and walked past a couple smoking in front of the doors. Kieran scrunched his nose before we were back on the street, and I took him in the other direction than where we had come.

"Much to do," I repeated, turning a corner.

"Like what?" Kieran asked, keeping pace.

"Oh, I have a list."

"You're kidding."

"A little." Kieran picked up the pace as we made it across the street. "I figured you'd like it though if I said that I did. There's plenty to do in the city that never sleeps. There are museums and bookstores—"

"Bookstores?"

"Absolutely. There are little parks and random other things always happening."

I pulled out everything I had heard of and everything I thought I would've done already since I had gotten here. Plus, I hadn't planned the day extensively mainly because of one big problem that had to be at the top of my mind—money. Or in our case, the lack thereof. But that still left us plenty to do.

He raised his eyebrows, as if impressed by my list.

"The city is our oyster." I ended my speech. After another

minute to catch my breath, I turned to look up at Kieran next to me.

He was already looking at me.

I squinted. "What?"

"Nothing. I was just looking at you." He pressed his lips back into a smile.

I rolled my eyes, swinging my arms as we walked. "How is everyone at home?"

"They're good."

"What about Jenna and Gabe? They had the baby, right?"

Kieran nodded. "If they didn't, that would be one massive kid."

"Stop it."

"They're good too. The baby is good. Nothing crazy has happened besides the regular crazy."

"Are you calling childbirth and pregnancy crazy? It's a very natural part of life." Even if I wasn't sure I ever wanted to experience it.

"It is." Kieran laughed.

"What?"

"It's just wild. The whole thing, let alone the fact that people we graduated with less than a year ago are now parents."

I guessed it was. Sort of.

"Seriously, you should've seen how big Jenna was by the end. I mean, Gabe was no small guy, but it was ..."

"Wild?"

He smiled, but his eyes were wide with whatever it was they must've told him. I wished I had been there.

"I went over once after they came home from the hospital. They looked tired. Happy though."

"So, I guess we can count you out for becoming a parent."

"Not in the immediate future," he said with a dramatic shiver.

I laughed as we continued to walk.

"You want to be a mom?" Kieran asked after a moment.

"I don't know. I'm not sure I'd be a very good one, to be honest," I admitted.

Kieran looked at me closely. We took the turn and walked across the street, where I could see the entrance going underground.

"I'm sure you would be."

Either way, it didn't really matter.

"What else is new back home? You know, besides the miracle of life?"

Kieran pursed his lips in thought. "Not much. I've met up with everyone who is still nearby every other weekend, so there's that gossip, too, though I think I already filled you in on some of it on our last call. Amy and I went out the other weekend again to see that new movie they finally got in at the cineplex."

I stared at him in outrage. "The one we wanted to see this past summer, but they didn't have it?"

"Yeah." He laughed.

"Traitor."

"It was pretty good, but not as good as our last rom-com we saw. Amy really liked it though," he said.

"That's good," I said slowly, imagining the two of them.

Kieran and Amy had probably sat in our usual movie seats. They probably got there early to watch the previews, which was Kieran's favorite part. They might've even gotten popcorn, using one of the coupons Kieran's mom clipped. Though Amy had likely conceded to no butter and no salt for Kieran. I usually forced him to suffer through trying to do half and half of the value bag.

"We can go again if you want. You're going to come home soon, right?"

"Yeah," I said. "I can't come home on the weekends, like some people I know are able to, but I'll be home for the holidays and break."

"So, Thanksgiving?" he clarified.

"And Christmas."

"Seems far away."

"You'll just have to soak all my presence in for the next month or so now," I said.

Kieran chuckled as I tugged on his hand down the stairs to the L train. "Where are we going again?"

"Our first item on the list to make sure you experience New York City ..."

"Is?" Kieran led off, waiting patiently.

"The subway."

The subway took us uptown to the Metropolitan Museum of Art. No matter how terrible Kieran was at blatantly lying to strangers, we tried to sneak in for a penny each by pretending he was a student.

"He forgot his ID," I insisted.

The man behind the desk rolled his eyes at the entire exchange but gave us the stickers to get in anyway, which we slapped on our chests. We walked through each exhibit, pausing at the statues and the paintings as big as walls until, at some point, we made it back to where we had started all over again. Down the steps, we turned right and continued to walk until Kieran stopped on the edge of the sidewalk.

Looking in one of the small storefronts, I grinned. "Want to go in?"

We pushed through the heavy door into the bookshop,

where there were piles of old editions on one side and new books on the other with crisp spines, never read before.

Kieran immediately drifted toward the used novels. He let the pages skim through his fingers as he took a deep breath of paper and dust. "Ah, that's some good stuff."

"You're probably inhaling someone's skin cells right now from whoever owned that book last."

Kieran rolled his eyes. "You just don't appreciate the little things."

"Sure, that's what we'll call whatever this is," I teased.

After he purchased a hardcover to add to his future personal library, I put the novel in my bag for safe keeping and slung it on my back. We headed to the next street over until trees were arching across the one side of the street.

"Is this a park?"

"Not just any park," I said, as if in a big reveal. "Central Park."

"Really?"

"Yeah." I laughed.

This might be the only place where I somewhat knew where I was going now after a solo adventure. It had led me to being lost in Central Park for a few hours, walking in circles and being too much of a coward to ask anyone for directions so that I could make it back for my afternoon class.

There had to be nearly a hundred blankets spread out across a wide yard with people listening to a small band of performers play music.

Without pausing, Kieran collapsed down onto the grass, stretching his legs out in front of him. "Ah."

"Not used to walking so much," I said, feeling the same way. Now that we had stopped moving, my legs ached and felt as if they were going to go all wobbly, like Jell-O.

"And for so long," he moaned, but happiness was etched on his face.

I lowered myself down to the grass with him. I leaned back on my hands. The band playing was actually pretty good. I wondered if this was what it was like for all my classmates who had their groups they sat out with together. It was nice. It was peaceful, even with all the noise.

A band played on and on until Kieran reached for my hand.

"Really?" Out of everyone, I hadn't expected Kieran to want to do anything in front of so many people, especially not after how red I had seen his cheeks turn during karaoke last year.

I took his hand and stood up.

"We aren't the only ones."

He was right. Along with a lot of the people talking and relaxing, there were a few clusters of people dancing right along to the music, screaming words that went with the lyrics and even ones that made no sense at all, and no one seemed to care.

"No one knows us here." Kieran started to wiggle his shoulders to the soft beat. "Right?"

Shutting my eyes, I shook my head. When I opened my eyes again, Kieran was still doing his sorry excuse for dancing.

I started to shake my shoulders with him. "Right."

And we danced like we didn't have the worry of the world, let alone anyone staring at us. We jumped and shimmied, and Kieran grabbed my hand and gave me a twirl, which gave me permission to do the same back to him. He was pretty good at twirling. The only person who mattered was right next to me, grinning so hard that his eyes squinted in the corners.

I was loving every second of it.

So, I danced some more. Kieran danced right alongside me, just like he always had.

Holding on to each other's hands, we stretched our arms out

between us, like a bridge connecting us. Our chests rose and fell with the exertion as we stared at each other and around the park, no one the wiser of the moment we were having as the sun started its steady descent. The sky cast off shades of orange and gold.

"Hey," said Kieran.

"Hey," I replied.

I looked up at him, and his blue eyes looked down into mine. A long moment passed, where we stood just like that, until I dropped a hand and turned away. My cheeks heated for a different reason, one I thought they wouldn't do anymore under Kieran's study.

"You okay?"

Better than.

I was starting to see what people meant when they said that living in the city was a unique kind of magic.

"I'm starving," I said. I groaned with my hands on my stomach in exaggeration.

"I am too," agreed Kieran.

"All right. We can head back near campus," I said, looking up at the darkening sky. "I think I know exactly where to go."

I bit my lip and waited for Kieran's reaction to what might be the largest slice of pizza he had ever seen. The piece of pizza was bigger than Kieran's head, and I laughed at the awed expression on his face when the man slapped it down in front of him on a flimsy paper plate.

"For two dollars?" he asked, shocked.

The quick stop was much to the delight of the college students surrounding the place. The parlor probably made more money this way, being known for massive, cheap slices of pizza that students traveled an extra block for. Plus, it was really good pizza.

We both leaned against the wall outside of the shop where there was a perch in the brick. Holding the pizza with two hands, Kieran took a huge bite, biting down on the thick cheese that came away with him. I laughed, taking a bite of my own slice of pepperoni as I watched him struggle.

His eyes shut. "So good," he moaned.

I took another big bite until cheese caught on my chin. "So good."

He chuckled as I closed my eyes and savored my next bite. "Do you come here to this place a lot?"

I shook my head. "Once."

He nodded slowly, carefully taking his next bite.

"I kind of was wondering when you were going to introduce me to your friends," said Kieran.

I nearly choked on cheese. Coughing, I wiped my mouth with the back of my hand. "Oh, they're, uh, not around today."

He narrowed his eyes. "Oh."

"Yeah, everyone's so busy and everything."

"Right."

"Yep," I said.

It was clear by his confused expression that Kieran saw right through me. I didn't know why I had thought he wouldn't. "Do you not want to introduce me to them, Sylvia?"

I sighed. "No, that's not it."

"Okay," Kieran said, though he sounded a little down.

He didn't get it.

"It's not like that," I insisted. My shoulders slumped. "I don't ... the thing is ... I don't really have any friends here to introduce you to."

"What are you talking about?"

I shrugged. "You know, it turns out that I've never been great when it comes to making friends."

"When you talked to me on the phone about the places you were going and the classes you were in, I thought that you were making all these friends."

I lied. I purposely hadn't corrected him when he asked about the voices around me when I was talking on the phone or who I was hanging out with even though that had only happened once with a group project so far. "Sorry."

"Why are you sorry?" His face fell.

I took another bite of pizza. "Because you're looking at me like you want to pity me."

"Being sad for you and pitying you are two very different things, especially when it comes to my best friend, Sylvia," said Kieran. "I'm sorry you've been alone since you got here. What about your roommate?"

"About that ..."

He groaned in sorrow for me.

It made me laugh.

"I did have a roommate." I sucked in a breath through my teeth.

"Did?"

"Yes. *Did.*" I made sure to enunciate. "She sort of had a minor mental breakdown and ended up going home about a week into the semester. I went to class one day, and when I came back, all her stuff had mysteriously disappeared."

"Jeez."

That was one word for it.

"It's not a big deal."

"Aren't you ..." Kieran looked around at the city, and in the silence, all the sounds from the sirens to the cars came back in full force. We could even hear people yelling at one another down the block. "I don't know ... lonely?"

"No," I answered hastily.

It was like I was talking to my mom when she would call me every week, which had turned into every other week. She'd ask me how I was doing and if I was enjoying the city. The answer was always *good* and *yes* and *I'm having a great time*.

But I knew Kieran, and I knew he could tell when that wasn't the whole truth.

I leaned against him for a moment, letting my head rest on his shoulder. "It just makes me even more glad that you were able to come visit me."

Kieran nudged me. "I'm glad I'm here too."

"Do you want to stay?"

He laughed, resting the side of his head back on top of mine.

"You could transfer schools. I'm sure if you applied, NYU would even squeeze you into my dorm room. They are very coed progressive," I said.

Kieran chuckled some more before the sound died out. He lifted his ear back from the top of my head and took another bite of his pizza. After another moment, I did the same.

We finished eating our bargain dinner in the darkness. The lamps lit our way back along the sidewalk toward campus. Or at least, I thought we were going toward campus.

I turned around and looked at the street signs. In a city people described as being like a rectangle, I never thought I'd get constantly turned around.

"Are you doing okay there?"

"Yep, just making sure we are taking the fastest way back," I said.

"We lost?" asked Kieran.

"Sidetracked."

Kieran's calm disposition since the pizza shop fizzled, but he didn't say anything as we made our way back toward the residence hall. Eventually, with enough turns, it would have to show up back in front of us again even if I wasn't sure if we'd make it before the slow drizzle of impending rain began.

By the time we made it around the next block, I turned to look at the next sign, but stopped. I paused in front of the large window of the storefront that was still on in the darkness.

"What are you looking at? If you really are lost, you can just stop and ask someone for directions." Immediately, when Kieran took notice of the sign, he shook his head. There was a stern press to his upper lip. "No."

"It's on the list," I argued.

"It shouldn't be," he debated right back.

"But, Kieran"—I pulled on his arm toward the illuminated sign on the shop, seeing the moment he started to give up the fight—"it's on the list."

THIRTY-ONE

NOW

EACH DAY FELT like a daydream that I'd had many times before. The dream was simple.

In the mornings, I woke up and trailed Kieran in silence—the best way to begin any morning that started earlier than the sun—to the bakery. Some days, I unraveled lights for Kieran and his father until my fingers turned numb. On others, I dropped off deliveries to the offices around Marshall. There never seemed to be a shortage of holiday luncheons.

Kieran caught the eye of more than a few older ladies at the retirement home. I teased him the entire way home until his cheeks turned a red brighter than the velvet holiday bows that hung off the gazebo in the center of the town.

Yesterday, we had helped Lori wrap presents, checking another item off my list. Two days before that, Kieran had thrown a snowball at my head, and we had gone to the final Christmas market night in the center of town—check and check.

We strung popcorn and watched all the old Christmas movies we used to as we ate dinner together on the couch most evenings.

We talked about everything—or what felt like everything.

We spoke around topics before shuffling away into our own nighttime habits whenever we got too close to what had happened between us—though neither of us breached that barrier. No matter what Lori had told me, I couldn't.

I couldn't risk it.

The days were in limbo between snowfalls and holiday madness, where, somehow, Kieran and I were good friends again. After all these years, I would still give anything for it. Ezra might've been right. I was willing to risk it all by keeping the peace, by keeping close to Kieran, for better or for worse.

For him.

Because, God, he looked good when he was happy.

"You look a mess."

"I look amazing," I insisted, jutting my chin out at Kieran as he walked by the bakery kitchen with another round of pink delivery boxes.

I had just helped bake nearly ten dozen cookies. I only knew how to make the one with the raspberry filling, but there were still ten dozen cookies. Minus one I had eaten.

That was why they had created the baker's dozen, wasn't it?

Whether or not I had flour on my cheeks and down the length of my apron was beside the real point.

Lori laughed as she carried out a tray to the display case, warding off Kieran's grabby hands offering to help with her elbows.

As I cleaned up, Kieran passed by, leaning over my shoulder. The heat of his chest pressing into my back caused me to halt in place.

"Go home or take a break. You've been working on the same thing for too long."

"What are you talking about? There are no rules," I said. "You're not paying me."

"The amount of baked goods you've eaten says otherwise."

I stuck out my tongue like a child.

Kieran laughed before he headed out toward the back door.

"You two seem to be getting on well."

I stared at her for a moment.

Lori nodded swiftly as she made her way back to her station, which she cleaned off and reset. "Understood. I won't pry anymore."

I shook my head as the grown woman I'd known as my second mother for all my life tried and failed to stifle a laugh.

"I still think you should come clean."

"I just thought you said you were done," I scolded with a light gasp.

If it was possible, Kieran's mother just rolled her eyes at me.

"I'm happy right now. And it's best this way. For now anyway."

"When does *for now* end?"

"I don't know." But for once, I was going to be happy for the *for now*.

"Go home and get cleaned up. You look tired."

"Are you sure?"

"We're covered," Lori assured. "Go."

THIRTY-TWO

BEFORE

"THIS IS SO STUPID."

"It's not that stupid," I insisted as we were led back toward the tattoo chair after signing away what I could only assume was our lives. "It's a memory. Plus, I did put it on the list."

"I erased it. It was blacklisted from the list during the creation of the list," Kieran argued.

"Then, like I said," I repeated, "a memory."

"A very permanent memory."

"Isn't that the best kind?" I teased him.

His leg bounced up and down as the tattoo artist smiled, listening in on our conversation. Bonny's Tattoo and Art Studio was painted in the loveliest shade of green with dozens of frames along the walls. Inside the glass featured other intricate tattoos as well as articles praising no one but Bonny herself. We were in fine hands. Plus, the shop was clean—almost too clean—so Kieran couldn't find anything to complain about.

"Would you rather get your belly button pierced?" I asked him.

He quickly shook his head, fear and frustration the only

things on his face right now. It made me want to laugh harder. "No."

"Fantastic. Just take a deep breath in ..." I waited. "Kieran, you're supposed to breathe in with me."

The tattoo artist looked between the two of us like we were paid cable, giggling to herself as she pulled latex gloves over her long black fingernails.

"Don't worry; you chose one of the best places in the city to get a last-minute tattoo. Usually, I don't have openings," Bonny said. "A client canceled theirs tonight though. It's almost like this was meant to be."

"You hear that, Kier? If you're not going to listen to me, listen to Bonny. It was meant to be."

He stared at the station like it was coming to bite him. Technically, it was. "I heard her."

"Okay, so you're up first?" Bonny asked Kieran.

I nodded for him. "I figure if he doesn't go first, he'll be a runner."

"Always good to plan," said Bonny. She lifted a sealed package. "I just need you to confirm that you see that this is a fresh needle, completely new, just for you."

After a second, Kieran sat up straighter. "Yes."

"Good stuff. The hard part is over. Now, you just need to lie back and let me do my work. Let me know if you start to feel like you're going to pass out." She gestured for me to go next to him.

I held Kieran's hand and took a deep breath. This time, he followed it with me. In and out.

The tattoo gun hummed as it stuck into Kieran's skin one line at a time. I swiped my thumb back and forth over Kieran's hand as he squeezed, though not as hard as I had expected.

"You'd better not back out on me now," Kieran threatened, a little out of breath when it was over.

The artist chuckled at the two of us as she lifted the next sealed package of the new needle to show me before she got to resetting the station.

I laughed as I leaned back to lie down where he'd been a minute ago. "Not a chance."

Afterward, I lifted my hair and turned to look in the mirror while Kieran twisted his neck around to do the same. I couldn't help the smile that pressed against my lips at the two tiny roses in the reflection. One behind my ear and his on the back of his neck, right where his apron strap always sat when he worked in the bakery.

"Look good?" the tattoo artist asked.

I looked up at Kieran. Pressing his lips together, he nodded, his eyes soft.

"It's perfect," I told her.

"Good. I really like that one. Simple but pretty," she said. "You two are a cute couple."

"Oh." I tried to stop her by shaking my head. "We're not—"

Kieran caught my hand, smiling as he turned his attention away from his tattoo in the mirror to address the artist. "Thanks."

"Absolutely. I'll even give you two a first-timer special tonight since it's slow."

She rang us up. I didn't care if it wiped out all my savings to have Kieran this content with our adventure.

"Have a great rest of your night."

I extended my hand toward Kieran, and he rushed to take it. "We will."

Rain pelted and dripped down my shoulders until it was cut off by the door. Using the back of my hand not still holding Kieran's, I flipped my head back, spraying water everywhere. Kieran shook his head, spraying me with more droplets, like a dog after a bath.

Both of us squealed.

The two of us weren't done running though. We headed toward the stairs and rushed to the fifth floor in a blink of an eye, passing other students who looked at us with raised eyebrows at the way we were soaked. Shutting the door behind us, I twisted the lock and took a deep breath.

"Made it."

Kieran laughed. "Just about."

I shoved my hands in my pockets as I looked around. It wasn't the best room I'd seen. Others had tons of decorations and things that made their space fuller, but I was determined not to be one of those people who showed up on moving day with a million pieces of luggage. All I'd needed was to be labeled high maintenance by anyone on my first day.

Kieran was still smiling, though concern flickered as he glanced around the room again. As quickly as it had come, however, it faded. "Do you have a towel or something?"

Nodding, I opened my tiny wardrobe and threw him one of my folded towels. I grabbed the other one that was left on the doorknob to dry. Leaning back against the bed, I squished the water out of my hair while Kieran did the same before reaching for his duffel bag and pulling out a pair of sweatpants. Reaching toward our bags, I tossed him his New York University T-shirt I bought him.

"Try it on," I said, "I want to see you representing the big city."

Still grinning, he got undressed, and I decided that it was probably the best time to do the same. Leaning down to my drawers underneath my bed, I slipped out my pair of light-blue plaid pajama pants. I shoved my jeans down my legs and stepped out of them, leaving them in a heavy, wet lump on the floor, along with my underwear. I didn't bother to reach for another pair, opting to slip on my pajama pants and one of Kieran's oversized T-shirts I stole from him before I left Marshall Falls.

When I turned around, Kieran was in a dry pair of lounge shorts and his NYU shirt, which fit him perfectly.

His eyes latched on to my chest before snapping back up to my face.

"I know. I lied. I took your shirt," I admitted.

Kieran blinked, as if he had just noticed. "Oh, right."

"You'll have to pry it out of my cold, dead hands though if you want it back."

"I wouldn't dare," he attempted to joke, but all the laughter in the past few minutes fled the room. There was a small smirk on his lips.

Clearing my throat, I turned back to the room. Though it was nice to have a single and not share with anyone, it was still an obscenely tiny space.

"The best way to probably go about this is to move the mattresses onto the floor and take our chances that way," I suggested, already yanking one down before getting a few more blankets. It wasn't going to be a comfortable night, but I figured that we'd end up watching movies for a little while anyway.

My heart was still running a mile a minute.

Coming up next to me, Kieran helped to rearrange the space until we created a nest on the floor under the window, piled with sheets and fluffy blankets. It was tight, but it would do. It wasn't as if we hadn't shared a bed before. This way, we could be more comfortable than squished.

Taking a deep breath, I leaned against the pillows. Kieran

stretched his arms above his head. He flinched before reaching toward the back of his head, almost touching his tattoo.

"Regret it yet?"

He shook his head. "Nope."

"I'm impressed."

"At my sudden spontaneity? Yeah, me too."

Now that we were back inside in the warmth, all the energy flowing through my body all day dropped.

I blinked a few times at him. "I missed you."

"I think you've told me that a few times already," he teased.

"Only because I really mean it. I'm still serious that you should transfer. It suits you."

"A day is different from a life. I don't know if the city is for me." Kieran looked around.

I shrugged. "Maybe for a little while, it could be. With me."

"Maybe," he whispered, tilting his head closer to mine as our eyes shut in the quiet. For a moment anyway.

The halls raged with something banging against the walls.

Kieran breathed a short laugh as our eyes popped back open. He touched the edge of my smile with his thumb. His lips screwed to the side. "I've really missed you a lot too, Sylvia. So much more than I ever thought I would."

"Wow. What a compliment."

"It should be. I miss you all the time. I miss you whenever you're not right next to me," he said. "Missing you some days is all I can think about."

"That can't be good for your productivity."

"Why do you think I failed my last American Lit quiz?" Kieran said, dead serious. Then, he said the words that he said all the time, almost every day we saw each other. But this time, it felt different. "You know I love you, Sylvia."

"I love you too, Kieran." Probably more than he'd ever realize.

But Kieran didn't leave it there. "Yeah?"

Without his glasses on, his deep, blue eyes were hooded, as if in a dream.

"Yeah."

But if he was dreaming, I was right there with him.

"Kieran," I whispered, my eyes fluttering back and forth between his mouth and his eyes, which were firmly locked between mine.

"Yeah?" His chin nudged against mine.

With that single touch, it was already too late to stop whatever was happening.

Kieran's mouth pressed against mine, and I lifted to meet it.

And I was kissing my best friend, Kieran Rose.

I was kissing Kieran, and it was everything. It was soft until we broke apart, gasping as if we had never breathed before. But we didn't stop. I was kissing my Kieran, my Kieran Rose, and I didn't want to stop.

We held on and didn't let go. Neither of us was willing to say a word and let this moment escape outside the space between our lips.

Oh, his lips.

He held on to me like he wasn't afraid that I would break. He held on to me like he was ready to invade my skin. I pressed right back into him, shoving the blankets between us away until I could feel his skin against my arms, where our shirts rode up along our stomachs. The entire room was buzzing, but all I cared about was how crazy this was.

How perfectly he kissed.

I moaned into his mouth.

"Fuck, Sylvia," Kieran groaned.

The curse on his lips tasted like sugar.

I shook my head, teeth scraping against his lips as I shifted again and felt him against my center. "Shh."

A breathless grunt slipped out from his lips as we pulsed, gently grinding ourselves together until we were a combination of stolen breaths. The deep kisses seeped into my bones, weighing me down. I grasped on to him to stay grounded, and moans ranged from every pitch.

His hands ran down my sides, cupping my breasts before playing with the edge of my plaid pajama pants. He fisted the waistband hard as we continued our frenzy, wanting every piece of each other. For the first time, we weren't holding back.

As we came back down, clutching one another like we were each other's own personal life raft, I waited for the fear. I waited for the panic to set in.

Only it didn't.

Somehow, in a building full of loud and awful human beings trying to get their degrees, there was silence. Silence and the sound of our heavy breaths passing between us.

I stared at Kieran, waiting for something to happen. Perhaps I'd look at him and he'd appear completely different than I had ever seen before.

I had just kissed my best friend. We had done a bit more than just kiss.

Yet there were still his blue eyes. There were his long lashes that he peered right back at me through, the picture of ease. His chest rose and fell as he caught his breath.

"Hi," I whispered.

Kieran chuckled. His eyes were closed as he licked his lips. "Hi."

I touched his collarbone before pulling my hand away. He put his hand over mine. I could feel his heartbeat.

I whimpered at the action as his hand stroked the back of my hand.

He cuddled me closer to him on the tiny mattress on the floor.

"Do we, uh, want to talk about it?" He took a deep breath into my hair.

"I ..." I forced my voice not to shake with uncertainty. "I don't know."

"Yeah." His hand still rested on me, held me as if he was afraid to let me go and stare me back in the face. "I mean, it was probably a mistake, right?"

A mistake?

I inhaled as if he had stabbed me, but I didn't dare move.

I stared down into his chest, where he held me until I was positive his eyes closed. I counted his breaths and lashes gently lying against his cheeks. I wasn't going to talk about it. We had both experienced what had just happened—or what I had thought happened.

I had kissed my best friend, and the only word I could think of to describe it?

Finally.

And what if he didn't feel the same? What if it had just happened because the day was over and it felt right, and in the morning, he actually did regret it? He had given me that chance last winter when I climbed into his bed and was nearly on top of him. Shouldn't I give him the same option?

He was going to go home. That was how it was right now. He was going to go home alone and see Amy, who he'd been going out with as much more than just friends. He would see and kiss Amy, who he always saw and kissed when he wasn't kissing me.

He was going to go home.

And I was going to stay right here.

My heart clenched so hard in my chest that I thought I was dying.

But I had to listen to the truth for once. The city might be made for dreamers, but it didn't mean that all dreams were meant to come true. That was just how it was, and for right now, I was going to burrow myself into his chest.

If I had to think that this was all a dream for him ... for me ... I would.

MY FINGERS HAD BEEN STRUMMING against the keys of my laptop every night for the past few days. The comments I responded to were no longer on my old posts, but new.

It was odd, working again. When I'd been in high school, I would write every day, whenever I had the chance. Tonight, after Lori had thrown me out of the shop to go home early was no different. I kept going.

Old, thrilled readers came to cheer on my strange, new list and homecoming to Marshall. Others quickly deleted notifications, according to my page readership count. *The List* wasn't as popular as it once had been, but I didn't care about that. I was writing.

Even in the darkness, much later than I probably should've been, I wrote.

I could hardly comprehend it, and to be honest, I didn't want to overthink it too much.

"It's nice to see you like this." Kieran sat down next to me.

I had holed myself up in a cocoon of blankets on the floor in front of the couch, helping to warm myself further while wearing one of Kieran's oversize sweatshirts. He'd laid one out for me ever since he had seen that I had stolen one the other day and I hadn't complained about how frozen I was since.

"Like what?" I asked after finishing the last sentence I had been on before I lost the thought altogether. Words were always fickle that way.

"Writing."

I offered him a small smile.

A strange sort of pleasure brought a blush toward my cheeks, from me, only for me. This was my love.

"Sorry, does the typing sound bother you?"

He shook his head. "No. It's fine."

The last thing I needed to get done was work out the final section of my post I wanted to put up by the end of the week. I'd look over it and edit all the misspelled and underlined words in the morning.

"I got a notification the other day that a certain blog I used to subscribe to had posted recently. More than once," he said quietly.

"You heard correctly."

"I'm happy for you," he said.

"I think I am too."

Kieran lifted himself up above me on the couch. His hands reached out and ran over my shoulders. I closed my eyes and melted back into his hands as he squeezed.

"Then, why do you seem unsure?"

"It makes me nervous," I admitted after a moment.

"Why?"

"Because what if this is it?" I waved a hand at my computer. "What if everyone was right and this is all I can ever write? Blog posts and community articles rather than actual newsworthy magazine work?"

"Who are these people saying this? Because I know for a fact that you've written a lot more than blog posts before. You've written stories and journals and apparently a semi-decent list recently," said Kieran.

"Now, you're just messing with me. And I'm talking about the people I used to work for and other editors I sent my work to that said that I was either too ..." I never knew what it was in the end.

The most notes I had ever gotten, which was few and far between when it came to a form rejection letter, said that I was either too commercial when it came to commerce pieces or too personal or too self-deprecating in lifestyle recaps. Overall, my writing, with all its flounces and ranting anecdotes, was too much.

Kieran shook his head. "All right then, what if?"

I twisted to look up at him.

"What if that's it, and this is all you write, and it's all you want to write because this is what you enjoy? That's it," Kieran elaborated. "Would it be so bad?"

"Kieran," I whined.

I knew what he was doing. Because, yes, technically it was bad. Adult me insisted it was bad, considering I still had to eventually pay for things like rent and food.

"Does it feel bad?"

I rolled my eyes. "No."

"Do people enjoy what you write?"

"Yes. Some of the time."

He shrugged. "Then, I think you have your answer and should do whatever you like with that. I won't hold you back. You need to sleep though."

"I will."

"Now."

"Once I'm done."

Kieran's hands ran once more over my shoulders and up the back of my neck. "Come on, little Sylvie."

"I hate that name."

Laughing softly, he stood and headed across the room. "I know, but at least now, you're moving."

"Only to kick your ass."

"So be it." He swung back the blankets on the bed. "Get in."

I paused on my feet. For the past few days, I had settled myself on the couch, even when Kieran moaned and groaned about how I was keeping him up with my constant repositioning and talking before I could fall asleep, which wasn't new. I hadn't pushed the bed issue, even when he got so frustrated that he practically yelled at me to get in with him and go to sleep.

"Seriously," said Kieran with another sigh. He walked over to the other side of the bed and yanked back the heavy sheets. "Get in."

I glared at him for another moment as I considered, but not for long. I sighed, my body aching from the work we had done at the bakery today before we got home. Sitting on the floor probably wasn't my best idea.

"Can you massage my shoulders again?"

He dipped his head, gesturing to the bed.

Walking across the floor to him, I thought about carefully climbing into his tucked bed. Instead, I flopped down onto the mattress and let him flip the blankets over me and himself as he crawled in.

"Roll over." He tapped my hip.

"Bossy," I grumbled.

"Do you want me to give you a massage or not?"

Yes.

I said nothing more aloud as I turned over.

"Thank you."

Reaching for the bottom of the sweatshirt, he pulled it up and over my head, leaving me in a thin T-shirt. Layers were amazing. Now even more so as I felt his hands travel up and down my back, tracing up and down my spine until I giggled.

"Shush," he scolded.

"You're tickling me," I argued, wiggling.

He grabbed me on both sides, making me shove my face into the pillows harder so he wouldn't hear my laughter. He sat up, straddling my legs to keep me still, and I froze. Before either of us said anything, however, his hands began a much gentler roam. He pressed down on my tense muscles.

I let out a tender moan as his thumbs worked under my shoulder blades and up my neck.

Dear Lord, that is good.

"Are you okay?" Kieran whispered, a hint of amusement in his voice. "You sound like you're praying."

"I'm not."

"Am I hurting you?"

"It feels too good. And painful. And good." I couldn't decide. Every option sounded right.

"Should I stop?" he asked.

"Don't you dare."

He chuckled and got back to work. He swiped and kneaded my muscles and poked at every freckle until I was a puddle beneath him. I hummed with each new place he found.

After another round up toward my neck, Kieran massaged toward the nape, and it felt so amazing that I nearly choked. When I gave a giggle, the movement caused a shift of his hips. The hard length of him pressed against my bottom. My laugh turned into a startled grunt.

We both paused.

"Sorry," he murmured.

I shook my head, not moving. "Don't be."

It didn't matter. Kieran pulled himself off me to the side and collapsed on the bed.

I turned my head and blinked, drowsy now that my muscles had been worked quite thoroughly. "Thank you. I see now where the perks of being with a baker can come in handy."

All that kneading.

"Amy must've been pleased all these years."

Kieran snorted, getting comfortable. The silence went on, even when he reached for the lamp next to the bed, plunging us into darkness. We forgot to turn the tree off again, however. It lit up the room just enough for me to still be able to see Kieran's face in an orange glow.

"This reminds me of when you used to sneak into my room," Kieran said after a moment.

"Your mom was never very happy about that."

He shook his head. "She thought it was funny after a while. So did my dad. I can't believe your parents never noticed."

"They did," I said, licking my lips, remembering back to those many years throughout school.

There had been a period of time where I spent more time in Kieran's bed than my own. At first, I had blamed it on nightmares, and then I stopped coming up with excuses at all. I didn't need to. It had become our normal. Our us.

"Once or twice. Then, they turned a blind eye to it. I'm pretty sure that's the reason my mother insisted on giving me the sex talk herself. Rather late, mind you. It was awkward for us all."

"I can only imagine."

"I could probably reenact it, if you want. I'd need to find a banana though."

Kieran laughed. "Now, you're joking."

"Only for effect."

"Much it helped us." Kieran snorted.

"What do you mean?"

Eyes half closed, he spoke, and our conversation took on a

lulling hum, as if we were in a dream. Maybe we could be. I'd sometimes had a dream like this over the past few years, being safe in bed with Kieran again. "Neither of us were the most sexually active people in Marshall."

"I thought you and Amy were together in school."

"Well, yeah. Not until junior year though. And you and Dylan ..." He laughed now, as if it was funny.

I narrowed my eyes.

"What?"

"Nothing ever happened between Dylan and me," I told him.

"At the party even? Not even at senior year?"

"No. I told you that. I told you that nothing happened. I left a little after you did, and then I crawled into your bed ..."

We had talked about a lot, but never that silly night. Silly to him anyway. To me, it was one of those memories that kept me up at night, thinking of all the ways it could've gone differently. Better.

"That was the night I told you that I thought we should have sex. Remember?"

Not saying anything, Kieran nodded.

"I wasn't sure if you and Amy had the last time you were together at that point until around graduation, and I thought it would be nice if we both shared that first together, considering ..."

"Considering what, Sylvia?"

"Considering that everything was changing, and I loved you. Even then."

Then.

Then. Why did I say then?

Kieran didn't seem to notice. "I thought you had forgotten about that night."

"I never forgot," I said. It was hard to forget getting turned down, as if the guy I had been into for years wasn't interested in the slightest. "I just didn't bring it up again."

"Why not?"

"Because you told me not to."

Kieran cringed, as if the statement hurt him. "I did not."

"You did. I'm pretty sure you did. You told me to stop talking and put me to bed with the phrase, *You won't even remember this.*"

"I thought you didn't."

"Well, I did."

"So, you're telling me you weren't drunk that night?" he asked.

"Only a little. More than just a little, maybe. Either way, I was more than a little embarrassed," I admitted. I was surprised how easy it was now just to tell him the truth in the dark. All the truths.

"And so you hadn't been with anyone until after graduation?" he asked. "Not Dylan or Landon or anyone else?"

"Did you think I had a harem going, Kieran?" I asked. I knew what he was asking though. "I never was with anyone. Not until my second year of college. I went to a party and met someone. Let's just say, it wasn't the best first time."

Not like it could've been with you.

I wasn't sure if I said that aloud, though by Kieran's expression I could still see, I wouldn't be surprised if I had.

"Wow."

"Yeah." I shook my head. "Wow. It's not a big deal."

"I know it's not. I just never realized that—" He cut himself off because we both knew what he was about to say. He could've been my first that day back in the city even, and he had no idea. "I wish I could've been more for you, Sylvia. Then."

"I wish I could've been more for you too. Then."

"You were," he said.

I didn't understand. I clearly wasn't enough. That was what everything came down to. In the end. At the time. "I wish I could've—"

"You're so much more now than I could've ever imagined, Sylvia. I wish you could just see it. You always were so much."

"Too much, some would say."

"So bright," Kieran corrected as he swiped his thumb over my cheek, as if it was the most natural thing in the world. He let it travel up to tuck a strand of hair behind my ear, brushing against the rose tattoo hidden behind there. "And creative."

Our foreheads nearly touched as I let my eyes close while he continued to stare at me, and eventually, we both fell asleep.

Right on the edge of dreaming, however, I heard him whisper, "I was just always so unsure I'd ever measure up."

PULLING up in front of the cabin on the edge of the lake, I was out of the door before my driver even stopped talking about how long the winding roads had taken to get us here. Paul slammed his door before coming around to the side to me, where I left the window open.

"This it?"

I nodded. "I think so. I've only ever seen the place in pictures."

The photographs that I had been sent both did and didn't do the place justice. It looked like the cabin was listed on stilts and set perfectly into the side of the mountain, like some sort of woodsy tree house. Peaks and corners stuck through the green leaves, casting the road in shade. Everything was golden and green.

"We get in, have some fun, and then get back out and back to the real world. Yeah?" asked Paul.

He acted like I hadn't already noticed him checking his email on his phone whenever we had to stop at the gas station for fuel. Every time, I ignored it and noticed the way the air turned more humid and balmier.

Even with all the trees, it still put the city's hot and stifling heat in the summer to shame. There, it felt like the temperature was going to come up and out from the sidewalks beneath you and swallow you whole to the pits of hell. Here, it was everywhere, sticking to every hair and pore.

I looked around. No wonder Amy had talked about this place for every back-to-school essay for years when we were kids. "Behave, please."

I leaned back against the car and cocked my head just as he turned his at my hopeful demand.

"Since when have I ever not behaved?" he asked.

Did I have to name just one occasion? Though Paul was charismatic, he had trouble when it came to keeping his mouth shut when people didn't want to hear him speak, myself included. Though, sometimes, it came in handy.

Paul bracketed me in with his arms.

"Yes?" I asked him again, wanting him to acknowledge my request.

Closing his eyes, he slowly nodded his head.

"Thank you," I whispered.

"Now, sweet pea, we are going to have a good time, right?"

Up in the cabin I could see movement by the windows. "Of course. Why wouldn't we? Look at this place. It's beautiful."

"Just making sure you're keeping promises. All of them."

I rolled my eyes.

"My hot girlfriend." He cradled me in his arms. I almost shoved him away. It was too hot already, and I needed to get out of the jeans I was wearing. "You for real?"

"I'm for real."

"Good." He slapped the side of my thigh. "Let's get this party started."

I took a deep breath before we climbed the stairs toward the cabin. More than once, Paul's hands tried to squeeze my butt. I glared at him while he chuckled when I almost missed a step entirely.

"Hello?" I called up as we made it to the deck. I looked out from over the edge of the beautiful view. I sucked in a breath, but it didn't come back out. "It's beautiful here."

"Just wait until the sun sets."

Twisting on my heel, I widened my eyes at Kieran standing in the doorway. Before I could stop myself—I didn't even think as I dropped my bag—I sprinted toward him. I threw my arms around his neck.

He lifted me and gave me half a twirl before my toes met solid ground again. "Good to see you, Sylv."

"Ugh, it's so good to see you, Kieran." I squeezed him once more.

He was here, and I was here. Kieran in the flesh, and he looked ... he looked tan and as if he'd been working out, which confused me since the Kieran I knew would basically do anything to put something between himself and physical fitness.

"How are you? We keep missing each other's calls."

"Definitely not a game of phone tag I like," he agreed.

"Who likes phone tag?"

"It's good to see you. Why are you wearing jeans? You must be sweltering."

He wasn't wrong. I pulled back, not willing to let go of his hands until they swung between us.

Paul cleared his throat.

Kieran's hands fell out of mine.

"Oh, Kieran." I pulled Paul a step forward. His other hand, not locked in mine, remained in his pocket. "This is Paul."

After a second, Kieran extended his hand, ever the small-town gentleman. "Hey, Paul. As you can guess, I'm Kieran."

"Figured. That was quite the reunion." He stared down at my childhood best friend's hand, and I nudged him before he took it. He flashed a smile at Kieran as if there was no anger behind it.

I should've warned him better about Kieran, but then again, maybe I should've prepared myself better than to run back into his arms.

Why had I done that?

"Yeah. Sylvia and I go way back. It's been a while since we saw each other." Kieran chuckled, turning his gaze back on me. "Even last Christmas was touch and go when you came back."

"There was a lot of work and internship stuff I needed to get done before graduation."

All of us nodded as we stood. After another second, Kieran pointed back at the cabin slider doors.

"Amy is inside too," said Kieran.

"Right." I looked toward the doors, but couldn't see inside past the darkness. I put a hand up to my eyes to block the sun.

"Everyone else is in there too. We should probably go in. The air-conditioning sucks, but it's better than out here." With a wave, Kieran bent down and picked up my overnight bag before I could reach for it, leading us inside the cabin in the trees.

He shut the door behind us, and it was somewhat cooler inside. Not a lot cooler, but I'd take it.

Paul's eyes skimmed over the old orange wood dining set to the living room with the plaid furniture and television that looked like it had been here since the '90s.

Amy sat on the edge of the couch. Setting aside the paperback she had been reading, she stood up, wearing a two-piece and a cover-up.

"This is cozy," said Paul.

"I take it you're not much of a camper, like some of us?" Amy asked with a bright smile at Paul. She glanced between the two of us with the bright cheeriness I'd seen her give everyone but me. "Hi, I'm Amy."

"Paul." Paul introduced himself before glancing down at me. "I went camping with my parents once when they went to Joshua Tree. But that was more of a bungalow than a cabin. You've camped?"

"Only against her will," Kieran answered for me.

"It's sort of a rite of passage, growing up in Marshall Falls. The school even forced it on us when we had to go to camp for a week," explained Amy.

Paul turned toward me. "You're kidding."

I shook my head.

"Jenna and Gabe are in the back room, getting Delilah up and ready to head down to the lake. They should be out soon," said Amy, nodding toward the hallway.

"The baby is here too?" I had considered it, but wasn't sure that Jenna and Gabe were up to the task after hearing that the kid was basically a vampire. She never slept and sucked them both dry of any energy they had, the last time I had heard.

"She's older than a baby now."

That was right. She was basically a kid at four years old. A full-fledged child. She was another thing I had missed when I was busy during the holidays at home.

"How is she?"

"Loud," interjected Kieran, wide-eyed, as if the entire two days they'd been here already were horror-filled.

I couldn't help myself. I laughed, quickly covering it up with my hand.

"You guys should go settle into your room and get ready. We plan on heading down to the lake for the afternoon, if you're up for it," said Amy. "It's the only way to stay cool, basically, and the tourist crowd isn't here so much during the week. You're in the third room on the left."

"Got it." I reached for my bag that Kieran seemed to have forgotten he was holding.

"Oh." He passed it back.

"Thanks."

"Of course."

I glanced to make sure that Paul was following. I made it down the hall. Through the one door, I could hear Gabe making sweet, high-pitched voices at Delilah about putting on her swim floaties.

As I looked down at my feet and the knotty floorboards of the cabin, something loosened in my chest since we had first arrived in the car. I could hear Kieran talking behind me and all the voices of people I knew but hadn't heard in a long time. It was oddly, nice.

I pushed open the door to the third room on the left. One queen-size bed was in the center, taking up most of the room. On either side were small wooden nightstands. I heaved my bag up onto the end of the bed. The zipper slid down to open the bag, and I was already reaching inside to search for the swimsuit I had packed when I looked over my shoulder.

Paul shut the door until it clicked, but it didn't quite close, popping back open for a small sliver of light from the hallway to sneak through.

"Hey." I paused. "Is everything okay?"

"Yeah, it's just great."

"I'm sorry. I know it probably isn't what you expected when I said beach, lake, whatever. It's okay to be a little uncomfortable," I said with a small shake of my head. I reached up toward my hair, running a hand through it. "I should've told you more. I wasn't thinking about how the rest of us would know each other and you wouldn't."

He shrugged. "It's fine."

"Is it?" I asked. "I mean, if you really don't want to stay, we can ..."

Go? Leave?

I swallowed, unsure of where I was leading with that. Because we could leave. It wouldn't be the first time I headed out early from a gallery party or something that wasn't exactly our style.

"We can do something else if you want."

"We already drove," he sighed. "It's fine. You're right; it's just different. I don't know what I was expecting when you talked about it. It's an adventure, right?"

I bit my bottom lip. "Right. It's like you said before at the car. This is going to be a good trip. We'll be in and out this weekend. We're going to have some fun."

"You're right; we did say that." Paul's shoulders relaxed as he dropped his duffel bag on the floor. He stepped toward me, bracketing me against the edge of the bed, like he had at the car. Only this time, he didn't hold himself back from putting his mouth down alongside my ear and all the way toward my neck in a way that made me shiver, even when he bit down.

I braced my palms against his stomach, pushing him back as he made his way lower toward my chest. "Stop. We need to get ready to go before everyone leaves."

"It's not like we won't know where they went. We'll catch up," he said, glancing up at me with his cool brown eyes before getting back to where he had left off.

I felt my body begin to melt and give in as he started to kiss down my neck again, pushing at my tank top until the cups of my bra were brushed down toward my ribs.

Gabe's voice traveled through the crack in the door from the hallway, laughter in every word. "You're going to need to flap your wings if you're going to make it down to the beach. Come on now, Delly."

Paul moaned into my chest.

I pushed him back again. With him leaning down over me, it

was easier this time. "Come on. You don't want to make a bad first impression. I haven't seen them all in a while, and I'm hot."

"Yeah, you are."

"No." I forced myself not to cringe as I turned back toward my bag, still looking for my old swimsuit. "I mean, the temperature is hot. Let's go to the lake and cool off. It will be nice."

Paul groaned as he turned to pick up his own bag and sorted through it. "Fine. But you owe me."

It turned out, my bathing suit was a little older than I had thought. I hadn't had much of a chance to wear it in the past few years. It traveled with me from school to home, but the last time I had put it on, it seemed that I'd had less, well, everything.

I adjusted my boobs, trying to make them stay contained and not overflow out of the top.

"Wow, not keeping much to the imagination there, are you, Sylvie?" said Paul, smacking me on the ass.

He didn't notice my frown as he headed toward the bathroom. I adjusted the seersucker material one more time before putting on my cover-up. I guessed I didn't need to take it off. It wasn't as if I planned to go far into the water. I wanted to cool off, but one of the worst things I could imagine was being stuck in dark water, only to feel something brush up along your leg.

Gave me the heebie-jeebies just thinking about it.

Grabbing my bag with a book and my sunglasses, I headed down the hallway toward where voices gathered in the kitchen.

"I wanna go! I wanna go swimming," screeched the child with ducky floats on either arm.

"We're heading down in just a minute. We need to wait for our friends, just like our friends waited for you, Dell Bells," said Gabe.

Red faced and covered in sunscreen beneath her tiny purple bucket hat, Delilah crossed her arms and huffed, but didn't argue. To be honest, I was impressed.

"Sorry I took so long," I said.

"No problem," said Gabe, reaching out for a hug. "It's good to see you, Sylvia. Seriously, it's been too long since we've all been together like this. Most of us anyway. Landon and Dylan said they were hoping to make the trip out sometime next week if we manage to stay here that long."

"Bored already?"

"Nah, not yet. But eventually, Delly is going to run out of coloring book pages, and the television isn't the best when it rains out here whether or not it's a little paradise for now." He looked around. "Are we waiting on anyone else?"

"Oh, yeah." I waved a hand behind me. "Paul is—"

"Right here." Paul came up from behind me and flung an arm around my shoulders. "Are we ready to go?"

"You got it. Nice to meet you, Paul. I'm Gabe, and this is my wife, Jenna. And this one is Delilah." He introduced his daughter, who looked in the other direction.

"Wow, you guys really got started early, huh?"

Jenna narrowed her eyes from where she had been happily adding more snacks to her bag. She glanced up, looking Paul up and down in a way that used to make girls rethink their lives on the track team. "Sure."

Paul laughed as if she had told a joke.

"Let's head out, shall we?" Kieran clapped his hands together and stepped toward the slider doors. Opening it up, he flourished his hand toward Delilah. "After you."

Giggling, she jumped over the metal door ramp and ran toward the stairs. Gabe quickly paced after her, warning her to slow down on the steps.

"Can you help me carry the basket, Paul?" Jenna asked,

barely waiting for an answer before she pushed the basket, filled with snacks and plastic buckets and shovels, into his hands.

Paul glanced back at me before looking at Jenna like this was a great honor other than likely earning Jenna's passive-aggressive attitude in record time. When I didn't say anything, it seemed to encourage him.

He headed out the door ahead of me. "No problem."

Amy walked with Jenna, chatting about something or another by the time I made it out the door. The humid air stuck to my skin again. I twisted my hair over one shoulder, though it was too short ever since I had cut it a few months back.

Kieran shut the door and twisted the safety lock behind us.

I walked alongside him back down the steps toward the lake, toward the tiny beach across the road. For a moment, neither of us said anything. We each exchanged a glance and an awkward smile.

"I didn't realize that you were with ..." Kieran's nose scrunched where he had put on too much sunscreen, creating a white haze over his freckles.

"I didn't realize things were so serious between you and Amy," I said, stopping his train of thought. "I mean, not until I got the invitation to come up here anyway. That's good. I'm glad you guys figured things out from last time or whenever that was."

"Yeah, well ... sort of. We have both been in town, so we've been giving it another go since a little before New Year's. She thinks it's a sign or something." Kieran rubbed the back of his neck.

I pressed my lips together with a single nod. "Makes sense."

"Yeah," Kieran said as we crossed the road. "It's good to see you."

"It's good to see you too."

"Hey, Sylv, get over here and help me lay out the blanket," Paul called.

I jogged over to Paul and the others, who began to set up their spot on the rocky beach. Amy and Jenna had it down to a science while Gabe ran into the water with Delilah. The two women pushed up the umbrella and settled their chairs beneath so their faces were cast in the shade.

Everyone started to pull off their layers, if they had any. Jenna shed her oversize T-shirt, and Amy settled into her chair as she looked up at Kieran. She tilted up her chin, and he leaned down for a quick peck of a kiss.

She reached for her magazine, showing no inclination to get in the water.

I didn't really want to either as I hesitated, fingering the edge of my too-thin white cover-up.

Paul nudged me with his elbow. "Come on. Don't worry about it. Let's get in the water."

"I don't know. I'm not a big swimmer really," I admitted. "I like the idea of the water more than I actually like the experience of being submerged in it."

"Let's do this. You wanted to come to the lake. The least you could do is get in," said Paul.

He had a point. Slowly, I peeled my cover-up over my head, making quick work to readjust my bikini again until everything was covered.

I could see Amy's raised eyebrows over her sunglasses as I quickly dropped my things and walked toward the water. Everyone gathered around Delilah, doing her best effort to repeatedly throw herself into the gentle ripples.

"Now, this is what I call summer," said Gabe. He looked between Paul and me. "I'm really glad you guys could make it."

"We are too." Paul splashed himself with water until the sun glinted off him and his black aviator glasses.

If I stayed in a few more minutes, I figured that would be a good enough time before I could retreat to land. I reached out and put a hand on Paul's elbow to tell him where I was going.

He turned the other way without noticing.

I took a deep breath, trying again.

"What's that over there?" Paul asked, pointing toward the rope wrapped around a thick tree limb, hanging over the water.

"That's the rope swing. I was just saying the other day that I probably still have some moves in me," joked Gabe. "I used to show up everyone when we came to the cabin in the summer. We'd do flips and everything."

Kieran held Delilah's hand as she jumped around before slumping down, out of energy. Both of us rolled our eyes at Gabe's overexaggeration of what he had done nearly a decade ago with everyone else who ran to the lake, away from tourist-filled summers in Marshall Falls.

Paul, however, was completely invested. He clapped his hands together. "We should go do it."

"We absolutely should."

"Do it!" Jenna yelled from the beach, cupping her hands around her mouth. "Gabe has not shut up about it for days."

Without pausing to laugh, Gabe walked Delilah back to the beach to lie on the towels. She was already half asleep from showing the water who was boss. Then, everyone started to swim over to the cove on the edge of the lake. The water was, no doubt, deeper than where we had previously stood.

I didn't move from where I was. The water was nearly at the middle of my thighs, and that was enough for me.

"Come on. You know you want to get up there and show up those other girls who won't even get in the water," said Paul.

Most of the time, years ago maybe, I would've said yes. Now, at this moment, even the sun was beginning to feel like too much.

"You know, I really don't like the water much. I'm not the best swimmer."

"It'll be fine. It's not that deep. We'll be there at the bottom to grab you if you need us. It's completely safe."

As he spoke, Paul led me farther out into the water with a hand on my back. When I bobbed up and down, I could still mostly touch the dirty bottom of the lake all the way to the edge, where Gabe and Kieran were already hauling themselves out to climb up to the short peak. By the time I made it up there with Paul behind me, his hands lifted so I wouldn't fall backward down the hill, which was turning muddy from our wet feet. Gabe held on to the thick rope. There was a knot at the bottom and frayed at the end.

Looking up toward the branch, I took a deep breath. We were high, but not that high in comparison to some things, like when I looked out the windows of some of my classes, but that wasn't what bothered me.

How many years had the rope been tied up there to the branch?

"Okay!" Gabe called out loud enough that the figures on the beach glanced toward us. "One, two, three!"

Lifting his feet off the ground, Gabe swung out into the air before letting go of the rope. He gracefully fell into the water, not doing any tricks, but coming back up from under the water with a grin. He swung back his dark hair over his forehead with a cheer.

"Your turn, Kieran."

Kieran looked back at me. His face wavered at whatever he found there.

I crossed my arms over one another to both shield the world from my chest, which clearly didn't fit into this bathing suit, and stop the chill that whispered up my back and over each drop of water still clinging to me.

"Are you really going to do this?" Kieran asked.

"Hell yeah, she is," Paul answered before I could.

Swallowing, I nodded. "It's your turn."

Kieran took a deep breath before swinging on the rope into the water. His entry was less smooth than Gabe's had been, but his expression flared with delight as he waded below alongside Gabe, who was carefully distancing himself to make his way back to shore.

"Your turn now, sweetheart," said Paul. Reaching out, he grabbed the rope and passed it to me.

I held on, feeling the prickly strings bite into my hands.

I could do this. All I had to do was hold on to the rope and then let go. A child could do it. It wasn't that hard. Hold on and let go ... at the exact right moment so that I wouldn't accidentally fling back against the rocky ledge and then hit the murky, fish-infested water and drown.

Pausing, I shook my head as I let go of one hand to turn back. "You know, I really don't think I want—"

I heard my scream echo over the water before I realized it was me. Partially, it was because of the amount of gross lake water that got into my mouth when I finally hit the bottom. I gasped for air as I flung my body back up toward the surface of the water, arms automatically reaching out for something that wasn't there while my eyes were a haze of sun and water clinging to my lashes.

As I tried to catch my bearings, my hand finally connected with something. Hands yanked me toward the body they were connected to.

Kieran lifted me up out of the water, pulling me against him so I could catch my breath. His eyes were wide with panic. "You okay?"

Coughing a second as water was expelled from my lungs, I

nodded. I hadn't hit the ledge, and I hadn't drowned. My fingernails, however, bit into Kieran's shoulders. "I'm fine."

After the confirmation, his eyes were no longer on me though as he turned toward the bank, eyes on the laughter coming up from the edge, where Paul was still standing.

"You okay there, hon?" Paul called from above, letting go of the rope and jumping in himself.

A large splash came up and over the top of my hair. I coughed again while Kieran held on to me. His eyes pointedly stared at Paul until he was right up alongside me.

"I didn't realize you weren't ready."

"I kind of said that," I said softly. Because I hadn't been ready. I hadn't even wanted to do the stupid thing at all, but I held back the sharp words.

"I wouldn't have pushed you if you hadn't wanted to go. I just thought you said that you wanted to have a bit of fun."

I was having fun. Somewhat at least. "It's okay. I think I'm done swimming for now though."

"I'll help you back to the side," Kieran said carefully.

"Don't stop your fun because of Sylvia being a puss, man. I got her."

Kieran's sunburned face turned a deeper shade of red as Paul directed me away from the water and closer to the side.

"I'm sorry, hon, seriously. I thought you were just playing."

I shook my head. "It's fine."

When I stepped out of the water, the sun felt even hotter than it had before. Scooping up my towel, I wrapped it tightly around my shoulders. Taking another deep breath, I willed my heart, still racing, to calm back down.

"Hey," Amy said, leaning forward from her seat under the umbrella. She watched as Paul retreated into the water, flopping on his back when he was deep enough. "Are you all right?"

"I'm fine." I wiped my face with the edge of the towel. My eyes burned from sunscreen. "Thanks."

"He was kind of rough, wasn't he?"

I stepped under the umbrella shade while I had the chance. Carefully, Jenna got up from between us and moved toward Delilah. Jenna slipped off her arm floaties as she wrestled with them.

"He thought I was messing around. We were before, so I guess he didn't get it."

"Okay," Amy said. "You realize you don't have to do that here, right?"

"What?"

"I know I'm a bitch, but you don't have to pretend like it's all right when your boyfriend is acting like a douche."

I blinked. I never thought Amy would ever say anything kind to me in my life. This wasn't kind, and yet it was still something. I could tell even behind her large bug sunglasses.

"It's fine, Amy. It was an accident."

"All right."

"Thank you," I said.

She sat back on her plastic fold-out chair in the sun once more. She reached into the cooler and handed me a canned drink.

When I stared at it, she shook it at me until I took it.

Amy got one for herself and cracked open the fizzy alcohol, taking a sip. "I have a feeling this weekend is going to call for a lot more of where that came from."

Jenna rounded us and sat back down with Delilah in her arms, wrapped in a pink-striped towel. "Pop one for me?"

Back inside the air-conditioning, though it wasn't much, felt like a blessing. I forced myself not to pass out on the bed for a late afternoon nap the moment I changed into dry clothes. My loose T-shirt and linen shorts didn't feel like they were strangling my ribs.

Paul smiled the whole time, talking about Gabe after he got a shower and ready for dinner. "I thought you'd be happier about us all getting along."

"I am," I said. "Sorry. I'm tired."

"Well, get untired. Dinner is in a bit, isn't it? You should probably go help."

Nodding, I took a moment to squeeze in the mirror to comb out my hair before heading to the kitchen. Jenna handed me the plates to set the table as everyone worked in a gentle silence, refueling after a day in the sun.

One by one, the rest of them slowly came out of the rooms to help. Kieran set out napkins before supervising Gabe, who was cooking on the grill, where he mostly didn't burn anything. We kept the door open as the sun went down, and a cool breeze drifted in from the deck, ruffling my hair as we sat down and ate together.

I drank a large gulp of water from my glass. Kieran chuckled as he grabbed the pitcher behind him to immediately refill my cup.

"Thanks," I whispered.

He nodded, not smiling, just watching.

"So, Paul, I didn't get to ask. You graduated with Sylvia, right?"

Chewing, Paul shook his head. "No. I work in business management."

"That's interesting."

"Yeah, business is where it's best to be right now, especially in the city. Some people think that dressing up and looking your best every day is sort of stuffy, but I like it."

"Do you help a business or …" Jenna drifted off, as if her family didn't own two businesses in town. They did and would eventually pass them on to her. "Sorry, I don't know much about what goes into the title of business management."

"That's okay," said Paul. "It's complicated. Like I said, not for everyone."

"And, Sylvia, you graduated earlier this month, right?"

The only people who had come out to graduation were my parents even though I had made sure to invite Kieran as well. He was busy in town, he had said, even though he had graduated back in the winter an entire semester early. I had missed his. So, really, I couldn't blame him. The trip was long on the train, too, unless he managed a ride with my parents, and the entire graduation had been boring.

"Yeah, I'm looking to get a job or another editorial internship, I think. It's what my advisor recommended anyway. I've been trying to get my website together as sort of a portfolio," I said.

Paul clacked his fork against the plate, taking another bite of potatoes. "Yeah, her little blog is definitely something, though it's not going to get her far when it comes down to it. I keep telling her if she wants to do that kind of stuff, she should've switched her major before it was too late. Get into marketing. That's what all the girls do in the business school. High-end brands and public relations. You'd probably be good at that, huh, babe?"

"I've never really wanted to be an administrator in a cubicle." I leaned into my one hand, preparing myself for whatever else he planned to throw out there. "Or at least not exactly."

"Isn't that what you'd do anyway—sit around all day, doing those off-beat articles for magazines no one has heard of? What was your last one? Froyo toppings for each zodiac sign or some shit?" He had a point, yet I didn't reply. "PR girls get into all the good parties eventually, too, if they're any good."

"Not all girls like parties." Kieran spoke up.

"All the girls who are forming professional connections like parties," Paul said. "How else are they going to find their next position without a few drinks and sitting in a few laps? Helps to rise above the competition if the industry already knows who the hell you are."

My lip curled. "Paul."

"What is it, sweetheart? You know I only want to help you."

Right. Of course. Yet, in the back of my mind, I couldn't help myself.

Who is this asshole? I always knew Paul wasn't the best, but now I wanted to shrivel under his arm, disgusted.

"You shouldn't talk about her like that." Kieran looked down at his plate, gripping his fork tightly in his fist.

"You like how I talk to you, don't you, Sylvie?" Paul's hand slid up my back toward my nape. Usually, I thought that hand was warm and heady, possessive in a way no one had ever been for me before.

I rolled out my neck.

"Her name is Sylvia."

Paul's eyes trailed back over to Kieran, narrowing. "Yeah, I know that."

I stood up. All eyes turned to me.

I waved a hand in front of my face, an easy cover-up with how red my cheeks had turned. "Sorry, all the drinking today is making me hot. I think I'm going to step outside for a minute. I'll be right back."

Before anyone could say anything, I rounded the table and headed outside onto the deck. I didn't stop walking until I hit the very edge, overlooking the lake and trees. Some strung with lights were just beginning to turn on.

What had I been thinking, bringing him here? What had I been thinking, coming here to begin with? I laughed out loud at my complete stupidity, hoping it would cover up the fact I really wanted to cry.

"Something funny?"

I flung myself around to face Kieran as he slipped out of the house. Behind us, I could hear the rumble inside, picking up a new conversation.

I took a deep breath. "Life."

"Makes sense." Kieran paced for a moment before coming to stand next to me at the railing. "That was ... Paul is ... I don't dislike people, Sylvia. At least, I try not to, but Paul ... he—"

I know.

My body felt like it was covered in a rash, and I couldn't stand to look at Kieran and see what he must've seen. It was all pathetic, but Paul did like me. He did and had said so right to my face the first time we met.

I thought I liked him, too, though I couldn't come up with a reason why when all the air was squished tight in my lungs.

"Your taste in guys is just getting worse and worse," Kieran said, exasperated. "You're lucky I don't punch him ... how he talks to you."

"You would punch someone for me, Kier?"

He shook his head at me back and forth, loosening some anger. He ran his hands through his hair.

I wasn't sure I had ever seen him like this. Upset, frustrated? Sure. But never angry.

"Kieran ..."

"I miss you, Sylv."

"I miss you too."

"No," he said, taking a deep breath. "I really miss *you.*"

The two of us stared at each other. I looked down at the lack of space between us before I looked up at Kieran's face. How easy it would be to bridge that final inch gap between us, just like in New York—though neither of us spoke about it, so much so that I was pretty sure it had all been a dream.

Kieran cared about me. I cared about Kieran. But that was all it was meant to be, wasn't it?

I took a step back because it had to be.

"We should probably get back inside, huh?"

He stared down at me, still unmoving from where he stood. His chin dipped in a small nod.

He sighed. "Probably."

We probably should've done a lot of things.

THIRTY-FIVE

NOW

MY EYES SNAPPED BACK OPEN. *No*, sleep was not going to stop me now. I forced myself to sit up in Kieran's bed, even after my muscles were lulled into a false calm.

"No," I said.

"What?"

"You know that isn't true. Please, if anyone was cast in one of our shadows, it was clearly me in yours. You were always the amazing one, Kieran."

"No, I wasn't. I was the smart one."

I rolled my eyes even though it was one hundred percent true.

"I was terrified of everything. I didn't have a talent, and I wasn't good at anything, like you. I told you that I couldn't even leave Marshall Falls, like you did."

"That doesn't matter."

"It did though," Kieran said, voice turning hard before he shook his head. "It did matter, didn't it?"

My lips parted, but no words came out. We were both very awake now.

"It did matter," repeated Kieran. "I might've made friends in school and gotten the grades, and I was a decent son."

"More than a decent son," I said.

"But in the end, I look around these days and wonder what it mattered. I didn't get the life or the purpose ..."

"What are you talking about, Kier?"

"I didn't get you," Kieran forced out the admission.

I nearly jumped back. Kieran didn't let me as he wrapped a hand around the back of my neck.

I sputtered.

"You asked me the other night when I dragged you back here if I ever forgot about you." Kieran shook his head, his gaze flickering between my eyes, which were suddenly met with damp pressure, and then lower. "Shit, Sylv. Sometimes, I feel like I never stop thinking about you. Every day since I first met you, I think about the times we've spent together and how I've felt about you. You're all I've thought about in my life—every minute."

Our heads were pressed together so that we shared heated breaths.

"I've only ever thought about you that way too, Kieran."

Before I could comprehend what exactly we were doing next, Kieran's lips scraped against mine, as if somewhere in our conversation, we had leaned into each other too close as we spoke. But quickly, it held, lingering in a short, tender kiss. Unfortunately, I wasn't willing to let it end there, like a passing whisper in the late of night.

My hand shot up to hold him at the back of his neck, mirroring him. I tilted my head to the right until we lined up as if our mouths had been made for each other.

The small kiss breathed into wanting to devour, and we gave in to it. Our bodies molded together. I breathed into him when we tangling ourselves until there was no backing away. I was unwilling to let him go.

Kieran let out a small, almost-keening sound as he kissed me back.

Because he did. He kissed me back.

I gasped on a cry, almost unable to believe it.

But I had to because when it ended, the feeling ached in my chest like nothing else in the entire world ever would. I never thought I would kiss Kieran again, and he tasted ...

"Fuck, Sylv. You taste just like I remember."

I huffed a laugh, thinking the same thing.

But then he was shaking his head. "We can't."

Why not? I wanted to scream, but I shut my eyes and sealed my lips tight together in a line.

His thumb pulled out my bottom lip. "We *really* can't do this again."

"The past few days," I said, agreeing, "it's been better than I could've ever hoped for. I'm sorry. I thought I could do this."

He studied me, but he didn't let go. He wasn't letting go of me, and I put a hand on top of his to stop him for even an extra second if he tried, feeling his smooth calluses against my skin.

"Do what?"

"I thought I could let this go and follow through and let myself be with you, even for this short amount of time, so that I knew you didn't hate me because I couldn't stand it. I never could stand it."

I shut my eyes again so I wouldn't have to witness my confessions. "I love you, Kieran Rose. I've always loved you, and you know it. You must know it. That stupid night four years ago and those stupid, stubborn fights don't change that. Right? You do know, don't you?"

When I peeked my eyes back open, Kieran remained staring at me.

"You must know that I wanted to come back all this time. I wanted to come back and make things right. But then your mom got sick. It's no excuse, I know. But I didn't know until I was too late because I didn't pick up the damn phone. All I wanted was to be here for you, but then, yet again, *there* was here. There was town and Amy. I knew she was better for you than I was. Then there was work, and it was all so much. So, I didn't decide. Though that sort of was deciding, wasn't it?"

"You're rambling."

"I know I am. I'm just trying to say I'm sorry. So sorry for everything and that I still love you so much that I made a stupid list to even try to win back your love—"

"I knew the list was a ploy."

"I thought I could at least get you for a little while, whether you wanted me or not, which, yes, was selfish, but I thought I could fix things and just have a piece of you—my best friend—for a little while again. We didn't need to talk about this or what happened or how much I missed you. Because I did. I missed you so much that I sincerely thought after work, I could collapse on the subway steps and die there."

"If not from that, from the tetanus."

Both of us shared a small laugh.

"I get it, okay? We don't need to talk about it if you don't want to. I can handle just having a little of you for now, if you let me." I was one second away from begging.

"Please, Sylvia. We both know that we suck at moderation."

"Even when it comes to each other?"

"Especially then," he said, looking down at us in the same bed all over again.

History was repeating itself, only instead of hopeful kids, we were now adults with painful, broken hearts, tattered and cut to sharp edges.

"I'm really sorry."

"I thought we were done saying sorry."

"I don't think I'll ever be done saying sorry to you, Kieran. I have too much to be sorry for at this point, so I understand if you just want this to be it too. A clean slate. We can walk away from this all after the holidays. You get to live your life and get back with Amy and fall in love and have your family here. It'll be like you always dreamed of, without me in the picture after everything and all the complications that come with me being here."

"You think I want that?"

I shrugged.

"I feel like we keep having this same conversation. Look at me, Sylvia. For once, take my words for what they are. They aren't people-pleasing or trying to say something other than what I mean. Ready?"

I nodded.

"Amy and I were never going to work out. Ever."

"What? Of course, you could—"

"Let me keep going," said Kieran. "Amy was never going to be anything more than my girlfriend since the first time we got together. We were good together. We fit because all we both ever wanted was to be happy enough, content. But someone along the line messed that up for me. Content wasn't what I wanted anymore. I wanted you, Sylvia. From middle school or even before that, I wanted you. No matter how hard Amy and I wanted it all to be simple and talked about making the best of things, nothing ever could be that way because I was in love with the least simple person in any room. I didn't want a family out of high school and to throw dinner parties every weekend. I wanted you. Always you."

I wasn't sure I was breathing.

"But we can't do this again, Sylv. I've been through too much the past few years with my mom and you. If we mess anything up again like that, I don't think I'll survive it. I don't think we will. You understand what I'm saying?"

I quickly turned to get out of the bed when he didn't say anything. He reached out and grabbed my waist before I could move an inch.

"Stay," he repeated. "But we can't. Really, this time, I know that it's not what you or I want ... not again, Sylv. Not if you aren't sure that this is all enough for you. That I'm enough for you."

"You've always been enough for me."

His thumb brushed my chin.

"Please, Sylv?" he begged softly. "You know this is it? My hat has been in the ring forever. I've always been here whether or not it's a good idea. Us. But I can't keep doing this. I can't keep having and losing you all over again. You're either mine or ..."

Or we would turn to nothing.

"Okay. I understand. Okay."

Kieran, as if he couldn't help himself, tilted his head up and kissed my forehead. "You know, if we close our eyes like this, I can almost believe we are fifteen again."

So could I.

A tear at last slipped down my cheek, and Kieran knew better than to say a word about it as it collected into a puddle around my nose.

"But we aren't fifteen anymore. We're pieces of who we are, and *now Kieran* knows that I won't be that stupid boy that I let myself be all those years ago. I will be all the best pieces of myself for you, if you want me to be. But you have to know what you want, Sylvia. Do you? Because if not, right now, we can't do this. I know you don't want to risk it."

"I ..." I thought I did. "I don't want to risk this."

"Then, promise."

No.

I didn't answer as we stared at each other, but it didn't matter. I could feel my heart race faster as the realization that by the end of this week and the holidays, this had to be it. One way or another.

Like Kieran said, we were never good at moderation.

I BROKE UP WITH PAUL. We hadn't made it long after we got home from the lake. I had held on for a few weeks. I had to. I couldn't just give up. I didn't want to be alone even if alone was better than with Paul.

He hadn't even seemed to mind after he blew up at me about ditching him and said that I never saw him as someone as amazing as he really was.

I guessed both of us just hadn't been enough for each other.

With all my extra time, I applied to so many jobs that my fingers nearly gave out before I was able to post on my blog at least once or twice a week. I needed something to go right after all. So, I wrote.

I wrote about the city, and I wrote about my awful jobs without naming the place I worked at. I wrote about the parties I had gone to and the ones I had dodged to stay home and eat too many wavy potato chips by myself with the latest best-selling book in my lap. I had picked it up after I saw it on a brownstone front step, along with a few other hardcovers, with a note saying, *Free to a good home.* I wrote about Kieran and when he called and long-distance friendships.

The only phone calls I had answered lately were the ones from him.

Each call filled me with new ideas and possibilities as I pitched articles I knew would sell and ones I knew were too personal and too kitschy for anyone to pick up at all—because as Kieran had said, what could it hurt?

The List skyrocketed in views. My work was getting out there even if no one knew it was me talking about the best places to go in the city when you were young and broke. Both things I absolutely was as I signed my first big-girl lease with five other girls, squeezing into a fifth-floor walk-up, where the only window was facing a brick wall. There were two full bedrooms with the rest of us creating walls with curtains and bookshelves when we found them on the side of the street.

Luckily, a few months later, an expensive train ticket was purchased, and I no longer had to listen to doors slamming from the odd hours my roommates kept. Trees passed by, more and more already losing their leaves the farther north we went, and the sky took on a gray hue, even as the sun attempted to peek out between the clouds.

Anxious giddiness pooled deep in my stomach.

I jumped off the train and onto the platform the moment it stopped with no one else getting off. I raced down the steps, narrowly missing one and going sprawling over the concrete. I barely saw my driver back into town. He stood against the side of his dad's old cherry-red pickup truck.

I crashed into his arms with a string of laughter between the two of us.

"You miss me that much, Silly?" Kieran chuckled, using my ridiculous nickname that I hadn't heard him use since we had been in high school, and even then, it had been few and far between.

His arms wrapped around me tighter as he nearly lifted me off the ground.

My face pressed into the space between his neck and shoulder. He carried the scent of vanilla from his mother's bakery and pine from whatever deodorant he'd worn since high school, and I sucked a deep breath in.

Well, I was definitely here. I was back in Marshall Falls. With Kieran's arms around me like this, it felt good.

"Yes," I admitted, holding on to this hug for one more second.

"Not even going to lie and pretend that you didn't?" He chuckled again.

I shook my head into his skin before we slowly pulled back apart. Kieran opened the passenger door and swung my bag inside.

"Nope."

Clipping my seat belt, I rested my feet on my bag. Turning toward me as he pulled himself into the driver's seat, Kieran smirked at me.

I studied him. "What?"

"You." He turned the key and started the truck. "You're basically shaking in your seat. Did something happen? Did you commit a murder and that's why you are so excited to be home—because you know I'll pretend to be your alibi?"

"You would lie about an alibi for me?"

Kieran narrowed his eyes, as if the question was utterly ridiculous. "Um, yeah, I would. My mom made an extra two dozen batches of raspberry shortbreads for you. She'd be disappointed if you were carted away before she could see you somehow eat them all in one go."

Now, I knew what I wanted to do first when we got to Kieran's house. As if to punctuate the fact, my stomach rumbled.

"Good," I said. "I saved room."

Kieran laughed, reaching for the radio. A gentle noise of holiday music was everywhere at this point. You couldn't get away from it.

I leaned back in my seat. "Tell me what I missed."

"We just talked last night."

"Enough time for something crazy to happen."

"Where do you think I live again?" he asked.

"Come on. There has to be something. Did your mom try anything new at the bakery that you forgot to tell me? New espresso machine?"

"We got a new one last year."

"Right," I said, not remembering that, but I nodded nonetheless. "How about Jenna and Gabe and the rest of the crew? Are they doing anything fun?"

"I helped them put up their second tree a few days ago."

"A second tree?"

"Yeah, the first one they chose for the house fell over."

"You're kidding."

Kieran shook his head. "Nope. The whole thing basically snapped in half for no reason. Jenna's dad thought it was funny. Everyone else was just glad they hadn't decorated it yet."

"What else?"

"Uh ... Dylan is dating some girl."

"Someone in town?"

He shook his head again. "No, he went on a trip with people from school and came back with this girl. Or so we think. I never met her. They talk on the phone a lot, but Landon and Gabe tease him that she's probably fake."

"Why would they think that?"

"He says she's from Canada."

I barked a laugh. That did sound fake. Poor Dylan.

"Okay then, what about Amy? Have you two gone out and done all the romantic holiday traditions and experiences this year? Was there looking at all the Christmas lights and sipping hot cocoa on the bakery porch?"

He gripped the wheel. "Amy and I ... we decided to take another break for a while."

"Oh." I paused. "Really?"

"Yeah. We decided it a while ago, back in October or so actually."

"You didn't say that on the phone."

He looked a bit sheepish. "I probably should've. Sorry."

"Was it because of the phone calls?" I asked.

"No. Of course not."

He didn't sound one hundred percent honest. Or maybe he really didn't know. I didn't press any further.

"Okay. I'm sorry."

"Don't be. Like I said, Amy thought it was a sign since we were still here in town, and it was..."

"Like magic?" I tried to tease, but it came out flat.

"Convenient." Kieran blinked and turned to glance at me before focusing back on the road. "That sounds really awful, doesn't it? I didn't mean it like that."

"No, it doesn't sound awful. It makes sense. We all want to have someone there for us, Kieran."

I couldn't be that person. We came back around to this conclusion again and again. Or at least, I did.

"We're still friends," said Kieran.

"That's good."

"It is," he agreed, serious.

Sensing the change of topic, I looked out the window as we made it into town before speaking back up.

"Okay, so what do we need to fit in during my time home here?" I asked. "Come on. I know you probably made a list for the two of us."

"You know you could make a list sometime. Put in some of

the heavy *listing*."

"But I know you love it."

Kieran rolled his eyes. He totally did love making a good list. Who was I to take that away from him?

Slowly reaching down into his jeans pocket, Kieran procured a folded piece of paper. He handed it to me between two fingers.

"Why, thank you." I scanned the list.

Everything was laid out in perfectly straight lines with checkboxes. Christmas morning gift exchange, looking at the lights, watching holiday films even if we probably wouldn't get through all of them by New Year's ...

"The holiday party?" I asked, looking up.

"Yeah," Kieran huffed, as if, for a second, he thought I was joking. "Mom's going to be so happy that you're here for the party."

"I didn't miss it?"

"Psh." He glanced at me as he pulled up to my house. I could already see my mother peeking through the front living room curtains. "Oh, you're serious."

Kind of.

"It's the twenty-third. It's always the twenty-third. Of course you didn't miss it." He laughed as if I had said something completely ridiculous.

In the world of Marshall Falls, it was.

Then again, I guessed I was the one who had forgotten.

"Seriously, you need to be dressed and ready to go by seven so my mom doesn't freak out. She's been extra uptight about the party this year for some reason."

"I'll be ready by seven," I assured.

Kieran studied my sincerity. "Better make it six thirty for you. Or maybe you should just show up when your parents do if they get to my place before."

I rolled my eyes. "Six thirty then."

"Good."

Reaching across the center console of the truck, I wrapped my arms back around Kieran. This time, our hug was softer.

"It's good to see you," I mumbled even though I really wanted to say that I had been counting down the days I could see him in person because the phone calls just hadn't been cutting it for a while now.

As if he could tell, Kieran gave me a squeeze. "Yeah, me too, Sylv."

My father stood in front of the front door on the stoop the moment I made it out of the passenger seat and tugged along my heavy duffel bag, bursting at the seams. Hands on hips, my father tipped his head at Kieran, who idled in the driveway.

"Hi, Mr. Calasis," said Kieran through the rolled-down window.

"Hey there, Kieran. We'll see you at the party later."

Kieran smiled with a wave as he watched me get to the door. "I'll be there."

"Does your mother need anything beforehand that we can help out with?"

"Nope, I think we're all good at home. She's been planning for weeks. Sylvia!"

I turned back, halfway past the screen door.

"Six thirty." He pointed at me.

I rolled my eyes and headed inside, where my mom was already waiting.

"You're late."

"I am not. It's seven. We both knew that when you said six thirty, that was what you meant."

Kieran pulled me inside the house.

The party was just getting started anyway by the way others rolled in through the front door behind me.

"My mother was insistent that I wash my hair with 'non-city' water and make myself look presentable."

"So, that's why it took forever?" Kieran joked.

"Don't be mean."

He chuckled, eyes scanning me up and down. "You look nice, Sylv."

I honestly hadn't been sure what I was going to wear for a nice night back in Marshall Falls. All my clothes from high school were still packed together in a dresser in my old room, but nothing either fit right or felt right anymore. I had picked up the tight sweater dress on a whim from a thrift store down in SoHo. The deep plum color was the first thing that had caught my eye even though it wasn't exactly one of the more traditional Christmas colors.

I looked down at myself again, oddly feeling a rush of heat flood into my cheeks.

"Thanks." I smiled.

"Ready?"

"For the party or for you to show me where the two dozen cookies are I'm very prepared to consume?" I asked. "Because yes to both."

"Come on, cookie monster." Kieran waved a hand for us to move away from the door as more people pushed in.

"Is anyone else here? The group should be coming, right?" I said, meaning Gabe, Jenna, Dylan, Landon, and Amy at least.

They always showed up, especially if their parents were coming and to get one of the best holiday meals of the year.

Kieran shuffled his feet halfway into the living room. Most of the guests milled between there and the kitchen, where all the delicious food and confections made by Lori were likely to be, which I'd been waiting all night for. I could already imagine them—no, smell them.

"They should be here eventually."

"So, it's not me who is late," I pointed out.

Kieran rolled his eyes.

A round of claps in beat started to sound through the living room. Pausing, I looked around, finding eyes on us and above our heads.

I tilted my chin up to see the piece of leaves hung by a string between the archway we had paused below.

Everyone continued their hoots at the sight of us not realizing. Mistletoe.

"Come on. It's tradition!" someone called out.

I looked at Kieran, who shifted before staring down at me. Our eyes met, and for a moment, I could see the two of us not hesitating at all. He would already be holding me, and kissing me would be like breathing air.

But we weren't like that. I had to keep reminding myself of that.

"Just a kiss," I whispered.

The corner of his mouth curved upward as he leaned down. A quick peck that ended all too quickly. We pulled away, and a few of the Roses' guests clapped before the next group would be sacrificed to their mistletoe wager.

Making our way through the living room, I took a few steps away from Kieran and stopped at what I saw on the kitchen counter. I shoved a cookie in my mouth, tasting the tart sweetness of the raspberries. Immediately at whatever sound I must've made, Kieran's mom's eyes turned and found me.

"I'm so happy you're here," she said before whispering, "I have an extra batch of them hidden away for you."

Kieran wasn't kidding.

"Best. Christmas gift. Ever."

Lori beamed at my reaction and patted me on the shoulder before moving on to her next guest. I moved on to the next cookie.

How could I ever go so long without them every year?

After consuming more than the appropriate number of cookies and washing them down with whatever was in the holiday punch bowl, I realized that Kieran never followed me to eat. Maybe one of the guys had shown up. I rounded the corner back into the living room. Kieran sat on one end of the couch.

From this angle, it was easy to see how much work Lori had put into this get-together. The lights in the house were dim, except for the ones brightening up the room from the roof outside and rounding the tree. The cozy holiday even transcended upstairs this year, looping around the staircase.

Sitting down, I squeezed up next to him, and my feet kicked out in front of us before I got settled. Holding two cookies in my hand, which I had brought with me in case of a party emergency, I offered one to Kieran, waving it in front of his face as he zoned out.

After a second, he took it.

I bit down into mine. "Now, this is the kind of holiday I'm talking about."

Looking down at the little heart imprint of his cookie, Kieran shrugged.

"What? Not in the holiday spirit suddenly?" I asked, finishing my own last bite. I really needed to stop eating and brushed off my hands for good measure. "Come on. We still need to add our decoration to the tree."

Patting his leg, I pushed up off him and headed toward the tree. No one else was there yet. A few ornaments adorned the branches. That left a lot of room for decisions.

Reaching down, I dug through the brown paper bag on the floor until I found an ornament that I didn't think I'd ever noticed before on the Rose tree. Sparkling and covered with snowflakes, I gently picked it up and held it until it glimmered in the low light.

I might not have been a traditional holiday girl, but I could appreciate the pretty parts of it.

One branch at a time, I scanned for the perfect spot for the perfect ornament. I held on to the metal wire until I bent down, right toward the front of the round tree. As I looped my snowflake-painted ornament around my chosen branch, Kieran did the same with his old family-made decoration a branch away.

We were nose to nose, and I chuckled, ready to compete in some sort of staring contest if that was what it was going to take to perk Kieran back up out of whatever mood he was in. We stared at each other for a minute, and then without hesitation, Kieran kissed me.

THIRTY-SEVEN

NOW

I SQUINTED at the screen after looking at it for so long. Not only that, but looking at so much silver glitter really hurt the eyes, which I had learned after helping Lori and the rest of the Roses get set up for the annual holiday party tonight.

It was a full schedule. Lori had been running around with her fine hair in rollers most of the morning. Not only that, but it wasn't the only party Kieran and I had to juggle. Somewhere in the past few years, Jenna had taken it on herself to assume the hostess position of the next generation, which I could totally see.

With the holiday music sweeping through the main house and everyone posting their own holiday lists and Christmas happenings online, I could almost feel the swirling spirit that I hadn't had since I had been a small child. It pooled in my stomach as I worked on *The List* and made sure to schedule updates over on social media in case I forgot. So far, I'd posted a holiday party style guide as well as books to complete a yearly reading goal on a high note.

Kieran had helped quite a bit with that one. He also helped me figure out how to best upload all the photos I'd been taking onto my old laptop I desperately needed to look into upgrading.

Crossing my legs where I sat in front of the coffee table, I hit publish on a new section on the website, smiling as I did. It had been a long time coming, but I couldn't help but get excited about what was slowly but surely happening next. Who would've thought my little blog would matter so much to me all over again?

Where's KIERAN??? a longtime blog reader had commented on my small-town tree decorating post after catching a stray hand that clearly wasn't mine in the photographs. *Is Kieran still around in Marshall Falls?*

A few below responded with their own guesses, along with, *I always thought they were a one true pairing in real life.* And, *If he's still there and she doesn't take him, I might need to schedule a hiking trip for a cute small-town man to come save me when I wander off the trail.*

I rolled my eyes. As if Kieran would save anyone on a hiking trip.

I allowed them to entertain themselves as I chose a few other comments to reply to—not including the ones begging for gossip on Kieran. To be honest, I wasn't sure what to say.

I had an entirely newfound respect for devoted readers, however. They felt almost like a strange little online family with never updated, early chat-room nicknames, like *Rebex42* or, even better, *cinnamontoastluv4eva.*

That was some serious loyalty.

I clicked my next tab, going back to my email. I had been slowly clearing out and reorganizing the past few days. I finally made my way through enough for it to be considered a decent-sized dent.

A new, unopened email sat in bold at the top, right above the last email I had hastily replied to a few days ago. I narrowed my eyes toward the unknown name.

Hello, Sylvia Calasis.

We've recently come across your updated website, The List, as well as its developing up-and-coming media channels. We are highly impressed, and we would be honored to invite you ...

"Are you still sitting on the floor?"

I quickly looked above my screen toward Kieran. "Hmm?"

Kieran narrowed his eyes at my wide pair. "Whatcha looking at?"

"Nothing."

"Okay then," Kieran replied slowly. "It's getting late. You should probably change unless you plan on going to your first non-Rose-hosted Marshall Falls holiday dinner party looking like a pubescent me. Though I doubt my mom will find it anything but hilarious when we get back to her party."

I chuckled, shimmying back and forth where I sat. "You think I'm hot."

"Oh, yeah, that old hoodie you stole from my closet definitely makes you look hot."

"You think I'm hot," I sang.

His cheeks flushed a shade darker. "Be quiet."

"Never." I grinned, knowing that I was walking a fine line since the other night.

Though things had been better since I had started sleeping back in his bed with him, including my sleep, other things had been on edge. Every movement we made almost felt too close to one another, a brush of a hand too friendly.

And I couldn't help but want more of it.

He waved me off. "I'm getting a shower. Do you need to get into the bathroom?"

I shook my head. "Go ahead."

"Get dressed," he reminded, watching me turn back to my laptop, peeking back down at the email sender.

"I am!" Standing up, I shut the lid.

At some point in the past week, Kieran's closet had begun to hold more and more of my clothing that had made its way out of my suitcase. I was fine with having a little spot on the floor, but every time I left something somewhere, Kieran would hang it up. My shirts were in the closet. My jeans were on top of his dresser, and my shoes were neatly tucked underneath the edge. Usually, everything was folded better than I had ever left it, incorporated into all his own things.

Pausing before the closet, I listened to the cascade of water falling inside the bathroom. I turned my head to the side and saw the door had been left an inch cracked open.

Unable to help myself, I peeked through the crack. I saw nothing other than the foggy glass mirror inside.

What would he do if I walked in?

What if I left everything out here—from his worn sweatshirt, which still smelled a little like him, to my underwear—and got into the shower with him? Where would his eyes land and his hands touch?

I shook out my hair and fixed my makeup by the time the water cut off. We had a few days left before the reality of the new year hit and the world came crashing down on us, and then—

Kieran came out of the bathroom, his towel hung low over his hips.

I swallowed, hoping it wasn't audible as I inched my tights up over my thighs. They snapped into place at my waist.

I stared at Kieran. He stared back until my dress fell over my lower half.

His hair stuck up from the water. "You look..."

I look down at myself and away from Kieran's gaze. He cleared his throat by the time I looked back up.

"I know. I clean up nice after a good sleep and living with you for the past two weeks, huh?"

"You look good. I'll get dressed, and we'll head out, okay?"

I pressed my lips together. "Sounds good."

"Good," he said, turning around toward the bathroom. I watched his back as he went, nodding to himself. "Good."

"Look at me." I turned around in a small circle. "I have a jacket and everything."

The thick fabric fell behind my knees. Though I was supposed to be saving money, I could only go on for so long throughout the winter, wearing Kieran's coat. It had been a necessary splurge, especially as I watched Kieran laugh at the extra-thick fleece lining.

"You must be so proud."

"You have no idea."

Kieran led us down the path to his car. He held out his hand to steady me on my short heels. It was different to be in actual clothes again, ones that I wasn't going to be getting flour or random iced baked goods on after helping at the shop.

"You're really stepping up in the world, actually taking notice of the weather for once."

He opened the passenger door for me. I gave him a little curtsy.

Both of us were laughing by the time we made it down the street, barely noticing the fact that the car was still pouring out cold air from the vents when we stopped in front of a small ranch home. Dark purple shutters were more pronounced from the few holiday lights and obnoxiously large wreath on the front door.

I took in every inch of the small family house, framed by snow-covered bushes.

"I've never seen where Jenna and Gabe live," I said. "For some reason, I still imagined them crammed into Jenna's house with her parents, like they were after Delilah was born."

"They were with their parents for a while after the first baby, yeah. They moved in here about three—no, nearly four years ago, I think." Kieran shook his head, as if he couldn't believe he'd almost forgotten.

Parking the car, he unclipped his belt and was around the other side of the car before I even reached for mine.

He opened the door for me. After a moment, he bent down. "Are you ready?"

The door and the windows lit up with holiday lights. Forms of people were moving behind the curtains.

"You sure they don't mind that I'm here?"

"What are you talking about?" he asked. "Jenna invited you. Or don't you remember?"

I rolled my eyes. I had been a little off that night when I first confronted Kieran at the bar, but I remembered.

It felt like months ago.

"I know," I said. "But I didn't want them to think they had to invite me because I was there."

"They did."

"Only because you were there. They probably felt bad." That was the sentiment that had always happened between me and Kieran, growing up.

"When are you going to realize that they have always considered you part of the group, Sylvia? You're part of here, and you always have been whether you wanted to be or not."

It was hard for me to see it that way, though she had a point. There were few things I hadn't been invited to or incorporated in. I'd always thought it was just because of Kieran, and yet ...

I had gotten a Christmas card every year from Jenna and Gabe before I moved in with Ezra.

"Now that we're done with that, get your butt out of the car, and let's get inside," said Kieran. "We're going to make today worth it, okay?"

I wondered if he felt as much pressure tonight as I did.

With a huff, I unlocked my seat belt. "Bossy."

"Uh-huh. Move it before we both freeze out here." Kieran kept a hand on me, as if he thought I was going to bolt, all the way up until we made it to the front door.

In true Marshall Falls fashion, he knocked once before letting us both in. The door was unlocked and teeming with voices inside.

"It's going to be a good time," Kieran said softly again as he stepped through the entry. "Just like old times."

"You really think Dylan will be inside yelling at us to take a shot the moment we pass the threshold?"

Kieran unzipped my coat for me, pulling the zipper down until he was bent down low in front of my face. His hot breath swept up the side of my neck as he whispered, "You never know."

"Sylvia!" cried Jenna.

I tore my attention away from Kieran. Jenna's short hair flopped this way and that as she jogged toward us from the kitchen at the back of the house.

Kieran stood up and undid his own jacket, hanging it next to mine on the coat rack.

Jenna wrapped me up in her arms against her soft cable knit sweater. "It's so good to see you. Excuse my lack of holiday clothes. Whenever I think I'm going to wear something nice, my toddler has other ideas."

I chuckled. "You look great."

She smiled wide and looked next to me. "Good to see you too, Kieran. The boys are having snacks before dinner if you want some. You, too, of course, Sylv. Are you hungry? Of course you are."

"Have fun," Kieran murmured down into my ear.

His hand slid over my arm before he walked back toward the kitchen. My arm vibrated at the touch.

"Well, don't just stand there. Come on in." Jenna tugged on my hand.

Jenna led me to where a few others were, chatting around the tree. Her two daughters stuck their heads underneath the branches to see the glow of the lights from a different angle, giggling.

The tree was covered in family photo ornaments that must've been gifts for the kids every year since they had been born. It was mismatched and full of color, but ultimately joyful.

Amy watched the two girls play, knocking into small gifts already laid underneath as they rolled this way and that. She caught me standing on the edge of the room, giving a short wave. "Hi again, Sylvia."

"Merry Christmas, Amy."

She smoothed her hands down her cheery red dress. "Merry Christmas."

"You too look so good! Stay right there." Jenna crawled up on the floor next to Delilah and her other daughter.

I didn't want to admit I didn't know the name of their most recent addition.

Jenna cupped her hands around her mouth. "Gabriel! Get in here for a second. This is our chance!"

Amy laughed as she watched Gabe eventually make his way into the living room and crawl up next to Jenna and the kids. Dylan made silly faces to take the little family photo.

Eventually, Jenna stood back up, brushing herself off as the kids seemed to get a second wind, running around the room to play with the toys already out.

Jenna grinned. "Well, I figured that was never going to happen. We have to take cooperation where we can get it."

"You look happy," I said quietly.

She cocked her head, as if it was a crazy thing to say. "I am."

It was hard not to think back to Jenna sitting next to me, near tears after she had first found out she and Gabe were going to become a family. How far they'd come, so full of love.

I never thought Jenna wasn't a great friend, but she was someone who always made Marshall Falls feel less empty. Maybe she could be a good friend, if I gave in and let her, even after all this time.

"It took a bit, I'll admit," Jenna said. "Things aren't meant to go to plan though. That's what makes life fun. Gabriel certainly taught me that, if nothing else, all these years."

"Hasn't it been ten years already?"

"That we've been married," Jenna confirmed. "I know, right? It's wild. But a good wild. We'll be that decrepit, old couple that will practically have been together as long as we've been alive."

"I'm happy for you," I said.

Taking a deep breath, Jenna studied me. She reached over and squeezed my elbow, leading me a room over to the kitchen. The house was cozy and warm, though it didn't have the open concept that most modern homes did and people vied for. No one seemed to care right now. Photographs lined the wall. Old wallpaper, which I could only imagine they never got to remove yet from the last owners, peeled at the edges. Horses and cowboys littered the repeating print. Yet, somehow, it worked.

"I'm happy you're here." She repeated her previous sentiment when I had arrived. "We should get you a drink before we sit down to eat."

Some of the guys leaned around the counter, filled with crackers and cheese.

Gabe caught us as we entered, reaching for Jenna. She quickly evaded him, heading toward the counter.

"Wine, Sylvia?" she asked, raising a bottle.

"Sounds great."

Kieran caught my eyes and flared his own, as if in giddy warning of the last time I had admitted to drinking wine. I was only going to have one.

Taking the glass, I took a sip. It was much better than I'd expected.

Maybe I'd have two.

Kieran shook his head as he chewed on a piece of candy next to me, as if he could hear my internal monologue. It was good to see he still wasn't afraid to spoil his appetite with sweets.

I reached for a chocolate myself, biting into a caramel.

"It's good to see you again, Sylvia," Gabe said.

I spoke around the chocolate. "It's good to see you too."

"Did I see that you've been working in the bakery with Kieran?" he asked.

"Probably. I've been staying with Kieran and the Roses since my house isn't exactly the warmest right now."

Landon barked a laugh around the top of his beer can as he came in from the living room. "Yeah, her parents' entire heating system is shot. Your dad gave us a call a few days ago though."

They hadn't even called me.

"He did?"

"Yeah. Your place should be a toasty sixty-eight degrees by the time they get home."

"Great." It was still about a week away until they got home, but I wasn't sure if I wanted the heat to be fixed just yet. The thought of going back to live alone in the empty house didn't sound at all appealing.

Now, without living with Kieran, it would be lonely.

Gabe studied me. His eyes turned back and forth between

Kieran and me. "You've been fitting right back in since you got back to town then."

"Seems that way," I said carefully. "It's been nice, being back."

In the other room, a little girl let out a loud wail.

Gabe pushed away from us, glancing at Jenna. "I got it."

I turned and watched as he scooped up the upset child into his arms, who had wandered through the kitchen archway.

Gabe carried her down the hall as he spoke in a low tone. "It's time to get you ready for the sugar plums to dance in your head, young lady."

His older daughter rubbed her eyes and trailed after the two of them without question.

"They're not joining us for dinner?" Amy asked as she followed into the kitchen, where everyone was.

Jenna shook her head. She handed Amy a new glass of wine to enjoy with us. She took it without question.

"No. They ate earlier. Honestly, it will be nice not to have a battle of carrot throwing."

Amy chuckled, looking back toward the girls going down the hallway.

"I'm sure they'll see more of their aunt Amy tomorrow," said Jenna. "If not later for dessert. They'll be up for hours, unable to sleep anyway."

Everyone continued to talk until Gabe came back down the hallway without the two girls. He washed his hands and helped Jenna as she slowly began moving things toward their long wood dining table.

"Let's sit down and get ready."

Squished around the small table in the kitchen, Jenna and Gabe sat at one end. Amy was across from me with Dylan and Landon on the other end. Next to me, Kieran shuffled the chair back and sat down.

"Everyone!" Jenna said. Gabe gently rubbed her back as she spoke with her glass raised. "It's wonderful to have everyone here. Feeling very grown-up these days, having our own little party."

"Took them two kids and being married," joked Dylan.

We all chuckled.

"To friendships. They never really do end, do they?" said Jenna with a small curve of her lips. "They only grow."

"How adorable," chimed Landon, lifting his cup.

"Here's to that," Gabe agreed, shoving his glass up higher.

The chime of glasses echoed. Everyone reached over to tap the rim of their wine against mine, and I did so back.

Had it always been this way with all of us? I'd never thought so, but then again, I'd never quite given it all a chance to be like this.

Kieran tipped his glass of water in my direction. I tapped my glass against his with a low, resounding ring before we all turned toward the dishes. I didn't know what to expect, but certainly not the wide variety of bread and pasta laid out along the table.

"I might like to host a party, but it doesn't mean I've gotten to be any better of a cook," joked Jenna.

Gabe rubbed her back, not that it mattered. We all dug in, filling our plates full of noodles and different sauces.

I lifted my fork up, and Kieran's eyes caught mine.

Carefully, we dipped our forks to touch.

"Christmas pasta," he said, voice low for our inside joke.

He had promised to make up for all my lack of carbs the past few years, though I doubted he'd had anything to do with tonight.

"Christmas pasta," I agreed, unable to help my giggles as I took a bite.

Everyone looked as pleased as we were, eating. Even Amy

regarded the two of us, her eyes soft as she took a bite and washed it down with a smile and her wine.

My stomach ached from how full it was. I could hardly imagine indulging in Lori's holiday party for the rest of the night with the collection of confections that were bound to be there. Then again, I'd make room.

Leaning against the arch connecting the living room and kitchen, I watched Kieran play with the girls, who had come back out, just as Jenna had predicted. They set up milk and cookies for Santa, half asleep, but not wanting to miss the fun.

Kieran eventually trailed after Gabe to put them back to bed. My body softened.

"I saw that."

Jenna snuck up next to me. "What?"

Her eyes flicked between her husband and Kieran and back to me.

"You saw nothing," I said. Because that was what it was, clearly.

"So, you're still a liar?" asked Jenna. "A terrible one at that."

I rolled my eyes and took another sip of wine. Unfortunately, it was my last one, hitting the bottom.

Jenna hummed, not letting up. "You two sure looked a lot cozier than you did at the bar the other night."

I shrugged. "We haven't seen each other in a while."

"Must be all the living together in that tiny apartment of his for the past, what, almost two weeks? Because it sure doesn't look like two friends just catching up, if you know what I mean."

"It's been nice."

"*Nice.* That's it?" she teased.

"Yes."

"I bet it has."

I nudged her with my hip, forgetting just how much of a gossip Jenna was. She had always been Amy's eyes and ears when it came down to it back in school. Such a fact was easy to forget.

"Stop it."

Jenna barked a laugh. "I need entertainment. Especially when the two of you have always been so obvious."

"You know that isn't true."

She raised her eyebrows.

"Not always," I insisted. "There was always him and Amy. Not to mention, they made sense, and then I left."

Jenna made no noise for such a time that I turned to look her in the eye. The expression on her face stared back at me, as if I was still the most ridiculous thing she had ever seen in her life. My excuses were falling on deaf ears, and frankly, they were sounding a little sad to my own at this point.

"Don't—"

"I know that you and she never got along well, Sylvia," said Jenna. "But Amy ... she's never been stupid."

"I never said she was," I sighed.

"I know," said Jenna. "I'm telling you that if you seriously can't see what I see—if Kieran doesn't see it still at this point— well, we're all doomed."

I turned my attention back to the living room, taking a step. "We need to stop talking about it."

"Why?"

"Because," I huffed, "it wouldn't work. All we did was hurt each other when we tried."

"Ah."

"Yes, ah," I said. "We have finally gotten back to a good point, and things have been happening. We can't risk it."

"I get it."

"Do you?" I asked.

Jenna glanced behind me. A hand touched my shoulder.

Spinning around, I expected Kieran to be there. Instead, it was Amy.

"I'll just leave you two to it," said Jenna as she pressed her lips together, looking as if this was the most fun she'd had in ages. She waved a finger between the two of us, as if Amy could understand what that meant.

I glared at her as I turned to look at Amy, who rolled her eyes at her best friend.

"I assume you were listening?" I asked.

"Not intentionally."

I wasn't sure if that was the truth.

"I see you didn't quite take my advice from the other day at school to heart."

"It's not like that," I said. I really didn't want to have this conversation with Amy. At least with Jenna, it was like a friend. "Kieran and I ... he's my best friend."

Amy nodded.

"He's always been my best friend, and it's nothing more than that."

She scoffed.

"What?"

"I'm pretty sure Jenna just told you straight up that if you think that, you're kidding yourself. I already told you that a week and a half ago."

Not in so clear of words.

"Nothing is happening," I restated.

"I'm not here to talk about your and Kieran's love life, Sylvia," sighed Amy.

"I just don't want you to think that during all these years, I ..." *I was in love with him all this time and was keeping him from you.*

Because that was exactly what had happened. This on-and-off friendship. This on-and-off love that I wanted so badly with Kieran must not have just hurt us.

"I knew." Amy stopped me before I could ramble on further. It was beginning to sound pitiful. "I knew everything."

I narrowed my eyes. "You knew?"

"I knew about how close you two were all my life, and yet, for some reason, I thought I had this chance with him for years," said Amy. "I thought I had a chance with a nice guy. But obviously, I didn't. Not when he already had who he wanted, always right there in a way that I never could be."

Just like me, she had a hundred memories of Kieran. Only for her, I had been in them too, hadn't I? All the time, I had been there because even when I let him go—God, I could never let Kieran go.

Amy shrugged, as if she was completely over what she was saying at this rate. "I knew about you two basically sleeping together for most of high school, even when he was seeing me."

"We didn't—"

"I knew that you guys had those phone calls. They interrupted our time together when we all went off to school. If you called, the world stopped," said Amy with a long pause. "It was just you and him. For hours, if you could come up with that many things to talk about, you and those phone calls were his world. I knew there was no denying it when he went to New York to visit and came back, all weird. I knew that something had happened between the two of you. It did, didn't it?"

I opened my mouth to answer, but she swiftly shook her head.

"No, I don't want to know," Amy decided. "Yet still, it was like you two were blind, and I just kept hoping there was a reason for that. A reason for me, even after that and the lake house. It's kind of pitiful for me to keep listing all this off, so please stop me whenever you are ready."

I didn't know what to say. "You deserve a nice guy, Amy."

"Thanks. I'm going to find him eventually," she said, as if anything else was completely preposterous. Though her eyes dipped low. "Like I said before though, don't screw this up. If not for me, for everyone else who has had to put up with you two all this time."

"I'm going to try not to."

"Do more than try," said Amy, turning back to look around Jenna's overly decorated home. "At this point, you basically have a toxic fan club going, and if you mess this up, not only won't we forgive you again, but I doubt he will either. You're not perfect, and he sure as hell isn't either, but then again, I think that's why you two are meant to be, or whatever we want to call that romantic crap. You both fuck up a lot. Fuck up together."

"Thank you, Amy."

"Don't mention it. Seriously." She waved me off toward where Kieran was eyeing us, as if he couldn't comprehend what he was seeing. "I can't believe I'm saying this, but if you need anything, I'm here. Or, ya know, consult the phone chain."

"There's a phone chain?"

"Of course there's a phone chain, Sylvia. This is Marshall Falls." Amy rolled her eyes, holding her almost-empty glass of wine with both hands. "Man, I can't stand this time of year."

Huh.

That made two of us.

THIRTY-EIGHT

BEFORE

KIERAN WAS KISSING ME.

His lips were on mine, soft and supple, just like under the mistletoe. Only this time, it was more than a peck. The sounds of the party around us faded away until he was all I could focus on. His hand cupped my cheek. And this kiss? This kiss held on. It turned into a slow, even kiss. It was warm and wonderful as Kieran leaned in and kissed me like I remembered that one time in the city, as if we were both too overwhelmed to stop—until he did.

The holiday music and voices of people caught up in their own conversations flooded back in.

Breaking apart, he licked his lips, pausing. "I wanted to do that right."

That kiss was certainly more than just all right.

I didn't know what to say. Kieran stood back up to his full height, making his way toward the staircase leading upstairs. By the time he was halfway up the steps, I finally got my legs to move again and followed him.

"Kieran."

He didn't say anything as he made his way around the corner toward his room.

"Kieran, hold on a second." I was relieved when I found that he hadn't closed the door. I slipped inside and closed it behind me. "Are you okay?"

"I'm fine." He shook his head, however.

This wasn't fine Kieran. This was frustrated, confused Kieran, who would lock himself away for days if I let him, over-thinking everything that could possibly be on his mind.

"It was just a kiss." I tried to console. "It's okay."

"It wasn't just a kiss. It could never be just a kiss between us. Ever."

"What are you talking about?" I stared at him as he paced back and forth.

Holiday music beat up through the floorboards, meeting each of his steps.

He ran both hands through his hair until it stuck up at the front. "You're not getting it, Sylvia. I miss you. I miss you so much that it hurts, and I don't want to go back. I don't want to go back to phone calls and talking about our lives. I don't want you to leave and run off with all those amazing people you met. I want you to be with me."

"I want that too." I had always wanted that even though things didn't seem to work out the way we had planned or wanted them to, and I was starting to understand that was just how things happened.

"I want to live my life and make sure every second is worth it with you."

"What?" I still couldn't comprehend. I couldn't assume. I knew better than to do so.

Until he said the words.

"I love you."

My heart pounded in my chest. He had said that phrase a

million times to me before, but this time, he said it in a way that we both knew it was different.

Kieran loved me.

How many times had I thought of those words on my own? How many times had I wished that Kieran weren't so dense when it came to going after things he wanted? And now, that thing he wanted was ... me?

I had thought about this moment for months, years, decades.

The time on the mountain, when we had been thirteen, I'd stared at him and wondered what it would be like to kiss a boy, not realizing how much it was really that I just wanted to kiss him. In high school, when we had lounged in bed, all I had wanted was him close. In fact, it had felt like the most peace I'd ever had in my life when I was next to him. I thought about the phone calls that had made me feel like I was dying inside, a fine line before being brought back to life by his voice cheering me up and cheering me on.

I wanted Kieran. So many times, I had wanted him and needed him, and I knew that this right here was exactly the person I was supposed to be with all my life whether or not it seemed the best choice when it could break us as easily as make everything so much better.

So much more.

I wanted him so bad.

My eyes burned with pressure, though I didn't know why in the world I would possibly cry right now. How could this have taken so long? How could neither of us have just said something when I saw the pain and frustration behind his eyes now, as if it had been building for years, like it had been mine?

Years.

But all of them had still been spent with him.

Kieran's eyes widened. "I'm sorry if ..."

I cut him off, grabbing on to his sweater and pulling him

toward me. We both knew what I was about to do, and neither of us wanted to stop it. Kieran bent low and kissed me. I lifted myself onto my toes and kissed him right back. Or maybe it was the other way around. It didn't matter.

"I love you," I said.

He blinked, as if he couldn't believe the words coming out of my mouth. "You do?"

"I love you so much, Kieran Rose," I rambled. "I've loved you since I got you stuck in a tree."

"That long?"

"Longer. Probably when I first saw you on the steps, looking like a homeless boy who belonged in a cupboard under the stairs."

"Why didn't you say anything?"

"I did. And I didn't."

All this time.

"Why didn't *you* say anything?"

"I did," Kieran repeated, cupping my cheeks with his hands. "And I didn't. I couldn't risk this."

I knew what he meant, but now, we had gone and thrown that all out the window. Whether or not we could play pretend, like we had after his trip to New York freshman year, now, there was no hiding. There was no going back.

Good.

"You really mean it though?" I asked, my voice cracking.

For the first time perhaps, Kieran saw right through me to the deepest crevices of my insecurity that I'd hidden for years. His thumbs swiped back and forth over my cheeks.

I reached up to hold the back of his hands right there.

"It's always been us, Sylvia."

"It's just us now. You actually want to be mine? Just like that?"

"I've always been yours," said Kieran. "And you're mine."

I moaned, running my hands over him. This was real, and this was happening, and there was nothing stopping us this time.

"It's us."

"Me and no one else ever again," he murmured into my skin. His head dipped forward. "No Dylan ..."

"No Paul."

"No Paul," he repeated, nearly growling at the word as he took my mouth once more, teeth sliding over my bottom lip.

Good. We were always so good, even when we shouldn't have been. Now, this was it. This was right. This time, we were ours.

"Maybe it was a meant to be this way," I breathed. "Practice makes perfect and all that."

"We were always going to be perfect. I don't want to hear you even say something like that," he said with a chuckle. "The only guy's name I want to ever hear you say when I have you like this is mine."

"So possessive."

"Of you."

"Then, no Amy?"

He shook his head. "Only yours."

"You've always been mine, Kieran," I whispered, repeating his words back to him. I still needed to somehow comprehend the honesty fully in that statement.

It was the truth. It always had been.

Kieran grinned, eyes soft in agreement. "Always."

He didn't hesitate when he kissed me again. Our mouths moved easily. They had to. We had taken decades to study one another.

I arched into Kieran as we moved and shifted on the bed until he was on top of me. I circled my legs around his hips and held him tightly against me, even as he hissed. I could feel how hard he was through his pants.

"God, Sylvia."

I felt it too. I felt all of it, and I needed it all right now. I slid my hands underneath his sweater, and when he pulled back, I nipped at his neck. He groaned as he threw off the sweater to the ground, leaving his chest bare for my hands to roam. He grabbed on to me to even the playing field.

"Lift your arms," he commanded, barely waiting for my hands to pass over his shoulders before sweeping my dress up and overhead.

The knit was thrown wherever his sweater had gone to the other side of the room, inside out and us past caring. Kieran was already moving on as his warm hands tickled my ribs until he found the back clasp of my bra.

The clasp on my bra came undone with a single hand.

"Impressive," I commented.

"Luck." He grinned into my mouth, both of us smiling so hard that it was difficult to kiss, but that was just fine with me.

We'd seen each other naked before. We were never shy when it came to our bodies, growing up. It had always just been us. But this was different.

I looked at him and he looked back at me as if we could hardly believe that we were here.

I wasn't dreaming, was I?

Kieran chuckled as he ran a hand over my head, holding me up. His other hand teased, curving over the swell of my breast. Shivers cascaded across my skin.

"No, you're not dreaming."

I laughed with him.

"Thank God," he added, kissing me again.

He kissed me everywhere from my lips to behind my ears and down my neck until his mouth finally wrapped around my nipple and sucked so well that I cried out, and then he went to the next one, tweaking and caressing with his fingertips, completely content to take his time.

Me, however? I was a shaking mess as I watched and felt everything. I ached everywhere.

Why was he wearing pants?

Before Kieran could make up his mind, I did. I reached down to the button of his waistband, shoving his pants past his hips. While he stripped them off, I pushed at my constrictive tights. I wiggled the sheer fabric off before either of us could comprehend it or care about what I had done before we collapsed back against each other on the bed.

Kieran's fingers dipped past the elastic of my underwear.

"Sylv," he groaned as he felt me.

I gasped, forcing myself to keep my eyes open. I didn't want to blink. I wanted to be right here for all of it and prove to myself that this was real.

I reached down. His previously loose briefs were taut. He watched as I took him into my hand. I nearly moaned at the velvet skin that met me. Kieran did. His hips pitched into me as I tugged and squeezed.

He wanted this. I wanted this.

Neither of us could help it as the sounds of our want took over, and that was the only thing I could hear—or ever possibly wanted to hear again.

The past two months, I had struggled, and I had missed him, and now, this—this moment and choice were entirely ours. It didn't matter if it was right or wrong. I'd never felt something so wonderful in my entire life. I'd never heard something so good as I listened to Kieran come undone, our hitched breaths gasping together until there was nothing left of us.

Kieran rested the head of himself just barely inside of me. I already could feel the adrenaline coursing through me at the pressure and stretch. I looked down to where we cradled each other.

"You still okay?" Kieran asked for permission, breathless.

I needed him right now. "More than. I've wanted you more than anything. Please, I need to feel you. I might cry if I don't."

He chuckled, flashing his teeth. "We can't have that."

Dropping his forehead against mine, he slowly shifted his hips. I flinched when he pushed further, meeting some resistance.

"Are you okay?"

I shut my eyes for a moment, taking in the new and wonderful sensation. "Mmhmm."

Kieran ran his hands down either side of me. Cooing like I was something he needed to soothe. "Eyes open. I want you looking at me. We want to remember this, don't we?"

I nodded, opening my legs wider.

"Lift your hips for me. I got you," Kieran said as he slowly thrust, one shift at a time until he was all the way inside of me.

I could feel his skin, hot and as needy as I was, flush against mine.

My mouth opened, as if I were in shock as I looked down at myself. This was really it. This was happening. I couldn't believe it, how perfect and how right this felt. After so long, I didn't want to leave this moment. I didn't want to move. I wanted to stay right here forever.

That was, until Kieran gave me a little nod and began to move.

I cried at the sudden shift from pressure to pleasure. I held him tight between my legs, lifting to meet him halfway with every thrust.

So many years, we had been together, yet no moment felt more right than this one. We watched each other, listening to the sharp, aching sounds escaping between us.

I was causing Kieran to look like he couldn't believe what was happening right now. I had caused that moan. I had caused that shudder that rocked through his body before I hit a peak so high that I couldn't stand it any longer.

Kieran collapsed on top of me, our skin hot and heady with what we'd done. I could feel it as I ran my hands up and down over his back, one hand tangling into the short hair on the nape of his neck where there was a tiny tattoo.

He panted into my skin.

"You still there?" he asked, never used to me being quiet so long.

"Still not dreaming," I confirmed.

THIRTY-NINE

NOW

"DID I really just see you having an actual conversation with Amy?"

"It's a Christmas miracle," I joked.

Kieran chuckled. "Ready to go? Everyone else who isn't staying in tonight said they might stop by the house with us eventually too."

"Don't want to keep Lori wondering."

"Definitely not."

Yeah, I thought. *She probably thinks we ran off with one another, like everyone else at this point.*

Over the past few days, the Rose house had been upgraded from gentle holiday cheer to full-out Christmas wonderland. The wreath lit up the door with poinsettias and green and white lights wrapped around columns and everywhere they could land. The pathway up the door was lined with lanterns, and it didn't stop when we made it inside.

When I stepped through the front door of the tall colonial home, the assault of piano Christmas music and voices felt almost as if I had stepped through a portal to fifteen years ago, coming to my first Rose holiday party.

Back then, my mom had stuffed me into a sweater dress that wasn't all that unlike the formfitting material I wore tonight over sheer tights. When I had walked through the door then, immediately, I'd had one thing I was looking for, whether or not he wanted me to. Kieran. I had found him gorging himself on cookies and watching an animated film about a Christmas cow in his parents' room upstairs.

I might've never had a good Christmas itself, but this party Lori threw usually turned out to be one of my favorite days of the entire year. Or it used to be.

Now, Kieran wasn't hiding. He was right at my side, and I walked into the house as if on eggshells, waiting for something or everything to come crashing down in a fiery inferno. The door, however, shut behind us, and nothing happened.

Kieran's hands brushed over my shoulders as he slid my coat off and tucked it into the hall closet, away from the other pile of all the other party guests' outerwear.

"Are you okay?" Kieran asked, curling his head around my shoulder.

"I'm great. Sorry. I just had a little déjà vu."

A smile curved at the one corner of his lips as we headed down the hall, past the crowd of people. Nearly everyone in Marshall Falls had been invited to stop by. Before we made it into the kitchen, I was pushed to the side. Arms were thrown around me.

"Oh!" I stumbled.

Kieran laughed.

His mother held me tighter. "I'm so happy you are here with us."

I squeezed Lori back, tight to me before we both pulled back to look each other in the eye. "I'm happy I'm here too."

Her hands squished my bicep. "Good. Go on through and

get some food if you're not already weighed down. Get a drink or anything. And don't forget the tree."

My cheeks started to ache as I looked across the room to Kieran, who found his dad by the kitchen table. "I'd never."

With another pat of her hand on my back, Lori rounded the counter toward the rest of her guests. She was a hostess unlike any other I'd ever witnessed. She paused for Kieran's father to give her a short kiss. Then, he watched her go with a soft, knowing look of his own as she took on her favorite night out of the year.

That was always something that I'd noticed was the biggest difference between Kieran and me. Our parents. Both pairs were still together. They worked. Yet, always while growing up, I couldn't help but notice just how right Lori and Dave were for each other. They just fit, as if nearly the same person. Or perfectly practiced over the years to be that way, careful, loving glances thrown to the other even when the other wasn't looking.

My parents had to work to be good together. They had to plan trips and double-check things. There were highs and lows that I never wanted to be present for when they happened, but they always had when I was little until I had Kieran's steady house, full of undeniable and unconditional love, to run off to whenever I was no longer sure if I deserved it.

I took a glass of the red punch. Though it wasn't the wine at Jenna's, it still tasted sweetly pleasant with cranberries. With another small sip, I wandered into the living room. It was lit with the fireplace going, and people sat on the couch or stood wherever there was room. In the far corner, the Christmas tree stood tall and glimmering.

Unlike most festive Christmas trees, Lori's was bare. There was not a thread of ribbon or ornaments on the tree. There was nothing aside from the star on top and white lights wrapped around the center. It shone like a beacon through the living room.

As the guests milled around, drank, ate, and conversed with the other friends and family stuffed in every corner of the house, the tree was decorated. Someone would add an orb from the box Lori had left out. Another brought a new ornament they wanted to give. More than just a few friends laughed as they looked at an old picture of Kieran with his oversize glasses as a child before hanging it on the tree. Slowly, the tree was decorated, filled with memories right alongside new ones being made.

Reaching down into the old, slightly ripped box, filled with tissue paper, I saw the ornament I had put on the last time I was here. Four years ago, the ornament had caught my eye, unlike any other. An antique glass ball, the shell was covered in snowflakes and sparkles. Rounding the tree, I took my time to find the perfect branch.

I placed the metal hook on, adding to the spirit with every swing back and forth the decoration took.

I remembered the last time I had hung it right out front for everyone to see. Then, Kieran had found me and grabbed a random ornament of his own and put it right next to mine until we were nose to nose and ...

"Did you find your ornament?"

I nearly fell into the tree. Kieran bit his lip so not to laugh. "It was saved just for me."

He bent down to grab an ornament of his own, setting it on the tree after one look over for the ideal spot.

"I love this."

"I'm glad," said Kieran, glancing around the space. "It hasn't been the same without you here. I love this too."

I bit my lip, wanting to say it so badly.

I love you too.

Whatever was on my face was clear enough.

Kieran's face pinched. "Don't. You promised."

No, I didn't.

I might as well have said it aloud.

"Not tonight, when we don't know what we are doing. Let's just be happy and be satisfied enough."

"What if, for once, I know exactly what I'm doing?" I backed up from the tree toward the window, leaving room for others to decorate. "What if, for the first time in my entire life, I'm seeing clearly right now, and I know exactly what I want and it isn't to be *satisfied enough?*"

Kieran's eyes widened.

Oohs and aahs came from the room loud enough to cover the steady thrum of holiday piano music.

Kieran looked up above us before I did this time. It used to be under the archway as people paused, coming in the front door. Now, the mistletoe was beneath the front bay window.

"Kiss!" someone called out.

I stared at Kieran, remembering how this had played out before. It almost felt meant to be. A second chance.

I sure as hell wasn't going to waste it.

Luckily, for once, finally, we were on the same page.

"This is such a stupid, childish tradition," muttered Kieran as he tilted his chin.

Our mouths bent to touch together. This was no chaste, quick kiss. He held on to my back as we arched together. With this kind of kiss, heat rushed all the way from the tip of my tongue down to my toes.

I felt off-kilter and about to fall over when we pulled apart. Kieran looked down at me, eyes dilated and breathing heavy as he held on to me.

"Is that what you wanted?" Kieran asked. "More than satisfied?"

I could still feel him on my lips.

"Cheers!" a few other voices called out.

Loudest of all was behind us as Dylan and Landon pushed through the front door. They patted Kieran on the back before heading toward the kitchen, leaving us standing as everyone returned to what they had been doing.

Kieran was still holding on to my hand. His fingers slipped up toward my wrist. He looked down at my wrist, eyes lighting up in surprise.

"I didn't know you put this on." He continued to stare at where I had put on my charm bracelet, out of my memory box.

I hadn't worn it in years. At some point, it had begun to feel too gaudy and childish.

It didn't feel that way right now. "It felt right tonight."

"It looks nice."

I stared at Kieran, letting the mess of words just keep coming. "I wanted tonight to be perfect for us. I need to make up for all the years I missed so that, at least for a little bit, I know that I was something worthwhile. For you. For me—even if it's only ever going to be here, tonight."

When he didn't respond, I tried to take a step back.

Kieran grabbed my shoulder before I could retreat. He forced me to look at him. "I get it. Trust me, I do. But you were already something to me. You've always been something to me," he said. "Always."

"You mean that?" I whispered.

He let out a harsh breath, as potent as a swear.

I was right there with him.

"You were always everything to me, Kieran," I told him, not breaking our stare. "More than. There was nothing more you could've measured up to because you were always just how you were supposed to be—perfect for me."

Kieran stared at me with wide eyes. "Do you want to get out of here for a little bit?"

Taking a deep breath, I looked down to where he took my hand and nodded.

Our time dancing around the topic and dancing into us was over. That was clear. I didn't know how this holiday would end between us, but it was time, and we were ready for it.

"More than anything."

FORTY

BEFORE

WHEN WE WEREN'T SPENDING time with our families, trying to pretend nothing had happened, Kieran and I couldn't keep our hands off each other.

After all these years, there finally was no longer a need, and we took advantage of it. We pulled one another into different rooms no one else was in. We even drove away in my dad's truck, telling him we were going for a ride to pick up a few things before heading back into town to meet up with everyone for New Year's Eve.

Which was partially true.

If anyone noticed, they didn't say anything. It was as if Kieran and I had always been this way or were meant to be, even as we met back up at Dylan's house for our own New Year's celebration.

There were only a few minutes left until midnight.

Kieran laughed, lips spread wide in a grin as he slugged back another drink with everyone. I never saw him so at ease, drinking, or relaxed with everyone in general. Then again, it had been a long time since I last had the experience to see him that way. We hadn't been in the same place long enough the past few years.

Now, we were going to have to change that. Because I was not spending another second without him by my side.

We had so many more adventures to go on now.

"It's time for the countdown!" Dylan hollered.

Everyone, including quite a few faces I didn't recognize, pooled into the cramped living room. The television displayed the sparkling clock in Times Square.

To think that I had walked there and been there.

Maybe it wouldn't be too long until I was back in the city, for real this time with everything finally perfect.

"Three! Two!"

Kieran tugged on my arm, pulling me away from the crowd. Everyone found a partner to kiss, lips puckered for a peck. Kieran led me until we were all the way outside. I didn't even care about the cold.

I was so giddy at his spontaneity that I nearly slipped on a patch of ice. Everyone behind the front door cheered. Outside, silence hung all around us. Admiring me, Kieran bit his lip as he pulled me against him. For balance maybe, but really, as he breathed against my mouth, mainly just to kiss.

I laughed against his mouth. We were all teeth as we swayed to the sound of snow sprinkling down from the gutters.

"Happy New Year, Silly."

"Happy New Year," I agreed, rubbing my damp lips together. "Guess what."

He kissed me again. "What?"

"I have something to tell you."

His eyes flashed behind his slightly foggy glasses, and there was only delight. "Want to leave first? No one will notice."

That sounded like the perfect way to bring in a new year.

But right now, I was watching Kieran's slightly loopy smile. There was no place I'd rather be.

I wanted to soak in this entire moment.

"Kieran, you are listening to me?"

"Course."

"I have something to tell you."

"Tell me then," he said.

I took a deep breath, holding on to his arms. "You know how I've been writing a lot? Well, the other week, one of my articles from the blog got picked up. They really liked it. They want me to write more for them as a staff writer."

"That's amazing, Sylv!"

I grinned. "Then, the other day, a magazine contacted me too."

Kieran gaped, his hands on my hips. "No way."

"Uh-huh. They want me to work with them. I applied to them so many times. Now, they finally looked at my stuff and want me to join *their* team. I'm going to be a real writer."

"Congratulations!"

I shook my head. "A real writer," I repeated.

"You've always been a real writer. You should be so proud."

"I'm honestly super nervous. I still have some things to get together..."

The list of things I needed to get done since I had accepted the position over email the other day was astounding. I needed to pack my things and see about new apartment options since I certainly couldn't stay in my lease with four other girls if Kieran was going to be there too. For one, he'd probably pass out if he saw the bathroom situation.

There was also an insane amount of onboarding paperwork I had to fill out for *Main Attraction*, half of which I didn't know the answers to.

"Wait, what do you mean?" Kieran's smile faltered, twisting with confusion.

"I know that it's last minute, but I figured it would be a sort of new year surprise. New year, new us. I know it's a big deal, but we can do this."

"Right, but wait a second. You need to explain." Kieran took a step back, putting a hand to his head.

"I have to go back to the city, Kier."

"New York City?"

"Yeah." I chuckled, reaching for his hand. He grasped it limply. "What other city? It's last minute, but they need me in the office by Monday. They had me get a train ticket for tomorrow."

"You're leaving tomorrow?"

"You don't seem as happy anymore."

"It's not ..." His forehead creased in frustration. "You're leaving just like that?"

"No. I mean, yes, I'm leaving. But I figure I can get to New York while you can pack up, and I'll find us a decent place to stay. Everything will be great. It'll all work out, Kieran. Just like you and me. It's going to work."

"But ..."

I must've missed what he had said. "What was that?"

"You said you were going to stay with me."

With him. "Right. With *you*. This job is amazing though, Kieran, and in the city, no less. It'll be great."

"I don't have a job in the city. I have a job here."

"You can find one. It's not like the bakery and doing odd jobs with your dad around town were ever your career dreams in life," I reminded him.

"How do you know that? I like what I do every day."

"You could like something new and exciting with me. In the city too. There are bakeries and bookstores. People do it all the time. They take a chance and run off to the city, and they find a job and their people."

"You're my people, Sylvia."

"You're my people too. I just mean, more people. With me."

"Do you?"

"Of course I do."

Did he need me to say it again? I stepped forward and reached out.

He stepped back. "I guess that's that then."

"What are you talking about?"

"I thought that you'd found her. I thought that I'd found that girl—my best friend again—when you got off that train the other day," said Kieran.

"Kieran. What's happening?"

"Nothing. I just see the kind of life you want. You were right; our lives just don't make sense together. I was kind of stupid."

I had to have heard him wrong.

"Or is that how you've always thought of me all these years? Stupid Kieran pining over something he can't have, something too good for him?"

"I've never been too good for you."

If anything, it was the opposite. Clearly the opposite. How could he not see that?

"I love you, Kieran. I do. I love you. You're right. I should have talked about this and told you sooner, but don't do this. We've been drinking. This isn't right. I love you."

"I haven't been drinking."

"Yes, we both have. I just don't understand." I ran a hand through my hair, my bracelet getting caught in the strands. "I thought you understood that I couldn't stay here if I wanted to write professionally."

"I don't know what I was thinking. I guess I just didn't

consider that you'd be fine with up and leaving now. I can't leave, Sylvia. I can't just leave Marshall."

"That's okay." The air felt like it had been squeezed from my lungs. "We'll figure this out."

"I'm sorry."

"Sorry?"

"I'm not going to stand here. I can't keep waiting, Sylvia. I can't keep waiting for you to choose me."

My lips quivered. I didn't understand.

"I saw this happen when you left the first time," he said. "I can't do it again."

"This is different. We told each other how we felt, and we can work through this."

"It isn't. This just isn't going to work. It was stupid to believe we could do this. I have a feeling I know the ending of us too. You were never going to write a love story for me, were you?" he asked.

"Stop, please." My voice cracked as I reached back for him. My hand found nothing. "You're asking me to stay here. You want me to give up my writing?"

"I'm not."

"You are," I said, trying to make him hear himself. I had a feeling we were only making it worse. "You're asking me to give up everything that I've worked for. This is everything we both have worked for. *Everything* since we were kids."

"It isn't everything I've worked for, Sylvia!" Kieran yelled. I wasn't sure I'd ever heard him raise his voice so loud. It bounced off the snow and the space around us. "You were the thing I wanted all this time. You."

"Kieran." I shifted on my feet, wrapping my arms around myself. "Don't do this. Don't ruin a good thing. I don't know what you expected of me suddenly. I'm still the same person I always was."

"I *know*."

It dawned on me. "I'm not Amy."

"Are you kidding me? I know that!" he cried out, flinging his arms to either side. "Trust me, I know."

"Then, you must know that I'm not going to be satisfied, living here. I don't want to be in Marshall Falls for the rest of my life. I'm not going to pop out babies like Gabe and Jenna just because you're too scared to leave. Is that what you want me to say right now? You want me to throw everything I've worked for away for you?"

"What if I do?"

I recoiled.

"You've never even been happy in the city," he said.

"Fine!" I yelled. "If you want to, this is your chance. Go. Run back to Amy. I'm sure she'll take you back with open arms."

"This isn't about Amy! But at least she cared about my opinion. At least she cared to let me have some sort of input. She would say something before buying a fucking train ticket and running off to God knows where, doing who knows what." Kieran started to pace.

"I've never belonged here." I whispered the words.

He knew that. He knew that this wasn't it for me. I couldn't let it go. Why couldn't he just understand?

"You belong with me."

"Then, why can't you just accept me right now? Where is Kieran who would be so proud of me, who'd want to go on one more adventure?"

"That Kieran grew up. Maybe he's tired of adventures and realized that some things just aren't meant to work out the way we want."

He might as well have punched me.

"So have I, if that's what you want," I whispered. "Once I

leave this place, I'm never going to come back for anything. Ever. Then, I guess we really won't work out, huh?"

His face broke, lips curling. "You don't mean that."

"I do."

"If you mean that, then, damn, Sylvia, I wish you'd never come back. I would've been better off if I'd never met you that day you came knocking on our door with your mom all those years ago."

I opened my mouth, but no words came out.

He thought that. He didn't want me around him ever. He wished that he'd never met me.

My heart was so far up my throat that I was sure he could hear it beating ... or breaking. I'd thought a lot of things about us, but never this.

"I'm sorry," said Kieran, his voice much softer than before.

"Why?" At some point, my throat clenched as I cried, gasping between words. I wanted to stop, but I couldn't.

"I just need some space. This isn't me."

Then, who is it?

"You're right; we both had too much to drink," he finally admitted.

"Okay."

"Tomorrow morning, we'll talk about this," said Kieran. "We just need to take a second, and I need to screw my head on straight."

I nodded again, not even wanting to look at him.

"I'm serious. We can't do this. I'm not going to just give up on us like this. Not now."

I'd never imagined that my declaration tonight was going to go down like this. I had no idea even why it had exploded in my face. One minute, we had been perfect, and then it was like neither of us cared about what happened to the other at all, shoving each other away as if we couldn't do it fast enough.

"Okay, Kieran," I agreed, not having anything else to say when all I wanted was him to wrap his arms around me and tell me that it was going to be all right. That *we* were going to be all right.

But he didn't do that.

"Tomorrow. Before your train, okay? I just need to cool off. I need to figure some things out. I need to..."

For the first time, I was unsure what he planned to say next as his words drifted off between us.

"Okay."

FORTY-ONE

NOW

KIERAN DIDN'T LET my hand go. He constantly touched me all the way through the backyard and up the stairs to his apartment.

One step at a time upward we moved toward something, my heart hammering in my chest so loud that I was sure that Kieran could hear it. He didn't say anything, even as he closed the door behind us, sealing us and the warmth inside.

Walking through the space, he kept himself moving. He hung up our coats and plugged the lights back in until our ugly tree glowed in the dark. The furnace hummed, and he clicked on the lamp lights, never the overhead, until the space was exactly how we'd been living—at peace each night after a long day.

Only this day wasn't over.

Kieran glanced down at the coffee table, adjusting papers and straightening my laptop I'd left charging. He paused at the crumbled holiday to-do list.

"We don't have much left on your list," he commented.

I shook my head, still right where he had left me a few steps from the door. "We were never really good at finishing them anyway, were we?"

"No, I guess not. But we made a good go at them, didn't we?"

"Yeah, we did. We probably still would have finished our last list four years ago if we'd had more time. I know we planned to."

We'd had one or two items left that we let sit but joked about on the phone all the time.

We'd planned to go skinny-dipping in the lake come summer and stay up late enough to see the sunrise. It was odd that we'd never managed that one. If we had, we wouldn't have been paying attention to the sunrise at the time.

"We put aside a lot of things that were important to us the last time we were here." I hesitated, but this needed to happen.

Kieran shut his eyes and took a deep breath. Visible nerves coated him. "You really want to have this conversation? The real conversation?"

If we did, this was going to be it—I could feel it. By the look on Kieran's face, he was just as frustrated, just as torn.

"When I got back and saw you, you asked me if I just wanted to ignore it and pretend everything was fine ..." I had known my answer then, but now, I was able to say it. "Yeah, I want to have the real conversation."

"Right now?"

"We need to. I mean, I know what happened. I just—"

"Do you though, really?"

"Yes." I stared at him. "I do. I know that I ruined us. You even said so."

His face screwed up as he shook his head. "Let's hear it from your side then."

What other side was there? It was all a mess. I was the one who had caused it. I didn't want to rehash it all like this, but we could if that was what he needed to do. Put all our sins out on display.

"I got a job in the city," I recalled. "I got the job that I'd dreamed of after my article was picked up in another magazine. *Main Attraction* didn't want them poaching me. I didn't care about the reason. I already had my bags packed and was out the door the moment I saw the email. I didn't even tell you."

"But you did," countered Kieran.

"Too late," I maintained. "I didn't even think to take you or your feelings into consideration before I took it and assumed that you would just follow me along because..." That was what he had done when we were kids. "I was stupid and selfish."

"But you did end up telling me. You didn't leave me behind. You never planned to. That was on me. For so long, I still couldn't comprehend that you wanted me like the way I wanted you. Then, the job came, and I figured..."

"Figured what?"

"I figured you wouldn't want me anymore. Or you wouldn't want me in the long run."

I couldn't believe this. "You knew how I felt. I told you. It was my fault. I should've consulted you and told you what was happening before I accepted the job so that we were completely on the same page. If I'd listened to you..."

Kieran stepped forward to grasp my shoulders. "Stop. Sylvia, you're not understanding. I was wrong. I should've gone with you! If I hadn't been so much of a coward or so anxious all the damn time, I would've gone."

"You know you wouldn't have though." I saw everything so clearly now. I never realized how much weight from that night Kieran was still holding.

I had broken us. Or I'd thought I had. All this time.

"Not to mention, you couldn't have," I said. "There was the

fact that you didn't know what you were getting yourself into. There was no plan. Then, Lori got sick."

"I didn't know any of that at the time."

"But it matters."

"Does it? Because in my head, when I think about that night, all I think about is us yelling at each other right after we both said we had everything in the world we wanted. I regretted not following you even if I wasn't sure that you wanted me the same way we had said because I couldn't handle what it all meant and how it was all happening so quickly."

"But you were so sure then."

"Out loud. We were young and stupid, and even when we decided to split for a breather so that we didn't say anything else we didn't mean before regrouping—"

"Only you didn't show up," I whispered, cutting him off.

"I didn't show up."

FORTY-TWO

BEFORE

I WIPED AWAY TEARS. They coated my face and kept falling, no matter how many times I chastised myself.

I shouldn't have come back here. I should've listened to everyone. I should've listened to the stupid, irritating words of advice from Paul and the people from my classes. I should've taken to heart all the stories of writers who had made it in the city and what it took and took and took.

Yet I couldn't stop myself, all this time.

I had to come back and see him. And now, it was all for nothing. Worse than nothing.

I felt like nothing.

For years, we had been working toward this moment. Us. Now, it was all crashing down. It was all ruined within a few minutes, and I couldn't understand why.

It didn't matter though. He didn't show up.

I waited.

I stood outside my house a half hour earlier than I was supposed to leave for the train station, and I waited. I had my dad drive by his house on the way. There was no movement. I got all the way to the station and had my dad drop me off with plenty of time to spare. There was still time.

He could still make it here, driving up slightly over the speed limit in his car, smeared with slush and road salt.

No one ever came but the train.

He'd promised. He'd promised that he would show up and that we could talk about this.

I thought maybe there would be relief or some sort of understanding that settled into my chest as I got into the train car, lugging my suitcase behind me. I was leaving Marshall Falls. I was going to the job and the place I'd always imagined myself in. I was going to become me.

I was going to become extraordinary.

I should've felt happy and amazing and excited. Despair was so much more potent.

Nothing felt different or changed anywhere but in my chest as my heart shattered with each mile the train traveled away from Marshall Falls.

Kieran was still mine every time I thought about him. That was clear. Every single detail.

Maybe he would be forever.

Only now, it was too late.

FORTY-THREE

NOW

"I DIDN'T SHOW up the next morning for you."

"I thought that was because you were angry and that you couldn't forgive me." My throat was thick with emotion as I remembered that morning. "I thought you didn't want me. I thought everything you had said to me the night before was true. I knew that you had been drinking and I had been drinking, but still. You let me go."

"And I thought you didn't care because you hadn't stayed," said Kieran. "I understand what you thought now, and you had a train to catch, but I still just let myself believe that you didn't actually want me because that would mean—"

"We wasted so much time."

Only now, we'd wasted so much more.

"I wasn't there that morning because after I left you, I went back to Dylan's."

"You did?"

"I met up with everyone. I didn't go home, like I'd said I was going to. I'd lied. Then, I got even more drunk. I got so drunk that I can barely drink at all anymore, thinking about it. The next morning, I was sick. I felt like I was going to die. Not only because I was physically stuck to the toilet, but also because I knew the moment I woke up and you weren't there, I was too late. Whether that was true, I told myself that. I manipulated myself."

"I should've found you. I left you here," I countered him.

"Fine." Kieran shrugged. "We both screwed up. Fair?"

"Yeah." I would've laughed if I wasn't so close to crying.

"We screwed up big time because we were both too messed up and scared for so many reasons besides the obvious one."

"The obvious one?"

"I wanted you so badly. Neither of us could handle it," said Kieran. "We weren't ready. *I* wasn't ready, no matter how much I wanted to be. You had to go. You had to see if you could write. We both needed each other to go after we got together and everything between us happened so fast."

"I didn't answer the phone though, even after. I never answered when you called."

"You didn't."

"I thought that I could be this famous writer. I thought I could be great without you, even when, in the end, the best part of me was you—or who I was with you. I don't know. I've loved you with all my heart every single day of my life since we were kids, and I just threw it all away. I don't see how you can forgive me for that."

Kieran took a step toward me while I remained frozen in place in the middle of the room.

"I can forgive you for not showing up. I never held that against you," I admitted. It was so low on my radar of things that had gone wrong. I'd cared about him, and I had thrown it all away. I'd let him down. I'd let Lori down. I'd let everyone who cared about me in Marshall Falls down. "I can't forgive myself."

Before I could even finish the thought, Kieran's arms wrapped around me. He pulled me into his chest. I didn't fight it. I couldn't. It felt too good. I'd been holding back tears, but with him, I couldn't help it.

"I loved you so much that I felt like I would never be near you like this ever again." I shook with my tears.

"Loved?" said Kieran. "Past tense."

I pressed my forehead into the soft knit of his sweater.

"Love," I corrected him. "Present tense."

Kieran hummed, taking a deep breath, as if to calm himself down. I'd always thought, out of the two of us, he was the more emotional one, but something had obviously switched along the line.

If we both started crying now, it was over. I would collapse in a puddle of tears.

"Always present tense," I whispered. "I can't get past it, Kieran. I knew there was a reason you didn't show up to fix things, but I still left because I think it was just easier not to fix it at that point. I regret it so much. I think about it all the time."

"It was my decision too. I feel like you forget that. I let myself forget that for a long time."

I shook my head.

"I wanted nothing more than to go back to that night four years ago and do things differently. I hated myself for wanting that, too, but it doesn't make it any less true, Sylvia. Any of it."

"You don't—"

"You can't just stop loving someone the way I love you."

Love, present tense.

"We both get to be people who were young and stupid enough to make bad decisions we regret, Sylvia. You don't get to proclaim all of that as yours," Kieran said. "You have no idea how many times I thought of getting on a train and tracking you down through Manhattan. I bought a ticket more than once, but then Mom got sick ..."

I shut my eyes.

"And I started to worry you weren't the only thing I was going to lose."

I pressed my hands to my face, not wanting to look at him and also knowing I couldn't turn away to look at anything else. "I'm so sorry."

"I'm sorry too, Sylvia. I wasn't the person you needed, and I just let you go. I should've chased after you. I should've, for once in my life, done *something*."

"I left," I said, the words tasting wrong and bitter. "I left and didn't even look back when everything was behind me. You were my everything. You are."

"You mean that?" Kieran's thumb tilted my chin up to stare him in the eye. "You still think you're mine?"

"Always."

His breath shuddered between crying and relief.

"We've wasted so much time," I wept.

"Better not waste any more of it then."

I brought my forehead up to his so that I could speak the words against his lips. "Please, Kieran."

"Yeah?"

"Just kiss me again?" I was no longer above begging.

A good thing because not a second passed before he claimed me as his own again and our lips sealed us together.

We were past the point of awkward hands, not knowing what to do. The two of us had waited too long for this. We couldn't stop ourselves. We tore at each other's clothing.

Kieran's mouth was on mine and on my neck. His lips trailed over the tiny rose, tattooed forever on my skin, as he whispered into my ear.

"Have you thought of this ever since you left?" he asked,

hushed, as if no one else in the world deserved to hear him speak. "Have you regretted not being able to have me touch you like this every day?"

"Every day," I agreed. "I've thought of it every day."

No matter what, I couldn't stop remembering the last time we had been in this same position. Even whenever I had sex with Ezra or touched myself, there was one fantasy, one memory I kept coming back to, and it was him. Even when I hadn't wanted him to be, he had been there.

It had always been him.

"This?" His hands skimmed down to the hem of my dress, lifting it up over my hips.

There were far too many layers between us.

"You."

I tugged at his shirt until he lifted his hands. We took turns undressing each other. Every layer of clothing that came away produced a more pained hiss from Kieran. I chuckled at the sounds he made. Heat flooded me, knowing that I was the one causing them as my tights were yanked down my legs.

"You think it's funny now?"

I nodded.

"You think it's funny how much I care about you? How much I've always loved and wanted you so badly?"

"Like in this way?" I ran my hand down his stomach toward his waistband.

He inhaled, backing us until my thighs knocked into his bed. "In all the ways you'll let me. We aren't letting us go this time. I'm not going to let us."

"You're not?"

He shook his head.

"Good." I was breathless. "I'm not either. You've been mine ever since I saw you, Kieran Rose. My best friend, my soulmate ..."

He liked that one.

"My everything," I said.

"Finally, we're telling the truth."

Finally.

I kissed him hard until he groaned. We were on the bed. I pressed myself against him as hard as I could. I wanted to melt into him. That way, we could never be pulled apart again. I arched into his hips as he pushed me onto my back, kissing down between the swell of my breasts. Quickly, my bra followed the rest of my clothes, and I was below him.

His hands gripped my hips, roughly pressing himself between my legs as if he couldn't help himself.

A good thing. I wanted to kiss him everywhere, down his neck to his chest.

His palm slipped down to cover my panties and he swore.

I lifted my hips. "Have I brought you to swearing again?"

"You brought me to say a whole lot of things."

The quiet Kieran I had known, growing up, had a whole different side of himself in the bedroom. Maybe it was all the books he'd read—from the classics filled with elaborate prose to the most sinful of erotica novels he couldn't help but dive into after seeing them on the dusty shelves of Pauper's Used Books. It was, after all, where all the women dropped off their latest book club picks when they were finished.

"For research," he had once told me.

Now, I was going to reap every single benefit of it all.

I arched as his mouth trailed down my collarbone, and I gasped when I ground myself into his hand.

Kieran moaned at the sound, as if he could taste it. "You're so beautiful. So hot. I can't wait to hear you come for me."

At this rate, it wasn't going to take long. Just him looking at me made me feel like I was about to burst.

"Please, Kieran. Touch me. Please, please."

"I'm going to do a lot more than just touch you, Sylvia." He pulled back to stare down at my pleading, pinched expression. "You just said, after all, you're mine now."

I always had been, but the statement made me gasp. "Yours."

Take me. I wanted to cry at the sincerity of every touch. *Make me yours and never let me leave again.*

His tongue trailed toward my navel, and before I could comprehend it, Kieran's mouth settled between my legs.

I cried out, feeling him taste me. His tongue lingered between my folds, spreading me out. I couldn't help myself as I turned into a writhing mess. Kieran sighed in satisfaction of the obscene sounds I made, but that didn't stop how badly I wanted him.

"I need you," I whispered—cried. "I love you so much, Kier."

He twisted me until I was straddling him. "You still want me, Sylv?"

"Always." I nearly laughed as I reached for him and lined him up with my opening. Rocking myself over him, I whimpered before I fit him into me, taking him slow. Then, I was all the way down, pressing against him.

"God, Sylvia. You feel so good," he grunted as I started to move, rolling my hips.

Nothing had felt this good—ever.

Kieran cupped me against him, thrusting into me as we both cried out into each other's mouths, feeling every movement and every second as I contracted around him with a shout.

The world was him, nothing else but this.

I wanted to stay here forever. How could we have been so stupid to think we could let this go? How could we have ever thought we could let each other go?

"What's wrong?" Kieran's thumbs brushed at my tears that

continued to flow with no chance of stopping. He held me to his chest, where I could hear the steady cadence of his heart. "Why are you crying?"

"What if I hadn't come back? What if—"

"We never need to think about it. I don't plan on leaving your side ever again."

And he proved it.

FORTY-FOUR

BEFORE

I BRUSHED AWAY the tears and took another short walk outside, away from the doors of the building I now officially worked in. The area by the plants was always covered in a thick waft of stale air and cigarette smoke. The bitter smell wasn't the reason that I wiped my eyes against my sleeve, smearing my mascara, however.

The first few months of a new job were supposed to be hard. I knew that. I was sure that I knew that. I just hadn't expected it to be quite this difficult for so long.

Swiping through my phone, I looked at my last missed call and cringed. Turning the corner, I waited until I was alone. Or mostly alone. On this side of town, inside or out, I barely remembered the last time that it had just been me and no one else.

Even the siren calls of police and taxis honking their horns sliced through my head, as if I suddenly wasn't used to the city since going home for the holidays four months ago.

I pressed the phone to my ear and listened to the saved voice message.

"Please, answer the phone, Sylvia. I'm sorry. You're sorry.

I'm really freaking sorry. I was drunk and upset, and I don't even know … I just need you to answer the phone because I know me and I know you. I know you'll hate yourself if you don't call me back right now. I can't handle the thought of you hurting after what I said. So please, *please* just answer or call me back. If I don't answer, call the house. Just call," begged Kieran.

The ache in his voice was unmistakable, even over my own tears that had at some point started to pour down my cheeks again. *Damn it.*

I hit the next message still sitting in my inbox.

"If you don't pick up this phone, I'm going to forget you ever happened to me if it's the last thing I do, Sylvia. It'll be like you were always nothing to me. You need to answer right now, so pick up the freaking phone." Kieran gritted out one word after another.

He had left that message nearly three weeks ago.

I bit my lip, unsure I'd ever heard Kieran sound so angry. No. Maybe he was sad? What had happened? I didn't understand. I didn't understand anything.

I didn't even understand why I hit the next button and waited as it rang.

"Hey, this is Kieran. Sorry I can't come to the phone right now. Please leave a message."

I should just leave it like that. I'd tried. He hadn't picked up.

Looking around the street, I took a deep breath. I knew his home phone number by heart. I knew it from years of using it since I had been seven years old, and like most things in Marshall Falls, it hadn't changed.

It rang.

The phone would keep ringing until Lori or Dave picked it up, surely, and then what would I say?

I bit the corner of my fingernail. At least if one of them picked up, I would be able to say something. Because the longer

I waited, the more I replayed all the things Kieran had said to me and all the messages he'd left. Maybe at this point, he really didn't want to hear from me. Maybe me not calling back, holding him back, was a good thing.

Maybe it'd even made him finally do something big, like move out or go on his own adventure he had gotten to choose without me. If he did, he might've even had his own place or shared it with one unbelievably clean roommate by now.

We used to think a year could change a lot. Sometimes though, it only took a few months.

Maybe he even shared that apartment with a girlfriend.

The phone rang—

"Hello?"

Kieran deserved a pretty girlfriend who doted on him. One who was pleasant and sweet. He deserved everything, especially someone who could be there. For him.

Unlike me.

"Hello? Is anyone there? If it's a wrong number, sorry." Kieran gave an awkward chuckle. "Hello?"

Kieran.

He hung up the phone with a click.

I let my phone drop to the ground, not even caring as my body turned slack. I looked up and around me to the gray buildings and dead plants that still hadn't given in to even try and blossom yet. I let the phone sit there in the dirt after adding another crack to the screen.

FORTY-FIVE

NOW

I COULDN'T IMAGINE what my hair looked like. Kieran grinned at me from the moment I sat up. Blankets were tucked around the two of us.

We had never ended up going back to the Christmas party. For the entire night, we talked about the last few years. We talked about before then, and we talked about now, in between other things. In fact, we had done about the same thing straight through Christmas Eve until Lori called to make sure that we were coming for dinner last night.

I never wanted to leave this little holiday bubble we had created.

Kieran pressed his lips together as he looked at me again, happy and flushed. "Merry Christmas, Sylvia."

I leaned in until our lips were almost touching.

It was official. I was addicted to him.

"Merry Christmas, Kieran."

"Speaking of ..." Kieran leaned over the edge of the bed and produced a small, brightly wrapped box.

I stared down at the box. "I don't have a gift for you."

"Don't." He stopped me. "You're my gift."

"That's so cheesy."

"Not when it's true. You came back. For so long, I wanted you. You're enough. You'll always be enough."

My heart ached. "You're enough for me too, Kieran. I'm sorry," I added, thinking about the last time we had been right here, stuck in this almost moment. Only this time, it wasn't almost.

It was.

It couldn't not be, and the pain of realizing how late I was to understand that must've shown plain on my face.

"We aren't going to worry about that today." Kieran squeezed me into him. "We already worked through it, and it's going to be fine. We are going to make it fine from now on. Agreed?"

I nodded into him. Pulling back, I stared down at the wrapped box.

"It's really nothing special."

Before he could discount his gift any more, I ripped the wrapping paper off. I paused at the wide lid. Lifting it up, I barked a laugh. "Socks."

A pair of rolled-up light-blue polka-dot socks was tucked inside. As I pulled them out, however, a small ting sounded at the bottom. Forehead creasing, I peered into the bottom of the box. Inside ... my breath caught in my throat.

"Kieran."

"You weren't the only one trying to hold on to pieces of that night, trying to make it all make sense."

I lifted the tiny silver charm into my hand.

"I noticed you didn't wear your bracelet anymore until the other day at the party—"

I cut him off, unable to look away from the little typewriter. "I love it."

"We never gave each other gifts four years ago either. We must've forgotten. But I still always had it."

Carefully, I added the charm to my bracelet that sat on the nightstand, giving it a nice weight. A reminder. Next, I unraveled the socks and put them on my feet.

I wiggled my toes inside them, admiring them in front of me.

Kieran laughed.

"They're perfect. Thank you. I mean it," I said.

He nudged me. "I'm starving."

"I need coffee," I complained with him.

"Are you going to serve me for my Christmas gift?"

Rolling my eyes, I got up and headed toward the kitchen, pausing at my computer as I went. I hadn't checked it in the past two days. It was fine, but it would be nice to send out a little happy holidays update. Eventually, I'd have to write another more detailed blog post—with Kieran included.

I could only imagine how wild some of the loyal readers would go at that.

Smiling, I left the screen open to restart as I headed into the small kitchen. I dumped coffee grounds into the filter, and the coffeepot groaned as much as I did when waking up before slowly starting a steady hot water drip.

"Did you want anything specific for breakfast?" I called over my shoulder. "Just remember, the most I can do is toast, cereal, and if you have any of those little premade packets of oatmeal. You like the peach ones best, right?"

Kieran had made his way out of bed, as if he was going to join me in the kitchen, but he didn't make it that far. Turning around, I narrowed my eyes. He blinked as he looked down at my computer. All my pages were still open from the last time I'd used it.

"What are you doing?" I asked.

"What is this?" He pointed down to the email, as if I couldn't already see what he was looking at.

My eyes widened. "Kieran, stop."

"Is this what I think it is?"

I opened my mouth, slowly shaking my head. "*Main Attraction* emailed me a few days ago. They noticed that my personal blog was back up because a different magazine had reached out to them about it."

"I shouldn't have thought—I mean, I get it." The happy expression Kieran had had in bed moments ago fell from his face. He took a deep breath, though his fists were tight as he kept whatever he was feeling contained. "I told myself that I would understand. I don't want to hold you back. I'll move and go to the city ..."

"You'd do that?"

He considered it. "I told you I'm not letting you go again, and I mean it. You're going to have to force me away."

"I definitely don't want that."

"There came a point when I decided if we were going to do this—really do this—there were few things I wouldn't do for you, Sylvia."

I shook my head at his devotion. "Listen to me. You are listening closely, right?"

He nodded.

"I'm not going back to *Main Attraction*."

Kieran reeled. "You're not?"

"I told them no."

"You told them no?" He was clearly confused.

"I didn't even have to think about it. I told them in no uncertain terms, no," I said.

Kieran's breath came out in a heavy gasp, as if he was stunned. "You shouldn't have done that though. You should go back now that you're writing again. Everyone deserves to see you write."

"I wasn't happy there. It wasn't what I wanted to do."

"You deserve to write."

"Thank you." The one side of my mouth curled. "But you don't need to worry about me."

"I still can't let you do that."

"What?"

"I won't let you give up what you love for me." Kieran ran his hands through his hair, making the ends stand up.

I put my hands up until they framed his face. "Look at me. I'm going to keep writing. *Main Attraction* isn't the only way I can write even if I thought that for a long time. In fact, they reached out to me because another magazine had reached out to me first."

"To work for them?"

I shook my head. "They want to feature me in a sort of online writer roundup. You can imagine how excited they felt when they realized that their rival magazine had let me go right before the holidays. They might want me to write on a freelance basis, maybe."

"You're going to still write?" Kieran asked again for clarification.

I nodded.

"In New York?"

"I don't know. It doesn't matter. I can do it right here if I want to," I told him. "If I'm writing, that's all that matters at this point. A brand reached out to me. So did a few others. It's been kind of wild since a lot of my readers who loved the blog to begin with are now older and have careers of their own. They are happy to share and include me. They want me to be a part of their media campaigns and work for their sites. This is good, Kieran. This is really good."

"This is good," he repeated, as if still comprehending everything I was saying.

"I'm going to keep my blog. I'm going to do what I love, and I'm going to be able to do it right next to the person I love, all because you forced me to start writing online back in high school."

I laughed at his stunned expression.

"I can't tell if you're joking."

"I'm going to keep writing and start up even more pieces with reviews and a book club now that I might have some extra time. A subscription box also wants to get their name out online. They are going to sponsor me. It's everything I once talked about."

"You're serious."

"I'm very serious." I beamed at him, watching as he started to get as excited as I was. "I'm not leaving you. Not again. Because you're right. I'm not leaving what I love."

Kieran's hand came up to cup my palm, still holding on to him. A shaky smile coated his lips.

"No matter what it takes. Even if I'm staying in Marshall Falls all my life, just like my mom, maybe that's what was meant to happen. I feel like I let a lot of people down."

"You didn't."

"Either way, I still have plenty to make up for myself. I'm going to do that with you. You were always my person who made me happy. I plan on staying around from now on until you get sick of me again."

"That's not going to happen. Like I always said, Sylv, if I was going to get sick of you, it would've happened by now. I figure we have a few good decades left in us."

I shook my head at the tease. "You promise?"

"I will every day if I have to," agreed Kieran. "Actually, don't make anything to eat yet."

"Other than the coffee," I said. I needed a big cup if this was how the day was already starting.

"All the coffee."

I snorted a laugh.

"I'm going to see if my parents are still doing anything for brunch. They mentioned it, but I don't want to interrupt their morning after we stayed up with them so late last night," said Kieran.

Grabbing his coat, he wasn't paying attention, nearly knocking the entire coat rack over. My coat, as well as the thin jacket I'd worn when I first arrived in Kieran's apartment, fell to the floor, along with a slip of paper folded in fourths.

"What's this?"

I cocked my head to the side before clear understanding swept through me. Making my way across the room, I moved to stop him.

"You probably shouldn't—"

"*Dear Kieran, I have loved you from the day I met you and have regretted not telling you since the moment I stepped on the train out of Marshall Falls. The first time, the second time, the last time ...*" Kieran trailed off, his voice getting progressively softer.

He looked up at me with wide eyes. His heart was all over his face, let alone out on his sleeve.

I blushed.

"Sylvia, is this a love letter?"

I rolled my eyes.

"How much did you plan to keep from me today?" he asked. "When did you write this?"

"Somewhere between the first few sips of wine and when I thought it would be a better idea to try to con you into loving me through a holiday-themed list."

Kieran barked a laugh. He tipped his head back down, reading the rest of what had to be a note littered with typos.

I hadn't even realized I'd kept hold of the thing since that night.

"Are you telling me this was in the other pocket of your jacket the entire time?" He smiled, but I could tell there were tears in his eyes. His glasses were starting to fog.

I pulled them off his face to wipe them but ended up laughing with him.

"I'll just take that." I reached for the note.

"No, this is going to be my favorite Christmas present." Kieran held the piece of paper out of reach. "I'm keeping it. I might go and share it with everyone. I'm going to scream it off the rooftop, just how much Sylvia Calasis has always loved me."

"You'd better not."

"I am."

"Fine." I gave up. "Enjoy it."

"I will. You meant it though, all of it?"

"All of it. I never want to leave, Kieran. Never again, so long as I can be right here." I held on to his glasses before I looked back up into his blue eyes. I was once and for all prepared to drown in them, just so that he could save me. We could save each other, just like we always did. "You'll still keep me, right? Even now that you know I've been holding out on your love story?"

"Sylvia, you never had to ask." He breathed against my lips as he took a taste. "And don't worry; we're making our own love story. I'll give you plenty of inspiration."

AFTER

KIERAN GAVE me more than just inspiration.

From the first moment we were about to walk into our new-to-us one-bedroom apartment, Kieran swept me up into his arms and carried me across the threshold.

"You're marrying me," he murmured into my ear, brushing his slightly prickly jaw against my cheek.

I whacked him in the chest with the back of my hand until he set me down in the middle of what was going to be our living room.

"Stop," I grumbled.

"Absolutely not," said Kieran, not falling a step behind me. "I always promised that I'd marry you if we were both sad and alone at thirty."

We were neither of those things. Yet anyway, and when we were it would only be the latter.

"If I have to propose five more times, I will."

"What about seven?" I teased.

"Done."

I groaned. "We've been together for a year."

"We've been together our entire lives."

Semantics.

Carrying each box into the apartment, we slowly filled up the small, empty space with old furniture and decorations, the more we unpacked. And then there was the tree, of course.

We might have had to move in quickly to get this place right before the holidays, but it was worth it to have some holiday spirit when we still could. Even in the form of the silly plastic tree from my parents' basement.

We hadn't moved to New York City. We hadn't even decided on Boston, but Burlington, Vermont, would do. Plus, their coffee shops rivaled anything in the city.

It was also a short trip back to Marshall Falls for Kieran to check in on everything, including the flagship Rose Bakery. The second shop was set to open soon, starting the Roses'—and thus Kieran's—own little franchise. He had crunched the numbers for months on end.

He probably would've second-guessed for years if I hadn't put an end to it.

We were done waiting and wasting time. With us together, we got this.

If the past year had proven anything, it was that everything fell into place somehow when it needed to. That was proved alone somewhere along the line of when my parents got home from their cruise after the holiday, shocked by both the bill to repair the heat and finding out that their daughter was back in town, living with her childhood best friend as a permanent fixture.

Everyone else who had seen me and Kieran during the holidays didn't look surprised in the least. Like Kieran, they were just curious when the next big Marshall Falls wedding was going to be. Even my various blog commenters were questioning it, ever since I had written the life update post on *The List*. I shared vague details of Kieran and what was coming next for me, my writing, and the blog.

Which was a lot.

I just didn't want us to get ahead of ourselves. We had learned what happened when we did that even though I doubted anything could break us apart now. We wouldn't let it, even if it came in the form of Kieran and our mothers getting out of hand with possible future wedding planning before we were even engaged.

Our schedules were packed enough as it was. I was hosting a book club in person in Marshall Falls and online, alongside my new writing schedule, posting for myself while working with other websites consistently every single day.

Though, I had to admit, some days were always more interesting than others when it came to what I wrote.

Especially when I was working on a special project I'd been holding on to for the past few months.

When Kieran finally fell asleep, tucked into freshly washed sheets and tuckered out from all the unpacking, I slowly peeled myself out of bed. I maneuvered down the hallway, around half-emptied moving boxes.

The living room overlooked a glimmering street, almost as spirited as Marshall Falls this time of year. A few presents were already under our makeshift tree. Kieran's were clearly better wrapped than mine.

I pushed a few gifts aside before I could slip in the final one —tied red bow—beneath the branches. I couldn't wait to see Kieran's face when he opened it in the morning. After nearly fifteen years, he'd finally get what he was owed since following me on one of our first adventures.

Kieran was finally going to get his own personal love story—the one he likely thought I'd never write for him—in print.

It was ours.

Kieran, Sylvia, and the List.

With plenty of romance, just as promised.

I smirked as I nudged the thickly bound document pages farther back. I wanted it to be hidden away from the front so he'd open it last. The corner, however, caught on something.

I hadn't noticed it until I nearly pushed the tiny box under the tree skirt.

Leaning down on my side, I reached for the small object. My eyes widened at the velvet box in my hand.

No. It couldn't be.

Inside could be anything. It could be earrings or the world's tiniest pair of socks ...

I couldn't help myself. I lifted the lid and inhaled on a gasp.

"You just couldn't wait, could you?" A voice chuckled behind me. Kieran walked out from the short hallway, rubbing his eyes behind his glasses, and wearing only his plaid pajama pants. He knelt. "Why am I not surprised?"

I looked between him and the contents of the box.

Kieran cupped his hands around mine. "May I?"

I bit my lip, letting go.

Grinning, he was unable to stop his quiet laughter at my awestruck expression.

I was unable to take my eyes off the perfect ring that could not be anything else but an engagement ring inside the box.

"I'm honestly a little nervous that you are about to say no to me again, but I really never thought it would take a ring for you to be stunned silent," Kieran said as he picked it up.

He waited for me to look him in the eye before he slipped

the ring onto my finger. The clear stone glittered in the dark glow of fairy lights.

"How about I rephrase my request?" he said, voice groggy and his glasses a little crooked as he focused on me. "You'll be mine forever?"

Immediately, I nodded. "And after."

ACKNOWLEDGMENTS

Call You Mine didn't start as a childhood best friends love story. In fact, it barely started as an idea at all. When I first pictured *Call You Mine*, the only goal was to produce a holiday romance book by the end of the year. I figured it would be short and sweet. It would be the perfect gift, following the extremely done and redone plot line of a girl coming home to her small town from the city only to fall in love. Easy.

Then, I met Sylvia, and almost more importantly, I met Kieran. Quickly, I realized that he was not going to be a character I could gloss over. No. He was dedicated. Most importantly, he forced me to realize that *Call You Mine* and his relationship with Sylvia would never be the story it could be without the *before*.

Kieran never wanted to be the center of attention, but there was one thing for sure. He wanted his love story.

Over a year later than planned, he got it. But that's sort of the story writing itself, isn't it?

Call You Mine has proved itself to be one of my favorite stories I've written yet, and with writing always comes thanking a variety of people who assisted in me not giving up every single day.

I always want to thank my fellow indie authors always willing to listen to me rant about my latest writing woe or lend a hand and answer any questions I may have for them. I learn something new each time I publish a new book. I'm so grateful to be in such a welcoming online community of writers.

To my parents (especially my father), thank you for the constant loop of cheesy Christmas movies that come on around the holidays. Without them, I'm unsure if I would've ever made it my mission to write my own. And to my mother, a special thank you for being my final set of eyes on *Call You Mine* before it went to print. You're the best proofreader, and mom, I could ever have.

And to my readers, thank you. As of the time this book comes out, there is only a small group of you, but I am so thankful for you spending your time reading my stories. Even more than that, loving these characters and stories enough to share.

ABOUT THE AUTHOR

Kendra Mase is the author of sweet, steamy, emotional romance novels including Call You Mine and the Ashton and Barnett Witches series. She holds a degree in English Publishing and Editing and is a graduate of The Columbia Publishing Course in New York City.